PRASE FOR
What You Need

"Deliciously real, modern, hot and funny."
—Katy Evans, *New York Times* bestselling author

"Relentless chemistry and sizzling romance make this book a must-read!" —Laura Kaye, *New York Times* bestselling author

"This refreshing new series by James is a tender excursion into the lives of an uptight billionaire and a company employee."
—RT Book Reviews

"Fun, sweet and sexy. Lorelei James captures the angst and anticipation of a slow-burn family-run-office romance with engaging characters. . . . Fans of Jaci Burton and Shiloh Walker will enjoy *What You Need*." —Harlequin Junkie

"If you're looking for a quick, sexy read, this one is definitely for you. I can't wait for the next! Well-done, Lorelei James! Very well-done." —The Reading Cafe

"The characters are perfect; the romance is perfect and takes things step-by-step. Not too rushed, not too slow. . . . This is a series I'll be looking forward to seeing more of soon!"
—Under the Covers Book Blog

"[James] has blown me away with a beautiful romance that is sexy and sweet, and I loved every second of it!"
—...eviews

I Want You Back

LORELEI JAMES

JOVE
New York

A JOVE BOOK
Published by Berkley
An imprint of Penguin Random House LLC
1745 Broadway, New York, NY 10019

Copyright © 2019 by LJLA, LLC
Excerpt from *When I Need You* by Lorelei James copyright © 2017 by LJLA, LLC
Penguin Random House supports copyright. Copyright fuels creativity, encourages
diverse voices, promotes free speech, and creates a vibrant culture. Thank you for buying
an authorized edition of this book and for complying with copyright laws by not
reproducing, scanning, or distributing any part of it in any form without permission.
You are supporting writers and allowing Penguin Random House to continue to
publish books for every reader.

A JOVE BOOK, BERKLEY, and the BERKLEY & B colophon
are registered trademarks of Penguin Random House LLC.

ISBN: 9780451492746

First Edition: April 2019

Printed in the United States of America
1 3 5 7 9 10 8 6 4 2

Cover images by Shutterstock
Cover design by Rita Frangie

Prologue

Chicago (AP)—Jaxson "Stonewall" Lund announced his retirement from the NHL at a press conference held in conjunction with the Blackhawks organization. The statement, read by Lund himself, immediately ended speculation that the all-star defenseman was a possible trade option to the Minnesota Wild. "I'm proud to have spent my entire professional career with the Chicago Blackhawks, and retiring from this sport that has given me so much is bittersweet. The amazing Blackhawks coaching staff formed me into the player who could help bring the Stanley Cup to Chicago three times. I'm grateful for the fans who supported us year in, year out, in memorable seasons and those seasons we all wish we could forget. I'm thankful to my teammates, not only for their *fierceness and loyalty on the ice, but for friendships we built year round. In a perfect world I could play another decade, but I'm no Gordie Howe. As much as I'll miss being a Chicago Blackhawks hockey player, I'm looking forward to returning home to Minneapolis, reconnecting with my family and starting the next chapter of my life."*

One

LUCY

"Mommy. What time will Daddy get here?"

Whenever the hell he feels like it.

Not an answer I could give my precocious eight-year-old daughter, even when it was the truth. "He said after six. Since it's now six fifteen, he'll be here at any moment."

Mimi sighed heavily. Then she kicked her legs up and hung upside down from the back of the chair, balancing on her hands. It was obvious to everyone she inherited her natural athleticism from her father. Embarrassingly I was one of those people who trip over their own feet . . . and everyone else's.

"You sure that hanging like a monkey in a tree won't upset your stomach?" I asked her. "Or give you a headache? I'd hate for you to miss an overnight with your dad."

"I have to practice so being upside down doesn't make me sick," she replied with another sigh, as if I should've already known that.

"Ah. So what are you practicing for this week?"

"It's between a trapeze artist or an ice skater. If I decide to have a partner I'll have to be used to being upside down."

Last month Mimi wanted to be an astronaut. The month before that a dolphin trainer. While I've always told her that she can be whatever she wants to be when she grows up, it's exhausting finding an activity that holds her attention. After spending money on dance lessons, gymnastics classes, martial arts classes, T-ball, soccer club, fencing, swim team, tennis lessons, golf lessons and horseback riding lessons, I'd put my foot down and said no new organized activities. If none of those worked then she needed to wait until she was older to try others.

Still, I feared she'd play the guilt card and I'd find myself buying tickets to the circus, a Cirque du Soleil show or a Disney on Ice program. Or . . . maybe . . .

"I'm sure your dad would love to take you to a performance." Not really dirty pool—Mimi's father, Jaxson Lund, was a member of the billionaire Lund family as well as a highly paid former pro hockey player, so money had never been an issue for him. And there was nothing he loved more than humoring Mimi's requests, even if it was to alleviate the guilt that he'd missed being a regular presence in her life for most of her life.

The doorbell pealed and Mimi squealed, "I'll get it!" twisting her lithe little body sideways from the chair to land lightly on her feet, agile as a cat.

I heard her disengage the locks and yell, "Daddy! I thought you'd never get here."

He laughed. That sweet indulgent laugh he only had for our daughter. "I missed you too, Mimi."

"I got my stuff all packed. I'm ready to go now."

Without saying good-bye to me? That stung. But I sucked it up and started toward the entryway.

"Sure. Just let me get the all clear from your mom first."

Then Jaxson Lund and I nearly collided as we turned the corner simultaneously.

His big hands circled my upper arms to steady me.

I had to tilt my head back to look at him as he towered over me by almost a foot.

It was unfair that my ex actually looked better now than he did when he and I met a decade ago. His dark hair was shorter—no more long locks befitting the bad-boy defenseman of the NHL. No scruffy beard, just the smooth skin of his outlandishly square jaw and muscled neck. His eyes were clear, not bloodshot as I'd usually seen them, making those turquoise-hued eyes the most striking feature on his face . . . Besides that damn smile. Hockey players were supposed to have teeth missing from taking a puck or two hundred to the face. I knew Jax had a partial, but he'd never removed it when we were together. The lips framing that smile were both soft and hard. Druggingly warm and soft when pressed into a kiss, but cold and hard when twisting into a cruel sneer. A sneer I'd been on the receiving end of many times.

That shook me out of my musings about Jax's amazing physical attributes.

"Hey, Luce."

Jax had called me Luce from the first—a joke between us because I warned him I wasn't loose and wouldn't sleep with him on the first date. An inside joke made me feel special—he made me feel special—until I realized Jaxson Lund used that killer smile and those gorgeous twinkling eyes as a weapon on every woman he wanted to bang the boards with; there wasn't anything special about me.

I forced a smile. "Jaxson. How are you?"

He retreated at my cool demeanor and dropped his hands. "I'm fine. You're looking well."

And people thought we couldn't be civil to each other. "Thanks. You too."

"Anything I should know before Meems and I take off?"

Meems. He'd given our daughter another nickname, even when Mimi was already the shortened version of Milora Michelle. "Nothing worth mentioning. She's been looking forward to this all week."

Those beautiful eyes narrowed. "So don't disappoint her, right?"

"Right."

"Luce. I'm not—"

"Daddy, come *on*. Are we goin' or what?" Mimi demanded.

"We're goin', impatient one." Jaxson hauled her up and cocked her on his hip with seemingly little effort, because his eyes never left mine. "We can do the switch back at the Lund Industries thing on Sunday afternoon?"

"You'll be there?"

"I work there, remember?"

In the past six months since Jax had joined the family business, I'd hardly seen him hustling around the building in a suit and tie, so I had no idea what his actual job title was. As far as I could tell, he didn't "work" there like I did. Sunday's event was a retirement party for a woman I doubted he knew personally. "I'm surprised. I wasn't aware that you knew Lola."

"The poor woman was tasked with getting me up to speed on all departments when I started at LI. I'd still be aimlessly wandering the halls if not for her."

"Lola will be missed, that's for sure. So if you want to bring Mimi's things on Sunday, that'll work. I planned on going for the two hours."

"Sounds like a plan. Speaking of . . . what are your plans for the weekend?"

None of your business. "Oh, this and that. Mimi has more

things planned for you two than you could fit into two weeks, say nothing of two days."

His dark eyebrow winged up. "Now I'm taking that as a personal challenge."

Mimi held her arms out for a hug. "Bye, Mommy."

"Bye, wild one. Behave, okay?"

"Okay."

"Promise to call me tomorrow sometime."

She sighed heavily. "I'd call you all the time if I had my own cell phone."

I chuckled. "Nice try. Use Daddy's phone. Or Grandma Edie's."

"But all of my friends have iPhones."

"Eight-year-olds do not need a cell phone." I sent Jaxson a stern look as a reminder not to swoop in and buy her one just because he could. Then I kissed her cheek. "Love you, Mimi."

"Love you too."

Jaxson gathered Mimi's stuff with her chattering away at him like she always did. I wondered how much of it he paid attention to.

Not my concern. I'd had to learn to let go of a lot of my issues with Jaxson's parenting style since he'd returned permanently to Minneapolis.

I waved good-bye and locked the door behind them.

As I readied myself for my first date with Damon, my thoughts scrolled back to the first time I'd met Jaxson Lund a decade ago . . .

I'd left work early to take my mother to the doctor. After I'd dropped her off at her place, I pulled into one of those super fancy deluxe car washes that offered one-hour detailing inside and out. Winter in the Twin Cities meant tons of road salt and freeway grime, and my poor car needed TLC. Not that my Toyota Corolla was anything fancy, but it'd been a major purchase for me after I'd graduated from college. My first new car, and I took good care of it.

With an hour to kill, I grabbed a magazine and a Diet Mountain Dew. The lobby wasn't jam-packed with other customers—which was a total contradiction to the lines of cars outside—but I embraced the quiet for a change and settled in.

My alone time lasted about five minutes. A guy blew in—the wind was blustery, but not nearly as blustering as the man yakking on his cell phone at a thousand decibels.

"Peter. I told you I'm happy to stay at the same salary." Pause. "Why? Because a salary freeze for a year isn't the end of the world for me. Especially if that means they can use that extra money to lure the kind of D-man we need."

I rolled my eyes and wished I'd brought my earbuds.

"No. What it speaks to isn't that I'm not worth more money. It shows that I'm a team player."

I tried to ignore the annoying man. But he paced in front of me, forcing me to listen to him as well as watch his jean-clad legs nearly brush my knees as his hiking boots beat a path in the carpet. From the reflection in the glass that allowed customers to see their cars going through the automated portion of the car wash, I knew he was a big man; tall, at least six foot four, with wide shoulders, long arms and long legs.

And huge lungs, because his voice continued to escalate. His pace increased. He gestured wildly with the hand not holding the phone. He couldn't see me scowling at him, as his head was down and his baseball cap put his face in shadow. Not that he'd looked my way even one time to see if his loud, one-sided conversation might be bothering me.

Look at me, look at me! My job is so crucial that I can't

even go to the car wash without dealing with such pressing matters.

Ugh. I hated when people acted inconsiderate and self-important.

He stopped moving. "Fine. It's stupid as shit, but an increase of one dollar if it'll make you happy to have on record that my salary went up again this year. I'll let you keep one hundred percent of that dollar instead of your usual twenty percent commission." Pause. "Do you hear me laughing? Look. I'm done with this convo, Peter. Call me after the trade is over. Bye."

I flipped through a couple of pages.

He sighed and shoved his phone in his back pocket. Then I sensed him taking in his surroundings for the first time. The lack of customers, no car going through the car wash to entertain him.

Please don't assume I'll entertain you. He was definitely that type of guy.

I silently willed him to go away. But I'll be damned if the man didn't plop down on the bench directly across from me. I felt his gaze moving up my legs from my heeled suede boots to where the hem of my wool skirt ended above my knees.

Continuing to ignore him, I thumbed another magazine page and took a swig of my soda.

"Ever have one of those days?" he asked me.

The smart response would've been no response. I'm not sure what compelled me to say, "One of those days where you're enjoying a rare moment of quiet and some rude guy destroys it with an obnoxiously loud phone conversation? Why yes, ironically enough, I *am* having one of those days right now."

Silence.

Then he laughed. A deep rumble of amusement that had me glancing up at him against my better judgment.

Our eyes met.

Holy hell was this man gorgeous. Like male model gorgeous with amazing bone structure and aquamarine-colored eyes. And his smile. Just wry enough to be compelling and "aw shucks" enough to be charming and wicked enough that I had a hard time not smiling back.

"I'm sorry. I don't normally carry on like that, but he was seriously missing my point."

"So I gathered." Dammit. I'd confessed I'd been listening in.

He leaned in, resting his forearms on his knees. "I'm serious. I'm not that annoying cell phone guy."

"Maybe not normally, but you were today."

"You don't pull any punches, do you?"

"No. Also now you've moved on from being 'annoying cell phone guy' to annoying guy determined to convince me that he's not annoying cell phone guy . . . which is even more annoying."

His grin widened. "I'm supposed to apologize for that too? Okay. Sorry for interrupting your quality time reading"—he snatched the magazine off my lap—"*Redbook* and this article on how to prioritize organization in day-to-day life."

My cheeks flamed even as I scooted forward to snatch back my magazine. "Gimme that."

"After you answer two questions. First, are you married, engaged or currently involved with someone? And if the answer is no, will you go out on a date with me so I can prove that I'm not annoying?"

I laughed. "I actually believed you couldn't get more annoying, but I was wrong."

"Are you single?"

"Annoying and tenacious—there's a winning combo," I retorted.

"And she hedges yet again. Fine. Don't answer. I'll just

read this fascinating article that's got you so engrossed you can't even answer a simple question."

"Gimme back my magazine."

He lifted a brow. "I doubt it's your magazine. I'll bet you took it from the stack over there that's for customers to share."

"Fine. Keep it."

"Let's start over." He tossed the magazine aside and offered his hand. "I'm Jaxson. What's your name, beautiful?"

Calling me beautiful threw me off. I automatically answered, "Lucy," and took his hand.

"Lucy. Lovely name. Please put me out of my misery, Lovely Lucy, and tell me that you're single."

"I'm single but I'm not interested in flirting with you because you're bored at the car wash and I'm convenient."

He flashed me a grin that might've made me weak kneed had I been standing. "I'm far from bored. Let me prove it by taking you out for dinner. I promise I'll be on my least-annoying behavior."

That's when I realized he still held my hand. That's also when I realized I was a sucker for his tenacious charm, because I said, "Okay. But if that cell phone comes out even one time I will snatch it from you and grind it under my boot heel as I'm walking away."

"I'd expect nothing less."

I tugged my hand free before he did something else completely charming like kiss my knuckles. "Are you single?"

"Yes, ma'am. And this is the first time I've asked a woman I met at a car wash for a date."

"This is the first time I've agreed to a date with a man I find a—"

"Attractive?" he inserted. "Amusing? Feel free to use any A-word except the one you've repeatedly overused."

"Calling you an asshole is an acceptable A-word?"

"Damn. Opened myself up for that one, didn't I?"

"Yes, in your arrogance."

Another laugh. "I'm definitely not bored with you. Now where am I taking you for our dinner date?"

I smirked. "Pizza Lucé."

"Hilarious, Luce."

"I'm serious. That's where I want to go."

"For real?"

"Why does that surprise you?"

"I figured you'd pick someplace more upscale."

"Sorry to disappoint, but I'm the pizza and beer type."

He leaned in. "I'd ask if this was a setup, with you being a sharp-tongued brunette with those big brown Bambi eyes, because you're exactly my type. But I stopped here on a whim, so I know my friends and family aren't fucking with me."

"Mr. Jaxson, your vehicle is ready," a voice announced via the loudspeaker.

I cocked my head. "You refer to yourself by your last name?"

He shook his head. "Long story that I'll explain over pizza and beer."

"Miz Q, your vehicle is ready," echoed from the loudspeaker.

Jaxson—Mr. Jaxson—whatever his name was—winked. "Lucy Q? What's the Q stand for?"

"Nothing."

We stood simultaneously.

"Come on. Tell me," he urged.

"Maybe, as a single woman in a public venue, I didn't use my real name or initial as a safety precaution."

That declaration—a total lie—was worth it to see his smugness vanish.

Outside, the attendants stood by our cars.

No surprise that Mr. Annoying and Tenacious drove a Porsche.

But my eyes were on how spiffy my beloved blue Corolla looked. I smiled at the attendant and slipped him five bucks. "Thank you."

"My pleasure."

I looked across the roof of my car to see my date staring at me. "I'd say the last one to arrive at Pizza Lucé has to buy the first round, but my Toyota is at a disadvantage in comparison to that beast."

"I planned on following you, in case you decided to make a detour."

"Worried that I might come to my senses and change my mind about this bizarre date?"

"Yep." He grinned at me. "Lead the way, Lucy Q. I'll be right behind you."

The doorbell rang, pulling me out of the memory.

I slicked on a final coat of lip gloss and went to meet my date.

Damon smiled. "Lucy. You look fantastic." He handed me a bouquet of mixed flowers.

"Thanks, Damon, they're lovely." I stepped back to allow him to come inside. "I'll just take a minute to put these in water."

"No rush. Our reservation is at eight. We've got time."

Damon wandered through the main room, looking at the artwork hanging on the walls and the kid stuff that seemed to multiply across every horizontal surface every time I turned around. Points for him that he didn't react to the chaos that was our living space.

Surprisingly I wasn't nervous for this official first date. The potential of a second date would create more nerves, since most men never made it past the first date with me.

I'd met Damon at a business function. We'd hit it off and

exchanged emails, then phone numbers. We'd met twice after work, so when he'd asked me out for dinner, I'd said yes without hesitation. I liked him. He was low key, but not so low key as to have no personality like some of the business-type guys I worked with.

I arranged the blooms and set the vase on the dining table. "Thank you again for the flowers. Great first-date behavior."

"You're welcome." He frowned. "But this is our third date, counting meeting for coffee once and cocktails once."

Jaxson's sexy warning from years ago on our first date echoed in my head . . . *"By our third date you will know how perfectly wicked it'll feel to have my mouth all over you."*

Was that what Damon was hoping for? By assigning this outing a number? So if we made it to date five, then I'd fall into bed with him because it was time?

Wrong.

And here was yet another reminder of why I didn't date. I managed a smile. "Semantics."

Then he looked around. "Your daughter isn't here?"

Here was the awkward part. If I said she was with her father for the weekend, would he take that as the all clear for an adult sleepover? Or did I lie about having a babysitter so if the night sucked I could use Mimi as an excuse to end the date?

After I opted for a simple "No," Damon smiled. "Maybe I'll get to meet her next time."

"Maybe. For now, let's go. I'm starving."

Two

JAX

I shifted Mimi off my back to punch in the alarm code for my apartment.

She scooted inside with a happy, "Yay, my princess room," and disappeared into the bedroom I'd let her decorate however she wanted, which meant an explosion of pink and purple, sequins, lace, satin ruffles and a canopied bed fit for . . . well, a princess.

Since my return to Minneapolis six months ago, I'd been temporarily living in Snow Village, the two-building apartment complex for professional athletes who specialized in "winter" sports that my cousin Jensen Lund owned. It fulfilled my security requirements, and the complex had plenty of kids for Mimi to play with when she stayed with me.

So far her visits had mostly been on the weekends, since Lucy preferred getting Mimi to and from school. I'd tried not to be bitter about the fact she didn't even trust me to get our kid to school on time, but I had no right to bitch about it. I'd had limited access to my daughter for most of her life—with good reason due to my past bad behavior—so I needed to prove I intended to be a full-time father even if I only had Mimi part time.

During the years I played hockey, I only saw Mimi sporadically during the season, and hockey has a long damn season. Training starts the end of August, and the regular season ends for most of us in April, unless we make it to the playoffs, and then the season can extend into June. I traveled more than I was home, and even when I was in my team's home base of Chicago, I had grueling practices, home games and responsibilities to the club and fans that made a single-parent schedule nearly impossible.

But the shitty truth I'd had to face the past three years was I hadn't cared. I'd cared about one thing: hockey. Family time interfered with that. So even during our longer breaks, I didn't head to Minneapolis and demand to spend time with my daughter. Instead, I stayed in Chicago, basking in the glory of being a professional athlete in a city that revered athletes above all else. Even now my stomach roils when I think about blowing off my child to get blown by some nameless puck bunny. Nameless mostly because I was too drunk to remember any of it.

I'd lost plenty of sleep over that since I'd sobered up and now steered clear of alcohol.

But I was trying to move forward . . . and I had to do that at the pace Lucy allowed. For the past eight years she'd basically raised Mimi with no emotional support from me. And I'd been so bitter and nasty about the fact she was the only person in my life who called me on every bullshit lie that exited my mouth, that I'd pulled a total dick move and fought her in court for every single penny of financial support she asked for. Some nights I still woke up in a cold sweat when it sank in what low levels I'd sunk to when it came to getting back at Lucy. Mimi—Mimi's well-being—had gotten caught in the cross fire of my pettiness. If my brother, Nolan, and our parents hadn't intervened . . .

"Daddy?"

I shoved the guilt aside and looked into my daughter's sweet face. Mimi looked nothing like me or her mother. She had brown eyes, not dark like Lucy's but more the color of whiskey. Her dark blond hair had streaks of red—no clue where that came from, since my hair was nearly black and Lucy's was a rich chestnut brown. Mimi had freckles spattered across her nose and cheeks. I claimed that she inherited Lucy's stubborn chin; Lucy claimed that immovable set to Mimi's jaw came one hundred percent from me. Her button nose could've come from me. But since my beak had been broken more times than I could count, I don't even remember what my nose used to look like. I just knew when I was lucky enough to have that cute little face in front of me, smiling up at me, I felt grateful beyond measure to have been given a second chance. I tugged on her left pigtail. "What's up, squirt?"

"What are we gonna do tonight?"

"I thought I'd leave the choice up to you."

Her eyes narrowed—that look was one hundred percent skeptical Lucy. "You didn't make any plans?"

"Not for tonight. I've got a surprise for tomorrow night, so what would you like to do?"

"I wanna go ice skating."

That threw me. Naturally she'd pick the one thing guaranteed to send her mother into panic mode. So I hedged. "Wouldn't you rather go to Trampoline World? Or Chuck E. Cheese's? Or . . ." Anything else?

She shook her head. "You're like the best skater ever. You can show me how to get better."

Her buttering me up aside, I knew of no place that offered open ice skating on a Friday night.

That's because you haven't looked.

"Is there an ice skating rink in particular that you want to go to?"

She blinked at me.

Right. She was a kid. I was the adult. This was my job. "Look. I'll see what I can find. But no promises. It's kind of late to try and make this work tonight."

"Can't you call Axl? I bet he knows lots of places to skate."

Doubtful. He played for the Minnesota Wild, and they had a dedicated practice facility. If he showed up at a rink for open skate, he'd likely get mobbed. "He's on the road."

"Maybe you could ask Irina? Since she's a world champion figure skater she probably knows all of the good places," she suggested.

"When were you talking to Irina? She lives on the third floor of the next building over."

"When me 'n Calder were playing. I dared him to go up to the third floor. He wouldn't do it, so I did," she said proudly, "and Irina gave us Russian tea cookies for being brave spies."

"Do Rowan and Jensen know that you and Calder were running all over the building?"

"We weren't running 'all over the building,' Daddy. We went up to the third floor one time."

"But you were up there long enough to have conversation and cookies with Irina," I pointed out. "The only reason I let you go over to Calder's unsupervised last weekend is because I know Rowan and Jensen have strict rules and they expect Calder to follow them. Whose idea was it to break the rules?"

Mimi stared at me, and I could see her struggling to tell me the truth. "It was my idea."

"Milora Michelle Lund. We talked about this. Just because I'm not physically standing beside you doesn't mean the rules change."

Her eyes widened at my usage of her full name.

"I'm happy you didn't lie when I asked you about it, but you broke a rule. And there are consequences with me, just like there are with your mother, when that happens."

"Don't spank me." She took a few steps back.

Christ, just what I needed; my kid to be afraid of me. I crouched down so we were face-to-face. "Have I ever used spanking as a punishment?"

She shook her head.

"I'm not about to start now. The consequences I'm talking about? You lost your chance to go ice skating. And tomorrow you will apologize to Rowan and Jensen for convincing Calder to break the rules with you. Understand?"

She nodded and burst into tears. She said, "I'm sorry!" and launched herself at me.

Hard as it was, I forced myself to let her cry it out. I'd promised Lucy I wouldn't be that drive-by fun dad who left all the shitty parts of parenting to her, especially since she'd done most of it by herself anyway.

The rest of our night was mellow. We ate dinner and watched a movie, and she fell asleep halfway through it.

Barely ten minutes had passed after I'd tucked her in when I heard a soft knock on the door.

I peered through the peephole to see my cousin Jensen standing on the other side.

I'd texted him that we needed to talk after Mimi's confession, but I hadn't expected to see Jens tonight.

"Hey, cuz. I didn't mean to interrupt your night."

"You didn't. Ro and I just got back from a Vikings corporate event and I'm a little wired anyway."

I gave him a sharp look. "Is everything all right?"

"Yeah." He sat on the edge of the couch. "What's up?"

I told him about Mimi and Calder's spy excursion last week. Adding my own guilt for giving Mimi free rein for an hour so I could work out in the fitness center.

Jens waved aside my guilt. "She's eight and in a secure apartment complex with you at the other end of the building. It wasn't like you warned her to stay put while you flitted off to do your thing downtown. And Calder confessed their little adventure to us within two hours, since the guilt was eating him alive."

"Wait. You knew about Mimi being the ringleader and didn't tell me?"

He jammed a hand through his hair. "Rowan and I discussed it, but we decided to give Mimi a chance to come clean to you on her own. We dealt with disciplining our kid. Not our business how you discipline yours."

"This aspect is new to me. But that's part of the parenting gig, isn't it?"

"Yep. And it doesn't get any easier," Jens admitted. "It gives me a whole new appreciation for my parents finding balance with four kids so neither of them was consistently the bad guy."

"My folks were the same way. Mom never used that 'wait until your father gets home' line to pass the buck. If Nolan or I did something that warranted discipline, she meted it out herself." My mother still did that. She pushed her way into my life when I hit rock bottom, dragging my dad and my brother right beside her. I'll never forget the grief on their faces that they couldn't fix me or shoulder some of my burdens. Even after the truth came out about my alcohol abuse, none of them treated me with contempt. They freely, lovingly gave me compassion I know I didn't deserve.

Their unquestioning support humbled me. And I wanted to be the type of father that Mimi looked up to. The man in her life she could always count on.

"What else is on your mind, Jax?" Jensen asked.

"Parental protocol. Do I tell Lucy that Mimi broke the

rules when she was with me? Because that might bring me more trouble."

"Like?"

"Like why didn't I know that Mimi was running around in another building? What was I doing that I couldn't properly watch our child? Why hadn't I known she'd broken a rule until a week after it happened? I don't want to hand her a damn excuse to justify me spending less time with her. What sucks is that she has precedents for that type of reaction."

I fought the roar of frustration building inside me, a roar I used to drown in whiskey and women. Now I forced myself to utilize the redirection exercises my counselor suggested. Breathe in, clench my fists, breath out, release them.

After three rounds of that, I felt the frustration ebb. I opened my eyes to see Jensen studying me warily. My cheeks flushed with embarrassment. Goddammit. The last thing I wanted was for my youngest male cousin to see me struggle. To see me as weak.

But you are weak. Admitting that is the first step toward finding real strength.

I exhaled again. "Sorry."

"Dude. Don't apologize. I'm just happy to see that you have coping mechanisms that work for you."

"Thanks. Some days are easier than others."

Jens leaned forward. "You have people to talk to? Or is assuming that you do just another place where we've all failed you?"

"I see a counselor once a week. He heads up the group therapy sessions at Hazelden. After I completed the program he referred me to a colleague in Chicago. After I moved back here, he took me on as a private client. I'm lucky to have him."

"I'm really freakin' relieved to hear that." Jensen paused. "I know you're tight with Nolan, but if you ever need someone else to talk to, someone who understands the public demands of being a pro athlete, who feels the need to numb the constant aches and pains associated with using your body as a battering ram, call me. I'm not some punk-ass kid anymore."

I locked my gaze to his. "I know that. I appreciate the offer, so don't be shocked when I take you up on it."

"Good." Jens stood. "Now, come here, bro, and hug it out."

"Jesus. You sound like Martin."

"Wrong. Martin calls me brosky."

I laughed. We did the backslapping-man-hug thing. Then I followed Jensen to the door.

He faced me. "As far as the Mimi situation . . . you gotta tell Lucy what Mimi did and how you dealt with it. That said . . . Snow Village is secure. Emphasize that. Emphasize that you gave Mimi consequences for her behavior. She'll see your honesty as a step forward. Better to be up front now than for Mimi to spill the details in a few months, which will cause Lucy to wonder what else you'd kept from her."

"You're right. Maybe I'll find my balls and tell her about my upcoming move at the same time."

Jensen's jaw dropped. "Jax. Buddy. You still haven't told her?"

I shook my head. "The space isn't ready. They're finishing the trim work and final installation of the private elevator this week. Move-in date is still up in the air."

"Who all knows about this move?" Jensen asked, shooting a glance down the hallway toward Mimi's bedroom.

"You. Since you're my landlord."

"That's it?"

"I didn't bother to talk to your brother about taking on the remodel since he's focused on historical renovation."

"Your brother doesn't know either?"

"Nolan would try to talk me out of it."

Jensen clapped me on the shoulder. "Good luck telling her,

because you'll need it." He grinned. "Speaking of getting lucky, got to get home to my wife so we can end our date night with a bang."

After he left, I locked up, grabbed a sparkling water from the fridge and plopped into the recliner. I found it weird that married couples had "date" nights. Wasn't that the whole point of getting married? So you didn't have to come up with dating type stuff? Christ. I sucked at dating.

With the TV off and silence filling the space, I nestled my head into the cushion and closed my eyes. My mind wasn't calm. It zigged and zagged until it settled on a direction I hadn't wanted to go. To my very first conflict with Lucy and our first date, which, ironically enough, still was the best date I'd ever had . . .

On the drive to Pizza Lucé, I didn't let that little blue Corolla out of my sight to the point I was tailgating. Lucy already thought I was annoying; proving I was an asshole driver wouldn't come as a surprise to her. But no way was I letting her ditch me; I'd never been so drawn to a woman.

It'd been a long time since I'd met a woman who hadn't immediately known who I was. Not my ego talking, but the truth. Anytime I ventured out in Chicago, either alone, with my teammates or with a woman, I got recognized. After living out of the Twin Cities for several years, whenever I came home, the odds of anyone recognizing me either as Jaxson "Stonewall" Lund, Chicago Blackhawks hockey player and rival to the Minnesota Wild, or just as Jax Lund, one of the heirs to the billionaire Lund family fortune, were still pretty high.

The Lund family name was synonymous with power, money and prestige in the community. Plus, I'd been the high school hockey standout as well as part of the college hockey team that brought the Frozen Four championship to the University of Minnesota. So it'd been refreshing that Lucy had treated me like any other guy who annoyed the piss out of her with rude, entitled behavior. Add in the fact she was hot—man, I could worship those legs of hers for days—and unapologetically prickly . . . I wanted to see if she had that attitude in bed.

I parked quickly enough I was able to do the gentlemanly thing and help her out of her car.

She said nothing, just arched a brow at me. But she didn't remove my hand from the small of her back as I ushered her inside the restaurant.

The scents of yeast and basil, oregano and tomatoes greeted us. The male host said, "Two for the restaurant side or the bar side?"

Lucy answered, "Bar side, please. A booth by the windows if you've got one."

The host offered her a dazzling smile. "Whatever the lady wishes."

The smarmy asshole hadn't even looked at me.

Once we were seated, she held out her hand.

"What?"

"Your cell. Hand it over."

I leaned across the table and kissed her palm. "I left it in the car."

"Umm. Well. Okay."

That little peck on the palm flustered her.

Good.

The host cleared his throat.

I glanced up. I'd forgotten the little shit was still there.

He handed Lucy a menu, then me. "Wine list is on the back."

She smiled at him. "Sorry. Beer girl."

"A woman after my own heart. The beer on tap is listed on the second to the last page. And might I suggest you try the Spring Splendor from a microbrewery in Wisconsin? It's a full-bodied IPA with hints of apple blossom, green wheatgrass and honey. It's the quintessential beer for spring."

Fucking hipster.

"While my beautiful date is debating what her heart desires"—*besides me* went unsaid—"have the bartender pour me whatever seasonal Schell you've got on tap. Sixteen ounce."

The dude bristled.

Lucy said, "I'll have the same."

As soon as the guy left, she leaned in. "This date ain't starting out so hot, ace."

"Why? Because I was brusque to the server who was salivating all over my date?"

She blinked at me. "Salivating? Really?"

"Slathering on the flattery too."

She snorted and busied herself scouring the menu.

"Salivating and slathering is my job, hot stuff. Not his."

Without missing a beat or looking up from her menu, she said, "Hit me with some flattery."

"I can't decide if I'll wrap my fingers in your silky hair the first time I kiss you or if I'll curl my hand around the back of your neck as I taste my fill of those full lips of yours. I may not kiss you tonight, but by our third date you will know how perfectly wicked it'll feel to have my mouth all over you."

Lucy slowly lowered the menu. Her pupils had nearly disappeared in her dark brown eyes. "Are you a good kisser, Jaxson? Or do you just talk a good game?"

"Anytime you want to find out, baby, all you gotta do is ask."

She smirked . . . and damn if it didn't straddle the line between evil and challenging. "Fair warning that this verbal foreplay is all you'll get from me tonight: I don't fuck on the first date."

"So I can't call you loose." I smirked. "But then again, *Luce*, I guess I can."

She started laughing. The sound of it had me joining in. We were still snickering when the waiter—not the brown-nosing host boy—delivered our beer.

I raised my mug to hers for a toast.

But she beat me to the punch. "To loose women and annoying men."

"Skål."

After that first sip, I said, "What kind of pizza are we ordering?"

"Pepperoni and green olive."

I shook my head. "Sausage and black olive. With hot peppers."

She shook her head right back at me. "With green peppers and green onions."

"Nope. With purple onions and mushrooms. Chicago deep-dish pan style."

"Wrong. Thin crust."

The waiter returned. "Are you ready to order?"

I kept my eyes on hers. "We'll take a large hand-tossed crust, loaded with all toppings except anchovies."

"Extra cheese?" he asked.

We said, "No," simultaneously.

"The man can compromise," she muttered before taking another swig of beer.

I just smiled. "So, Lucy Q, are you a native Minnesotan or a transplant?"

"Native. Born and raised in the Twin Cities. How about you?"

"Same." If I told her I didn't live here now this would be our first and last date. "And your family?"

"My mom lives here. She and my father divorced when I was ten. My sister lives here too."

"Older sister? Younger?"

"Older by two years. What about your family?"

"Most of my family lives here. I have one brother. Younger by two years. I have a lot of cousins. We spent so much time together growing up that they're almost like my siblings."

"Sounds fun." She made a ring on her cocktail napkin with the bottom of her beer mug. "Ever been married?"

"Nope. Never came close."

"Me neither." She gave me a curious look. "What do you do for a living?"

"Guess."

"How did I know you were gonna say that." She continued her perusal of me. "You're a finance guy. Probably a stock-broker, given the annoying conversation about salary that I overheard."

"Nope. Not even close."

"Is Jaxson your first name or your last name?"

I said, "First," and nothing else.

"What's the big deal about you not telling me your last name or what you do for a living?"

I slumped back in the booth with a sigh. "Me telling you will change things. And I like you and how this is going, so I'm not ready to wreck it."

Her eyes searched mine. "I'll let you hedge. For now."

"Sounds like you've already made up your mind there will be a second date, despite your erroneous statement that this date wasn't going well. What do you do for a living?"

"Guess."

I had that coming. "You're a baker."

"What about me caused you to make that claim?"

"Because you smell amazing. Like lemon cupcakes coated with sweet buttercream frosting."

"That's my body lotion," she retorted. "Try again. You have two more guesses about my occupation."

"You're a . . . nurse."

"Sort of. But that's not what pays my bills."

"How can one 'sort of' be a nurse?"

"One guess left."

"What do I get if I guess correctly?"

"Nothing, because you won't figure it out."

I took a swig of beer. "She has a high bullshit meter. She likes to argue. She has a haughty demeanor. She dresses well—feminine yet professional. I'd say a high-powered attorney, but if that were the case you'd be driving a Mercedes, not a Corolla. So my final answer is . . . you're an advocate in a social services department."

She made a deep-throated "you missed" buzzer noise and I burst out laughing. Not what I'd expected from her. At all.

"In a show of faith because I'm proud of the fact I graduated from college, I'll tell you that I'm a graphic designer. Which means I can't draw for shit, but I'm creative and excel at organizing computer images into functional graphics."

"Do you like your job?"

"I love it. It's nearly impossible to find a stable, full-time job now in our industry. Too many graphics people are stuck with freelancing jobs because companies prefer to hire out for specific campaigns, rather than having an in-house graphics department."

"What do you do for fun?"

Lucy cocked her head, sending that glorious hair cascading onto the table. "What's with the twenty questions? I thought you intended to prove that you aren't annoying. Being grilled by a guy who's embarrassed to confess how he makes a living or refuses to divulge his last name skirts the line from you being annoying into you being an arrogant ass."

"Point taken." I smiled and brushed her hair over her shoulder. "I was going for mysterious."

"You failed, buddy."

I laughed. I couldn't remember the last time I'd laughed

so much. Especially at my own expense. "Ask me three things about myself."

"Do you have a closer relationship to your mom or your dad?"

Great question—and one I'd never been asked. "My mom."

"When was the last time you cried?"

Jesus. She could be a professional interrogator. "Two months ago."

"What made you cry?"

My subconscious said, *I got the fuck beat out of me during the final game of the season and I was pissed off that we lost*, but my mouth said, "I had a physical injury."

"What's your—"

"Huh-uh, Lucy Q. That was three questions. Anything you ask me from here on out? You have to answer too."

"Fine. What's your favorite song?"

"Today it's 'Brown Eyed Girl.' What's yours?"

She shot back, " 'King of Wishful Thinking,' " without missing a beat.

I laughed. God. This woman. I was already half-crazy about her. "Seriously, Luce. What do you do for fun when you're not working as a graphic designer?"

Lucy drummed her fingers on the table. "I pick up sexy, nosy, secretive men in car washes."

"Now I'm crushed that I'm not the first to fall for your prickly charms."

"Ah. But you are." Her smiled faded. "I'll admit . . . it's been a while since I've done anything fun, Jaxson."

I swallowed my flip response. "You're beautiful and you could go to any club or bar in the metro area and never have to pay for a drink. You wouldn't lack for dance partners. And you wouldn't have to go home alone unless you chose to. As a lifelong resident of the Twin Cities I'm guessing you've got tons of friends. You're honestly telling me that you aren't out and about at least some of the time taking advantage of being hot, sexy and single?"

"Will it put me in a different light if I admit if I'm not working or taking care of my mom I don't know what to do with myself?"

My eyes narrowed. "Taking care of your mom?"

"She was diagnosed with breast cancer when I was in college. Thankfully she had good health insurance and we were able to get her into Mayo. She went through two rounds of chemo, so my sister, Lindsey, and I moved back in with her. I deferred a semester of school, and Lindsey and I took turns taking her to appointments, because it's a bit of a drive to Rochester."

"That explains your 'sort of a nurse' response," I murmured.

"After the cancer went into remission, I refocused on school. Then I graduated and focused on my job. Pretty boring, huh?"

I snagged her restless hand. "Pretty fucking amazing, actually, that you'd put your life in a holding pattern to be there for your mom."

"She'd do it for me. And I wouldn't have been able to concentrate on school anyway, since I was so worried I'd lose her."

"Doesn't make it—or you—any less amazing, Lucy Q." I kissed the back of her hand. "I want to take you out and do every fun thing you've ever wanted to experience but couldn't because you were singularly focused on doing things for other people." I rubbed my lips across her knuckles and watched the pulse in her throat quicken.

"Why me?"

"It's not a line when I say I've never felt this kind of pull. I want to learn everything about you. Your likes, your dislikes. What makes you laugh. If you throw things when you're angry. If your skin tastes salty sweet. If I can make you melt on my tongue."

"Jaxson."

"Lucy."

"Even without understanding why you're determined to keep things from me, I know we're horribly mismatched, you and I."

"You can't know that after spending only an hour with me."

"Exactly. And you can't be that into me after just an hour either," she volleyed back.

Dammit. I kept my temper in check, but that allowed sarcasm to escape. "You're wrong. And your generalization is annoying."

"Poor man. The fact I'm always right is annoying to those who are usually wrong."

I laughed. "You don't fool me, hot stuff. I figured out a couple of key things about you in the past hour."

"Like what?"

"You get off on being argumentative." I watched as she struggled—and lost—against the urge to argue with me.

"I'm only argumentative when the situation warrants it," she retorted.

"You're stubborn."

"So? It's better to be a mule doing the kicking rather than be the one getting kicked around."

"You like me."

That caught her off guard. "I sort of like you."

"Then put that stubbornness aside and let me prove that we're not mismatched."

The food arrived.

I didn't push her to talk.

But I caught her sneaking thoughtful, slightly confused glances at me as I wolfed down all but three slices of our pizza.

After we'd finished our beers and I'd fought her on being allowed to pay the full bill and not going halvsies—whatever the fuck that was—with her, she cut right to the chase.

"You get one shot at proving you know me after only two hours in my company, Jaxson. Meet me back here tomorrow night at six P.M." She slid out of the booth and challenged, "If you don't show up . . ."

Then I'd have proved her "mismatched" theory.

The fuck that was gonna happen.

"Oh, I'll be here, Lucy Q. Count on it."

M y phone buzzed in my pocket, pulling me out of the memory.

I ended the timer that reminded me to take my medication before bed.

As I brushed my teeth, my mind was still in the past. Specifically how easy it'd been to be with Lucy from the start. I'd never had that type of relationship with any other woman, and it killed me—killed me—that I'd screwed it up so completely with her.

It was a long damn time before I fell asleep.

Three

LUCY

Sunday afternoon I'd arrived at Lola's retirement party earlier than I'd planned.

Jax wasn't there yet. And Mimi's phone call yesterday had been so brief I had no idea what fun things Daddy had planned for them.

Part of me was happy he took his daughter places for them to spend time together, just the two of them, doing whatever her heart desired, damn the cost. Part of me carried resentment that I'd never had the luxury of extra cash until four years ago when Jax stepped up his monetary support.

I made the rounds, chatting with other clerical staff members of Lund Industries. As much as I loved working for LI, there was a line between management and the rest of us—evidenced by the separation of the groups on opposite sides of the conference room.

I'd volunteered to help Lennox Lund decorate for Lola's party, since Lennox's pregnancy prevented her from standing on ladders. Lennox hadn't worked in Lola's department for a few years, but she still maintained tight ties with the "floaters"—the term given to the in-house temp service. As a party organizer, I had a legitimate excuse to disappear behind the scenes, restocking plates and forks. Refilling the punch bowl. I'd just cracked open a new can of nuts, when I heard, "Lucy, dear? Are you back here?"

Why had Jaxson's mother come looking for me?

"Yes, Edie. Be right there." I exited the pantry with the jumbo can in one hand and the can opener in the other. I smiled at her.

Edie Lund was a stunning woman. With her dark hair cut into an asymmetrical bob that brushed one shoulder, she looked hip and approachable, not like a stuffy socialite married to one of the richest men in Minnesota. Her clothing was stylish whether she dressed in a trendy business suit for her position at Lund Cares Community Outreach, or whether she was home, in cropped jeans and a gauzy blouse as she tended her gardens. She was shorter than me, which put her at around five foot two, but she always wore four-inch heels. I used to joke with Jaxson that even if the house was on fire, Edie would still take the time to strap on her stilettos.

Even in the darkest times between Jax and me, Edie was never cold or cruel to me or indifferent to Mimi. That's why I had allowed her to create a bond with her granddaughter. Edie never asked why I denied her son contact with his daughter, she never commented on the court battles Jax instigated, she never defended or attempted to explain Jaxson's behavior. The only time she voiced her opinion was when Nolan and his father, Archer, threatened to file for custody of Mimi. Edie refused to have any part of taking Mimi away from me, and she made sure I knew she'd fight her husband and her sons on their ego-fed scheme. She was a wonderful grandma, and anytime I needed extra help with Mimi, she jumped in, no questions asked.

"Well, lookit you, Lucy." Her eyes, identical to Jaxson's in shape and color, perused me from head to toe. "You are a vision in that dress."

I blushed. "Thanks. It's a little formal for daily office wear, so I pull it out when the occasion warrants it." I'd worn it on my date with Damon too.

"I have a closetful of special occasion dresses, most of which I've worn exactly once. Part and parcel of being wife to the CEO, but it seems like such a waste."

"You should take them to your seamstress. I've seen her work and she's amazing. She can repurpose and refashion them."

"I love that you're so practical. I was going to let Mimi have them as dress-up clothes."

"God no. She'd take scissors to them and make clothes for her stuffed animals."

Edie laughed. "True. Where is my sweet girl?"

I frowned. "She's with Jax this weekend. Didn't they hang out with you and Archer?"

"No. I didn't hear a word from them."

"Huh. Well, Jax is coming to this party with Mimi."

"I'll just text him and find out where they are. I think Lola is ready to escape, and he'll miss her if he doesn't arrive soon."

My return to the party went unnoticed—just how I liked it. I fussed around the food table. Rearranged the presents. Checked my watch.

Just then my little ray of sunshine burst in, looked around for me and then made a beeline in my direction. The girl was out of breath by the time she reached me.

"Mommy. You'll never guess what we did last night!"

"Wrestled alligators?"

She giggled. "No. Better than that."

"You ate the sundae extravaganza at Minnehaha Scoop?"

"Huh-uh. Even better than that!"

"Oh, sweetheart, there ain't nothing better than that."

She was shifting from foot to foot with excitement. "Cinderella is better than ice cream."

"What?"

"Daddy took me to see the play *Cinderella*! There was singing and dancing and princess dresses and it was so awesome! Then he bought me a sparkly crown and Cinderella princess pajamas! And he even let me wear the crown to bed!"

Getting tickets for a musical? That didn't sound like something Jax would do on his own. "Who went with you?"

"Nobody. Just me and Daddy."

Before I could ask her anything else, Jaxson sauntered into the room. He took in the crowd, giving a nod or a dip of his chin to people he knew. When his eyes met mine, he stopped moving.

Immediately I felt the silent pull between us that we'd both attempted to ignore. Even now that wistful feeling of want flowed through me. And the sardonic twist of his lips let me know he felt it too.

Jax started toward me, and I didn't feign interest in anything or anyone else.

With his long-legged stride eating up the distance between us, his eyes seemed to eat me up too. By the time he finally reached me, my heart pounded like a snare drum.

His big body blocked mine from everyone in the room. So no one saw him circle his massive hand around my biceps and lean in to brush those perfect lips over my jaw as he murmured, "Hey, Luce."

My breath caught.

"You look phenomenal, as usual." His lips skated up,

across my cheekbone to the spot in front of my ear. "Christ, you smell even better."

"Jaxson."

"There's Grandma!" Mimi said and raced off.

His sweet, focused affectionate side still had the power to affect me.

"Sorry we're late." He eased back just enough to look into my face.

"No biggie. I have to stay and clean up."

"Need some help?"

I locked my gaze to his, momentarily losing my train of thought when I saw the sincerity in those mesmerizing eyes.

He grinned. "Babe. That wasn't a trick question."

Babe. That term snapped me out of my moon-eyed gaze. Wasn't that Jaxson "Stonewall" Lund's default term when he couldn't recall his flavor of the night's name? "No need to stick around. I'm sure you've got better things to do."

Jaxson's smile dropped. "That wasn't what I asked. Are you pulling the 'I'm a one-woman band' bullshit line like you always do when anyone offers you help?" He paused. "Or is it only when I offer help?"

My cheeks flamed. Damn man saw too much. He always had when I'd interested him enough to look. "You want to vacuum up cake crumbs, have at it." I looked away.

"See?" He crouched down to force my attention back to him. "That wasn't so hard. And I'm fully versed in janitorial duties after another summer of pushing the broom at Camp Step-Up, remember?"

That caused me to smile. "I still can't believe that Jensen couldn't find a position for you besides in the janitorial sector."

"That's because my cousin is aware that I have few usable skills besides shooting a puck."

Automatically I said, "That's not true."

"Yeah? Ask me what I've been doing the past six months at LI."

"Okay. Jaxson Lund, eldest of the next generation of the Lund family dynasty, what have you been doing in these hallowed halls since your retirement from your glorious hockey career?"

"I've missed that sarcastic mouth. You still can't repeat back a simple question, can you?"

"Nope. That's what we graphic designers do—add extra flourishes. It's the same question, Jax, so hit me with your answer."

"I have no idea what I've been doing, Luce. Dad sends me to 'train' at various departments, but I haven't learned a damn thing besides how big and complicated this company truly is. I'm as lost as the intern I found sobbing in the break room last month. And trust me, I knew exactly how she felt."

His distress was so genuine, without thought I put my hand on his chest to try and soothe him. "Have you talked to anyone about this?"

"You're the first." He covered my hand with his. "My dad is the CEO. As the oldest Lund son, he was groomed for the position by his father. As my grandfather was groomed in the same way by his father. Now the grooming cycle begins with me. Except I've spent minimal time in these 'hallowed halls,' because from the time I held that hockey stick in my hand at age eight, that's all I ever wanted. Period. I only went to college to appease my parents and to play hockey. I have a degree in business and no idea how to use it to benefit a company this size. How am I supposed to talk to my family about this? Like you said, I'm the oldest. By all rights, and historically in the Lund family, I'm next in line for that CEO position. Imagining being at the helm of this billion-dollar company scares the shit out of me, Luce. Like panic attack type fear that's keeping me up at night. It's not me being macho or trying to save face when I say that none of my family members will understand—not my dad, not Ash, not Brady, not Annika, not Uncle Ward, not Uncle Monte, and especially not Nolan, who are all super invested and committed to LI."

"Oh, Jax."

"Everyone is cutting me way too much slack. They claim I'll find my footing. That I'll eventually settle in. But I know in my gut that's never gonna happen. So I've been playing along just the same as I've always done since they put me on the board of directors when I was twenty-two."

"What can I do?"

Jax rested his forehead to mine. "You're doing it."

"Just listening?"

"Yeah." He inhaled a deep breath.

His exhale fanned across my lips, and I steeled myself not to tremble from this intimacy.

"Shit. Sorry. I didn't mean to blurt all of this out. I know that we haven't been each other's confidants for a long time, but you were the one person in my life I could talk to." He squeezed my hand. "I miss that. I miss this. I never fully understood what I had with you until it—and you—were gone."

My entire body stiffened.

He sighed and retreated. "And there was another confession that I hadn't intended to make today."

"Just today?" The words slipped out before I could stop them.

His haunted eyes searched mine. "There's so much between us that we've never addressed. So much hurt and anger. Frustration and lies. I get that the past is the past, Luce, I really do. To some extent, we're both still stuck there. Or dwelling on it, which means we've never truly dealt with our past the way we need to. I wasn't in a position to ask for that from you. I'm not talking about forgiveness."

"Then what are you talking about, Jax?"

"Hoping at some point we can have a conversation. An uninterrupted conversation that has nothing to do with Mimi and everything to do with what happened between us. What went wrong when everything started out so right."

Your infidelity and your inability to see a life off the ice ruined everything.

"I can tell you want to say something to me, so just go ahead and spit it out."

The words that had been stuck inside me for so long dislodged themselves from that dark place and exited my mouth in a rush. "You're absolutely right."

Jax went utterly still. "Please say that again so I know I wasn't hearing what I wanted to hear."

"You're right. Before either of us can move on, we should deal with our past. We should . . . talk."

The relief on his handsome face and the way he suddenly had difficulty swallowing assured me I'd said the right thing, even if following through with this conversation would be excruciating for both of us.

"Thank you."

Before I could respond, Mimi crashed into us, worming her way between our bodies, which were way closer than usual. I stepped back, and if Mimi noticed I'd been touching her father . . . Oh, who was I kidding? She didn't pay attention to stuff like that.

"Mommy, can I have cake?"

I looked at Jax. "Has she already had cake today?" Mimi's favorite place was Wuollet Bakery because they crafted the most beautiful, elaborate cupcakes, and she begged her dad to take her there every weekend.

Jax shook his head. "After our late night at the play, we slept in today, so we didn't eat brunch until one. She had a waffle but no desserts."

"So is that yes?" Mimi demanded.

"Yes. One piece. Have Grandma help you."

Mimi's freckled nose wrinkled. "I'm not a baby. I don't need help getting cake."

She skipped off and I caught Edie's eye. She gave me a quick nod and arrived at the cake table at the same time as her granddaughter.

"Something did happen with Mimi that we need to talk about," Jaxson said.

My gaze zoomed back to him. "What?"

Jax barely took a breath as he relayed the incident, and I had to admit to myself that was probably my fault since I tended to interrupt him whenever we discussed a Mimi issue. I hadn't known how often I did that until my sister, Lindsey, had been at my apartment when Jax had dropped Mimi off and she'd pointed it out. So I swore I'd try to listen fully before I cut in.

After a long minute or so, time that Jax allowed me to think without interruption, I said, "You did exactly what I would've done. Not letting her play with Calder over the weekend . . . clever little bonus punishment, Daddy, because you know how much she loves her cousin."

He flashed a quick smile. "I hoped you'd think so."

"I won't bring it up with her unless she says something to me first."

"Cool. What else is on the Mimi agenda this week?"

"I'm working from noon to eight P.M. on Wednesday, filling in for Jonna. Could you pick Mimi up from school and take her to your place until I'm done? Then I'll swing by and pick her up."

"Why don't you have her spend the night with me? That way you can work as late as you want and not have to worry Meems is missing her bedtime. I'll get her to school on Thursday."

I glanced over at our daughter when I heard her laugh. My

eyes narrowed on the one piece of cake she'd chosen that filled up the entire plate.

Then Jax's hand touched beneath my chin, tipping my face back to meet his gaze.

"I'll get her to school on time. I promise."

"It's not that."

"Then what's the problem?"

"She . . ." *Just spit it out. Mimi is his daughter.* "She's really difficult early in the morning on school days."

Jax's gaze turned shrewd. "You think I don't know this? Or that I can't handle it?"

"You don't know about this bratty behavior because I'm so mortified by it that I haven't told anyone."

"Not even me?"

"No. It's my fault that I let her get away with it. I feel like a pushover and a failure, and yet I do nothing to change it."

His grip increased on my shoulder. "Is that why you never let me take her to school?"

I nodded. "It's a battle every morning. She yells and cries and is a total demon child from the moment I wake her up. When she's with you on the weekends, she gets to sleep in. Same goes for summer vacation. Same goes for when she stays with her grandparents. She's all smiles and sweetness. But on a day-to-day basis with me . . ."

"You've been dealing with this behavior with her for how long?"

"Since she was three." My voice became quieter with that embarrassing shitty parenting admission, and I hung my head.

Jax cupped the side of my face in his hand like he used to when we were together—a countermeasure against me closing down during an argument. Early on he'd figured out the best way to force my attention to the subject at hand was to force me to focus on him.

Then he was in my face. "Dammit, Lucy. I'm her father. I'm supposed to know this about her, not just the sweet, shiny, bubbly unicorn stuff."

"I know. I'm sorry. But you weren't—"

"Around? Well, I'm here now and we're partners. That means all of it; the good, the bad and the ugly. I get that it'll take some faith on your part to believe that parenting isn't a phase for me. I need to know you're willing to talk to me."

"That's never been my strong suit."

"Then it's time for you to learn." He smirked. "Practice makes perfect, babe. So let's start now. Tell me about her demonic behavior."

Babe again. Ugh. "Fine. I'll give you the lowdown on my oh-so-fun morning routine without any sugarcoating."

By the time I'd told him everything, his eyes had taken on a hard glint.

"No way am I putting up with that from her. No way. It'll be a shock to her little world that weekday rules at Daddy's are different than weekend rules."

"Jax—"

He leaned in closer. "Do you trust me?"

"With her? Yes."

He ground his teeth together with such force that I heard the tendons in his jaw pop. "You just had to qualify it, didn't you?"

"Yes. This trust is about Mimi, not about me. I just wanted you to be clear on how far the trust goes."

"It doesn't extend to you and me."

"Not yet."

Jax smiled. "Then there's hope for us." Then he softly pressed his lips to mine.

I froze.

He froze.

Then he retreated and muttered, "Shit." He scrubbed his hands over his face before he looked at me. "Kissing you after we exchanged words . . . sorry. Habit. An old habit that was more ingrained in me than I realized."

I tossed my head and said, "No biggie," even when it was.

Because Jax had been exactly right. It'd been so easy to slip back into those habits, those roles. Arguing. Him pressing his point. Me wanting to avoid confrontation. Him forcing me to listen, to be present with him in the moment. Then a compromise, followed by a kiss, which had always resulted in us getting naked and sweaty as fast as possible.

Yes, there had been a time when we rocked at conflict resolution—even if we'd had to rock the bed frame or the couch or the kitchen table to finish it out.

"I think about that too," Jax said softly, interrupting my thoughts.

My face and neck were hot when I looked at him.

"So, umm . . . yeah. I'll get started on cleanup." And he walked away.

Mimi crashed in the back seat of the car on the way home after the party.

Given her tendency to be crabby when getting woken up, I decided to go for a drive and let her sleep. It'd give me an opportunity to view the autumn colors exploding in reds, rusts and golds along the banks of the Mississippi River and to the farmlands, orchards and valleys outside of the metro area.

Who was I kidding? My brain would be replaying my conversation with Jaxson as well as that unexpected kiss.

Which was completely unlike the first time Jax and I kissed, when it was all about the tease and a challenge to test which one of us would succumb first . . .

———

After issuing the second date challenge, I was ninety-nine point nine percent sure that this Jaxson guy wouldn't show. I wouldn't have put it past him to be one of those guys who collected moments. Flirting and conversation with a woman he met in a car wash, sharing an intimate, yet bizarre dinner, but keeping the promise of more that would always only be that: what might've been.

And I couldn't fault him. How often had the reality of someone paled in comparison to the fantasy we'd built up?

I had a surprisingly giddy feeling, seeing him in the parking lot of Pizza Lucé, leaning against his car, looking the epitome of cool in his wraparound shades, dressed head to toe in black clothing.

I'd barely opened my car door before he was there, offering me a helping hand out and admitting, "I figured you'd blow me off."

"Our minds were on the same wavelength then; I pegged you for a no-show." Standing in front of him, the top of my head didn't even touch his chin. I'd worn flats and jeans, a lightweight thermal shirt covered in cabbage roses and a nylon jacket the neon color of a hothouse hibiscus. Wouldn't want him to think I was trying to impress him, so I went to the other extreme.

"You look . . . springy," he said.

"You look like a thug," I returned. "Although, if you donned an eye patch you could totally pull off the pirate look."

"Argh, me sees no humor in that, lassie."

I laughed. "So, Mr. Thug Life, what are we doing tonight with you wearing that getup? A little cat burglarizing? Reciting bad poetry in a beatnik club?"

"Hey, I don't look that much like a hipster or a criminal. I've got a scarf in the car that'll add a pop of color if need be."

"Pop of color? Dude."

"It's not a phrase I normally use, trust me. I heard it from my brother, Nolan, who is an unapologetic male fashionista."

He admitted that almost with . . . pride. "He chose that ensemble for you?"

"God no. If he saw me wearing this he'd harass me endlessly until I changed into something 'worthy of my station.'"

As soon as he'd said that part, he realized he'd revealed too much.

Hmm. So Jaxson Whoever-he-was had a station in life? That didn't help me decipher who he was since I'd already established that the man had money. Still, I couldn't let his slip slide. I cocked an eyebrow. "Station in life? Does that mean you drive a choo choo train?"

He grinned. "Whoo-whoo . . . nope."

"Ah. I get it. You're a radio jock. What station is it you command? I doubt it's easy listening. Given your clothing choice . . . rap?"

"Hilarious." His gaze moved over me from head to toe. "And you obviously assumed I'd be taking you to a fussy teahouse in a wind tunnel since you dressed for that type of outing."

I bristled at his accurate assessment of my matronly clothing. "Touché."

"Are we going on this date or what?"

"Yes. But before I get into the car with you, should I snap a picture of your license plate and send it to my sister so if you're a psycho Lindsey knows who to accuse of kidnapping and possible dismemberment?"

"Jesus, Lucy Q. I'm not a psycho killer."

"Okay. Speaking of Jesus . . . you're not like . . . a priest or something? On sabbatical and disavowing your celibacy for kicks for a few weeks?"

"Not . . . even . . . close to priestlike behavior." Then he flashed a sexy, devilish grin that gave me tingles. "Now will you walk those beautiful legs around the other side of my car and climb in?"

Didn't have to ask me twice.

Inside the fancy car, with its immaculate interior and new car scent, rap music played in the background. At least I'd gotten that much about him right. "Where are we going, Jaxson?"

"It's a surprise."

"Will people at this place know who you are?"

"Hoping for a hint before we decide when we're doing the big 'last name' reveal?"

I shrugged. "I suck at guessing games. Actually I'm not good at any kind of games. Video games, board games, games of chance."

"What about sports?"

"If I can't concentrate long enough to figure out that Miss Scarlet did it in the library with the candlestick, do you really think I have the ability to hit, kick, throw or catch a ball?"

Defensively he lifted his hands off the steering wheel. "Take it down a notch, babe. It was a question. And there are other sports besides ones requiring a ball."

I shifted in the seat to face him. "Name five."

"Cycling, boxing, gymnastics, swimming, ice skating, running, hockey, skiing, skateboarding—"

"All right, all right, you proved your point. We can just add all of those to the other list of games I'm not good at."

"You've tried them all?"

I shook my head. "Can we please move on from listing all the things I'm bad at?"

"Fine."

"But now you have to tell me at least three things you're no good at."

He tapped his fingers on the steering wheel and appeared to be thinking hard, the jerk.

"Oh, come on. You can't be good at everything."

"I can't cook worth shit."

So he wasn't some local celebrity chef. "And?"

"And I can't carry a tune to save my life."

Not a famous musician either. Wait. Backtrack. I said, "Do you play any instruments?" because he could be a famous guitar player even if he couldn't sing. He definitely had the charisma to be a rock star.

"Nope. Not even a kazoo."

He made a sharp left turn, and within two blocks we were cruising down a residential street lined with huge maple trees in that ugly prebud stage. I hadn't paid attention to where he'd been driving, but I recognized the area now. "We're close to Dinkytown."

"Yep. And FYI, I've never understood why this area around the U of M is called Dinkytown. It's stupid." He pulled up to the curb and parallel parked.

Before he released his seat belt, I put my hand on his shoulder. "Ah ah ah. Not so fast, buddy. You still have to tell me one other thing that you're bad at."

Jaxson slipped off his sunglasses.

God. Those eyes. In less than twenty-four hours I'd forgotten the hypnotic effect they had.

After several long moments, his focus dropped to my mouth. His nostrils flared, and I swear the temperature in the car went up fifty degrees. "I'm really, really bad at self-denial. If want something, I'll do whatever it takes to get it."

Although I'd fantasized about having his smirking mouth on mine and the slick glide of our tongues warring for supremacy as we thoroughly tasted each other, I realized the longer we dragged out that first intimate contact, the hotter—and the more memorable—it'd be.

So I lit that flame of desire by inching closer. I watched it smolder as I delicately traced the strong line of his jaw with the very tips of my fingers.

He made a noise, a low rumble, deep in the back of his throat.

I let my breath tease his lips, and I caught a whiff of the minty-fresh scent of toothpaste pushing past his half-parted lips.

I felt the fire between us getting hotter and more intense.

A warning buzzed through me as shrill as a fire alarm. *Blow out the flare now or you'll get burned.*

Somehow, through the drumlike cadence of my heart, I managed to pull off nonchalant. "See? That confession wasn't so hard."

He mumbled something and retreated. Then he exited the car in such a rush that I'd barely released my seat belt and he was right there, assisting me up and out.

His sunglasses were back in place, so I couldn't read his eyes. His sexy smile returned immediately as he offered his arm. "Shall we?"

"What is this place?"

"A community center. Small scale. It hosts art openings, a more personal variety than the major galleries in the Twin Cities. Occasionally there'll be a play read-thru or a poetry reading or a novel in progress. Kids can attend classes for free as long as there's a sponsorship of some sort by an adult."

I frowned. "Sponsorship? I don't follow."

"The concept is community based. Members use the facility for free, but they have to share their skills as a form of payment. So no one can just sign their kid up for basket weaving. If they want their kid to take a class, they have to contribute to the community aspect somehow."

"But what if the parent has no artistic or creative skills,

but their kid does and a place like this is the only affordable and local option?"

"Then that parent can volunteer to clean up the facility or provide snacks or supplies. It's still a pretty new concept, and they'll work out the bugs as they go. But it was intentionally structured not to outgrow this space. It's an experiment to see if it will evolve into whatever the locals and the volunteer teachers need it to be."

Dumbfounded, I paused on the sidewalk and looked up at him. "Is this what you do, Jaxson? Are you some kind of entrepreneur turned benefactor for the arts?"

He shook his head.

"Then how do you even know that a place like this exists?"

"My mom volunteers here sometimes."

"And?"

"And that's all I know. I've been here once before. Let's check out this month's exhibit." He slipped his callused hand into mine, and it felt as if he'd done it a hundred times before.

At the door, Jaxson handed over cash. The woman said, "Due to the nature of the exhibit, there are rooms where no talking is allowed so visitors can concentrate on the written words. But in the main performing area where the exhibition ends, feel free to discuss what you've seen. The music you'll hear, written and performed by Angelique exclusively for this exhibit, is a joyful celebration of life-sustaining relationships. Please, take as much time as you need to fully enjoy the exhibit."

"Thank you. We will." Then Jaxson ushered me around the corner.

Before we entered the "no talking" room, I crowded him against the wall and tried to look intimidating as best I could, given the fact he topped me by nearly a foot. "Is this some Holocaust exhibit guaranteed to wreck me?"

"No." He shoved his sunglasses on top of his head. "Just keep an open mind, okay?"

"No promises," I shot back.

A large chalkboard by the door explained the purpose of the exhibit.

As I read through the explanation, a hard lump formed in my throat and my eyes burned. The exhibit was comprised of stories from cancer survivors, from age five to age one hundred and five. The stories weren't about the survivors themselves, but the people, the family members and friends who supported them during diagnosis and through treatment. Cared for them. Cheered them on with every tiny medical victory. Cried with them over setbacks.

Even if speaking had been allowed, I couldn't have forced out a single sound as I strolled through the first room. Some of the survivors had drawn pictures. Some had created a collage of photographs. One had made a mobile out of IV tubes and attached pictures of her caregivers on the ends so she could see their faces last thing at night and first thing in the morning.

Jaxson squeezed my hand and it startled me.

How had I forgotten we were still holding hands? I glanced up at him and he dabbed the corners of my eyes with a tissue, which made me want to cry harder. Between the flirting and clever one-liners, he'd actually listened to me . . . he'd heard me. He understood that dealing with my mother's cancer had been a defining moment in my life.

I started to speak, but he placed his fingers across my lips and shook his head.

Two hours later when we finished the exhibit, I was drained, but in a happy way. My mother could've written a piece like any of these. At one point she'd even said that she wished she had the skills to articulate what it'd meant to her to have both of her daughters there without question when she needed them the most.

I didn't speak at all until we were in Jaxson's car.

"Luce? You okay?"

"Yes. And no." I managed a smile. "Thank you. And while the obvious reason you took me there instead of the current textile exhibit showing at the Walker is because of my mom's cancer, that wasn't the only reason you chose that gallery."

He shifted smoothly as we accelerated onto the freeway. "What's the other reason?"

"If I were an optimist I'd say to remind me that every cloud has a silver lining."

"What's pessimistic Lucy say?"

"It's not necessarily pessimistic to see that pain and loss is universal and constant. While we think we're alone in our experiences, we're not. There can be a sliver of happiness even in sorrow." I paused. "How'd I do?"

"My thought processes don't run that deep, sorry to say."

I considered that response as I considered him. "Is there someone in your life who died that you wish you could've been there for like I was for my mom?"

"Nope. I've not had to deal with family death—or the possibility of it. When my grandfather died everyone was relieved because he was a nasty guy."

"Jaxson. That's horrible."

"Yes, he was. What really sucks is I was named after him." He shot me a dark look. "I never want to live up to his name or his reputation."

"I can't blame you." I studied his beautifully masculine profile. "But that's not the reason you haven't told me your full name."

"True."

After he parked alongside my car, he reached for my hand and kissed my knuckles. "You all right, Lucy Q?"

I shrugged. "Surprised . . . maybe a tiny bit confused."

"Confused because I proved that we're not mismatched?"

"Yes."

That earned me his wolfish grin.

"But I'm still curious."

"About?"

"Why I'm willing to agree to another date with you even when we're still playing the no-last-name game."

"Have dinner with me tonight—right now—and I'll tell you everything you want to know."

"I can't." Such a lie. I could, but he had me so twisted up I needed to regroup.

"When can I see you again?" he demanded softly.

"Monday night is open for me."

He nodded. "That'll work. But I can't be out late since it's—"

"A school night?" I supplied. "So that makes you a teacher, Mr. Jaxson?"

"Funny girl, but no."

I studied him closely.

"What?"

"Are you a philanthropist?"

"No, but I've been accused of being a philistine."

"I can scratch comedian off the list of possible career options for you," I said slyly.

"So for this date on Monday night," he continued, "it's your turn to choose what we do. Since you challenged me to prove we aren't mismatched . . . I'm giving you a challenge."

Please challenge me to rub my naked body all over yours to determine if we're sexually compatible.

He leaned in. "What went through your mind just now that put the hungry look in your pretty eyes?"

"It's a secret. What's the challenge?"

"The date has to involve an activity you've never done before."

"Okay." That left my options wide open. "Anything else?"

Jax granted me that cocky grin. "We exchange phone

numbers in a gesture of good faith between us. No chance of you disappearing on me, Lucy Q."

M ommy?"

Thoughts of the past faded and I focused on my daughter. I smiled at her in the rearview mirror. "Hey, sweetheart. You were really tired."

"Uh-huh. I'm hungry too."

"Good thing we're on our way home." I took the next exit and headed toward our apartment. "So tell me about all the things you and your dad did this weekend."

Four

—

JAX

I tried to avoid my brother on Monday morning by showing up at Borderlands first thing. I knew from talking to Simone, my business partner in this bar, that Nolan normally checked in after lunch.

No such luck for me.

I'd made it about twenty steps when I heard, "Stop me if you've heard this one. An alcoholic walks into a bar he owns . . ."

Simone snapped him with the bar towel and he yelped.

I plopped next to Nolan at the long, wooden hand-carved bar. "Don't you have a corporate schedule to keep? An admin who rides your ass when you screw up her hard work of trying to keep you on track?"

"Britt is home with a sick kid today," Nolan retorted. "Besides, I'm not the only one who's supposed to be at Lund Industries right now."

As if anyone would notice that I wasn't there. "I'm on my

way. But I wanted to see the sales receipts from the weekend."

Nolan spun in his barstool to face me. "Why?"

I gave Simone a nod of thanks when she slid a glass of sparkling water in front of me. I knocked back a swallow and focused on my little brother.

Little. Right. I had the distinction of being the oldest—as well as physically the biggest. Nolan's physique leaned toward that of a runner. He accentuated his long and lean form with expensive, trendy clothes, giving him the sophisticated, debonair look women went crazy for. The employees at Lund Industries called him "the Prince," which might've fit him if he hadn't been closer to James Bond—the Daniel Craig years. Power and grace on the surface; explosive temper with highly physical abilities under his snappy suits. And like Bond, I wondered if Nolan would ever settle down with just one woman.

He probably wonders the same thing about you.

Lucy's beautiful, smiling face flashed in my mind's eye.

"Jax?" Nolan prompted.

I shook my head to clear it. "I want to see the receipts because I own the bar, bro."

Nolan and Simone exchanged a look.

"What's the silent communication between you two about?"

"You turned the bar over to me and Ash, remember? So none of us—and yeah, Simone, I'm including you in this—understand why you show up as if you care what's going on here."

And . . . I'd had enough. I pushed to my feet.

Since the place wasn't officially open for the day yet, I didn't bother locking the front door. I said, "Get Ash on the phone now," and crossed the space to the swinging door that led to the back of the bar and the storerooms. I called out, "Dallas? Darlin', are you in here?"

My youngest Lund cousin popped her head out and grinned at me. "If it isn't the big, bad boss man. Good to see you, cuz."

"You too. Meeting out front."

"Now?"

"Right now."

Her big blue eyes went even wider. "Guess you are in big, bad boss man mode."

"Yep."

Another grin lit up her face. "About damn time."

Back out front, Nolan's cell sat on the bar. I pointed to it. "Is Ash on speaker?"

"Yes, I am," my cousin Ash, the COO of Lund Industries, said in his booming baritone. "What's going on?"

"Meeting of the minds. Plus, it's past time to get a few things straight." I inhaled a deep breath. "Look. When I turned over control of this bar to the two of you to run with my partner, I was under the impression that I shouldn't set foot in a bar—any bar—because it would be too much temptation. But the longer I live a life of sobriety, the more I understand that booze does not have the same power over me that it once did."

"And we're all so damn proud of you for that," Nolan interjected.

"Thanks. But with that realization comes the hard truth for both of you—Ash and Nolan. You dropped the fucking ball with this place. I didn't give you the go-ahead to become involved so you had a personal place to kick back with a cold one on the weekends when you weren't fulfilling your duties at LI. I was serious in telling you I wanted new concepts for this space that would make it successful. A year and a half later, every time I look at the monthly P&L, I see that we're limping along, business as usual. Making enough to pay Simone and the waitstaff and that's it. Again, that isn't a change of any sort. I released funds to foot the bill for a full remodel, but I've yet to hear a new idea about what this place could become, let alone see a single blueprint."

"That's where you're wrong," Nolan said. "You shot down our initial idea of this place becoming a sports bar, with memorabilia from your hockey career, and Jensen's football career, and Uncle Monte's basketball career. Sports figures are a huge draw in this town, Jax."

"This town doesn't need another damn sports bar just like the two hundred other sports bars on every damn corner."

I looked at Simone and she stared back at me. She wasn't surprised that it had come to this. In fact, she'd warned me when I'd brought Ash and Nolan in to manage my half of the partnership that it wouldn't work. For them, running a bar was a hobby. For her, it was the business she'd gotten stuck with by trusting me.

"Okay, Jax, I'm relieved you're airing your grievances," Ash said. "But—"

"But I'm not done. And you will listen to me until I am done, and not a word of this conversation leaves this room until I'm damn good and ready for it. Understood?"

Around me Nolan, Simone and Dallas nodded, and Ash said, "Understood."

I did two rounds of my deep-breathing exercises before I spoke. "The truth I've had to face in retirement is that I do not want to work at Lund Industries. In any capacity. I've been going with the flow, faking interest while inside I'm a confused mess. That's the type of feeling that'll drive me back to the bottle. Not that I've been tempted," I clarified at Nolan's look of concern, "but it's far more likely to happen if I'm unhappy in my day-to-day work life, in a job I hate, than here in this bar where I have ready access to every kind of booze imaginable."

Silence.

Then Ash's whistle echoed from the speaker phone. "That's

some serious stuff to throw at us out of the blue, Jax. You honestly hate spending time at LI?"

"Yes."

"If you've felt that way for six months, why wait so long to tell us?" Nolan asked.

"Because I thought I was doing the right thing joining the family business. Problem is, I don't understand the family business. At all. And I realized I don't want to understand it. You guys have been part of LI since our dads first put you to work there. I'm not the best qualified to take over as CEO when my dad retires just because I'm the eldest Lund. It should not be my birthright." I looked at my brother. "That job is ideal for you, Nolan. You've got the charisma and the knowledge. You've spent your life learning the ropes. It's a total dick move on dad and the uncles' parts to even consider putting me in a position I don't deserve."

"And don't want," Dallas said quietly.

"Exactly." The fierce support in her eyes . . . there was something going on with her too. She hadn't taken a permanent position at LI after she received her business degree, despite having worked there as an intern throughout her college years. Having a heart-to-heart with her after I made it through this conversation was my top priority.

"Nolan?" Ash prompted. "Don't you have something to add?"

"Yes. Eventually. Right now I just need a moment to gather my thoughts. This has caught me totally off guard."

"Understandable. But focus on the bar issues, not your future at LI. So far we haven't heard a peep out of Simone. I'm sure she has opinions," Ash said dryly.

Simone snorted. Then she folded her arms across her chest and leaned back against the countertop. "I agree with Jax. I always have. This business was supposed to be an investment for me so I could shake off the shackles of corporate America and live my life. But this business became my life. Due to the fact my business partner had a hockey career that kept him out of running the day-to-day business, I had no choice but to become a bartender and bar manager. That isn't how I hoped this opportunity would play out for me. Every penny of my partnership money is in the physical aspect of this building. Jax has the capital to remodel, remake the image, change the concept. I don't. So I've been in a holding pattern until someone decides what this place could be."

"Simone, if Jax could buy out your half, would you take the cash and move on with your life?" Ash asked her.

Good question. I glanced over at Simone.

She shrugged. "There's no added value to the property since we purchased it, so he'd only have to reimburse me for what I initially paid. Which means the time equity I've invested doesn't equal squat. I'd be a fool to bail out now when there's potential to see our initial vision realized as well as return on my investment."

I could tell Nolan was impressed with her answer.

"Plus," Simone said, looking at me, "no matter what this space becomes, I don't see Jax as a hands-on owner. He won't fill in pulling taps when a bartender gets sick. If we end up installing food service, he won't hop in as a line cook if we're short staffed. He'll be in the background as the silent partner. Checking the P&L, looking to maximize profit, and that's the type of partner I always expected he'd be. I'm good with that . . . with some stipulations, of course."

"Jax. Is that true?" Ash asked.

"Absolutely. No matter what direction we opt to go, this place will still be a bar, geared toward building an evening clientele. I didn't move back here to raise my daughter only to be gone every night."

Dallas and Nolan both nodded.

"My concern now is how and when this news of you not

working for LI will be revealed," Nolan said. "Obviously we'll bring it up as a private family matter first, and then once that's settled, we'll have to take it to the board." He cocked his head and locked his gaze to mine. "You *are* planning on staying on the LI board of directors?"

"Yes. I care about the company. I care that it's being run right, which is why I'm happy to concede that my little brother is better qualified—is the better man—to do that."

Ash said, "I agree. The balance of power will remain as is with the three familial descendants of Jackson Lund— with me as COO and Brady as CFO and Nolan eventually CEO."

"Is that truly balanced?" Dallas asked. "Annika heads up the PR department. So Ward's family has two department heads, while your dad"—she pointed between Nolan and me—"and our dad each have one kid running a department."

"Without being cocky, the positions of COO and CEO are larger entities than the Finance division that Brady controls, and the PR arm that Annika runs." Ash paused. "You have a position at LI if you want it, sis. But we are covered too, if you're still figuring things out."

Dallas smiled at the phone. "Thanks, big brother."

"That still doesn't give me a timeline for when we're telling the family, Jax. It'll be obvious something is up if you stop coming into LI this week. Sooner is preferable to later for sharing this," Ash pointed out.

"Aren't the Vikings playing at home on Sunday?" I asked. "We could do it then, as long as corporate clients haven't been invited into the Lund family skybox."

"Great idea. I'll get the details sorted out and request family only at this game and keep you all in the loop," Nolan said.

"Excellent. Now, Nolan, get your ass to the office. Acquisitions has called my admin twice this morning," Ash said.

Nolan pushed to his feet. "On my way." He picked up his

phone and ended the call. Then he moved to stand in front of me. He kept his voice low. "You and me. Tomorrow morning at Brady's gym. Six A.M. Bring your sparring gear because I'm gonna kick your ass for keeping all of this shit from me."

"I'll bring it, bro. And a little tiny towel for you to wipe away your tears when I beat you."

He gave me his most evil grin. "Can't wait." He waved to Simone and scooted out the door.

I turned around to see Dallas and Simone both staring at me. "What?"

"How, during that revealing conversation, could you have forgotten to mention that in addition to owning this building, you now own the entire block?" Simone asked.

Damn. "Not kidding when I say it slipped my mind."

"Dallas, doll, keep an eye on the front while I make some calls from the office," Simone said as she sauntered over to stand in front of me." She poked me in the chest. "You and I will talk later."

"I look forward to it," I lied. Simone would press me on specific plans, and I hadn't made any. I hadn't shown up today intending to share any of what'd been churning in my mind, but the timing had seemed right, so I went with my gut and I wasn't sorry.

Then Simone leaned closer and murmured, "Talk to Dallas first. She has been working on a totally new, fresh concept for this building, and it's pretty damn impressive."

"I will. Thanks." I'd taken a rash of crap from my brother and my cousins for impulsively going into business with Simone, a woman I'd slept with a few times during my stopovers in Minneapolis. They believed she was just another puck bunny, but they couldn't have been further from the truth. While a sexual relationship between us had fizzled pretty fast, we'd become good friends. When the opportunity arose to buy this building, she was the first person I'd contacted about forming a partnership. I could claim altruism, helping her escape a shitty career situation—which was true—but she'd also been the first woman since Lucy who didn't pull any punches with me. She was smart and driven, yet she needed to reconfigure her life, and running a run-down bar gave her a few years to sort herself out. Simone also recognized my issues with booze early on, and she'd been the first person to push me into getting help. Ours was an odd relationship, but I trusted her without question.

"She's gonna bust your balls about this," Dallas said.

"I know." I focused on my baby cousin. She'd grown into a real beauty. Her gamine, almost elfin facial features belied the strength in her athletic body. If our golden-haired cousin Annika was considered the "Iron Princess" due to her cool demeanor, then Dallas was the "Fair Maiden"—we all felt protective of her and her delicate sensibilities. Dallas had a few quirks that might throw her into the oddball category if not for the Lund name (and money) that allowed her to be seen as an eccentric rich girl.

From the time she was a small child, she'd read people's auras, seeing spirits and harnessing positive energy through various techniques that have always made her a joy to be around. Plus, she has a sixth sense that is a little spooky. Our family lovingly accepted the "woo-woo" aspect of her, even if not everyone believed it.

Last year, after Ash let the Lund Collective—aka all branches of the entire Lund family—know that he and Nolan were dealing with my stake in Borderlands, Dallas begged Ash to give her a job. She'd worked in Personnel at Lund Industries during her last two years of college as an intern—a job guaranteed to turn into a full-time management position after she received her bachelor's degree. But something had happened to her in her senior year of college that sent her into near seclusion. We chalked it up to a bad breakup with her Russian hockey-playing boyfriend, who'd gone to Russia for a funeral and hadn't returned to the United States. In fact, he hadn't been heard from again.

After spending more time with Dallas in the past six months than I'd spent with her in her entire life, I recognized her indecision about joining the family business had nothing to do with a broken heart or bad relationship. Not that I had taken steps to talk to her about it . . . until now.

"So sweet baby D, what's been going on in your world?"

The bracelets on her wrists rattled when she crossed her arms over her chest. "My mom is hounding me."

"About?"

"Cochairing a couple of charity events. Then she sends me real estate notices about new places that have come up for sale on the market. She's even emailed me links to spiritual spa retreats in Bali. She doesn't act like this is a real job." She sighed. "I know her heart is in the right place. But I'm still dealing with the major aftereffects from the total solar eclipse, when Mercury was also in retrograde. It's such a powerful celestial event when darkness falls on the sun. It forced me to shed the mask I'd been wearing as well as accept that I have to admit to the outside world I need to honor who I truly am and step into the light again."

I leaned in. "Okay. Was that little segue supposed to reveal the real story on why you're not working at LI? I've heard from everyone that you were instrumental in revising the intern program, and it's been incredibly successful in all departments. Why aren't you basking in your success and outlining the next phase?"

"You would just get to the heart of the matter, wouldn't you?" She tipped her head and looked at me, yet beyond me. "I don't know why I'm surprised. The need for truth eclipses everything in your world these days too, doesn't it?"

Ironic she'd claim that, since I still hadn't come clean on

a crucial upcoming event, choosing to deal with mundane day-to-day issues instead. "This isn't about me, Dallas."

"It should be. You're the owner of this business."

"You know that's not what I mean." I paused. "Talk to me."

Those unnerving blue eyes connected with mine. "I like being the idea girl. I love when what I envisioned falls into place and runs smoothly. What I don't like? The pressure to have more ideas, better ideas on someone else's time frame. I freeze up, Jax. Not a little. A lot. I nearly go into a catatonic state. Then no ideas, no words, no feelings come. At all. The people that I worked with, the team I supposedly helped re-build at LI . . . when it happened, they didn't support me; they turned on me. My inability to contribute—their words—was construed as laziness. I was a Lund; I could skate by and collect a check without being subject to performance review."

My anger rose but I slammed a lid on it. "I imagine you tried to explain to them that in a collaborative effort everyone shouldered the blame when creativity slowed or even stopped?"

"Yes. But at that point they'd gotten so used to me contributing more than my fair share of ideas that they had no problem placing nearly all the blame for our lack of new progress on me. The negativity crushed me. I couldn't function at all. The only way to get out from under any kind of expectations was to not subject myself to them in the first place."

I took her hand. "I'm sorry."

"And before you ask, no, I didn't tell Ash. Or Annika. Or Nolan. Or Brady. Or my dad. None of our family have any idea what happened. They would've made it worse, going after the people responsible. Then it would've become a self-fulfilling prophecy; I did rate extra power and special treatment because of my surname. But it's not really been a better solution, letting the family think I'll return to the fold after I'm done 'finding' myself." She locked those vivid blue eyes to mine again. "I found myself a long time ago, Jax. The only time I'm not myself is when I'm at LI, pretending to be someone else." She paused. "And you get that, don't you?"

"Absolutely. And that's why I need your ideas for this space."

"Mine?"

"You just said you love being the idea girl."

"How do you know that I've come up with anything concrete?"

"You've worked here for a year. You just told me about the solar eclipse thingy that is forcing you to admit the truth."

Dallas rolled her eyes. "Nice try. Simone told you I've been working on it, didn't she?"

"Yep." I grinned. "Now hit me with it."

Barely a minute passed before she spoke. "I have two ideas. Not both for this space. One's for the tiny storefront down the block. I think for this building, you should divide it into two separate entities. That way you can go for two entirely different demographics."

"Keep going. I'm already intrigued."

"The upstairs right now is used for karaoke and it's hit and miss. Turn it into a barcade—which is exactly what it sounds like. Fill the space with classic arcade games and pinball machines, then customers can drink while they play *Pac-Man* or whatever. That vintage stuff is hot right now. Decorate the area like an '80s arcade or like someone's basement from that era. But no tickets-for-prizes type of machines, because they might as well go to Dave & Buster's. Just tokens that they can trade in for drinks if they want or buy more game time."

I let that sink in before I said, "It already has a separate entrance, so having two different spaces would be viable. That's brilliant. What else?"

She beamed back at me. "This one is totally fun. Use the historical aspect of the main part of this bar and turn it into a

speakeasy. Have a 'dummy' entrance. Heck, a small section
of the front of the house could even be a coffee bar, which
would be another moneymaker. Access to the speakeasy is by
password only. It'd have to be a word that changes frequently.
You might even take out online ads or buy phone app ads to
direct customers where to find the password. So it's all a
game and yet it's a tiny bit exclusive. If people show up expecting to get in, they can't. You can't buy your way in either.
And the speakeasy itself . . . How fun would it be to have
two-way glass? The people inside could see the ones on the
outside trying to get in, but the ones outside couldn't see inside. You could keep the time period intact by not allowing
the use of cell phones, playing music from that era, having the
bar staff dress in costume and play roles. God knows there's
enough wannabe actors and actresses in this town. Drinks are
handcrafted and high priced. People who go to the trouble of
finding the code to get in won't mind paying for the experience. So you can have high-end clientele on one end of the
building and trendy upstairs. The best of both worlds."

My mind. Blown. I pantomimed that and she glowed. The
light of excitement danced in her eyes, and I just wanted to
hug the shit out of her.

So I plucked her off the barstool and did just that.

I might've whooped and spun her around a time or two,
which caused her to smack me on the back and shriek, "Jax!
I am not Mimi! Put me down."

"I'm just so freakin' excited, Dallas. I want to get started
on this right now. Today. Close the bar down and start gutting
the place."

"Now hold on. There's a lot of other side things to consider. You want to make a big splash with this; PR and marketing has to be on board before a single wall comes down.
Word of mouth is what'll sell these spaces. And that has to

happen in stages. I'm not gonna lie, cuz. You need Annika to sign on for PR. She is head and shoulders above anyone in PR in this town. She will kill at this."

I felt a tug of resistance. Lucy worked for Annika, and I didn't want Lucy involved in this project. The fewer people who knew, the better. "Annika would need to freelance this project. Simone and I would have final approval on anyone who assists Annika."

Dallas blinked at me—a slow blink where, swear to god, I felt like she was reading my mind. "At LI Lucy is swamped with the layout for the spring spa line. Annika won't pull her off that. But Annika can't do it alone either." She flapped her hand at me. "We're getting off track. First discuss these ideas and changes with Simone. Then decide who does what. You've got a business degree, Jax. You know you need to set a budget, hire an architect and design firm—we both know who's going to get that contract."

Walker. My cousin whose construction company, Flint and Lund, specialized in restoration. His partner did the design work while Walker ran the construction crew. Not only would hiring family keep the concepts under wraps, Walker was the best in his field, so a win-win there.

Before Dallas started rattling off more ideas, I made the time-out sign. My poor head was spinning. "Okay, baby cuz, you're hired."

"Hired. But . . . hired to do what?"

"Implement ideas. You work well with Annika. And Simone. Walker adores you. You're the logical choice to spearhead these projects since it's obvious that you've been thinking about it for a while. And before you get that panicked look, I'll let you decide your own level of involvement. If it gets to be too much, we'll reassess, okay?"

"You're sure?"

"Positive."

"Yes!" She did a shimmy-shake thing that was her version of a fist pump.

I'd nearly made it through the swinging door, when I remembered Dallas mentioning the small empty storefront on the end of the block, so I stopped and faced her. "Oh, hey, you mentioned an idea for that tiny storefront too?"

"Yep. Ghost tours."

I froze. Of all the things she could've suggested . . . how had she come up with that?

"This block is haunted, Jax. Like seriously haunted. I feel it. I did some research on the history, and there were a bunch of murders around here that never were solved. The Mill District has a violent and criminal past. Sharing those stories . . . lots of juicy stuff, and no other tour company is working this angle. It would be seasonal, so if we kept it open in the off-season, we could also sell books on local legends and period-authentic trinkets, which would fit into the speakeasy theme."

"It's something to consider after we're done with the bigger projects."

She smirked. "At least you didn't say no outright."

After I passed into the storage area, I pressed my back against the brick wall and closed my eyes.

Ghost tours.

I hadn't thought about that in a long damn time.

Weren't you just mooning over the first time you met Lucy? It shocked the hell out of you that she'd picked something so random for your third date . . .

Once again we'd met in the pizza parking lot. This time Lucy insisted on driving.

It'd rained off and on all day. The air remained oppressively damp with a heavy mist that created sporadic banks of fog.

Lucy wore a smirk during the drive to wherever she was taking us. A smirk and a trench coat. My mind drifted to a scene where lovely Lucy wore that trench coat, a pair of fire-engine red stilettos and nothing else except a naughty challenge in her big brown eyes.

"You okay over there?" she asked, ripping me out of the fantasy.

"Yeah. Why?"

"Sounded like you growled."

Busted. "Nope. Just cleared the frog out of my throat."

"Well, it's the weather for it."

This relationship was still too damn new for our small talk to revolve around the weather. "This miserable drizzle doesn't put a crimp in our date plans?"

Her smirk bloomed into an all-out grin. "Actually it's the perfect condition for tonight."

"It's pointless to ask where you're taking me, isn't it?"

"Downtown St. Paul."

I'd spent some time in St. Paul—growing up in the Twin Cities, the suburbs flowed together. I'd spent the most time at the Xcel Energy Center playing hockey. I knew she wasn't surprising me with tickets to a hockey game since the Minnesota Wild had blown their playoff chances the same as we had.

The silence between us wasn't awkward, just there. That's probably why I noticed steel guitars and tight harmonies drifting from the radio.

Interesting. I wouldn't have pegged her as a country music fan.

Lucy took us straight into the heart of downtown and chose a nearly empty parking lot close to the capitol building.

Before we exited the car, I said, "Did you bring an umbrella?"

"Shoot. I forgot one." She reached over and popped open the glove compartment, the underside of her arm brushing the inside of my knee as she rooted around for something. "Aha, got it."

I eyed the piece of plastic that looked like a curved set of teeth. "How exactly is that supposed to keep us from getting wet?"

"It's not." She laughed and then twisted all that glorious hair into a knot at the back of her head and attached the big clip thingy. "There. Now at least my hair will be out of my face when we do get drenched."

I felt desperate to know what she would do if I leaned in to taste her beautiful neck, trailing my mouth from the hollow below her ear down the side of her throat. Would she squirm away from me? Or melt into me?

"Come on, we have to check in."

Please, god. Let us be checking into the Saint Paul Hotel just down the road.

She reached for my hand, and we started off at a good clip down the sidewalk. That's when I noticed she wore rain boots. Not just any rain boots, but screaming-ass red rain boots dotted with sunflowers. That quirky touch was as damn sexy as my vision of her sauntering toward me in high heels.

If I didn't get to touch this woman soon I might lose my mind.

We passed the Saint Paul Hotel—pity that—and crossed the street. The buildings here were a little worse for the wear, and I couldn't imagine there'd be any date-worthy activity down here.

That's when we stopped in front of a recently renovated storefront. The fancy lettering in the glass pane above the door read: HISTORIC TOURS.

I felt Lucy watching me and I met her gaze. "What's this?"

"A ghost tour."

"Seriously?" I paused. "Did you choose this because I mentioned you disappearing on me?"

"Maybe. But since neither of us are history fans, I figured taking a historically based ghost tour isn't something we would do on our own, so this activity fulfills your date challenge to me, doesn't it?"

I tried to hold back a laugh but couldn't. "Jesus. You are a literal smartass."

"Aww, Jax. You say the nicest things."

I stalked her until she retreated with her back pressed against the big paned window. Although it was dark outside, a streetlight amplified the misty air, sending a soft wash of gold across the windowpanes, front-lighting her like an angel. "I'm glad you didn't disappear on me."

"Me too."

"Still . . . I'm half-afraid you aren't real." Slipping my hand around the left side of her neck, I let my thumb stroke the sharp edge of her jaw from the tip of her stubborn chin to her ear.

"I'm real." She blinked those enormous brown eyes at me, and I noticed condensation clinging to her long eyelashes. In that moment she was the most exquisite woman I'd ever seen. Nothing could've stopped me from leaning forward and tasting her lips.

Nothing.

I absorbed the dew on her upper lip in a slow slide of my mouth over hers. Then I let my mouth travel across her cheek, up to the corner of her eye, where I placed another soft kiss.

She rewarded me with a tiny gasp and her eyes fluttered closed.

By the time I'd finished exploring the planes of her face, her lips were parted as she exhaled rapid breaths. I increased my grip on the back of her neck and brought her mouth to mine.

Probably I should've eased her into this first kiss, but my

hunger for her was overwhelming. After fastening my lips to hers, I devoured her. Each glide of my lips over hers forced her to open her mouth wider, to accept the teasing and plundering of my tongue.

That first taste of her made me ravenous. Reckless. I couldn't hear anything over the roaring in my head.

Her pulse leapt beneath where I'd pressed my thumb into her throat, and then I felt her fingers sifting through my hair as she pulled me closer.

The thought of ending the kiss had me gripping her tighter. She must've felt the same, because my scalp started to sting from her hands fisted in my hair.

A truck door behind us slammed hard enough to rattle the window I had her pressed up against. That startled us both into backing off.

But we maintained eye contact. Neither of us felt the need to play it cool, acting as if that explosive connection was no big deal.

The huge smile on my face had her responding with a grin of her own.

"Well, I guess that answers that question," she said with a laugh.

"Luce. I—"

She placed her fingers over my mouth. "I want to do that again, and again, and again with far fewer clothes on. But I paid for that damn ghost tour, so put away that pout, Jaxson, and prepare for a fascinating history lesson."

I nipped at her fingers until they fell away. "Oh, there's a lesson in this all right."

"What lesson is that?"

I angled my head and lightly sank my teeth into her bottom lip, watching her eyes turn molten.

"We might suck at history, but babe, we've got this chemistry thing locked down."

———

J ax?"

The voice yanked me back to the present. I glanced up to see Simone looking at me strangely. "Yeah?"

"You okay?"

"Just thinking. Why? What's up?"

"I've got the current income and expense report pulled up, if you want to look at it."

"Gimme a sec and I'll be right there."

Simone gave me another strange look but she let me be.

I closed my eyes, wanting to get back to the memory. I couldn't recall a single thing about the ghost tour, but that first kiss still haunted me.

I wondered if Lucy ever thought of it and if she could keep it in that original context or if our past and my actions had distorted everything that had been good between us at one time. I'd ask her when we had our talk, even if the truth—her truth—might be hard for me to hear.

Brooding about what I couldn't change . . . pointless as usual. I shook off my melancholy and got to work.

Five

___

LUCY

I hadn't seen Jax at Lund Industries all week.

On Wednesday afternoon, he texted me after he picked Mimi up from school. Then I had a brief conversation with our daughter a few hours later, right before her usual bedtime.

And I could admit that it had been easier that Mimi was with Jax when I kicked off my heels at ten thirty P.M. I fixed myself a gin and tonic, filled the tub, dropped in a bath bomb and fully relaxed before sliding into bed an hour later.

I felt only marginally guilty for waking up refreshed.

I wondered how Jax was faring this morning with the demon.

So when he strolled into the PR department half an hour after the first school bell rang, his square jaw tight, his hair sticking up all over and his tie askew, I knew it'd been a morning from hell for him, like it usually was for me.

Jax slapped his hands down on my desk. "We need to talk."

"I can take a coffee break in a couple of hours—"

"We need to talk now while the horror is still fresh in my mind."

I glanced around the office. No one paid attention to us, even when there was extra interest when one of the Lund bosses showed up. I grabbed my coffee mug and stood. "Fine. Lead the way."

I'd expected Jax to take us to the employee break room on the fourth floor. Instead, once we were in the elevator, he poked the up button. "Wait. Where are we going?"

"To my office."

I felt his gaze burning into me and I bit the inside of my cheek.

"For Christ's sake, Luce, just say it."

"You have an office?" rushed out in the shocked tone he'd expected.

"Yes, I have an office. Where'd you think I spent my time?"

"No clue."

Jax muttered something and I opted not to ask him to repeat it.

On the twenty-seventh floor, we turned right instead of left. Left led to the board of directors' conference room and the on-site shredding room. Halfway down the hallway he stopped and pushed open a door. "After you."

"I didn't know there were offices on this floor."

"There aren't . . . except for mine."

I tried not to be shocked by such a nondescript space for the man rumored to be the next CEO. The room had one small window, one small desk, one visitor's chair, one filing cabinet. I managed to say, "The built-in bookcase is nice."

He snorted. "It's ironic that this room reflects my position in the company."

A Keurig coffeemaker sat on the edge of the bookcase, and he hit the power button. Apparently he needed a moment to gather his thoughts as he brewed the coffee. And maybe it did give me a warmish feeling that he fixed my cup exactly as I liked it: two sugars and one creamer.

What other things does he remember about what you like? Does he remember how much you loved it when he came up behind you and used his teeth on the nape of your neck whenever you cooked dinner? Or the panting sounds you made when he—

"You deserve a fucking medal, Lucy."

I wrapped my hands around my mug of coffee and refocused. "Mimi wasn't on her best behavior because she was with Daddy?"

"No. I even warned her that she'd have to be up fifteen minutes earlier than normal since I live farther away from the school. She was all smiles, talking about what kind of cereal she planned to have. Then this morning I awakened the beast. I had to literally drag her out of bed. She locked herself in the bathroom, which I hadn't prepared for, and that was a wasted twenty minutes."

"Did she emerge on her own? Or did you have to pick the lock?"

Jax's cheeks turned crimson. "I had to resort to pretending that Calder had come to the door."

I laughed. "Ooh. High five for that trickery, Daddy-o."

"She glared at me as I made her get dressed in her room with the door open. She hid behind her cereal box during breakfast. And she was really pissed when I . . ." He paused.

"What? Come on, don't be dramatic."

A sheepish look crossed his face. "Don't get pissy with me, but I was so goddamned mad at the sheer amount of both of our time that she wasted by being a brat, that I refused to comb her hair."

I choked on my sip of coffee.

"I told her we were out of time and had to leave."

Mimi always thrashed in her sleep, turning her hair into a snarly mess in the morning. At age eight she hadn't taken any interest in styling her own hair, and honestly it was just easier and faster for me to do it for her. But to say, "To hell with it, I'm not putting up with your attitude," and making her go to school with bedhead? I grinned and lifted my mug to him. "Brilliant, Jax. Seriously. I'm a little jealous of your hard-ass parenting stance with her."

He raked his hand over his scalp. "Don't be too hasty in your praise. She refused to give me a kiss good-bye or to even say good-bye when I dropped her off."

"And the next time you see her, she'll be just fine," I assured him.

"I figured you oughta know what went down so you're not shocked by her appearance when you pick her up today."

I shrugged. "Maybe you should pick her up and see how her day went."

Jax narrowed his eyes at me. "Why the sudden change?"

"Hey, you pick her up sometimes. It'd stave off the blame game, Mimi complaining to me that you didn't do her hair this morning. In the past I would've gotten pissy on her behalf." I looked him dead in the eye. "She's smart enough to play us against each other, and I've been bitter enough to let her do it. No more. We are partners in raising her. Even if we disagree behind closed doors we have to provide a united front or she will run roughshod over both of us."

"Agreed." Then he offered me that smile, the one I'd always considered mine; softer, smirkier, more secretive than his usual wide grin. "Can I say that I'm glad we're able to talk about things like this now?"

"Me too."

"Want me to keep her overnight tonight? See if a back-to-back dose of discipline dad can tame the morning beast?"

Automatically I started to say no. But I was working on a

major project right now, and extra hours in the office tonight with no interruptions would get me caught up. "You're sure it won't interfere with your . . . ?"

Jax leaned forward. "With my what, Luce? My big, exciting life?" He laughed harshly. "I live by myself in a rental apartment. I'm not dating anyone"—his eyes turned hard—"and I'm not fucking anyone either. The only other thing I do at night besides sleep is work out if the insomnia is too bad."

I reached for his hand. "You're still dealing with that?"

"Yeah, well, it's worse now. Before I'd just drink until I passed out so I could sleep. That's no longer an option. Now I lay in bed, staring at the ceiling, reliving all the shitty things I did during my drinking years and feeling guilty about all the times I blacked out and don't remember the shitty things I did." He exhaled. "Maybe it sounds stupid, but I sleep better when Mimi is there. I don't feel so . . . isolated."

It squeezed my heart that he'd substituted the word *isolated* for *lonely*.

My pride snarked back, *Don't feel sorry for the cheater; he's always had women lined up around the block and the rink to ensure he was never alone.*

For once I ignored my pride. "I used to clean the apartment when I couldn't sleep and you were out of town." Wait. Why had I admitted that?

"I've never forgotten that I always slept better next to you," he murmured.

I couldn't come up with any kind of response to that.

Jax seemed to catch himself. He slipped his hand free and leaned back in his chair. "I'll pick Mimi up from school tomorrow too, but I'll drop her here first so she can go home with you and get whatever she needs for the weekend."

Would I ever get used to Jax taking Mimi on the weekend? Now that he was aware of morning devil child, maybe he could have her during the week sometimes and I could have a full weekend with her. Something to bring up at a later date. "Sounds good." I stood. "I'd better get back to work."

He got up and walked me to the door, which was ridiculous given the size of the room.

"Oh, there is one other thing."

I paused in the hallway. "What?"

"Sunday. Vikings home game and we're having a Lund family thing in the skybox."

"Mimi will love that."

"I want you to come." He inhaled a deep breath. "Actually I need you to come, Luce. Please."

Now I was alarmed. "What's going on?"

"Just say you'll be there."

I'd never been to a football game in the new U.S. Bank Stadium, say nothing of getting to sit in a luxury skybox. It'd be a new experience for me, if nothing else. "Okay." I smirked. "I'd request that your admin send me the details, but since you don't have an admin . . . ?"

"Ha ha. Rub it in. I'll give you the ticket and all the passes tomorrow when I bring Mimi by."

"Cool. And have her call me tonight before she goes to bed."

"Will do."

I'd spent the weekend doing the autumn purge; swapping out my summer wardrobe for my winter wardrobe. Living in an apartment meant limited storage, but thankfully this apartment building had decent-sized storage lockers in the basement, where I could keep out-of-season clothes and seasonal decorations. Since Mimi grew so fast, I took the clothes she'd outgrown to a secondhand clothing store for kids for credit.

Damon had called and asked me on another date. I liked

him, but I didn't feel like dressing up, so I promised I'd let him take me out the following weekend.

Early Sunday afternoon I suited up in the Vikings jersey that had accompanied the packet with my ticket to the game and passes for parking and the skybox. I felt ridiculous wearing a jersey; I'd worn Jaxson's Blackhawks jersey only a couple of times. I'd never been a sports girl. Even being involved with a professional hockey player hadn't changed that about me.

I finally made it to the Lund skybox and found myself in a sea of purple jerseys with #88 and the name LUND emblazoned across the backs.

Mimi noticed me first. "Mommy!"

I scooped her up, hating that she was getting too big to comfortably lodge on my hip. "Hey, sweet girl. What's up?"

"Me and Daddy were the first ones here so we got to go down onto the field and say hi to Jensen! He was in his uniform and everything!"

"That's pretty exciting."

"Uh-huh. And then Rowan came over and hugged me and I got to hold her pom-poms! They're so shiny! Daddy took me to the gift shop and bought me my very own pom-poms, 'cause I'm pretty sure I'm gonna be a Vikings cheerleader now, like Rowan."

Of course she was. "That would be pretty awesome."

"Oh, and I saw Calder." Mimi noticed me looking around, and she placed her hands on my face, forcing my attention back to her. "He's not up here. He's in the stands with his grandpa and grandma and Uncle Martin. So I'm the only kid here . . . except for Runner and Trinity's baby."

Jax appeared behind Mimi. "It's funny that she still calls Walker 'Runner.'"

"Why's that funny?" Mimi demanded of him.

"Because it'd be like me calling you . . . Youyou instead of Mimi."

Her nose wrinkled. "Huh?"

"Never mind. Go finish your lunch."

"Okay."

She slid down my body and scampered off, leaving me face-to-face with Jax.

Again.

"I'm so happy you're here."

I looked away and let my gaze zoom across the others in the skybox. It was all Lund family members. And me. Even when I knew all of them, and they were related to my daughter, it made me super self-conscious that I wasn't one of them.

Jax took my elbow and led me to the refreshment table. Before I said anything, he said, "Don't freak out about this."

"Why shouldn't I? I don't belong here."

"Yes, you do. Now, what are you hungry for? There's a full menu as well as a small buffet."

"The buffet is fine."

It didn't escape anyone's notice that Jax showed me around and damn near doted on me, like I was his girlfriend or something.

Annika was the last Lund to arrive with her hot, Swedish, hockey-playing husband. She immediately went over to her sister-in-law Lennox and put her hands on Lennox's rounded belly. Working with both of them, I knew they maintained a more formal relationship at the office, so seeing Annika, aka the Iron Princess, being so touchy-feely with Lennox, and baby-talking to her nephew Liam, gave me a deeper sense of being out of place.

"I barely remember when Mimi was that little," Jax said beside me, his gaze on Walker holding Liam.

"Me either."

"But not for the same reasons I don't," he said softly.

"We can't change it, Jax, so it serves no purpose to dwell on it."

He stepped in front of me. "Why are you cutting me slack now, Lucy Q?"

"I'm not. But I'm tired of being angry and hurt about it. I'm tired of my guilt. It's taxing."

"Can you stick around after the game so we can talk?"

I shook my head. "Lindsey is coming over for dinner tonight. I haven't seen her in a month."

"Ah. Okay. I'll touch base with you this week and see if we can't set something up."

"Jax. What is going on?"

His dad called him away and I didn't get an answer. I was alone maybe four seconds before Nolan sidled up. "Lucy."

"Nolan."

"Mimi seems happy to be here."

"She's in heaven. She'll eat twice her weight in chicken strips and French fries."

"I'm happy she's here." A beat passed. "I'm happy you're here too."

I tilted my head to look at Jax's younger brother. Although he wore the same Lund jersey we all did, it looked better on him. Classier for sure. He'd added a long-sleeved, high-necked white silk undershirt that muted the vivid purple. He'd tucked the bottom of the jersey into his jeans, creating a tighter, leaner look. "Why?"

"Because it makes Jax happy."

"I feel weird. Selka keeps looking over here like I'm trespassing."

"Ignore Aunt Selka. She always gets weird when her son Jens plays."

"And where's your flavor of the week?"

"I'm done with that."

I laughed.

"I'm serious. I've been so busy, if I have time for a little down-and-dirty action, my partner has to be happy being my flavor of the day."

"Well, you learned that from the best."

"Jax? Man. He is not like that anymore."

Hard not to shrug.

Mimi bounded over.

Then Jax moved to the center of the space and called for everyone's attention. "Before the game gets started, I have an announcement. After some soul-searching and a lot of sleepless nights, I've decided that I'm not a good fit for an executive's position at Lund Industries, so I'm resigning from the company effective immediately."

Shocked silence distorted the air.

"I've been grateful for these past months, getting to see how this amazing company that you all built works. It's mind boggling and daunting for a guy like me, who's spent most of his life on the ice, making decisions on the fly. While I appreciate the tradition and the chance to prove myself, what it's proven is that I'm underqualified to transition into a leadership position."

Stunned, I stared at him in silence, as did all the rest of his family members.

"I'll stay on the board of directors and fulfill my volunteer duties for Lund Cares Community Outreach."

"What else will you do, son?" his father asked.

"That is a damn good question, Dad. We're making changes with the bar business I co-own with Simone, so that will take a good chunk of my time. I'm fully invested in raising my daughter, so I don't know that there will be much time left after that."

It seemed everyone started talking at once. Mimi leaned back against me and watched with wide eyes.

Not everyone was tossing questions at him. Nolan stayed mum.

"You knew this was coming, didn't you?" I said to him.

"Yes. And I know he'll be happier in the long run."

"Working in a bar?" I said sharply. "Really, Nolan?"

Nolan set his hand on Mimi's shoulder. "Hey, girlie, I think your daddy could use a hug, so why don't you scoot over there and offer him one, okay?"

Mimi skipped off without question.

"That was my first thought too, Lucy, believe me. But Ash and I never did squat with the place when Jax entrusted it to us. Last week Jax pointed out it was a hobby for us—which is entirely true. I think his decision to leave LI boils down to his need to restructure every aspect of his life—personally and professionally. Up until now both of those aspects of his life were dictated by the hockey season. One of the first things he said was after the initial renovation is done, he intends to have minimal interaction as an owner. He also reminded us that he hadn't moved back to the Cities so he could spend his nights in a bar, ignoring his kid."

"Oh. Well that's a relief." I felt Nolan studying me. "What?"

"Jax's change of . . . well, everything, doesn't surprise you as much as I thought it would."

I shrugged.

"Come on, Lucy. Did Jax talk to you about any of this?"

"You'd hate that, wouldn't you? If your hero brother spilled his life plans to his demonized baby mama before confiding in you."

"Not fair," he said crossly. "My offers to help you out have always been shot down. But that's not what I'm talking about. I'd be happy if Jax had talked to you about this."

"Why?"

"Because at least he was talking to someone. It's ridiculous that he's more of an island here than he was all the years he lived in Chicago."

I exhaled the angry breath I'd been holding in. "I'm sorry. I know you've supported Jax no matter what stupid shit he's done. I know you tried to fix him when no one else was aware he was broken. I know you tried to balance your hero-like worship of him with the harsh realities of what kind of a man he was becoming. I never envied you that, Nolan. And I don't know if Jax fully realizes everything you've done for him. So while you and I haven't always agreed, I've never questioned your loyalty to him and your love for Mimi. I know it hurts you to see him struggle."

After several long moments, Nolan reached down and briefly squeezed my hand. "That might be one of the best things anyone has ever said to me, Lucy. Thank you."

"You're welcome." Then I bumped him with my shoulder. "It appears you'll be filling your dad's shoes after all. Good for you. Nolan Lund, CEO, sounds damn good."

"Doesn't it?" He grinned. "It'll be a while before Archer is ready to retire, and I've got a lot to learn before that day finally comes, so I'm in no rush."

I stayed in the background as each member of the Lund family took their turn talking to Jax. Ash and his sister Dallas spent the least amount of time chatting with him, since I suspected they too knew about this development ahead of time.

Mimi scampered off when Jax's dad, his uncle Monte and his uncle Ward circled him. A muscle ticked in his jaw, and he'd folded his arms over his chest in a defensive posture, but really . . . what could these men do? Jax had made up his mind. And I, for one, was proud of him.

Brady said, "Game's about to start."

Everyone scurried to their seats. Even Mimi crawled onto Grandma Edie's lap to watch the players' intro.

Jax looked around until he saw me. He slowly ambled

over, keeping his back to the room. When he loomed over me, blocking my view, I didn't really care. And since no one could see us, I placed my hand on his chest and felt his heart racing. I smiled up at him. "Perfect timing for your little bombshell."

"It went better than I expected."

"Really?"

"Fuck, Luce, I had no idea how they'd react."

"Really? You're a Lund. Aren't they obligated to support you no matter what?"

He shook his head. "You remember my cousin Zosia? Her dad was my granddad's younger brother. He hated my grandpa, hated him to the point he threatened to kill him. Jackson Lund conspired with his other brother, and they cut him out of Lund Industries completely. My great-uncle didn't marry until way later in life, so our cousins Zosia and Zach are actually my dad and uncles' first cousins. He left the Twin Cities with an old deed to a fishing fleet and made his living that way. I might've been set adrift the same way."

"Your dad and your uncles aren't assholes, Jax. And you're not the only Lund not to go into the family business. Walker didn't. Dallas hasn't so far. And Jensen won't have to make that decision for a while."

Those beautiful eyes burned into me with an intensity that sent my pulse tripping.

Automatically I attempted to retreat, but Mr. Quick-Handed hooked his fingers into my belt loops, holding me in place. "Not so fast. Drives me crazy that you can say such sweet or thoughtful things to me, about me, and then figure it's acceptable just to run off." He tugged me closer. "Not. Happening."

I froze.

"I miss this," he said softly. "This ease of talking to you. Of being with you. Not just because you said nice things to me instead of nasty."

"Jax."

"Have you ever had anything like this with another man, Lucy? The connection, the passion, the sense that this is what everyone looks for in an intimate relationship?"

When I didn't answer right away, a spark of fear danced in his eyes, which he replaced with that look of cool indifference that I hated.

That jarred me. Hard. My brain started picking out images of other times I'd seen that look in Jax's eyes. How hadn't I noticed that aloofness manifested after he'd opened up and he feared I'd go for the quick kill, the nasty remark, the easy shot at hurting him?

And after his infidelities came to light, I hadn't had a single conversation with him without pointing it—them— out. Not that any of the blame for his cheating behavior fell on me, but I never, ever, ever let him forget how badly he'd fucked up and that I was the wronged party. Even if our discussion had nothing to do with our conflicted past, I'd find a way—or ten—to remind him that he was a cheating bastard.

Ooh, you can get in a really sharp dig right now. Tell him he'll never find that intimacy with any woman if he continues to use his dick as a judge of depth of a woman's character.

I opened my mouth.

Shut it.

Broke my gaze from his and glanced down at my hand still resting on his chest over his heart. "No, Jax, I haven't had that connection since . . ." *You* went unsaid. "It's easier on my heart and mind if I forget something like that even exists."

"I can't forget. I don't want to forget. I dream of getting it back, knowing this time I'd treat it like the special thing it is."

Maybe I got a little dizzy feeling his hands on me and my hand on the warmth and hardness of him. His scent, his heat . . .

"Mommy?"

Mimi worked her way between us until I stepped back, giving her room. "Yes?"

"Can we go shopping for Jocelyn's birthday gift after we leave here?"

"Who is Jocelyn?"

"A girl from my class. I got invited to her birthday party this Saturday!"

"I planned to tell you about that," Jax interjected, "but we got a little sidetracked."

Understatement. We'd gone off the rails completely. I looked at our daughter. "We'll have to shop another day after school this week since Aunt Lindsey is coming over for dinner tonight."

She clapped. "Yay! I'll get to show her the cheerleading routine Dallas taught me."

My gaze met Jax's. "She already learned a cheerleading routine today? I didn't think I'd arrived that late."

He grinned. "Dallas called her a little sponge. Said she noticed even at camp that Meems has natural athletic ability."

"Guess we know where she gets that."

Mimi lifted her arms. "Come on, Daddy. Let's go watch the game."

I wandered to the buffet and filled a plate. But I wasn't alone for long; both Edie and Archer decided to eat. Coincidence? I think not.

Edie brushed her hand up my arm. "We're so happy that you could join us today, Lucy."

"Jax's invite surprised me, to be honest. But now I know why he insisted on me being here."

Archer moved in and spooned a pile of beans and weenies on his plate. "So, you had no idea he'd planned this announcement?"

"None. I guess the question is . . . did you?"

He stood in front of me. Archer Lund was a big guy, but not nearly as big as Jax. Both of his sons had inherited his striking good looks. Even at his age—what I guessed to be his early sixties—he was a stylish, distinguished man who commanded a room. That kind of power absolutely scared the crap out of me, especially after I'd gone to work at LI. While the CEO wasn't my direct boss—he was still THE boss. I'd seen him in several roles: the devoted husband, the softhearted grandfather who made time for his only grandchild, the ball-busting CEO of a multi-billion-dollar family conglomerate. I'd never seen him as the flummoxed father, fishing for information on his son, as he was obviously doing now with me.

"Honestly? No. I believed his lack of enthusiasm was from getting acclimated to a different daily schedule, in a different town, with different people. I'd been prepared to give him another six months to let him settle in. I assumed . . ." His eyes moved to Nolan and Jax standing together chatting. "Seems I should've been listening to him, watching him more closely than just assuming. I admitted this to him, and to Nolan, so I'm not talking out of turn by admitting to you that Nolan and I have gotten into our own routine over the years, and neither of us considered what it would mean bringing Jax into it."

I'd suspected Archer had separated me into various roles also: Jax's former girlfriend, Mimi's mother and LI underling. But his confession seemed a little personal for his son's ex-girlfriend, so maybe he'd assigned me another role?

Edie slipped her arm around her husband's waist. "Which just tells me that some part of you acknowledged that Nolan would be better suited for the job." She smirked at me. "Literally. His tailor will be a busy man."

I loved how perfectly Edie soothed her husband and brought humor into a situation that'd caught them off guard.

I really hoped Jax understood just how lucky he was to have such supportive parents. But I still felt the need to relay a concern they hadn't mentioned. "I spoke with Nolan a little about Jax's plans with the bar and property he owns, because I don't know that running a bar would be the healthiest option for him. Or for Mimi, for that matter."

"That occurred to us too," Edie murmured.

"Nolan believes Jax's claim that he won't be more than financially invested. He wants to make it a success and reap the profits."

Archer smiled. "True Lund business acumen, right there."

I smiled back. "Who knows? Maybe in a few years when he has more experience to bring to the table, he'll ask to rejoin LI in some capacity."

"I hope so." Archer gave me a one-armed hug. "Damn, lady. You shouldn't be toiling in PR. You should be putting your brains and common sense approach to work in HR. We could use someone like you."

That perked me up . . . even when I had no interest in switching departments. I was just happy that the CEO saw me as an adaptable employee. If that was the new role he'd put me in? I'd take it. "You really think so?"

"Absolutely. I'd offer to nose around to see if there are openings, but I'm aware you abhor personal favors, so check into it on your time frame, if you're interested. I can clear a path for you if you meet any resistance."

"Thank you, sir."

"Sir. Bah. We're beyond that." He waved me off, took his plate and rejoined his brother Ward down in the front seats.

Edie caught me before I could escape. "I'm not wrong in believing that you and Jax are getting along better these days?"

"We are. It's easier now that he lives here. Now that he's retired the Jaxson 'Stonewall' Lund persona."

"I agree. And unlike Archer, I have no problem talking out of turn."

My belly did a little flip.

Her eyes, identical to Jax's, searched mine. "Something to keep in mind, sweetheart. You're the only woman Jaxson ever brought home to meet the family. You're the only woman he ever lived with. You're the only woman he's ever let see the real him beneath that hockey mask. I'll never condone his actions with you—any of them—but people do change. It'd be sad if they didn't. It's sadder yet to go through life believing no one can ever change. There are no absolutes . . . except change is inevitable." She leaned in and kissed my cheek, then walked away, leaving me with a whiff of her jasmine perfume and a boatload of questions.

Since everyone was watching the game, I settled in the back of the suite, picking at my food, letting my mind return to the time I did believe in absolutes, and how Jax had reacted when I shared mine with him . . .

Jax greeted me with a kiss on the cheek for our fourth date. A lingering kiss where the soft brush of his longish hair tickled my face and I got a lungful of his enticing scent.

"Thanks for meeting me here, but I would've rather picked you up."

I pointed at the restaurant sign boasting fresh baked goods. "You chose Perkins, a pancake and bakery restaurant, for our date. There's no way I want you to see me shoveling in breakfast food and then witness me ordering half a dozen muffins to go after the meal. Driving separately means I can sneak back and load up on baked goods after you've driven off."

"Sneaky." He kissed me softly. "But what if I have plans after we finish eating?"

I shrugged. "You'll still have to drop me off here when

we're done." *Because I'm not going home with you tonight* went unstated, but his expression said he'd heard my message loud and clear.

Placing his hand in the small of my back, he directed me toward the entrance. "What's your favorite kind of muffin?" His lips touched the top of my ear. "And saying, 'A stud muffin like you, baby,' won't offend me."

"Dream on."

Since it was only late afternoon, we scored a window booth seat. A few members of the senior set were the only other patrons. I'd been surprised when Jax had suggested this place since it catered to families during the day and the bar rush crowd late at night . . . until I remembered he'd mentioned his love of breakfast for dinner during one of our epic text conversations the past week.

The waitress appeared. "What can I get you to drink?"

Jax and I said, "Coffee," simultaneously.

He ordered the Perkins famous "magnificent seven" breakfast—two eggs, two pieces of bacon and three pancakes—and I opted for a waffle, bacon and hash browns.

I stirred two packets of sweetener and one creamer into my coffee. "What's on the agenda tonight, stud muffin?"

Laughing, he picked up my hand and threaded our fingers together. "Just your average date. Food. Conversation. Groping under the table."

That's when I felt his other hand on my knee.

His faked innocent look cracked me up. But I managed to keep a straight face. "In your delusional dating timeline, the first date we talked, the second date we held hands and hugged, the third date we kissed, so the fourth date jumps to us touching each other's naughty bits?"

"Only if the mood strikes you to—"

"Stroke you?"

Jax squeezed my knee. "You're sassier than usual tonight."

"You bring out the best in me."

"I think you meant to say I bring out the *beast* in you, baby." I laughed.

"God. You are even more beautiful when you laugh."

"Slathering on the flattery? You really want to get to third base tonight, don't you?"

"I'm just happy to be here with you. It's been a long week."

The ghost tour was the last time we'd been together, although we'd been texting like crazy. "Your out-of-town trip was successful?" He hadn't told me where he was going, and I hadn't asked.

"I guess. It seemed like a waste of time and something that could've been handled over the phone."

That's when I pounced. "Level with me, Jax. You're some kind of investment banker." I still had no clue what he did to earn a living. It'd become more of a joke between us, but in some ways, I liked that I didn't know, because I'd gotten to know Jaxson in a different way than I had other men. We talked about everything but how we spent our workdays.

"An investment banker? Seriously? Do I look like I've got a stick up my ass?"

I opened my mouth and he stopped me before I gave him an honest answer.

"Try again." He shrugged. "Or don't. Because you're not gonna guess right."

"Then I give. No, wait. You're a commodities broker."

He blinked at me. "Lucy Q, I don't even know what the hell that is."

"Me neither, but it sounds rich and fancy. That type of job would totally explain the car you drive. Maybe I'll call you Mr. Rich and Fancy until you get annoyed and confess to being a car salesman, just to shut me up."

He snorted. "Not a car salesman either."

"Yeah, you smell too expensive to be hawking cars—even luxury models."

Another slow, sexy blink from those arresting eyes made my heart race. "How does one smell expensive?"

"Your cologne is a custom blend, isn't it?"

Surprisingly he nodded.

"I knew it! I've never smelled anything like it. Wearing a custom blend signals your need for exclusivity, which equals you've got the ka-ching to afford that privilege."

"You've sniffed a lot of guys, have you?"

I tapped my nose and then his. "Careful, Mr. Rich and Fancy, or I might suspect you're jealous that my nose has been in a lot of different guys'—"

"No need to finish that sentence," he supplied.

Our food arrived.

I had three plates of food . . . to his one.

"You sure you'll be able to eat all of that?" he asked.

"Watch me. I'll even mop up every bit of syrup with my bacon."

Jax teased me for using half a container of apricot syrup on one side of my waffle, and half a container of twinberry syrup on the other side.

I made a gagging noise when he dumped a pile of ketchup on his scrambled eggs.

He returned the sentiment when I covered my hash browns in Heinz 57.

Just normal date behavior for us.

With the exception that I'd never had a man look at me the way Jax did, with longing, lust, amusement and exasperation. Lately, though, the look of lust had gotten way more intense.

And I also really liked his affection, his need to be touching me in some manner, which further cemented this connection strengthening between us.

He finished his meal first and sipped his coffee, wearing that bemused smile as he watched me finish every bite.

The waitress cleared our plates.

"I am stuffed. That was so good. Great date idea."

"You weren't lying when you promised to eat it all."

"Why would I lie about that when I don't lie about anything else?"

Jax gave me a considering look. "You don't? Not even a little white lie here and there?"

"Nope. Lying was my father's specialty—a trait I'm very proud that he didn't pass on." As soon as the words tumbled out in a bitter rush, I wished them back.

"That's the first time I've heard you say anything about your dad."

"That's because the man isn't part of my life."

"Now? Or when you were growing up?"

"Both. I told you my parents divorced when I was ten. That event didn't change anything about my day-to-day life, because Mom got the house and us. He moved out. As far as I know he paid child support, but we never saw him. He never called. Never came to any of our milestone events. When he ditched Mom, he ditched us too."

Jax curled his hand around the side of my face. "I don't know what to say to that, Luce. Sorry . . . Doesn't seem like you're sorry he moved on."

"I'm honestly not. He was a salesman for a pharmaceutical company, with a big territory across the Midwest, so he came home every other weekend. If he wasn't golfing on that Saturday, then he was at the club with his cronies. My mom half joked that he was too busy dipping into his pharmacy samples to make it home. It didn't hit me until I was older that Mom had been referencing 'male enhancement' drugs, since Daddy-dearest was a proud philanderer."

"He bragged about fucking around on your mom?"

"He didn't hide it. I guess he didn't apologize either. He maintained the 'what are you going to do about it?' attitude because he was the breadwinner and she was the home-maker. Anyway, it doesn't matter now." I reached for my wa-ter to try and break Jax's hold on me. "So fill me in on our postdinner plans, Mr. Rich and Fancy."

Jax kept a gently commanding hand against my face. "Don't try and change the conversation."

I tried to avoid those cool blue eyes but he wouldn't allow it. "I hate talking about this."

"Because it's a painful part of your past?"

"No. Because I have an unpopular opinion on relation-ships. Which is why most men don't make it past the first date with me."

"You're talking in riddles, babe. Since I'm the rare mysti-cal male creature in your world that's made it to the fourth date with you, that means you talk to me, not at me, not around me, not in generalizations. I've got nowhere else to be. We can stay here all night if that's how long it takes for you to believe that I can handle the truth."

God. He was so pushy. So determined to dive beyond the surface layer with me. So freaking sexy because of all of that.

I locked my gaze to his. "The truth is all men cheat."

That caught him off guard. "Some, yeah, but not all men."

"Says you. A man," I scoffed. "All men cheat is my truth, not my opinion. I've never been proven wrong."

"Never?"

"Never. Needless to say, I have trust issues. I've consid-ered that they might also be 'daddy issues' because my first male influence was a cheater, but none of the males since, whether they've been friends, acquaintances or lovers, have changed my truth."

"You've been cheated on?"

"Every woman I know has been cheated on because men are incapable of monogamy."

I watched his reaction closely. A narrowing of his eyes. The tightening of his jaw. The need to defend or explain the male species.

So what Jax actually said next shocked the crap out of me.

"You're sure this is your truth, Lucy? And not a warning passed down from your mother that you've taken to believe is the gospel truth about love?"

"This has nothing to do with love. I believe in love. But I don't believe love is a magical talisman that alters a man's desire to cheat. A guy can proclaim his love for his woman to his family, friends and even god, and still be banging his assistant in the break room. But because he doesn't 'love her' "—I made air quotes—"then it doesn't count. Men have all sorts of reasons and excuses that justify their cheating ways."

"Like what?" he demanded.

"Like the example I just gave you. Like what happened to my sister. Her boyfriend of two years got caught cheating after my sister moved back in with me and Mom during her cancer treatment. Notice I didn't say he 'started cheating,' because I fully believe that asswipe had been cheating on my sister all along. But he had an excuse that he truly believed: It could only be considered cheating if they were married. It didn't 'count' if they hadn't officially exchanged rings in front of friends, family and a preacher." I paused to take a drink. "Never mind the fact he'd pledged his love to her and that should've been enough to keep his dick in his pants."

"Jesus."

"Not to mention the dozen or so examples I could share when guys' significant others 'don't understand their needs' so they troll 'just for sex' elsewhere—giving them the best of both worlds, a variety of sexual partners when they want to get kinky, and a companion to come home to who washes his fucking socks. Or they're working away from home so they invoke the 'what happens on the road, stays on the road' cheaters clause. Or it's not 'cheating' if it's a one-night stand—even if the dude has a different woman / one-night stand every damn week. Or the 'you don't pay attention to me so I found someone else who did' excuse, which conveniently puts the blame on the woman for his cheating behavior. Or there's the—"

He pressed his thumb over my lips. "Enough. I get it. It's depressing as hell because you're not wrong."

I waited, my heart racing, for what would come next.

Jax focused on my mouth, feathering his thumb across the swell of my lower lip. "I can't explain away your fears or the idiocy of the male species. I can't change how you've been treated in the past. I won't discount your truth. But I can ask you to give me a chance to be the exception."

"For how long? One night proves nothing."

"Sweetheart, one night would never be enough with you."

Desire unspooled in my core so fast I felt dizzy.

Which pissed me off, because we were having a conversation about cheating—sex should be the last thing on my mind.

"Whoa there, lady. Your fiery glare is starting to melt my manflesh."

His use of *manflesh* made me snicker and provided some levity.

"That's my clue to whisk you away to the second half of our date, where you can release some of that aggression in a productive way." He dropped a fifty on the table and slid out of the booth, waiting while I did the same.

Jax didn't give me space as we walked out. In fact, he draped his arm over my shoulder and tucked me close to his body.

When we reached his car, I finally said, "Where are we going?"

His dangerously sexy grin set off tiny warning bells. "Someplace where it's all fun and games."

Everyone started yelling, "Go, go, go!" bringing me back to the present.

I hopped up and squinted at the field, watching as Jensen Lund reached the end zone.

It was easy to get caught up in the Lund family's excitement.

Confetti actually rained down from the ceiling inside the suite.

Had all members of the Lund family acted this excited during Jax's hockey games when he played well? Archer and Edie had taken Mimi to several of Jax's games the last two years he played, but they'd never invited me. Not that I would've gone if they had. Mimi was part of this family, not me.

The servers cracked open bottles of champagne. I watched as Jax shook his head at the waiter. Then Edie appeared with another waiter who poured glasses of sparkling cider for Jax and Mimi as well as Lennox.

Yes, the Lund family definitely took care of their own, and I couldn't be unhappy that my daughter would always have whatever she needed from them without question.

Six

—

JAX

Normally when I had Mimi I was fully invested in whatever she was saying. I'd worked at becoming an "active listener"—a term my counselor used. That had been something I'd needed to grasp was a constant problem with me. No clue how long I'd been a narcissist, being in my own head, more concerned with creating my response to the conversation without paying attention to what others said. I'd been a piece of work before my issues with alcohol had overtaken my life.

You're doing it now . . . thinking about your issues instead of listening to your daughter.

Right. But Mimi had been babbling, her thoughts wandering all over the place, and it'd been easy to tune her out. I glanced in the rearview mirror and caught her watching me.

"You weren't listening, were you?" she accused.

"I'm sorry, Meems, my mind did wander. Sorry. You were telling me about . . . ?"

"Jocelyn's party tomorrow, geez, Daddy."

"You have a gift for her, right?"

She sighed dramatically. "Yes, but that's not what we were talking about. I said it's an ice skating party and I don't have any of the clothes and stuff to wear. And then I asked how come you never take me ice skating anymore? We used to go all the time."

Only because it suited my purpose. I could get Mimi suited up and ditch her with one of the ice rink attendants—usually they were starry eyed when I gave them my name. They were thrilled to work with Mimi while they watched me skate.

In the off-season, which was damn short anyway, I skated five days a week. And since I'd been spending part of my off-season in Minneapolis, I'd intentionally moved from rink to rink for the variances in the ice conditions. And I did spend time skating with Mimi, but after I'd done my own workout.

I'd been such a self-centered dick. I really hoped that Mimi wouldn't remember that about me.

"So how come you stopped taking me? Because you quit hockey? Because you don't like it anymore?"

"I love hockey. That'll never change. And I didn't quit; I just got too old to play with all of these young guys. But as far as why I don't take you skating anymore? I wasn't sure if skating was something you liked, or something you felt you had to like because I spent so much time skating."

"I like skating, Daddy. A lot. You're the only one who ever let me skate as fast as I wanted. Last Christmas I went with Mommy and Aunt Lindsey, but they made me hold their hands, the entire time, like I was some kind of baby on double training blades."

I bit back a smile at her indignation. I wouldn't have been surprised to hear that Miss I-Can-Do-It-Myself had staged a breakaway.

"Okay, sweets. Since you like it for yourself, and not me, next week I'll look for a rink with open skate times."

"But Daddy, I don't have stuff to wear for tomorrow. Mommy donated my old skates, and she said that I could just use the rink's rental skates at the party."

I nearly hit the brakes.

Oh fuck no. My kid was not wearing goddamned rental skates.

"I don't have gloves or a coat or anything either."

If she really wanted to do this, I'd make sure we did it right from the start.

"Well, squirt, looks like me and you are going shopping."

T he next afternoon, Nolan tagged along when I took Mimi to the birthday party.

I wasn't a drop-and-go dad; I walked my daughter into the rink and made sure there was adult supervision before Nolan and I hit the workout space at Brady's place, which housed a world-class gym and was only ten minutes from the ice rink.

My little brother tried to beat the fuck out of me . . . and he got in a couple of good shots. But ultimately I won our sparring contest.

For the tenth time.

Yeah, I probably rubbed that in his face.

We grabbed a quick bite to eat and then returned to the rink for the last half hour of the birthday bash. After snagging us each a piece of cake, we sat in the stands and watched.

Nolan bumped me with his knee. "You are such a sucker, bro."

"What?"

"Mimi. She manipulated you. She looks like a damn professional outfitted like that."

"Lucy donated her old stuff. She needed new gear, which I provided."

A moment or two passed and Nolan hissed, "Sweet Jesus, Jax. Is she wearing . . . hockey skates?"

"She wanted them," I offered as a half-assed protest. "All she could talk about was skating fast."

"Where'd you take her to buy this stuff?" Nolan asked without any casualness whatsoever.

"The Hockey Grail."

Another pause. "That store is for professional athletes! She's eight."

"*I'm* a professional athlete. She's my kid and she doesn't need to be out in public wearing borrowed sports gear that would catch the interest of the media more than if she's dressed in top-of-the-line equipment."

He laughed. "You trying to convince me that girl blends in?"

"Nope."

"Good. Because you're not an idiot, dumbass. She's skating circles around the rest of the girls. Someone is bound to notice that."

"Let them."

"I cannot believe you took her to the Hockey Grail."

I couldn't believe he was ragging on me about it. "She needed to test skates, and they're the only sporting goods store that also has a skating rink right in the store."

"Did she even try figure skates?"

"She wasn't interested. And now when she and I skate together, she'll be able to keep up better."

Nolan faced me. "You plan on taking her to the rink on a regular basis?"

"She said she missed it. And frankly I miss it too."

"Mama Luce ain't gonna be happy about this, bro."

"How will she know? I'll keep Mimi's gear at my place."

"Lying to her? Dude. That's never gone well for you."

"True. But I suspect chatterbox won't be able to keep a secret for long anyway, so I'll deal with it as it comes up."

Just then Mimi skated up. "The party is over. Uncle Nolan, can you help me get ready to go?"

"Sure. But why me?"

"Because I heard Dallas say you could get girls out of their clothes fast."

He choked on his last bite of cake.

Way to go, Dallas, saying that stuff to a kid who takes everything literally. "Sweets, that's not something that should be repeated, okay?" To Nolan I said, "I'll talk to Dallas about those type of slipups this week."

"You do that. And I'll do this." Nolan stood. "Lead the way, short stuff."

I'd started picking up the trash around us, when I heard, "Sir? Could I have a word with you?"

I offered the woman a quick smile. Getting recognized had always been part of the gig. "Sure."

"Does your daughter play hockey?"

Say what? "No. She doesn't play. Why?"

"I noticed she had on hockey skates, not figure skates." Upon seeing my frown, she clarified, "It can be an oversight for parents, especially if they're pink. Anyway, I'm the ice manager and it's my job to keep an eye on things. And your daughter certainly caught my eye. She's got a good, fast, solid gait on ice. Does she take lessons?"

"Uh. No."

"Well, she's got one helluva natural talent then. Have you ever considered putting her in a hockey program?"

My eyes widened.

And the lady mistook my reaction. She rolled her eyes. "It'll teach her team-building skills and make her a stronger girl. Hockey is great exercise; it strengthens hand-eye coordination—"

"You don't have to sell me on it. My daughter's mother would hate it, constantly worrying about head injuries, broken bones and missing teeth."

The woman opened her mouth. Shut it. Then she sighed. "Hockey is a contact sport. So those types of injuries are a possibility, but there's officially a 'no checking' rule in girls' and women's hockey."

A familiar quick whistle sounded, followed by, "Jaxson. I'm taking Mimi out to the car."

"Be right there." Then I faced the woman again. "I appreciate your input."

Her mouth hung open. "Holy crap. You're Jaxson Lund."

I grinned. "Guilty as charged."

Then she smacked her own head. "You just let me babble about the benefits of hockey and you've won the Stanley Cup three times. Three times! Good lord, man, I've been a Wild fan for years, but even I cheered on the 'hawks in the finals in 2015."

"Good to know. You should also know I wasn't critiquing your hard sell of your hockey program. All Mimi has said to me is she wants to skate fast . . . nothing about hockey."

She frowned again. "That's odd. She asked me to come over and talk to you about enrolling her in the program."

That's why the little sneak had disappeared with her uncle.

"We have a class for new players starting next week."

"This is something I'd have to discuss with her and her mother in depth."

"Understood. But this is a basic skills class. If she likes that, then you can address the possibility of her playing, even in a noncompetitive league."

I raised an eyebrow at her.

She laughed. "Right. Forgot who I was talkin' to for a moment. And you lived the dream that many of these kids strive for from an early age, so I don't gotta give you the spiel about commitment and cost, even on the recreational level."

"Recreational hockey is something I don't know a damn thing about. But I'd be grateful if you didn't mention to anyone the possibility of Mimi giving classes a try."

"This discussion and the follow-up is absolutely confidential, Mr. Lund."

"Please. Call me Jax. Right now I'm not a former pro hockey player, I'm just a plain old confused father trying to do the right thing for his kid."

She grinned at me. "I think we both know what that thing is." She pulled a business card out of the first aid kit attached to her belt. "I've got more time to talk in the mornings, so feel free to give me a holler if you need anything." She offered her hand. "Damn nice to meet you, Stonewall."

I glanced at the card. "You too, Margene."

I didn't say a word after I got in the car.

I didn't say anything for three solid minutes before Mimi piped up. "You're mad, huh?"

"I don't know yet."

"I really, really, really, really want to play hockey, Daddy. Please."

I held up my hand. "I would've been happy to discuss this with you. But you . . ." I inhaled and exhaled. I would not be the bad guy in this scenario. "Why don't you tell me what's wrong with how I discovered your interest in playing hockey." If she was old enough to use that kind of manipulation, she was old enough to understand why it was wrong, explain why she did it and take responsibility.

When Mimi remained mum several minutes later, my gaze flicked to the rearview mirror. Her brow was furrowed, but I didn't see that stubborn, mean set to her little chin.

Next to me, Nolan murmured, "You sure this is the best way to handle this, bro?"

"When you have a kid, feel free to do it differently," I said through clenched teeth.

"I'm sorry," Mimi finally said.

"And?"

"And I shoulda told you that I wanted hockey skates so I could play hockey, not because I was going to a birthday party."

I nodded. "Keep going."

"And I shouldn't have told that lady to go over and talk to you about putting me in hockey classes. Because I shoulda asked you first if we could talk about it."

I sent Nolan a smug look. *See? I can do this parenting stuff.*

"But, Daddy, even if you say yes, Mommy will say no and that's not fair! Maybe I could be a really, really good player like you and win championships and stuff, like you did! How will I know if I could be the best if I don't even get to try because you and Mommy will fight about it like you fight about everything else!"

And my pat on the back felt like a punch in the gut.

I hated that Mimi was aware that her mother and I sometimes had words. I really hated that Mimi tried to use it to her advantage now. Lucy and I had agreed to provide a united front. She was the one I needed to talk to, not a precocious eight-year-old with an agenda. "Your mom and I will talk about it."

"You mean yell about it," she said sullenly.

"Hey. And no back talk," I said sharply.

"I wanna go home."

"That's where we're headed."

"No, I wanna go home to Mommy."

"Jesus, when did this start?" Nolan said under his breath.

"Well, that's too bad, sweets, because you're stuck with me until tomorrow. But I'm pretty sure Calder is around if you wanna play until dinnertime."

She didn't respond, and the remainder of the drive to Snow Village was strangely silent.

I expected Nolan to take off, but he seemed content to settle into the couch with a soda while college football games droned in the background.

"I have to tell you something," he finally said.

I groaned. "I'm not gonna like this, am I?"

"It's not bad. I thought it was kind of sweet."

"What?"

"About the last year or so that you lived in Chicago, when-ever Mimi was around me, she asked a million questions about hockey. She always wanted to watch your games—even ones from years back before she was born. She thought it was the coolest sport ever, and she begged me to take her skating and to kids' hockey games around here. The girl was obsessed."

"Did you tell Lucy?"

He sent me an "Are you kidding me?" look.

"Why didn't you tell me?"

"I honestly thought it was a phase. A daddy-worship thing. She wished you were here, she wanted to be closer to you so she used her interest in hockey as a coping mechanism . . . blah, blah, blah."

"So you weren't surprised by her sneaky-ass actions to-day."

"Yes, I was surprised by the way she went about bringing it to your attention. But given the way Lucy would react if Mimi had asked her to enroll her in hockey? I'm not sur-prised that she had to figure out another way to get someone to take her seriously." He slurped his soda. "I'm just saying that her interest in the game is genuine. And it's not new. It's what she wants, Jax. How can you deny her the opportunity?" He smirked. "Especially now that she's got top-of-the-line hockey gear."

"Bite me."

"Pass. But you can't ignore this. Mimi will bring it up with Lucy, and then you'll take the brunt of the blame for keeping something from her."

"Add it to the other shit I've been dragging my feet on talking to her about."

"Do I even want to know what the hell that cryptic statement is supposed to refer to?"

"No. But it's time you knew anyway." I felt relieved to get my impending change of address off my chest. I figured telling my brother would be a good practice run for when I finally told Lucy.

Nolan took it in stride. "Your move makes sense, but dammit, Jax. Why have you kept this such a big secret?"

"Are you pouting because I didn't ask you for remodel and decorating advice?" I shot back.

"Yes." He stuck out his lower lip in an exaggerated pout and gave me puppy dog eyes.

"Pathetic." I flicked a piece of popcorn at him. "Is that hangdog look something that works with the ladies to get you laid?"

"Depends. Lately, though, I need more of a challenge."

"A potential conquest resisting your charms?"

He shrugged. "I had drinks with this woman Tuesday night. Testing the waters to see whether I wanted to spend time with her over the weekend. Everything was going fine. I excused myself to use the restroom . . . and she followed me. She got on her knees and blew me. Right there in the bathroom. Then afterward, she wandered over to the mirror and touched up her lipstick. She smiled and said it was still early in the week and she hoped when I was choosing a playmate for the weekend that her pregame preview would move her to the top of the list."

"And . . . did it?"

"God, Jax, that's not the point. The point is I've gotten into such a predictable routine with women that even the ones I'm going out with for the first time know what to expect. Makes me feel sleazy." He tossed a piece of popcorn in the air and caught it in his mouth. "So sleazy begets easy and I want to be done with it."

I snagged a handful of popcorn. "I don't know how you do the dating thing anyway."

"Like you have room to talk."

"I didn't date. I fucked. You wine and dine them. You bring them to family functions. Some of them you even see more than one time. That gives them a false sense of hope that they might be the one to get you to finally settle down." I pointed at him. "I never did that. Just sex, pure and simple. A drink in the hotel bar. A trip to my room. And if they really knocked my socks off, I'd order them room service the next morning before I hopped on the team bus and got the hell out of town."

My little brother didn't respond for several long moments, so I knew the bastard was stalling and whatever he wanted to ask me wouldn't be nice.

"What?"

"Was that how it played out when you were cheating on Lucy? You needed a warm body, she wasn't there, so any female would do?"

I stood and paced . . . Guilty feet couldn't sit still or something. "I never cheated on Lucy the first year we were together. Never. I couldn't wait to get back to her, even when I hated that she refused to move to Chicago during the season. So yeah, that was a point of contention between us. Then she was pregnant with my child, but she didn't want to be with me in the city where I was based. She needed her family, which totally bit her in the ass because both her mom and her sister moved out of the Cities within six months of Mimi's birth. She couldn't work because she had to care for our baby. The married guys on the team . . . their wives would've rallied around her and helped had she and Mimi been in Chicago. But no, she wouldn't even ask Mom and Dad for help here. And I know you offered, but she sent you away too." I faced him. "I'm not making excuses for fucking around on her. That is all on me. All of it."

"But?" he supplied casually.

"But nothing. Lucy shut me out from being with her and Mimi. Was it a reaction on her part to me cheating on her? Probably. If I never would've cheated would she have still shut me out? Probably. That is just how Lucy is."

"And you loved her anyway?"

"Yes." I sighed. "Christ. I think I was in love with her by our third date. The stupid thing? We didn't even know each other's last names at that point."

Nolan frowned. "Why didn't I know any of this?"

"Because it was our funny backstory. Our secret. And it . . . she . . ." I jammed a hand through my hair in frustration. "She liked me for me, Nolan. Not Jaxson, the pro hockey player. Not Jaxson, heir to the Lund empire. It was the first— and still might be the only—time I can say with certainty that the attraction was honest. Then I betrayed her and did the worst possible thing to her; the same thing her dad had done to her mother. That reinforced her belief men are incapable of monogamy and everything that had been good between us was just a lie."

A pause stretched for several long moments until Nolan spoke again. "Sounds like Lucy has always had some issues, bro."

"Yeah, well, don't we all? Mine has always been entitlement. And make fun of me or whatever, but Lucy giving me her heart, choosing to love me, wasn't an entitlement. It was something I'd earned. But instead of holding her heart like it was something precious? I treated that fucker like I could stomp on it, shred it, break it because it belonged to me."

"Jax. Man. Calm down."

I continued to pace. "This eats at me. If a man ever treated Mimi the way I treated Lucy? They'd never find his fucking body. How am I supposed to retain hope that Lucy could ever forget? Or forgive me? Am I just an idiot to think she'd ever want to get—" I snapped my mouth shut.

"Whoa. Are you saying that you want to get back together with her?" Nolan said.

"Yes. If she gives me the tiniest sign, I'd be all in with her again in a fucking heartbeat." I finally looked at my brother. "Why does that surprise you?"

"Because you're setting yourself up for failure with her again."

"So I'm doomed to want with her what we once had and to never get it back? Even if it'd be better this time because I know what we're—what she's—worth?"

"And what's that, Jax?"

"Everything."

Nolan just blinked at me in that slow, steady, considering manner of his.

My cell phone buzzed with a text message and I automatically checked. It was from Rowan, Jensen's wife.

RL: Hey, the kids want to go to the rec room. I'll take them if that's cool with you.

ME: That's fine. Sorry you'll get stuck playing pool with them again ☹

Across the room Nolan's cell rang. He said, "I need to take this."

"Go ahead."

Before he answered the call, he warned, "We're nowhere near done with this conversation, bro," before he vanished down the hallway.

My phone buzzed again.

RL: I wish. They're determined to play shuffleboard . . . I'll try and keep them from using the sticks as javelins this time, but no promises.

ME: Should I come down and supervise?

RL: Nope. I got this.

ME: K. Thanx. Let me know if you need anything.

I set my phone aside and heard Nolan still talking on his. I wandered over to the sliding glass door that led to a minuscule balcony that overlooked the courtyard. From here I could see the rec building. Mimi loved hanging out there with the other kids who lived in the apartment complex since it was packed with fun games like pool, foosball, air hockey, Ping-Pong, and shuffleboard.

Shuffleboard. I hadn't thought of that game in years, even when I'd walked over the painted outlines inside the rec center to get to the pool tables. Mimi hadn't shown interest in playing, and the last time I'd played was years ago with Lucy.

Man, that had been an eye-opening experience. I hadn't believed her when she claimed she had no basic sports skills at all—until she'd proved it without a doubt the night of our fourth date . . .

Y ou're joking," Lucy said as we stood outside the doors to the middle school gymnasium.

"Nope. I'm completely serious."

"This is one of my worst nightmares, Jax. Returning to PE class in middle school, where I didn't even have the humiliation of being chosen last for a team."

"What do you mean?"

"The PE teacher made me sit on the bench and watch my classmates play games. I never got to play."

I tugged her closer and kissed her temple. "That sucks. I'm sorry. But it just proves my point that you don't know if you're good at a sport if you haven't tried it. Your PE teacher was supposed to expose you to different activities so maybe one would click."

"Well, that didn't happen. And the only way this would be worse is if I have to get undressed in the locker room and shower naked with a bunch of strangers."

Curling my hands around her face, I tilted her head back, intending to say something to allay her paranoia, but no words came to mind, so I kissed her.

Damn, did I love kissing this woman. She never held back. No matter where we were, she was totally in the moment with me. No matter if we'd had a heated argument a minute before our lips connected. No matter if we were laughing and being stupid, it faded into the background when we fed this need.

I ended the kiss slowly, taking my time to memorize every luscious curve of her lips, every sexy sway of her body into mine, every throbbing beat of her pulse.

"Killer distraction, but still not good enough, buddy," she muttered as she caught her breath.

"One game. That's all I'm asking."

Lucy lifted that limpid gaze to mine and I almost said forget it.

Almost.

"Let me ask you something, Jaxson. If the situation was reversed and I dragged you to a cooking class, you'd be all gung ho about it?"

"Yes. Because that proved that you listened to me and wanted to do something thoughtful and personal for me that I'd appreciate, even if it made me a little nervous to try it."

"Oh."

"So this date-night excursion isn't an attempt to humiliate you. I just want to push you out of your comfort zone."

"Why?"

Because every moment I spend with you pushes me further out of mine.

But I didn't tell her that or confess this fun spring fling had turned into something real for me. Instead, I went for the flip response. "Because you're letting me."

Her jaw dropped and I stole another quick kiss. "Come on. I want to get the court before someone else does."

"This game involves a court?" She groaned behind me as I towed her along. "Is it volleyball?"

"Nope."

"Basketball?"

"Nope."

"The court of public opinion?"

I laughed. "Clever. But, no."

"See, if tossing out smartass quips were a sport, I'd be a champion."

"Of that, there's no doubt."

We entered the gymnasium. Half a dozen people played volleyball in one corner, and a few people were in the bleachers watching or talking, but besides them, the place was nearly empty.

A banner across the wall boasted

YOUR COMMUNITY GYM IS OPEN EVERY NIGHT
FROM 6 TO 8 P.M.!

"Do you live around here?"

"Nope."

"This is another 'community' option you just happened to know about?"

"Nothing but the best for you, baby." I stopped at the rack just inside the equipment room. "Grab two of those poles off the wall and I'll get the discs."

She blinked at me. "What poles?"

"The long ones with the pronged ends." I picked up the bins with the discs and carried them out to the courts.

Lucy followed behind me, and I heard her snort when she saw the elongated triangle that indicated what game I'd chosen.

"Shuffleboard?"

"Deck shuffleboard, actually. Regular shuffleboard is played on a tabletop with your hands. This one uses sticks called poles." I faced her. "Have you ever played?"

She rolled her eyes.

"Right. Okay. I'll explain the rules." After I finished, I said, "Any questions?"

"Are you a PE teacher?"

It appeared we were back to her trying to guess my occupation. "No."

"Are you an activities director for a senior citizens' home?"

What the fuck? "God no."

"Then how do you know—"

"Quit stalling. Time to play. You're yellow; you go first."

She put the disc down and lined the pole up. She went to push the disc but didn't maintain her grip on the pole and it went flying across the playing surface, while the disc didn't move at all.

For christsake, man . . . Do. Not. Laugh.

Then she turned and glared at me.

"You'll get it this time," I encouraged her.

Lucy managed to move all four of her discs. Two were completely out of play since they weren't even on the board. The other two were easy for me to knock out of play when my turn came.

At the end of the first round the score was Lucy zero; Jax . . . thirty.

It was tempting to throw the game, but I was too damn competitive. Plus, it would piss her off more if she suspected I'd let her win. So I did the same thing with the discs as I did with a puck: put it exactly where I wanted it.

End of round two, the final score was Lucy minus twenty; Jax . . . seventy-five.

"Yay, you won. Can we go now?"

I laughed. "No. It's the best three out of five games, not a single game."

"Then I concede."

"Huh-uh. This time I'll help you with your pole handling."

Her lips curved into a naughty smile. "I'm down with that."

I directed her into the 10-off zone, and stood behind her, with my left hand on her left hip and my right hand curled around the pole just below hers. "Now put the tip against the disc. Don't bump it; push it. Straighten your wrist and keep a firm grip on your pole so your hand isn't sliding up and down like this." As soon as my hand enclosed hers and I demonstrated that sliding motion, her breath caught.

She wiggled her ass against my groin and said, "So I'm

not supposed to use the pole like this?" She moved her hand up and down the pole in long, sensuous strokes, as if she had her fist wrapped around my pole.

Instant erection.

"Then I don't suppose I'm supposed to do this either?" she practically purred as she turned her wrist and slid her hand over the pole in short, fast bursts.

Yeah, baby, that's how I like it.

"I'd think it wouldn't matter how you held on to this thicker part of the shaft, because whether it's long and slow, or short and fast . . . it gets the job done," she cooed in a sultry tone.

"Lucy," I gritted out, "you're not supposed to move your hand up and down the pole at all. It's supposed to stay in one place."

"Oh. My bad." Then she squeezed her fist around the pole and released. Squeezed and released, perfectly aware that my hand was still on top of hers, so it felt like—

"Are we going to shoot this off? Or do I need more help on my pole-handling technique?"

I slid my fingers around her hip and spread my hand across her pelvis, pulling her ass more tightly against my crotch as I nosed aside her hair to reach her ear. "You've got exquisite technique, dirty girl, making my damn dick hard when we're playing shuffleboard."

She turned her head and captured my lips, kissing me with heat, teasing me with sugar bites and small flicks of her tongue, rendering me immobile since she controlled the angle of the kiss and I sure as hell didn't want to break the spell she'd put me under.

"Jax," she finally murmured.

"Yeah, baby?"

"Will you let me concede now?"

"No. Way."

A loud harrumph left her mouth, and she jerked on the

pole, surprising me and sending the disc caroming across the court.

It landed in the ten-point spot perfectly.

For a brief moment I wondered if I had a ringer on my hands, but then her next shot went as wild as her previous ones.

Even after I beat her all three games, I knew she'd had a good time.

Since she had to work the next morning, we ended the night early, but we lingered by her car in the Perkins parking lot like a pair of infatuated teens who didn't want to say good-bye.

"When's the next time I'll see you?" she asked.

"Not until next week. I've got a bunch of family commitments this weekend, and then as soon as that's over, I'm out of town for several more days." I brushed my lips across the crown of her head. "I'll text you. Or call you. Sorry that's how it'll play out this week."

"Okay."

When she didn't tack on a snarky comment, I nudged her chin up and stared into her eyes. "Talk to me."

"I honestly don't mind that we're not seeing each other every night. Don't get me wrong; I like being with you. But I also like getting to know you through text messages and phone conversations. The lust is starting to get pretty intense, and that's not all there is between us." She paused. "Am I wrong?"

"No, you're right. I didn't want to sound like I was feeding you full of shit, but even after just four dates and two weeks, you know more about me than I've ever let anyone else see. You've got no preconceived ideas about me. I can just be Jax, the charmingly annoying man you met at the car wash who interested you enough to keep going out on dates with him."

"That's true."

"And you can be Lucy, the most charmingly blunt and beautiful woman I've ever had the pleasure of spending time with."

She kissed me then. Sweetly, tenderly, softly. Her ability to recognize when I needed comfort instead of just passion absolutely bowled me over.

"Have a good week, Jaxson. I can't wait to see you again."

"Any idea when Mimi will be back?" Nolan said, bringing me back to the here and now.

"She and Calder are hanging out in the rec room for a while."

"Great. Then let's watch these Iowa assholes get their asses handed to them by the Gophers."

We returned to watching the game, forgoing any mention of our previous conversation.

Right as the game ended, the apartment door opened and Mimi skipped inside. "Hey, guess what? Calder got a cell phone!"

"That is cool," Nolan said. "Speaking of, girlie-girl, come over here and sit by me for a sec."

Mimi bounded over the back of the couch—damn Jensen for teaching her that little trick.

Nolan laughed. "Good thing your dad isn't paying too much for this furniture. I'd whoop your butt if you did that to my leather sofa."

She rolled her eyes as if that'd ever happen. Her uncle Nolan was a sucker for her and she knew it. "Am I in trouble or something?" she asked him.

"No. But I have something special for you."

While Nolan reached inside his messenger bag, I took the chair opposite the couch to see what he was up to. Nolan spoiled Mimi—he considered it his right as her only uncle—and Lucy and I mostly let him as long as his gifts weren't too outrageous.

Nolan set a box on the coffee table.

A cell phone box.

Mimi gasped.

Since Nolan knew me so well, he held up his hand to forestall my immediate "hell no" response.

"This phone is exactly like Calder's. It's from Grandpa Archer and Grandma Edie, just like Calder got his phone from his Grandpa Ward and Grandma Selka. It's not a fun phone for you to play games on, okay? It's a safety tool. And having it carries great responsibilities, understand?"

She nodded.

"You'll have to learn to put it in your backpack every day before school. You'll have to remember to charge it every night before you go to bed. We've already preprogrammed phone numbers in it, like your mom's and your dad's, Grandpa's and Grandma's, and mine, with our pictures, so it'll be easy for you to make calls. We've also listed 911 for emergencies, and the security desk at Lund Industries."

That made the hair on the back of my neck stand up. What in the hell was going on?

"So you'll have to be really careful that you don't accidentally call either of those numbers, okay?"

"Okay."

"But those numbers are important in case you ever get lost and you can't get ahold of anyone else on your phone contact list. Those are your safety calls."

Mimi gave him a thoughtful look. "Can I add my friends to my phone?"

Nolan shook his head. "This is a test to see if you're big enough to follow these phone rules first before you get extra privileges with this one."

Who did Nolan think he was, setting down rules for my daughter?

"Can I at least put Calder's number in it?" she pleaded.

"Yep."

She grinned and bounced off the couch. "I'm gonna go get him right now!" Then she looked at me. "Uh, is that okay, Daddy?"

"Make it fast, Meems."

And she was zipping out the door.

As soon as she was gone, I said, "What the fuck, Nolan?"

His cool, assessing eyes met mine. "You and Lucy have been arguing over whether Mimi is too young for a cell phone since you lived in Chicago. It has fuck-all to do with Mimi and everything to do with a power play between you two."

"Exactly. She is *our* daughter and we'll make the decisions about what she can and can't have. Not you. Not Mom and Dad. Jesus. Lucy is gonna blow her goddamned top over this. There's no way she'll believe I had nothing to do with it."

Nolan's eyes narrowed. "Do you hear yourself? That's why we took the decision out of your hands. It's not about which one of you can buy Mimi the fanciest cell phone and who she'll love more. This is strictly a safety precaution."

"Why?" I demanded.

"Last week, one of the Melgard grandchildren got separated from her class during a field trip. The outing was rural enough there were concerns about her roaming around lost in the woods, and the outing was just urban enough that there were four roads intersecting the area where anyone could've picked her up. There was a lot of ground to cover when she went missing. If she'd had a trackable device like this"—he pointed to the box—"as well as instructions on its importance to her safety and how to use it, then it wouldn't have taken them twelve hours to find her."

My gut twisted. I said, "Why wasn't this in the news?" even when "Lindbergh baby" popped into my head. That kidnapping and murder had happened decades ago, but no one had ever forgotten the horror of that sick incident. The Melgard family were titans in the Midwest, owning a chain of home-improvement stores that were worth billions, so our family similarities weren't lost on me.

"My understanding is the family immediately had their personal security firm handling the search, not the local authorities. The girl attends a private school, so no one spoke to the media. They found her sleeping in a barn, six miles from where her class had been." Nolan ran his hand through his hair. "She was scared and hungry and confused. But it could've turned out a lot differently."

"How old is she?"

"Six."

"Jesus."

"After the incident was whispered about among the Twin Cities elite at some fund-raiser last week, the Lund patriarchy met with our security detail. They made this decision for Mimi. And they volunteered me to be the messenger."

"Who got stuck delivering the message for Jensen and Rowan regarding Calder?"

"Annika."

I exhaled. "I suppose this is less invasive than embedding a microchip in the youngest Lund heirs."

Nolan gave me a wry look. "Don't think that option wasn't discussed. Both you and Jens are sports celebrities with fans, so it puts your kids at an even higher risk than them just being heirs to a billion-dollar conglomerate."

"Part of me knows that, but I still want Mimi to have a normal childhood."

"Part of her normal will have to be her awareness of her safety. If you ingrain it in her now, hopefully it'll stick."

I hoped Lucy wouldn't throw a huge fit about this. Maybe I could find a way to sugarcoat it. I glanced at my silver-tongued brother.

"What?" he said warily.

"I don't suppose you'd be willing to play the messenger again for Lucy?"

"Nice try. You're on your own."

"You suck."

Mimi returned with Calder. While Nolan let them add each other to their new phones and showed them how everything worked, I prepared dinner.

I'd had zero cooking skills during my hockey-playing years. It'd been easier to pay a personal chef and nutritionist to keep me on track health wise. After rehab, I needed an activity to fill my extra time, so I hired a few chefs in Chicago to teach me how to cook. Oddly enough, I discovered I enjoyed cooking. Every month I had a private lesson through the Minneapolis Culinary Institute, and now my cooking skills were above average. I couldn't wait to test out the custom chef's kitchen I'd had designed for my new apartment.

After Calder left, Mimi set the table for three—Nolan was always up for a free meal—and we settled in.

"Daddy, you made my favorite!"

I scooped a helping of orange sesame chicken with bok choy and pea pods onto the mound of cauliflower "rice," topping it with a mix of cilantro and crushed baked garbanzo beans for extra crunch. It amused me that Mimi had no idea that her favorite meal was extremely healthy; she just cared that it tasted good.

"Jax. Seriously, man. This is better than eighty percent of the food I'm served eating out."

"Only eighty percent?"

He shrugged. "You've yet to master desserts, and you know I need my daily dose of sweet stuff."

"Mommy is teaching me to bake cookies," Mimi added. "I'll save some for you next time, Uncle Nolan."

He leaned over and kissed her forehead. "Sweet cookies from my best girl. What more could a man want?"

I never would've believed my party animal, manwhore brother would be content spending an entire Saturday with me and his niece. Nolan and I had always been tight, but in the months since I'd returned to Minnesota and spent more time with him, I remembered why I'm so lucky that he's still my best friend.

"Have you tried out your new phone and called your mom yet?" I asked Mimi as I watched her playing with it.

"Huh-uh. She probably won't answer."

"Because it's an unknown number calling her?"

"Nope." She reached for more rice. "Because she's on a date."

I went utterly still. Even in all the times I'd been body-checked into the boards, I'd never had the wind knocked out of me so fast.

Lucy was . . . dating?

Why the fuck hadn't she mentioned that little fun fact to me?

"Maybe because it's none of your business," Nolan answered.

Shit. I hadn't meant to say that out loud. I sent Mimi a sideways glance, but she was too busy stuffing her face to point out my f-bomb slipup. But I couldn't keep from grilling her. "How do you know your mom is on a date? She told you?"

"Huh-uh. I heard her and Aunt Lindsey talking about it."

"Do you know the guy's name?"

She shrugged.

"Do you know how many dates she's had with him?"

"Jax," Nolan hissed. "Stop."

"What? I'm just expressing interest in—"

"What's clearly not your business, bro. If Lucy had wanted you to know about her private life, she would've told you."

I leaned in. "Which is exactly why I'm having this conversation with my daughter, to find out more information about this fu—"

Mimi looked at me.

"Fellow," I amended. Christ. I hoped my smile came off as reassuring to her and not as menacing as it felt. "Have you ever met this man?"

"Nope. But I don't think Aunt Lindsey likes him."

Now I was getting somewhere. "Why would you say that?"

"Because she called him a pencil-neck geek." She cocked her head. "What is that?"

"That is not a nice description for a man," Nolan inserted.

"Has anyone ever called you that, Uncle Nolan?"

He coughed. "Uh, no, but I have been called far worse."

"Like what?"

"Nothing worth repeating."

My gaze landed on my fitness watch. Eight twenty. Lucy and Mr. Pencil-Neck Geek were likely in the middle of dinner.

Or in the middle of something else.

No. I would not think about some other man's hands on her body. I would not imagine some douchebag's mouth on her soft skin, searching for all those secret spots that drove her wild, spots I was already intimately familiar with. I could not fathom some dickhead looking into those molten brown eyes as he drove his—

"Jax," Nolan said sharply.

"What?"

His expression said, "Take it down a notch," but his mouth said, "Mimi asked you a question."

I unclenched my fist and my jaw and forced a smile to my lips. "Yes, sweets?"

"Do you think I should call her on my new cell phone?"

"Absolutely. But let's text her first so she knows to answer when your number shows up."

Nolan muttered something that I ignored.

"But . . . I don't know how to text."

"It's easy." I scooted my chair closer. "I'll show you. And you can even add these cool little pictures called emojis that'll really get her attention."

Nolan pushed away from the table. "That's it. I'm out."

I smiled at him. Must not have been my nicest smile, because the smarmy fucker took a step back. "But you'll miss all of the fun."

He bent down and kissed the top of Mimi's head. "Now you have my number, girlie-girl. Call me if you need me."

Mimi grunted her response and then exclaimed, "Is that a mermaid and a unicorn?"

"It sure is."

Another gasp. "Daddy, there's even a hockey stick and a hockey net on here!"

"I know. You go ahead and use as many of those emojis as you want in your message."

"I'm sending it right now."

Nolan snagged his gym bag and scowled at me. "This antagonism will come back and bite you in the butt, Jax."

I lifted a brow. "And yet you're the one bailing so you don't have to face Lucy's wrath about the little 'safety device' you gifted your niece."

He smirked. "I've perfected my timing for an exit strategy in all situations. Later."

"Okay, Daddy, she just sent this text back."

I peered over Mimi's shoulder and saw a string of question marks. I didn't bother to mask my grin when I said, "Go ahead and call her now."

Seven

LUCY

Normally I didn't answer my cell phone during a dinner out.

Then again, my normal wasn't usually dinners out, without my daughter, on a date.

But as a mother, I needed quick access to my phone in case Jax called, which was something Damon understood.

Damon didn't understand why I blurted out, "What the ever-loving fuck?" a little too loudly when a text message came through from my daughter, from her cell phone . . . because the girl didn't have a cell phone. Or she hadn't had one when I'd kissed her good-bye twenty-four hours ago.

"I'm going to fucking kill him."

"Lucy?"

"What?" I snapped as I typed a string of question marks in the text window.

"Is everything okay?"

"No, everything is absolutely not okay."

"Could you keep your voice down?"

I glanced up at him, then at the tables next to us in the restaurant. No one paid attention to me as far as I could tell.

Just then my phone rang in my hand, the Eminem "Lose Yourself" ring tone blaring, so then everyone did stare at us. I answered quickly and as quietly as I could manage. "Hello?"

"Mommy! Guess what? I got a cell phone! And you're the very first person that I called!"

My temper rose and I knew I couldn't keep my voice down. I said, "Wow, sweetheart, that's really something. Hang on one second." I looked at Damon apologetically and left the table, walking through the restaurant until I reached the waiting area, which, thankfully, was mostly empty.

Mimi said, "Daddy helped me text you. Did you see the mermaid and unicorns in the message?"

"Yes, I did. Very cool. It was nice of him to help you out. Could you hand your phone to your father, please?"

"Don't you want to talk to me?" she said with a pout in her voice.

"Of course I do. As soon as I have a word with him."

"You're gonna yell at him, aren't you?"

You bet your sweet ass I am.

A clunk sounded on the other end, followed by muffled words. Then Jax's deep voice drifted into my ear. "Now hold on, Lucy, it's not what you think."

"Not what I think?" I hissed. "I think you bought our daughter a goddamned cell phone when I specifically forbade you to do just that, you jackass."

"She's sitting right here, and if you keep up that kind of language, I will put you on speakerphone to stop it, understand?"

God. I hated that I'd reverted to name-calling. What was wrong with me? "Sorry."

"That's better. Are you calm enough to let me explain why Mimi has a cell phone?"

"I'm not even fucking close to calm."

"I take it your date isn't going well, then?"

I held the phone out and glared at it, as if I could see Jax's smarmy face to go with the smarmy tone I was hearing from him. "How in the hell did you know I was on a date?" I spun around. "Did you have someone follow me?"

"Relax, Lucy Q. Mimi knew you were on a date and she told me."

"How did she know? I didn't tell her."

"Might wanna remember that whole 'little pitchers have big ears' thing the next time you discuss your love life with your sister."

"I don't have a love life—" Dammit, why had I admitted that? "Not that it's any of your business if I did," I retorted. "Leave it to you to wreck any potential love life with this stunt."

"Stunt? All I did was allow Mimi to call her mother when she had some exciting news to share with her. Not my fault if Pencil-Neck Geek boy can't handle the fact you've been briefly interrupted by our daughter."

I wanted to scream. This man could rile me up in no time flat. And why had Mimi picked up on her aunt's assessment of Damon and decided to share that with her father? Now Jaxson would think . . .

Why do you care what Jaxson thinks about your date?

Good question.

"I hear you fuming, Luce. I bet you've got that cute little crease between your eyebrows as you're silently cursing me." He paused. "I hear your heels clicking, which means you're pacing too."

I stopped moving. "This is just so typically you, Jaxson Lund."

"Throwing out bits of flattery when we fight? I'm touched you remember how we used to do this, babe."

Babe. That urge to scream arose again.

"I'm not doing this with you, Jax. Be at my place, with Mimi, and that blasted cell phone, in half an hour. You can explain why she has it in person."

"You're cutting your date short?"

"Gee, do you think?"

He chuckled and the sexy sound zipped down the right side of my body. "Pencil-Neck Geek boy can't handle you when you're like this, can he?"

"That is none of your concern, Lund. Thirty minutes. Every minute you're late, I will tear a new strip from you, understood?"

"Understood. And maybe it makes me a masochist, but I look forward to it, Lucy Q."

He hung up.

I let a little frustrated noise escape me. That conceited ass. When I got my hands on him . . .

"Lucy?"

I whirled around to see Damon staring at me with utter shock.

"I'm sorry, Damon. Family emergency. I have to go."

"I understand. I'll get my keys from the valet and take you home."

"No." I sucked in a quick breath. Not cool snapping at him. "Thank you for the offer, but I'll just grab a cab." I managed a tight smile. "I'm sorry the evening ended up this way."

"Are you?" he said coolly.

"Excuse me?"

"I overheard your conversation, Lucy. In fact, I'm pretty sure the entire restaurant did. Is this truly an emergency with your daughter?"

My confused look wasn't faked. "What else would it be?"

"You tell me." He crossed his arms over his chest. "Because it sounded like you were talking to that former hockey player, Jaxson Lund. It sounded like you're meeting him."

"I am meeting him," I snapped, my patience gone. "He's Mimi's father."

His condescending look vanished. "I knew you worked at Lund Industries, but you never mentioned your intimate connection to the family."

"Why would that have mattered?"

"I like to know everything about someone I'm getting involved with."

I poked the down button for the elevator, relieved when the doors immediately opened. I didn't speak until I was inside it. "Well, it's not something you need to worry about now, because we're definitely not getting involved. Good-bye, Damon."

For once the universe had perfect timing and the door shut in his face before he could respond.

J ax made it to my apartment with about thirty-five seconds to spare.

Mimi wasn't her usual exuberant self, but she did disappear into the kitchen for a snack after giving me a hug.

As soon as she was out of earshot, Jax's expression turned serious. "No name-calling. No swearing. No bringing up incidents or issues from our past. We keep this discussion polite and to the point. Agreed?"

I almost snapped that he didn't have to explain adult behavior to me, but that wasn't exactly mature, was it? "Agreed."

His gaze moved over my face, down my neck, across my cleavage—twice—then dropped to my lower half before taking a leisurely track back up to meet my eyes. "I hope your date appreciated how beautiful you are."

"Do not think that compliments will soften me up."

"Because that would be unforgivable, would it? That I remind you that I still find you as hot and sexy as every other man in the world does?"

Argh. What was wrong with him? "Jax. Focus."

"I am. I won't let you goad me into a fight with you, because clearly you're spoiling for one." He set his hands on my shoulders and squeezed. "Go put on some comfy clothes, because I'll be here awhile."

From the kitchen Mimi yelled, "Daddy? I poured your milk."

He smirked at me. "I was promised milk and cookies since we had to leave so abruptly before we had our dessert tonight." Then he walked off without another word.

In my bedroom I stripped out of my clothes and slipped on my satin pajama set with the full sleeves and long pants.

They'd finished their snack by the time I returned. Jax gave Mimi a piggyback ride into the living room, and we spread out, with them on the couch, me in the opposite chair and Mimi's cell phone on the coffee table between us.

"First of all, I didn't buy this for her. Nolan gave it to her only after Mimi found out Calder received a phone just like this today too. The phone is registered to the Lund Industries security division."

My heart raced. "Why?"

He explained, and with each point I felt more fearful instead of relieved, but managed to keep Mimi from seeing my concern. What wasn't LI security telling us? Were there threats against our daughter? I didn't care that she couldn't surf the Internet or use the device to play games or that none of her friends would have the phone number. I worried about why she needed a trackable safety device in the first place.

When Mimi sighed for the third time, Jax told her to start

her habit of plugging the phone into the charger before she went to bed, and Mimi happily escaped to her room, leaving us alone.

That's when Jax went into more details about why this was suddenly a necessity. After he finished speaking, we were both quiet for a few moments.

"It's just one of those things, Luce, given who she is."

"I get it. I see her as a normal little girl and forget that she's got these other aspects of her parentage that take her out of the normal realm. I can't let her ride her bike to a friend's house or tell her to go play at the playground." I looked at Jax, and in that moment our daughter's resemblance to him was uncanny, which freaked me out because Mimi looked nothing like either of us, saving us from any "mini-me" comparisons.

"We're trying to give her as normal a childhood as we can. It was easier for the Lund family to keep their kids out of the spotlight before all this constant bombardment with fifty different types of social media."

I snickered. "You weren't exactly the type to lay low, Lund. With your mad hockey skills from a young age putting you right in the spotlight."

He gave me a sheepish and utterly charming smile. "Only thing I cared about was advancing my skills so I could play more games at a higher level against better opponents." Then his handsome face shuttered and he locked his gaze to mine. "Speaking of a young hockey player, Mimi told me that she wants to learn to play."

I laughed. "Of course she does . . . today. Tomorrow she'll want to be a veterinarian. And the day after that she'll talk about becoming a circus performer."

"This is different."

"How would you know?" slipped out before I could stop it. "She's tried every sport—"

"Except for hockey," he interjected. "Tell me I'm wrong."

"What's wrong is you pushing her into thinking she wants to play hockey."

He shook his head. "She told Nolan she wanted to play." He paused, making sure he had my full attention. "Last year. And apparently when they've had free time together, she watches my old game tapes, and she convinced her uncle to take her to a few local girls' hockey games."

My mouth dropped open. "He did that without asking me first?"

"Mimi asked him to keep it from you because she knew you wouldn't like it. So I'm not pushing her into a damn thing. But neither will I ignore her interest in it."

"Yes, you will."

"No, I won't."

"She's not playing hockey."

"Not at first, no. She needs to take a basic skills class to see if she's suited for it. If she is . . ." He leaned forward, resting his forearms on his thighs. "I'll get her enrolled in a club. I'll take her to practices and games. I'll deal with her equipment until she's old enough to do it herself."

I threw my hands up. "Dammit, Lund, you've already made your mind up that Mimi will be playing hockey! And you'll just skate over any objections that I might have about my daughter involved in such a dangerous sport."

He flashed me a nasty smile. "She's my daughter too. You don't get the final say in everything she does."

Wanna bet? "She's doing this to manipulate you."

"Bullshit. You're saying no to manipulate her and me. You put your foot down and that's the end of discussion and I'm just supposed to accept that. Not this time."

I glared at him.

He glared back.

"We're done talking about this."

"We haven't even started talking about this, baby, so settle in."

"Don't call me *baby*, asshole."

"Ah. So we're to the name-calling stage. Didn't take you long to revert to your old habits, *Lucille*."

God I hated his pseudo calm tone of voice. "Don't talk down to me, Jaxson Lund."

"Fine. Let's dig in and get to the real problem. What is your biggest fear about Mimi playing? That she'll naturally be good at it? That she'll end up spending more time with me than with you?"

"No, you idiot, I worry that she'll get hurt! How many concussions have you had? How many teeth were knocked out? How many scars from stitches crisscross your body? How many times have you had your nose broken? Or your fingers? Or your arm? Or your kneecap? How many muscles have you torn? How many black eyes? How many bruises from getting whacked repeatedly with a stick? Or taking a puck to the shin or the chin? Or getting the crap beat out of you when you're repeatedly crashed into the boards during every single game!" My voice had escalated as I'd posed each injury question, and when I finished I realized I was on my feet, my hands fisted, my entire body shaking.

"I had very few injuries when I started playing at age eight, so let's focus on that, not what might happen years down the road. Now calm down and sit down."

"No, no and no."

Jaxson gave me a warning growl . . . which I ignored.

"Mimi will not be a broken and scarred girl because she's trying to ensure that you really love her and that you'll stick around this time by getting involved in the one thing you've always loved above everything else! Hockey!"

Jaxson jumped to his feet. "Goddammit, Lucy, that's

enough. Enough bullshit, enough playing the blame game. This is about what Mimi wants. But you're too blinded by resentment for me to see that you're projecting your fears onto her."

"And you're projecting some twisted need to stay relevant through her by putting a freakin' hockey stick in her hand!" I retorted.

"Relevant? Christ, woman, the only thing that is relevant in this conversation is your continual state of denial when it comes to me asserting my rights as Mimi's father."

"You have no right to put her in life-threatening situations."

"For the love of god, Lucy, what is wrong with you? You are being completely unreasonable!"

"Unreasonable?" I repeated. "No, being unreasonable would be me denying you access to your daughter."

He snorted. "That's gonna be hard to do, since in the next month or so I'll be living in this building and she can come up and see me any goddamned time she wants!"

Utter silence.

"What did you say?"

He scrubbed his hands over his face. "What is it about you that gets me so riled up I just blurt shit out without thinking?" He lowered his hands. "I didn't mean for you to find out this way."

"Find out what?"

"Find out that I bought the top floor of this building and over the past few months it's been modified into one apartment, which I will move into as soon as it's done."

I was so stunned by this turn of events that I couldn't speak. I just stared at him. With my jaw nearly hitting the coffee table.

"Come on, Luce. You had to know that I wouldn't live at Snow Village permanently."

"A, I didn't know that. B, who does this kind of shit? Buys a goddamned penthouse apartment in the same building that your baby mama and kid live in?"

"You are far more to me than just an ex-girlfriend, and I've never called you my baby mama. Ever."

Then why didn't you tell me? Why are you still full of so many secrets, Jaxson Lund? How am I ever supposed to trust you fully?

I swallowed yet another ball of anger. "How long have you hidden this from me?"

"Not everything is about you," he snapped. "I did this so I could be closer to Mimi."

"Answer. The. Question. How. Long?"

"Since I announced my retirement."

I started laughing. "Omigod. Your whole 'I was in the neighborhood' excuse when you just popped by wasn't a lie. You really were in the building, aka the neighborhood, checking on the progress of your remodel."

"This is a good thing for all of us. I'll be three floors away whenever you need me, not four miles."

"It'll definitely be handier for you to keep Mimi at your fancy penthouse apartment every night since you'll have to wake her up at the crack of dawn for hockey practice every morning."

He hissed in a breath. "Low blow."

"Why are you upending my life like this?"

"Your life?" he repeated. "What about my life? I'm doing everything I can to be an everyday part of our daughter's life, and you are blocking me at every turn!"

Four rapid knocks sounded on the door.

Jax and I both froze.

Before either of us moved, we heard the locks unclicking in the foyer, and then Nolan came around the corner, holding Mimi's hand, with her hiding behind him.

Mimi. Crap. We'd forgotten she was awake, in her room, listening to every ugly word her father and I spewed at each other.

Jaxson and I exchanged a look of horror and then shame.

"Those guilty looks are too little, too late," Nolan gritted out through his teeth. "Your seriously immature, seriously uncool display scared your child. I could hear the two of you yelling outside the apartment. Be thankful that she called me and not the police or you'd be talking your way out of a domestic disturbance charge."

I felt absolutely sick.

Jaxson's expression mirrored mine.

"Mimi. Honey." I started toward her, and she hid her face from me, making me feel a hundred times worse.

"Meems needs a break, so she's spending the night with me," Nolan said. "Then we're having brunch with Grandma and Grandpa and the rest of the Lund family tomorrow at noon." His hard, angry gaze moved between us. "I don't want to hear from either of you until you've figured this out like the responsible adults you're supposed to be." He picked up Mimi's bag, and they were out the door before either of us moved.

I'm not a crier. But I burst into tears anyway.

Then the last person I wanted comfort from was right there, wrapping me in his arms.

I fought him. "Let me go."

"Like hell. I need this just as much as you do right now."

I stopped fighting him. I was so damn tired of fighting with him. I just clung to him and sobbed and he let me.

I cried out of guilt. Out of anger. Out of frustration. Out of confusion. Out of embarrassment.

When I had nothing left except my stuttering breath, Jax gently tipped my head back and studied me. "I'm sorry."

"Me too."

"Let's never do that to her again."

"Okay."

"Can we take five minutes to regroup and then start this discussion over?"

"I'd like that."

Jax pressed his lips to my forehead, released me and wandered into the kitchen.

I hadn't forgotten how volatile things could be between us.

But I had forgotten how quickly he could soothe me when I let him.

In the bathroom I soaked a washcloth in cold water and pressed it to my face, welcoming the refreshing coolness against my tight skin. But with my eyes closed, my thoughts returned to Jax's favorite way to deal with conflict resolution, but no way was banging the hell out of each other until we were breathless and too spent to fight an option tonight.

Eight

JAX

After Lucy emerged from her room, I patted the spot on the sofa beside me. "Have a seat."

Lucy, being contrary Lucy, skirted the sofa, putting it between us. "Do you want a soda or water or something?"

"I'll take a soda."

She disappeared into the kitchen, and I let my head fall back onto the couch cushion.

I felt like I'd swallowed an anvil. A big anvil. A big, rusty anvil that scraped my throat, squeezed the breath from my lungs and settled in my gut, until my gut started churning and then it spun around and around, reminding me of its heavy, gouging presence.

How had I—we—forgotten that Mimi was with us? The look on her face . . .

The rusty anvil did another quick spin that made me want to hurl.

Lucy returned with two cans of Diet Mountain Dew and parked herself on the sofa, facing me, sitting crossways.

"What fun thing should we address first?" I asked before taking a sip of soda.

She blinked at me, almost like she was in shock.

Guess this would fall on me to start. "Back to the first discussion. Mimi's claim she wants to play hockey."

"Claim?" she repeated.

"It may not interest her after she learns that hockey is about ten percent game time and ninety percent practice. Or in some kids' cases, ninety percent practice and ten percent waiting for the coach to finally let them play for thirty seconds." I paused and looked at her.

"I'm listening."

"From what I understand, youth hockey has changed drastically since I was a kid. And I'm not just talking about the fact the hockey club I belonged to didn't have a single girls' team. I'd like to claim I paid attention to that type of stuff so you'd consider me somewhat enlightened, but the truth is, I didn't. I played with girls in the peewee leagues, but by the time it was decided that I had the skills for club hockey . . . no girls were around."

"I'm no more enlightened on the subject than you are, Jax. I didn't even pay attention to your hockey games, let alone anyone else's."

That stung, but I wasn't surprised. During the time we were together, she'd attended maybe half a dozen games. "The popularity of hockey has spawned lots of new opportunities for female players, on both the recreational and the competitive sides. I'm not sure how the groups are divided except that the players are still grouped by their ages."

"Let's say I agree to let Mimi try it. Would she have practice every day? Games every weekend?"

"Not at her age. After she's passed the basic skills class, and if she still likes it, then I'd suggest we put her in a recreational hockey program." That went against everything I'd had beaten into my head as a young player, but this wasn't about me.

Lucy frowned. "Recreational instead of . . . ?"

"Recreational games usually take place at community centers, where everyone gets a chance to play. Unlike club hockey, where you have to audition first and then you pay to play."

"That doesn't sound too bad. But if everyone can play, then do you know if they separate boys and girls?"

I shrugged. "Some organizations do, some don't; it depends on the enrollment. But regardless if she's playing in a mixed league, she'd be playing with boys her age. Even in a recreational setting, an eight-year-old girl won't be playing against a twelve-year-old boy. USA Hockey is very strict about that."

A look of relief crossed her face.

"To be honest, Luce, I don't know if they play actual league games at her age. Some programs focus on hockey basics. Learning about the different positions, stickhandling, skating. I remember hearing that some places don't even introduce the puck until midway through the season."

"How would that work if she wanted to be a goalie? She'd have to sit on the bench for half of the season? How is that fair?"

On the outside I merely smiled. On the inside I grinned like a damn fool. I had her. Lucy was this close to saying yes to letting Mimi try hockey if she was already worried about the fairness of ice time. "There are enough options in the Twin Cities that I wouldn't choose a venue or coaching staff that had that criteria. There's something to be said for playing it safe, but playing slow . . . that's not what hockey is about. Puck handling is the single most important skill she needs to master. Besides skating."

Lucy sighed. "Spoken like the pro athlete you are."

"Like the pro athlete I *was*," I reminded her.

Then awkward silence hung between us.

I let it. Lucy needed to come to terms with this on her own. I'd given her the information; I wasn't about to beg or badger her as she silently weighed pros and cons.

No idea how much time passed before I noticed she was about to crush her soda can between her hands, so I gently removed it from her grasp, set the can on the coffee table and took her shaking hands in mine. "Talk to me, Lucy Q. Like you used to. From that big heart of yours."

"I'm scared." She squeezed my hands. "For all of the reasons I mentioned during our discussion. And . . ."

"And what?"

"I'm afraid that she'll love it. There's no doubt in my mind she'll excel at hockey, because we both know she's ridiculously athletic. So I worry that she'll try it, love it and become obsessed with it, like you were. Her entire focus will be on hockey, and all traces of my Mimi, the child I've nurtured for eight years, will be gone."

Fuck. She could knock my legs right out from under me even without a damn stick in her hand. "Lucy. We can't know anything about how she'll react until we give her the chance to try it."

She looked down at our joined hands, but not before I saw the tears in her eyes. "I know. It's so freaking stupid, but right now, that's the thing that's stopping me from saying yes. Not that I'll lose her to you, but I'll lose her to hockey."

"Aw, baby, come here."

"Jax—"

"Come. Here." I tugged her to my chest and she came willingly.

All the harsh words from earlier vanished. We hadn't been this physically close since before Mimi was born, but we fit together like we hadn't been apart. Like our bodies knew what to do even when our heads and hearts hesitated.

After a few moments, she spoke. "Hockey was already your life when we met, Jax. You never pretended I would come first, because hockey had claimed you first. It might be hard to believe, but I never begrudged you doing something you loved, especially when you were so good at it. I can't claim that I was proud of you, because I had nothing to do with you reaching the highest level of the game. But with Mimi . . . it'd be different. I'd be invested. I'd have to be just as supportive as if she'd chosen to pursue ballet."

"Are you afraid you can't be supportive?"

"Maybe. I've never excelled at anything. That's not me fishing for a compliment. I'm just making an observation that while I know it takes hard work and dedication to become an elite athlete, I've never seen what it takes from the beginning."

"You're putting the cart before the horse. There's no guarantee she'll love it to the point she wants to devote her life to mastering it. It may end up being a fun outlet for her, nothing more."

"Was it fun for you?"

"Without question. Even a shitty day in the rink was better than a day not being on the ice."

"Be honest, Jaxson 'Stonewall' Lund. Do you really believe there's a chance she'll suck at this?"

"That's less likely than her hating it because she's my kid and everyone will expect more out of her than they would other kids, and the pressure will be too much."

"You've seen this happen with your hockey buddies' kids?"

I paused. "No, actually I saw it with my cousin Ash. His dad—my uncle Monte—was a basketball phenomenon. Broke all kinds of state high school records, and like LeBron—years and years before LeBron—he opted to go straight into the NBA right after high school. He didn't last more than a few years, but he talked about it so much that from an early age Ash was determined to be a basketball player. And he was an outstanding player, on track to be better than his dad. It confused the hell out of everyone when Ash refused to try out for any college hoops program during his senior year of high school. He told his family that he'd had enough and he wanted to prove to himself that he had other skills besides ballhandling."

"Wow. I had no idea."

"It's not something he talks about. But the same thing could happen to Mimi. She likes it for a while, has some success and decides it's not for her and she wants to explore other options." I sighed. "Look. We can go round and round with this speculation, but it's pointless to dissect potential outcomes until she takes that first class."

"Okay. She's got my support to give it a try." Lucy turned her head and looked up at me. "Promise me we'll keep a united front."

"I promise."

"Promise that you won't get super annoyed with me if I ask a bunch of newb questions."

"I promise."

"Promise you won't hide her injuries from me, no matter how inconsequential you think they are."

"I promise."

"Promise that you'll—"

"Lucy. Stop. I give you my word that I'll never shut you out. We're partners in this parenting gig. Remember?"

"I remember."

The way her gaze searched my face, she seemed to be trying to remember a lot more. "What?"

"Sometimes Mimi gets this look in her eyes that is so you, Jax. And then she stands a certain way and it's you all over again."

I waited.

"You've been out of her daily life for most of her life, so it's been easy to forget she gets half of her DNA from you, and easier yet to consider her just mine. But you being here now . . . I'm grateful. She needs you. And that's a phrase I never thought I'd say."

Keeping quiet was my best option, but I felt fidgety. I pushed a hank of glossy hair over her shoulder and skimmed my hand down her bicep. "It's one I didn't think I'd ever hear from you."

"I'd convinced myself I could fulfill both parental roles, given the fact my mother had done that too. But I can't." She paused. "The real truth is I don't want to."

"You shouldn't have to. But that's a moot point now."

"I know."

"I never wanted you to compare me to your dad—although I realize there are similarities between our actions."

Lucy lowered her head and pressed her cheek into my chest again. "Are we really ready to talk about our past?"

That anvil in my belly took another sharp turn. "I am. If you'd like to get resituated—"

"No. This is better."

Because she wouldn't have to look me in the eyes while we talked.

"So where do we start?" she asked quietly.

"With my apology. Again. And again, and again, and again." I plucked her hand off my chest and kissed her knuckles. "Christ, Luce, I don't know if I can ever say sorry enough times so you'll ever believe that I mean it every single time."

"Jax—"

"And I don't know that I ever said thank you for setting aside our differences and listening to me when I told you about my time at Hazelden."

"That surprised me."

"What surprised you? That I acknowledged my problem with alcohol and sought help? Or that I told you I'd spent six weeks in rehab?"

"Both, actually." She paused. "Right after Annika hired me at LI, Nolan came to see me."

My gut clenched. "Did he give you a heads-up about the changes in my life?"

"No. He apologized for being a tool and said that he never should've blindly believed things you told him about me."

I had no response.

So Lucy kept talking. "I could've relied on your parents and Nolan for help with Mimi. But I've been in Nolan's place, where you hero worship your sibling and feel there's no choice but to throw your support behind them no matter the situation."

"That's happened with you and Lindsey?"

She nodded. "Linds started dating that dirtbag Gene about the same time I found out I was pregnant. I didn't know him; I didn't like how he treated my sister. After it became apparent I'd be doing the single-parent thing, he started telling me what to do, using Lindsey as his megaphone. She'd never been the type to say, 'Sue him, make a big public deal about the Lund billionaire heir and superstar hockey player cheating on you during your pregnancy and then abandoning you and his newborn baby. That's guaranteed to set you up for life.' Yet that's exactly the action Lindsey kept pushing me to take."

My breath stalled. She'd never mentioned any of this to me.

"What really sucked? I'd lost both my confidants. You . . . for obvious reasons, and Lindsey because anything I said to her about my frustrations with trying to make it as a single parent, she repeated right back to him. Then I'd get more helpful advice, which I didn't need from the dickwad."

"Luce. I'm—"

"I know, you're sorry," she said with a hint of bitterness.

"But I couldn't talk to my mom either because she'd taken the 'he was a player; you should've known he'd cheat on you' tack. I hadn't been looking for sympathy, or someone to vent to about you; I wanted my mom's advice on Mimi's baby issues. Why she was gassy. Why she was crying. Why she didn't sleep. I didn't have any girlfriends who had kids, and I'd had to stop working, so I'd lost contact with all of my work friends too. Here I had this beautiful, healthy baby that I loved with my entire being, but I was so miserable and alone."

I didn't bother to swipe away the tears that leaked out. When one dripped on her forehead she cranked her head around to look at me.

Every bit of guilt and self-hatred for the type of man I'd been shone in my eyes, and again, I didn't mask it. I didn't apologize. I just let her see the misery I held on to now, for all the distress she'd dealt with back then.

Then she did the sweetest thing. She set her hand on the side of my face and wiped the dampness from my eyes.

An eternity stretched between us before I found my voice again. "Can we ever get past any of this?"

"Believe it or not, I *am* past a lot of it. You were who you were. That's who I fell for. So when you behaved exactly as you always had, I had to agree with my mom that my heartache over you was somewhat self-inflicted."

"Jesus, Lucy, no. You are not taking any of the blame for me fucking around on you."

She studied me. Opened her mouth. Closed it.

"What?"

"Dude, I've never blamed myself for your cheating ways."

I must've looked confused.

"I always knew you'd cheat on me, Jaxson. That's why I didn't demand a promise of fidelity from you. That's why I refused to marry you when we discovered I was pregnant. My heartache was self-inflicted because even knowing that eventually you'd fuck someone else, I couldn't walk away from you before it happened. After the first time I saw pictures of you with someone else . . ."

The guilt sent my heart racing but I forced myself to ask, "How did you find out?"

"A coworker saw that a puck bunny had tagged you in a tweet—complete with a picture of the two of you hanging out half-naked in a hotel room bed—and showed it to me out of concern. I laughed it off. But that was the beginning of the end for us as a couple." She looked away from me. "I'd considered playing like it hadn't happened, but that would've made me like my mother and every other woman who believes it was a onetime thing." She paused. "I don't know if that was the first time, but you made no attempt to hide it. You were aware of how I felt about cheating and that as soon as I found out that I'd be done with you, with us."

"I knew. But at the time? I didn't care because we'd been apart more than we'd been together. You were pregnant, you refused to move to Chicago and I was having the best season of my career. I wanted to celebrate with my team and anyone else who we invited to party with us." The advice I'd gotten had come from a veteran player I admired . . . all the more reason to consider it gospel. I realized now that I'd still had the ability to be starstruck, which zapped every bit of common sense.

"What aren't you telling me?" Lucy said softly.

"It's self-centered and crude, and I'm embarrassed that I actually believed the narcissistic bullshit that one of my idols beat into my head that championship year, so it's not something I want to relive or repeat."

"After that intriguing intro you have no choice but to share it."

My Lucy. I'd always loved, hated, and admired that she didn't pull any punches. "This bonus confession can't put me in any worse light, so here goes. At training camp I got paired for drills with my idol. After practice we'd go out and we were immediately surrounded. He wallowed in it; I ignored it. So when he asked why I wasn't balls deep in a different bunny every night, I told him you were pregnant. Called you my girlfriend, and his response was at least I hadn't fucked up completely by marrying you."

She mumbled something about dick-punching the douche-bag.

As much as it sucked to tell her this, Lucy had a right to know, since this dude's "advice" had been a catalyst for bad changes in my life. "Camp ended, the season started and he said we owed it to ourselves to live large during the season. And we earned our reputations with nonstop parties, booze, bunnies. It didn't occur to me until later that I was the only friend from our team that this man had.

"About two weeks after you gave birth to Mimi, a birth I complained about missing, he told me I could be a father after my hockey career ended. He gave me this spiel about our bodies being in prime form and we owed it to ourselves, our fans, our teammates, our club and the world to focus solely on hockey. After we retired, then we could be the hus-band, father, son, whatever role we'd neglected during our glory years. He pointed out that kids don't remember any-thing from the first five years of their lives anyway. So even if I ignored my daughter for a few years, the money I made being a franchise player would buy me back into her good graces. And I ate that shit up. It remained my mantra for the next six years. It wasn't until my counseling sessions in rehab that I understood what a narcissistic motherfucker I'd been, believing all would be forgiven once I started throwing money around. So yeah, I'm fully aware that time lost can never be replaced but money lost can. I'm trying to make emotional restitution."

"When did you start to do that? Because even before you hit bottom or whatever, the times you had custody of Mimi here in the Cities, you pawned her off on your mom and dad or Nolan. You might've had our daughter for a few weeks, but you weren't spending that time with her."

"She told you?" I groaned. "Christ, that hits me where it hurts. She was like . . . four."

"Wasn't like she tattled. And I didn't demand she tell me how you two spent every minute of every day. She just expressed disappointment that you weren't around as much as you'd promised."

"I was drinking heavily as soon as the season ended. Since I didn't have a house here, I crashed with my parents. They doted on Mimi and me, to some degree, leaving me alone to brood and drink while they did the activities with her that I was too drunk to do. Nolan called me out on it, and I was a total dick to him about it. I managed to keep up the appearance of being a good father when we attended Lund family functions. Wouldn't want my other family members to see how seriously I'd fucked up my life."

"Jax."

I pressed a kiss to the top of her head and she let me. "I hate telling you this, Luce. I hate that I was that guy. I can assure you that I'm not that way anymore. I've grown up, sobered up, wised up, but actions speak louder than words. I'm hoping going forward you'll judge me on the actions I'm taking now, not what I'd gotten away with for so long."

She adjusted her body and looked up at me. "You don't consider buying the top floor of this apartment building and remodeling it with the intent to move in and keeping it a secret from us . . . a douchebag move?"

"Maybe a little."

Those beautiful brown eyes continued to bore into me.

"What?"

"No excuses?"

"Nope. I should've told you. And Mimi."

"Level with me, sport. You didn't just buy the top floor. You own the whole building, don't you?"

I fought a blush and lost. "Yeah. In my defense, real estate is always a good investment."

She snickered. "There's a Lund excuse. 'It's just good business.'"

"And it'll be good for Mimi. We're both here."

"Kinda renders the 'she needs a cell phone' argument moot, doesn't it?"

"Hey. I had nothing to do with that."

"I believe you."

I brushed her hair from her forehead. "Thank you."

"For?"

"Talking to me. Listening to me. Being far more reasonable about all of these changes than—"

"You thought I'd be?" she supplied.

"Yeah."

"You weren't the only one who had to make personal and lifestyle changes, Jax. There were things about myself I didn't like either. Tendencies and traits I'd be embarrassed for my daughter to witness. Up until tonight I thought I'd done a good job keeping our interactions friendly. On an even keel." Her chin wobbled. "I guess I proved I can 'go big' when I fuck up."

"When we hit the boiling point, babe—look out. It's always been like that for us."

"I know. We still don't allow ourselves much time for a cooling-off period, do we?"

For just a moment, her eyes darkened and I could almost see the memories flying through her mind.

Fighting over everything because we needed an explosive moment as a catalyst to break down both of our walls. Then immediately we were climbing through the rubble to get to each other.

Did it make me an idiot to hope that tonight we'd leveled some of the walls between us? When I knew we still had several more obstacles in front of us?

Lucy's eyes searched mine. "Jax?"

I cleared my throat. "We haven't decided how we're going to deal with Mimi."

"She'll only care about one thing: whether or not she gets to try hockey. The minute we say yes, we're golden."

I grinned.

"Anything else we need to dissect right now? Because I didn't get to eat dinner and I'm starving." Almost on cue, her stomach rumbled.

The reference to her date doused my good mood. "Sorry about ruining your date, Luce."

"No, you're not."

She'd said it teasingly, but I wasn't sure if I could match that light tone.

"You're right. I'm not. If your sister called him a Pencil-Neck Geek . . ."

She groaned. "Mimi rarely pays attention to what Aunt Lindsey says, especially after the wine starts flowing, so of course she picked up on that. I'll be more careful in the future."

"Regarding future dates with this Demon guy?"

Lucy laughed. "Damon. And no. That ship has sailed."

Good fucking riddance.

"Seriously, Jax? Good fucking riddance?"

"I thought I'd said that under my breath."

"Since I'm only half a face away from your breath, you knew I'd hear that."

Of course I did. "Is 'half a face away' a new measurement I missed in math class?"

She poked me in the ribs. "You know what I meant, jerk."

"And you know that I meant good fucking riddance to him."

"Why?"

Because I want you—I want this—back.

But instead of blurting that out, for the first time tonight, I deflected. "How many times have you been out with Darwin?"

"Damon," she corrected. "I met him for coffee and drinks before I agreed to a date. We went out for dinner two weeks ago. Then dinner tonight. But I didn't count the friendly meet ups as dates, although apparently he did. He seemed insistent on calling it our fourth date, when I considered it a second date. But since tonight's date got interrupted, it doesn't count. So we've gone out once." Her eyes searched mine. "Why?"

"Just thinking about our first and second dates. Wondering how they compare."

"There's no comparison, as you're well aware."

"Yeah? Do you remember what we did on our fourth date?"

She shook her head . . . not very convincingly.

"How about our fifth date?" I prompted.

Lucy blinked those enormous brown eyes at me. "Um. Actually no, I don't remember."

I whispered, "Liar." Then, "Did you catch my meaning from half a face away? Because I can come in closer."

"Or I could make you back up."

I snagged her hand when she tried to poke me again. "No tickling."

"Hey! That's the only way I can level the playing field, because you're so much bigger and you'd squash me like a bug."

There'd been a time when she begged me to fully press my larger body over hers. With this body-to-body contact and the easy way we'd fallen back into being together, I was tempted to check her response if I tried to kiss her.

Patience, man. You pushed boundaries tonight and she hasn't pushed you away. Consider this a win.

Her stomach rumbled again.

I nudged her until she was upright. "The least I can do is feed you. Since we already have a babysitter, do you want to go out?"

"God no."

"Pizza delivery it is." I dug my phone out and called up the closest delivery place. While I waited for them to pick up, I said, "The usual?" to her.

"Sounds perfect, and don't forget to order—"

"Breadsticks with ranch, yeah, I remember."

Lucy stared at me with that "I'm ready to bolt" expression when she realized how quickly and easily we'd slipped back into being Jax and Lucy, the couple. Then she started to back away from me.

Oh hell no. She'd come this far on her own, and I couldn't let her retreat. "What's wrong?"

"I can't . . . We can't . . . I mean, what are we doing, Jax?"

I played dumb. "I'm ordering pizza."

"That's not what I meant and you damn well know it."

"This doesn't have to mean anything more than us sharing a late-night meal, Lucy Q, as we discuss our daughter's future activities."

Maybe she wanted to believe that lie as much as I did, because she smiled and said, "Fine, but if you're going to be here awhile, better add one of those big cookies onto the order."

Nine

LUCY

Jax and I stayed up late talking and online browsing the multitude of hockey clubs and ice centers that offered classes. When I realized it was one in the morning, I suggested he stay overnight on the couch instead of driving home. I even managed to pull off a joke about his previous drinking habits that he laughed at. It felt good to be breaking new ground with him.

It'd felt really good being with him like we used to be. I don't know why I hadn't fought him on how we positioned ourselves, both of us stretching out on the sofa, with me tucked against his chest and our arms and legs tangled. Maybe it had been ingrained behavior like he'd claimed when he'd given me that soft kiss last week. Maybe we needed the physical connection to deal with our emotional issues. Whatever the reasons, I wasn't about to regret it now, especially when our discussion had delved deeper than I believed it could.

Since I'd always been a morning person, I got up early

and made myself presentable. Then I tidied up my bedroom before I ventured into the living room.

Jax was still asleep. He dwarfed the couch, keeping one leg bent at the knee and resting it against the back cushion. He'd draped one arm across his eyes and the other arm dangled to the floor. In cataloguing his position, I also realized that Jax had stripped down to his boxer briefs as he lounged beneath the afghan my mother had made. An afghan too small to cover his muscular legs, and it barely reached the lower curve of his powerful chest.

Holy crap, I'd forgotten what a work of art his body was. Beautiful, deep-cut musculature everywhere. Wide shoulders, beefy biceps. Even his forearms were corded with muscle. And those hands. Mercy. Big and dotted with calluses. A ridiculously strong grip that could soften into a lover's gentle caress. Pity he'd hidden half of his face, but that square jaw covered in dark stubble jutted out at me. Even in sleep his sexy lips curved into a knowing smirk.

I must've been standing there gawking long enough that Jax sensed me perving on him. He drawled, "Our rule has always been the first one up makes coffee, babe. So, chop-chop."

Stunned, and embarrassed he'd caught me eyeballing his half-naked body, I said, "Chop-chop . . . ? Really, Lund?"

"Yep. I'm a guest. You're not being very hospitable, Lucy Q."

"I was being very hospitable by letting you sleep in for the past hour and not rattling around in the kitchen making coffee!"

"But I'm up now."

"Doesn't look like it."

He grinned. "And she still stands here indignantly, arguing, instead of hotfooting that cute butt into the kitchen and—"

He yelped when I ripped the afghan away.

"New rule, buddy. I—"

Words left me when nothing blocked my view of his pelvis and the thick ridge bulging against his too-tight boxer briefs.

"Gimme that," he said, and snatched the afghan back to cover himself. "It's just morning wood, Luce. Don't take it personal."

What? He did *not* just say that.

"It's not like you haven't seen it before."

"It's been a long damn time. And I had no idea that these days thinking about a cup of coffee is what gets you hot and hard first thing in the morning."

Silence.

That sounded way less suggestive in my head.

In the awkward quiet, the bang of the front door opening into the catchall table was as loud as a gunshot. Then, "Sorry, sis, it's just me, but I know you're up."

My gaze landed on Jax for a split second before my sister wheeled around the corner.

"Hey, good morning. I— Jesus Christ! There's a naked man on your couch!" Lindsey gasped. Then, realizing it was Jax, she said, "What the hell are you doing here?"

"Good to see you again, Lindsey," Jax said with a cheeky grin.

Lindsey's wide-eyed gaze winged between us. "I thought you had a date with Damon last night?"

"She did. There was a 'datus interruptus' incident with Mimi—"

"Speaking of interrupting . . . how about you let *me* explain what happened to my sister while you go put some clothes on."

"My clothes are right here. I'll get dressed when you're in the kitchen starting the coffee."

"You are such a pain in my ass." Before I headed to the kitchen I said, "I left a toothbrush in the guest bathroom for you."

"Thanks, my teeth are as fuzzy as my head. How much Diet Mountain Dew did we drink last night?"

"You drank a two-liter bottle by yourself."

"Better that than a two-liter bottle of whiskey, huh?"

"Word."

In the kitchen I held Lindsey off until I started the coffee. Then I gave her an abbreviated version of events, including the surprise he'd sprung that we were about to become neighbors.

Oddly she didn't jump in and voice her opinion, which freaked me out a little.

"What?"

"So all is well between you and Jax?" she finally asked.

"Better than it has been. Why?"

"Because you two are back to doing the bicker and flirt thing that served as foreplay."

"It's not foreplay." Was it?

"Don't you think it'll be weird having him living so close? I mean, say Mimi is staying with him upstairs and she forgets her pajamas. Instead of sending Mimi down to retrieve them, Jax grabs the key and pops in here unannounced. What if you're doing the nasty with your date on the couch? Talk about the ultimate 'coitus interruptus' courtesy of your ex."

"Lindsey!"

"It could happen." She cocked her head. "I was kinda hoping to show up and see that Damon had spent the night."

"Why would you say that? You don't even like Damon."

"What I don't like is the fact you're ignoring your sexual needs. Now that Jax has Mimi on the weekends, you should be reconnecting with your inner slut—"

"Enough. Speak for yourself, ho-bag." I held my hand out. "And give me my key back. Right now."

Lindsey grabbed my hand and pulled me in for a hug. "Fine. I'll shut it."

No surprise she didn't return my key.

Jax walked past us, snatched a cup from the mug tree. He filled the cup and slammed it before facing us. "Much better." He gave my sister a once-over. "Lindsey. You're looking good."

"Thanks, Jax. You're looking mighty fine too, not getting chubby around the edges like most former pro athletes."

He patted his super flat stomach. "My body is a temple and all that jazz." He flashed her a grin when she rolled her eyes. "You want a cup of coffee?"

What was up with him acting like the host in my house?

"Right after I pour one for Lucy, of course," he added, seeing my scowl.

"Sure. I'll grab the selection of creamers, since Lucy can't ever stick with just one kind."

I scowled at my sister's back. "I like a variety, okay?"

"I'm the same way with cheese," Jax offered as he filled my "World's Best Mom!" mug. "Some days I want sharp. Some days I want spicy. Some days I want creamy. Being indecisive . . . it's easier to have a selection right at your fingertips."

"You're talking about snacking cheese?" Lindsey asked, continuing the bizarre conversation about dairy products.

Jax shrugged and grabbed the coconut and almond creamer. "I use it in cooking too."

I said, "You cook?" and it slipped out like an accusation.

"Now I do." He studied me as he stirred his coffee. "Meems hasn't said anything about us eating at home for most meals?"

"I don't expect a full report on everything you two do. I assumed when she said you ate at home that you'd had take-out or delivery."

"Really? You have so little faith in me, Luce?"

"Oh, don't act indignant," I retorted. "You barely knew

how to use the microwave when we were together, say nothing of knowing how to cook a full meal."

"True. But it's different now. I took cooking classes in Chicago after I sobered up. I needed a productive hobby to fill my hours off the ice." He sent me a sheepish smile.

Don't smile back. Lindsey will think something is going on between you.

But that sweet grin did it for me every time and I smiled back.

Then I noticed Lindsey rooting around in the fridge.

She piled a carton of eggs, a bag of sharp cheddar cheese, a green onion, a package of crumbled bacon and a gallon of milk on the counter. "Prove it, Jax. Fix us breakfast."

To him, I said, "Ignore her."

To Lindsey, I said, "What the hell is wrong with you?"

"What? He said he can cook."

"That doesn't mean he wants to cook for you on command, dumbass."

Jax set his hand on my shoulder. "It's okay, Luce. I'll make omelets if everyone is cool with that."

"Fine by me," Lindsey piped up.

I sighed. "Some days I envy Mimi being an only child."

"Hey!"

But Jax was looking at me oddly. Probably because he didn't know where anything was in my kitchen. While I stacked a cutting board, knife, mixing bowl, whisk and pan on the counter, Lindsey started another pot of coffee.

And I still felt Jax watching me intently. Rather than snapping, "What?" I ignored him. Or tried to. But the man took up a lot of space. After the third time I smacked into him, I opted to sit at the breakfast bar, out of the way.

Lindsey hopped up next to me. "I'm beat."

"Then why did you show up here so early?"

"I was hoping Damon had spent the night so I could force him into a walk of shame. We both know you're too nice to tell someone when they've overstayed their welcome."

Thwak sounded against the cutting board.

"Sorry," Jax said smoothly. "My knife slipped."

"As soon as you're done stuffing your face, take off. You've overstayed your welcome, sis." I nudged Lindsey with my shoulder. "See? I'm not that nice."

Jax might've mumbled something too low for me to hear.

"Yay! Go you, showing that bossy side." She nudged me back. "I'm so damn proud."

Proud. I snorted. At least drama girl hadn't knuckled away a fake tear.

"So do you guys have plans today?" she asked Jax.

"We're having brunch with my family," Jax said as he cracked eggs one handed.

One handed! Even I couldn't do that, and I had much smaller hands than he did.

Wait a second . . . I glanced up at him. "I thought we were meeting Nolan, and then you and Mimi were having brunch with your whole family, not me."

"If I don't get to skip out on it, neither do you."

I watched him whip the eggs and milk and deftly pour the lemon-colored froth into the pan.

Without any shame whatsoever, Lindsey said, "I like brunch."

"You're welcome to come too," Jax said, never taking his focus off his omelet.

"Is Nolan going to be there?"

That got Jax's attention. "Yeah. Why?"

"Uh, have you seen your brother? That man is *hawt*. Like *rawr*. There's a tiger beneath those fancy-ass clothes he wears. I wouldn't mind rattling his cage a little."

"For god's sake, Lindsey. Show some dignity."

"Where's the fun in that?"

Jax laughed. "It's brunch with the Lund Collective at the club, so you'd have to be somewhat circumspect."

"*All* the Lunds?" Lindsey scowled. "Pass."

He finally looked at me. "We'll keep brunch short. We literally have a lot of ground to cover with Mimi today."

"Then we're on the same page."

"Good." He sprinkled the bacon, onion and shredded cheese on one half of the bubbling egg circle and folded it in half. After adding a little water, he placed the lid on top. He lifted a brow at me. "Might wanna get the plates out."

"Ah. Sure."

As deftly as a professional chef, he slid the omelet onto a plate and added a final flourish of toppings before handing the plate to me. "Enjoy."

"Looks almost too good to eat, Jax. Thanks."

He smiled shyly and ducked his head, like he was . . . embarrassed.

Oh fuck me.

I could handle aloof Jax just fine.

I could handle angry Jax just fine.

I could handle asshole Jax just fine.

But humble Jax, who not only cooked, but fed me first?

Resisting that Jax would be impossible.

When he watched me take the first bite and my response was a loud "mmm-mmm"—I swear the tension left his shoulders and he released a relieved exhale. Then I got that gooey melting sensation again, seeing that it'd mattered to him that I'd liked what he'd prepared.

Thankfully Lindsey kept up a steady stream of chatter during our impromptu breakfast since neither Jax nor I seemed inclined to talk.

Lindsey tackled the dishes while I changed into appropriate "brunch with the Lunds" attire—a plaid wool skirt, a burgundy Henley, a fisherman's cardigan flecked with gray, burgundy and black, and a pair of heeled boots. As I debated whether or not to braid my hair, Lindsey showed up in my bathroom.

She whistled. "Lookit you, hot mama. How you can make conservative clothes look sexy is a gift, sis, truly."

"Thanks. Think I should braid my hair?"

"No. You just need to fluff it up a bit. Here. Let me help." As she finger combed and rearranged my part, she said, "You put on a dress, did full hair and makeup on a Sunday. You sure you're putting in the extra effort for the Lunds? Or is it just one Lund in particular?"

Our eyes met in the mirror. Eyes identical to mine, but that was where our physical similarities ended. Lindsey had pale brown hair that she'd dyed a hundred different colors over the years. Right now her short bob was reddish black, as if she'd dipped her head into a vat of black cherry Kool-Aid mix. She topped me by four inches, and she was stick thin with enormous boobs, which she showcased at every opportunity. Luckily for her, her position as manager for a wholesale candy distributor meant a more casual approach to clothing styles.

"Don't clam up on me now," she warned, suddenly brandishing a flat iron at me.

"Fine. Yes, I'm dressing up because all of my bosses from LI will be at this shindig and I can't look like a bum."

"And that's the only reason?"

"No. I'm showing up with Jax, who rolls out of bed looking like a million bucks, and I've always felt people staring at us, judging me, wondering why he's with me."

"Lucy, I don't—"

"You don't know what it was like to be the object of pity. I can say his cheating was *his* issue and no reflection on me a thousand times, but my confidence took a major hit. So I feel more confident when I put in extra effort with my outer appearance."

"But you're not in a relationship with Jax."

"Exactly."

Lindsey looked confused.

And there wasn't enough time to delve into my neurosis, so I redirected the conversation. "I haven't heard from Mom this week. Have you?"

"Yeah." Snatching the can of hair spray, she aimed and fired, fogging up the entire bathroom in the process. "She and Benny were at the Grand Canyon. They had issues with the motor home, and the part wasn't coming in until tomorrow, so they were going white-water rafting." She paused. "Can you imagine?"

"God no. I never imagined Mom would contradict every bit of advice she'd ever given us, fall for a recently divorced guy a decade older than her, buy a motor home with him and flit off to travel the US together."

"Mom's relationship advice was based on her relationship with one man, Luce. Dad was a tool. Because of him, she made absolutes about how all men behaved, and stuck by her convictions until she met Benny and he turned them all upside down."

"I'm happy for her. But I miss her. Mimi does too."

"Now that Mimi has a cell phone, she can FaceTime with Grandma, right?"

"I'll have to ask about that since it's a security thing. And don't get your panties in a twist if your number isn't programmed into her phone," I warned.

"Panties. *Puh*-lease. No granny panties for me. I wear a thong, sista."

"Which means your butt floss is always in a twist up the crack of your ass anyway."

She laughed and hugged me from behind. "I love you,

Lucille Evangeline Quade. You're funny and sweet and patient. You are the best friend a sister could ever have, and I needed a dose of you today."

I wrapped my arms across hers and leaned back, keeping our gazes locked in the mirror. "What happened, Linds?"

"Just another week where nothing panned out as I'd hoped."

"A bad date?"

"It has nothing to do with a specific guy and everything to do with the fact I don't have a man in my life." She set her chin on my shoulder. "I thought I'd be married by now. Or at least settled in a long-term relationship. So every guy I'm even remotely attracted to . . . I wonder if I really like him, or if I'm so tired of waiting for Mr. Right that I'll settle for any man who's not a total jackass. Plus, my biological clock is ticking. I want a baby, but I don't want to do the whole parenting thing on my own for so many years like you did. And like Mom did."

"If you decide to go that route, you know I'll be here and eager to help out any way that I can."

Lindsey teared up. "Thank you. That's still one of my biggest regrets, following dickhead to Milwaukee after Mimi was born and not being here for you."

"I know. We've moved on from that. Put the past in the past, where it belongs."

"Are you doing that with Jax for Mimi's sake? Or for you on a personal level?"

I wasn't sure how to answer that.

"I don't know Jax well. I never did. It was easy for me to hate him and his behavior in solidarity with you." She paused. "But you never hated him, did you? Not even when he pulled all the bullshit with custody and fighting you on child support payments."

"I was mad and hurt and worried about Mimi's future, but no . . . I never hated him. How could I when the person I love most in the world shares half of his DNA? It'd be like hating half of my daughter."

"You're so much nicer than me," Lindsey groused. "I hold a grudge forever. That little fucker Mikey Speerbraaten? If I saw him walking down the street, I'd jump outta my car and dick-punch him for cutting off my braid in second grade."

I snickered. "I'd pay money to see that, sis."

"Sorry for that digression. I'm just asking you to be careful, okay? Jax is hot and he'll be living in your damn building. It'd be convenient to start up with him again."

I started to deny it.

But Lindsey steamrolled right over me. "Don't deny your attraction to him—I saw how you two were together. The man is sex on legs, and when he turns that charm on you, it'd be easy to get sucked in. He may act differently, but who's to say that he has changed? But the good news is if he does hurt you again I know where he lives and I'd have no problem dick-punching him."

"You're welcome to try," Jax drawled outside the bathroom door.

Fuck. Fuckity fuck fuck fuck.

I couldn't freaking believe that Jax had heard all that. My cheeks flamed, my heart sped up and I wanted to tit-punch my sister for having zero filter and kick my own ass for forgetting—once again—that there was another person in my apartment.

"Oh, hey, Jax. We were just talking about you," Lindsey said without missing a beat.

"So I heard." He leaned against the doorjamb.

"Is eavesdropping a new skill you've practiced too?" I asked, somewhat crossly.

Jax's eyes met mine in the mirror. "I wasn't listening in. I just got off the phone with Nolan, and it seemed to be taking you for fucking ever to get ready, so I came to see what the holdup was." His gaze traveled over my face, then he gave the rest of my body a thorough once-over before those stunning eyes reconnected with mine. "You look incredible, Lucy."

I wasn't expecting that or the way my body heated from his sexy perusal. "Thank you."

"We've gotta get going. I still need to stop at my place and change before we check out those facilities. I figured it'd be better if we met Mimi early and talked to her together about what happened last night before we see the rest of the family."

"Good idea." I brushed past him. If Jax could ignore the elephant in the room, I could too.

But of course my sister couldn't. I heard them speaking in fierce whispers, followed by Jax's sharp bark of laughter.

I truly didn't want to know what had transpired between them, so I didn't ask.

Ten

—

JAX

The next couple of hours were so busy I didn't have time to obsess about the conversation I'd overheard between Lucy and her sister. It wasn't Lindsey threatening to dick-punch me that'd stuck in my mind; it was that Lucy hadn't denied her attraction to me. Nor had she refuted her sister's accusation that it'd be "convenient" getting intimately involved with me again.

On one hand . . . that was insulting.

On the other hand . . . I'd be anything Lucy needed, including convenient, if I had even the tiniest opportunity for a second chance with her. Now that I suspected that she wouldn't slap me, knee me in the balls and yell, NO FUCKING WAY, WE'RE NEVER, EVER, EVER GETTING BACK TO-GETHER, if I let her know how I felt when the time was right, my outlook was vastly improved.

Lucy wandered through my apartment as I quickly changed for brunch. She didn't spend much time in Mimi's room besides a cursory look to see if the kid had made her bed and picked up her clothes. No, Lucy seemed to scrutinize everything else. The few pictures I'd put up, the reading material and DVDs on my bookshelves, the contents of my fridge and cupboards (I heard Miz Snoopy opening and closing cabinet doors). When she slipped into the main bathroom, I knew she was rifling through drawers and cabinets, searching for items that indicated I'd had female overnight guests. I wondered if she'd be relieved or disappointed her search would come up empty. The only female who'd stayed overnight in my apartment since I'd moved in was Mimi.

Before we left to meet Nolan and Mimi, I snagged Mimi's bag with her skates and rink wear. We'd have to make another trip to the sporting goods store to buy the rest of her hockey gear before she took to the ice.

Last night Lucy and I had narrowed down our program choices to three. She'd insisted on visiting the newest rink— the only one in the Twin Cities that was home strictly to girls' and women's hockey clubs. I wasn't sold on it for Mimi at her current age and skill level because I believed she'd be better off playing with boys and girls. If she continued with the sport, and when they separated gender, then it might be a good fit. And Lucy wasn't crazy about the rink I chose. She said it was too "industrial" and none of the kids looked like they were having fun.

Which left us to tour Lakeside, the rink where we'd been for the birthday party. Margene, the chatty rink manager, had the day off, but she'd set up a meeting with Gabi, the programs facilitator. She gave us the facility's history, a tour of the front end, which housed the offices and conference rooms, as well as a printout of the weekly schedule.

When I shot Lucy a sideways glance, I knew she was sold on this place as a testing ground for Mimi. While I agreed the curriculum had all the classes Mimi would need, something felt off about this place, and I couldn't put my finger on it.

On the drive to the club, I asked Lucy if she'd noticed it. She claimed the only reason it felt "off" to me was that Crabby Gabi hadn't fawned over me like everyone else had at the other facilities.

Maybe she had a point.

We met at the restaurant across the street from the club—which was packed on a Sunday; people filled the waiting area and spilled out onto the sidewalk. But Nolan had a table. In fact, it appeared Nolan had scored the best table in the house, a corner booth that managed to be both private and yet had a great view.

Mimi jumped up and hugged us both when we reached the table, but she was strangely subdued after she slid back in next to her uncle.

Nolan eyed us suspiciously, like we'd get into a shouting match again if he left us alone. I couldn't tell him that the previous night's shouting match had been a cleansing for Lucy and me, possibly even a clean slate.

Lucy and I exchanged a look and I nodded. She'd start the conversation and I'd join in. She leaned across the table and took Mimi's hands. "Honey, your dad and I are so sorry that we let our tempers get out of control last night. The last thing either of us ever wants to do is cause you to feel scared or unsafe. And we're very proud of you for calling your uncle Nolan to take you someplace where you weren't afraid."

"So you're not mad?"

"Not at all," I inserted. "That is what your phone is for. But that aside, your mom and I want to assure you that it won't happen again. After you left, we realized we needed to talk to each other, not shout at each other."

"And we were able to make a few decisions that have to

do with all three of us, separately and together as a family," Lucy said.

Her calling us a family . . . that just punched me in the gut. I wanted that so much. "First, I have a surprise for you."

Mimi grinned. "Is it a puppy?"

"No, almost as good as that."

"It's a kitty!"

Jesus. "No. The surprise is I'll be moving onto the top floor of your apartment building. So you'll have both your mom and dad close by. Won't that be great?"

Her gaze moved back and forth between us. "You won't live by Calder anymore?"

"Nope. I'll be living closer to you. And the apartment isn't done, but after we leave here, I thought we could all go check it out."

"Okay." She looked at us expectantly.

"What's wrong, sweetie?" Lucy asked.

"Can Calder come over and play sometimes?"

"Anytime you want," I said. "And we have some other good news. We talked it over, and we've decided to let you try hockey."

"For real?" She bounced in the booth seat. "Like playing on a hockey team and everything?"

"Yep. We signed you up for the basic skills class at Lakeside Ice Arena—where we were yesterday. Then if you like it, we'll enroll you at the Mite Team level."

"Did you hear that, Uncle? I get to play!"

"I heard that, short stuff. Exciting news. And you know I'll be there cheering you on at the games."

Mimi stopped bouncing and looked at Lucy. "What about you, Mommy? Will you come to the games?"

"Wouldn't miss them for anything," Lucy assured her. "I believe your daddy will handle taking you to most—if not all—of your practice times."

I leaned in. "But there is something we need from you, Meems, or this won't happen."

Mimi stilled, and I sensed Lucy looking at me, since we hadn't discussed this part.

"What?"

"You have to stop being a pain about getting up on school days. It's not fair to your mom. And if you stick with hockey? You'll have full practices early in the morning before you go to school, so it'd be best if you got used to the early hours now. No more bratty behavior, Milora Michelle. Understood?"

"I promise, promise, promise I'll do better." She held her pinkie up, and I hooked mine around it, watching as she offered the same pinkie promise to her mother and finally to Nolan.

"Good. After brunch we'll go buy the rest of your sports gear. There's open ice late this afternoon at Lakeside. We'll suit up and skate, since we didn't get to finish our weekend."

In a flash Mimi disappeared beneath the table, and then she was crawling between me and Lucy. She hugged me and then her mother. "This is the best day ever! I can't wait to tell Calder!"

"Can you hold off on telling him until after you're done with the skills class?"

"But Daddy . . . he's my best friend! We tell each other everything."

I heard Lucy suck in a sharp breath. I glanced at Nolan. He shook his head, indicating that Mimi hadn't relayed last night's events to her BFF, thank god.

"It'd be a way better surprise for Calder if you told him about playing hockey after you had two weeks of skills training," Nolan suggested. "When you're absolutely sure that you want to play hockey."

She considered it for a moment before she said, "Okay. I'll wait to tell him. But we don't gotta wait to sign me up for a team because I know I want to play hockey." She sighed with pure eight-year-old exasperation. "You've known that longer than anyone, Uncle Nolan."

Nolan shot me an "I told you so" look. "You are absolutely right. Now come over here and finish the picture you were coloring for me."

As soon as Mimi had fallen back into her own little world, Nolan's gaze zipped between us. "Everything all right?"

"It's great," Lucy said. "You coming to get her gave us the chance for a long talk last night."

"A long overdue talk," I amended.

"I'm happy to hear you both can adult when cornered," Nolan said with a smile.

"Hilarious."

"On a side note . . . it's been two weeks since you dropped the bombshell about ditching the corporate world at LI. The family is gonna grill you on what you've been doing."

"Is this your not-so-subtle way of asking what's going on with the bar remodel?"

"Yes. We didn't talk about it at all yesterday."

I wasn't sure if Nolan was testing me to see if I'd mentioned the full-scale remodel and reinvention of the bar spaces to Lucy, or if he worried I'd talked a good game and hadn't done anything to get the project underway. "I met with Walker and his partner Jase two days after our five-way phone conference. They assessed the room upstairs that'll be the barcade, testing it for structural integrity since it'll have to hold all those heavy gaming machines. The good news? No structural issues. The bad news is they're still waiting on permits to start the teardown."

"What's the time frame once the permits are released?"

I shrugged. "Depends on what issues they find beneath the lath and plaster. In the meantime, Dallas found a place that'll sell us fully restored machines. It's more money up-front, but they guarantee the games are plug-in ready, so that's one added expense I don't mind paying. She's also hired an online marketing firm in the Cities to incentivize the demographic we want into taking a quick poll so we have an idea of what types of games and drink specials will bring them to a barcade."

Nolan whistled. "So you haven't been sitting around polishing your trophies."

Asswipe. I scratched my cheek with my middle finger.

He laughed.

"Someone want to clue me in on what you're talking about?"

I glanced around to make sure no one was eavesdropping before I detailed the plans to demolish one bar and rebuild it into two vastly different clubs.

She blinked at me. "Jax. That's brilliant."

Inside I was grinning like an idiot from her praise. Outside, I played it cool. "You really think so?"

"Absolutely. I was sort of afraid you'd cash in on your name and turn it into another sports bar." She scowled. "Which are far too plentiful as it is."

I sent Nolan an "I told you so" smirk.

"Has Dallas started on PR yet?"

Was Lucy angling for a chance to help out? "Umm . . . not sure. That's on this week's agenda. Why?"

"Because you definitely should get Annika to spearhead your campaign. She'll know exactly what will make the biggest splash. But you need to get her on board ASAP because she tends to overextend herself on new projects during hockey season since Axl is gone so much."

I must've looked confused or surprised because she said, "What? You thought I'd ask to get involved?" Then she laughed. "Uh, no. Can you imagine us working together? We'd disagree on everything, and then everyone would disappear when we reverted to our loud and emphatically stated discussions."

I glanced at Mimi; she wasn't paying attention to our

conversation. "Yeah, we'd definitely fail at HR's suggested conflict resolution tactics." I bumped her with my shoulder. "Although there was a time when our unique approach to resolving our conflicts caused us both to forget what we'd been arguing about in the first place."

Lucy turned the same time I did. We shared the lovers' look that held secrets, desire and a smugness that no one else was welcome in our little world.

In hindsight, that's when I should've kissed her. Right there in front of our kid, my brother, and the entire restaurant, so she understood how much I wanted us to rebuild that little world starting right then.

Instead, in the sudden quiet, I heard Mimi say, "Uncle Nolan, are they gonna start yelling at each other again?"

"No, short stuff. I'm thinking they've moved on to another more complicated way to communicate."

Lucy looked away first.

I glanced over to see Mimi eyeballing us with suspicion. She said, "I don't get it."

"Join the club, sweetheart." Nolan slipped out of the booth. "Come on. It's time to be assimilated into the collective."

I used to dread Lund family brunches. In the years prior to my sobriety, at these gatherings I desperately tried not to drink too much so my family wouldn't see that I had a problem. Since they were a group of problem solvers, they'd butt into my business as if they could fix me, so I'd made sure none of them could tell just how broken I'd become.

The secrets, lies, deceptions I lived with still haunted me. While my family's love and support humbled me to my very core, I remained wary of revealing too much of myself.

But Lucy understood. I sensed her monitoring my mood from the end of the table. She knew when I'd reached the limit of my family togetherness. She worked her charm, and we bailed a full hour before I expected we could.

After we'd secured Mimi in the back seat of my car, I slipped my arm around Lucy's waist, pulled her in for a hug and whispered, "Thank you."

"Anytime, sport." She patted my chest to get me to release her. "Now let's finish the rest of today's trials so you can get to your happy place."

The dirty part of my mind piped up with, *Between your thighs?* but I ignored it and said, "Where's that?"

"On the ice."

I should've kissed her then. But I chickened out.

Again.

If I kept this up, I'd start sprouting feathers.

Shopping for hockey gear took half as long as I'd allowed for because Lucy kept Mimi focused.

Thankfully Lakeside had family changing rooms. I'd spent my life in locker rooms, so I thought nothing of stripping down to my underwear in front of Mimi and Lucy, so I could show Mimi the order she needed to follow to put on her protective gear. Even though she and I were working on skating basics, she needed to suit up fully, because there'd never be a time when she was on the ice without it.

Lucy sat in the observation area, wrapped in the blanket I'd stashed in my bag. Ice rinks were cold, and she'd dressed for brunch, not hockey practice. She'd seemed surprised I'd thought to bring it.

Once Mimi and I were on the ice, I crouched down to get her full attention. "Two things to remember today. First, you listen only to me. You don't look around at the other skaters; you don't worry what your mom is doing. Focus on me. That's for your own safety—and mine. Okay?"

"Okay."

"Second, we're done when I say we're done. There's no negotiating, no begging for more ice time. Again, this is for your safety, okay?"

"Okay."

I handed over her new hockey stick. "First thing about hockey. If you're on the ice, even during open skate practicing, your stick is always in your hand. Period." I held out my stick. "We'll start you out with the two-handed grip. One hand here"—I curled the fingers of her left hand around the top of the stick, and her right hand halfway down the stick—"and your dominant hand here. Got it?"

"Got it."

"Good. The blade is always on the ice. Your stick is always in your hand and the blade of the stick is always on the ice. Now skate forward. Keep your head up at all times." I started to skate backward. "See the logo on my shirt? Watch it as you're moving, that way you'll stay with me."

I grinned at her look of concentration.

We made it one full rotation around the rink before she fell.

As hard as it was to do, I didn't help her up. She needed to find her balance from the start, and me picking her up and asking if she was all right every time she fell? We'd get nothing accomplished. Beginning hockey players spent more time sprawled on the ice than they did skating.

I waited until she was upright before I spoke. "Why do you think you fell?"

"Because I looked at my feet."

"Exactly. Hockey players spend thousands of hours skating so it becomes as familiar as breathing. That's so when you're playing in a game, you're not thinking about skating; you're just doing it."

She nodded and put both hands on her stick. "I'm ready."

"No, you're not. What are you forgetting?"

Mimi lowered her blade to the ice.

"Good. Let's go."

At the end of an hour, she'd already shown such improvement that I let her take two laps around the rink by herself, as fast as she wanted. She fell twice but she got right back up both times and implemented the three basics without me having to remind her.

"How wide do you think she's grinning inside that helmet?" Lucy asked behind me.

"So wide she could pass for the Joker."

"Do you need to take some fast laps too, Coach Daddy?"

"Nah. I'm good."

"I'll say."

Her compliment surprised me. I turned and looked at her briefly before returning to watch Mimi.

"Well, you are. Mimi tends to tune out when she thinks she understands something. I couldn't hear what you were saying to her, but her body language said she was one hundred percent in the moment, listening to you. That is a commendable feat."

My neck burned from the praise. "It's the first day, Luce."

"How many days a week are you planning on working with her one-on-one?"

"Two. And she'll have an hour of skills classes twice a week." I groaned. "That's already more ice time than what I told you."

"A man who underestimates rather than exaggerates? That's novel." She laughed—a sensual rumble that flowed into my ear and vibrated through my entire body.

Christ. When we were together I'd craved hearing that sexy sound because I'd never heard her make that noise around anyone else.

Mimi headed straight for me at a speed she couldn't control, so I braced myself for impact.

Even though she was small, I let out an "Uff" of surprise at the solid hit she'd landed.

Immediately she started babbling. "Daddy! I'm so sorry! I didn't mean to! I couldn't slow down—"

"It's okay. But from here on out keep that speed down until you've learned forward stops, okay?"

She nodded.

"You and your mom can head to the changing room."

And like her mother, Mimi opened her mouth to argue, probably to tell me she wasn't a baby and didn't need help getting undressed. But at the last second, she nodded again and carefully walked across the mats to the locker rooms. Lucy took her hand and they turned the corner.

As soon as they were gone, Gabi, our crabby rink guide from earlier, skated toward me.

"I thought your daughter would be more advanced," she said without preamble.

"She's eight. How advanced could she be?"

She shrugged. "Some people start their kids when they're like three."

"Then hockey is the parent's choice not the kid's. I didn't assume she'd love hockey just because I did. Her wanting to try it just came up."

"She's lucky we have openings. Usually we're full. All leagues, all ages."

When I researched this place a little deeper last night after Lucy had gone to bed, I noticed the eight-year-old age bracket was the only one without a full roster. I'd wait to see if my suspicions were correct about that.

"I sent all the enrollment forms to the email address on your application. Bring them filled out when you come to skills class on Wednesday afternoon."

"No problem."

"You should remember that parental observation means observation only. No coaching from the stands."

Her brusqueness started to bug me, especially since Margene had been so helpful and friendly. "What level do you teach?"

"Why? Are you afraid you'll get me as your daughter's coach?"

"Afraid? Not hardly. I'm just curious if you're coaching younger kids or older. If you're part of the community skate or the club skate."

"I'm assistant coach to the fourteen-year-old club skaters. I also assist with the newbie classes."

"So you will be working with Mimi."

She narrowed her eyes at me. "I assist with the open eight-year-old class, which is boys and girls, not the closed girls' eight-year-old class."

"We're putting Mimi in the open class, not the girls' class." I smiled at her shocked expression. "Thanks for all your help, Coach Gabi. See you Wednesday."

Even after my short conversation with Gabi, I still beat Mimi out of the locker room. Once she emerged, yawning and holding her mother's hand while Lucy carried her equipment bag, I couldn't help but pick her up and carry her out to the car. Pretty soon Mimi would be too big for a "daddy carry," so I'd take it every chance I could.

We'd barely turned out of the parking lot and Mimi was sound asleep. Poor kid. It'd been a rough couple of days for her and she needed a nap.

I looked at Lucy. "Should we let her sleep? Or will that mess with her schedule?"

"If she's that tired then she needs it."

"Agreed. You want me to just drive around aimlessly? Or did you have a specific destination in mind?"

"I want to see the bar you own."

Shit. "Why? It's not open on Sunday."

"I wasn't asking you to swing by because I need a cocktail, Jax. I just want to see where it's located."

"Sure, if you'd rather drive through the city and not alongside the Mississippi River, leaf peeping at the beautiful fall foliage . . ."

"I've already done that. I want to see the place where you'll be spending so much time."

I should've been more prepared for this since I'd owned the building for almost three years.

This is just another secret you've been keeping from her, and she'll be pissed off about it. And maybe freaked out because it is sort of fucking creepy that you bought—

"Jaxson."

Her sharp intonation brought me out of my merry-go-round of thoughts. "Sorry."

"What were you thinking about just now?"

"Wondering if I had my building keys so I could take you inside if you changed your mind." Christ. Lying came so easy to me.

"A drive-by is fine. So chop-chop, Lund. Get a move on."

I laughed. "You've been waiting all damn day for the chance to say that to me, haven't you?"

"Yep."

We didn't talk during the drive, which cranked up my nervousness.

When we turned the corner, Lucy's back snapped straight. I inched past the first building on the block and parallel parked in front of the second building.

Lucy didn't look at me when she said, "You're joking."

"Not even a little."

"But this is . . ."

"Mine. My building. My business."

"It's the same sign."

"I didn't change the name either."

She stared out the window for the longest time before she spoke again. "Who knows about this place?"

"In my family? Everyone. But no one, not even my business partner Simone, knows the real reason I bought it."

"Why did you buy it?"

"Because I could."

"Don't be flip. Not now."

I sighed. "You're really gonna make me say it, Lucy?"

"You're goddamned right I am, Lund," she snapped.

"Because this was our secret spot. It was the first place we were together and the last place I remember being happy before everything went to hell in my life. I thought it might be a talisman. If I owned it then maybe I could own my life again. Maybe I could find my way back to a happier place." *Maybe I could find my way back to you.*

I paused to breathe. "Fucked-up logic, but true. I thought I could buy happiness."

The wait for her to say something was excruciating.

Without meeting my gaze, she said, "I need some air," and bolted out of the car.

Eleven

LUCY

After I scrambled out of Jax's car I felt ridiculous for say-ing I "needed some air" like a Victorian maiden with a case of the vapors.

But I had to take a moment to think.

I continued down the sidewalk at a decent clip. As I by-passed a couple, I offered a friendly smile that must've looked as fake and as panicked as it felt.

Just ignore the woman racing down the sidewalk, with no idea where she's going except away from her ex, who just informed her that he'd bought the bar they'd once considered theirs. That's not unusual at all. Neither is the fact the man also bought the apartment building she lives in and is taking the entire top floor. Totally normal, right?

God. Didn't Jax see that this situation was more than a little fucked up? I had a right to freak out.

Except did he freak out when he discovered you'd applied to work in his family's business?

Whoa. That thought almost brought me to a dead stop. I hadn't even considered how Jax might've reacted when I took the job at LI. What would be the mature reaction in this scenario? Believe Jax's claim that he'd bought the bar to remind himself of the good times with me?

True, we'd had lots of good times in Borderlands when we were a couple. Drinking. Dancing. Laughing. Mooning around in our own little world where no one recognized him. I hadn't understood his need for privacy until I learned who he was.

Stopping, I glanced up at the Borderlands sign. The big reveal had happened right here in this bar, a decade ago. But that night was still as vivid in my mind as if it'd happened last night . . .

And we meet again . . ." I smirked and sang, "at a place where no-body knows your na-a-ame . . . Including your date."

He smiled. "I'll spare your ears and not sing the next verse from your modified rendition of the *Cheers* theme song." He clasped my hand in his and said, "We're back here."

After we sat down, I looked around the dive bar. Didn't seem like his kind of joint. "Do you come here often?"

"First time."

"I feel overdressed."

"You shouldn't." He leaned over and kissed the corner of my mouth. "You look fucktacular."

"Fucktacular?"

"Uh-huh." His mouth migrated to my ear. "The definition of that word requires a physical demonstration, which I'd be happy to show you."

I shivered. The heat from his body, his breath, his words . . . the man wreaked sexy havoc, and I couldn't wait until he unleashed himself on me fully.

"Jax—"

"I'm getting ahead of myself, aren't I?" He retreated and smiled down at me. "Feel like drinking something other than beer tonight?"

I feel like drinking you down until I'm drowning in you. Until you're seeping into my pores and filling me back up again. And again.

Those startling blue eyes narrowed. "Hold that thought."

"Even if it's urgent?" I said huskily. "Or dirty?"

"Hold it close and tight and hard, especially if it's urgently dirty."

I giggled. Giggled. God. I never giggled.

"You, my beautiful Lucy Q, stay put. I'll be right back."

I remained standing so I could watch the muscles in that high and firm ass of his shift and pull against his jeans as he strode away. Then I felt like a perv and glanced around the bar to see if anyone had been watching me lust after my man.

Your man?

Yes, my man, I retorted to my snarky subconscious. So what if it was only the fifth date. So what if I didn't know his last name. For the past month and at least for tonight, that hot, hunky man was mine. I'd unlock my neuroses tomorrow.

It wasn't long after I'd seated myself that Jax returned with two clear glasses.

That's when I noticed the bartender carried an ice bucket and set it on the table next to Jax's chair. The bottle had already been uncorked, so he didn't stick around.

"Champagne? What are we celebrating?"

Jax brushed his lips over the shell of my ear. "Us."

Oh damn. That was really sweet.

He sat and reached for the champagne, filling my flute first and then his.

I lifted my glass, waiting for him to say something else sweet, or funny, or sexual, but he appeared at a loss for words, so I jumped in first. "To dirty cars, annoying cell phone conversations, to food and art and fun . . . all the things that have made us . . . us."

"Perfect."

We touched our glasses together and drank. "Wow. I wouldn't have thought a place like this stocked good champagne."

"I think it's been gathering dust since the building was finished last century."

I laughed. "It's very well aged then." I drained the remainder and held my glass out for more.

"Do you get tipsy from champagne?"

"Yep. That's the fun part of drinking it fast." I swallowed another mouthful. "I like how if fizzes on my tongue and then that fizzy sensation spreads throughout my body. No wonder they call it bubbly. That's how I feel when I drink it."

Before I took another sip, Jax moved my hand off to the side and leaned in so we were nose to nose. "I want to taste that fizzy, bubbly happiness on you, Lucy. Take another drink but don't swallow."

My internal temperature jumped to the combustible stage. Without breaking our sexy eye-fuck, I brought the flute to my lips. But I didn't tip it up and drink right away. Instead I traced the rim of the glass with the tip of my tongue.

Jax was so close to me that I felt his deep growl vibrate down my throat.

Oh, hello, sexy beast. That was the first time I'd ever caused a man to make that desperate, greedy sound, and I really, really liked it.

Was there anything better than this powerful feeling of being wanted?

I tipped the glass and filled my mouth.

Then Jax's lips were on mine as he curled his hand around the front of my throat, holding me in place. His coaxing kisses had me parting my lips, and he slipped his tongue into my mouth.

Cold fizzes of sweetness dancing on my tongue gave way to a deep suctioning pull that I felt between my legs as Jax sucked the champagne from my mouth into his. After he swallowed, he spoke against my lips. "Mmm. Sweet, wet and sticky." His kisses were deceptively erotic, a soft glide of his lips across mine, punctuating each word as he maintained his hold on me.

Maybe the champagne had gone to my head, because I heard myself say, "Now I'm sweet, wet and sticky somewhere else." I nipped his lower lip. "One guess where that might be."

"What do I get if I guess right?" he murmured as his lips toyed with mine.

"A taste of that too."

He groaned. "Jesus. We have to stop. I'm about to fuck you right here."

"Offering the patrons of Borderlands a live sex show? We'd never be welcome in here again."

"It'd be worth it."

I laughed softly. "Your challenge for me tonight was to experience something new. So bring out the exhibitionist in me, baby."

His mouth crashed down on mine.

This kiss was pure lust and I reveled in it. In him. In this moment.

Jax broke the kiss.

My eyes flew open and clashed with his.

"This passion is us too, Lucy."

"I know."

Satisfaction gleamed in his eyes, and he gifted me with a lingering smooch before his hand fell away from my neck.

He refilled our glasses, and I was surprised to see we'd almost killed the bottle.

"Drink up. Then we'll dance."

I peered over his shoulder. There was an open area ringed

by tables, and music was coming from somewhere, but I'd be hard pressed to call it a dance floor. "Jax. I don't think—"

"What will they do? Throw us out?" He tugged me to my feet. "I'd rather get tossed out for lewd behavior, so I'll let you choose."

"Dirty dancing it is." I poked him in the chest. "For now."

He granted me that sexy grin.

The first song was a soulful, bluesy jazz ballad probably from the '80s. We swayed together, adjusting our feet and hands and body movements. By the time the second song started, we were in sync. By the third song—yet another soulful slow piece, I had my arms twined around his neck and I felt a hard ridge pressing into my stomach.

"You move really well, Jax. Like you're aware of what every part of your body is doing at all times. So I'm thinking you might be a stripper."

He chuckled. "Would it bother you if I was?"

"Nope. I'd just demand a private show because your ass would look outstanding framed in one of those fancy silk jockstrap thingies. Do you have one?" I asked hopefully.

"No way. But I do have to wear a cup nearly every day."

"I think the time has come, Jaxson, to tell me what you do for a living."

He lowered his head and trailed his lips down my neck and then back up to my ear.

I held my breath, dizzy from lack of oxygen and from the drugging kisses he bestowed on me.

Finally he murmured, "I'm a professional hockey player."

"For real?"

"For real."

"No wonder you have such a fucktacular body."

Those warm, soft lips touched the shell of my ear again, sending goose bumps across my skin. "You're not disappointed?"

"No?"

"That's not very convincing."

"I've never dated an athlete, let alone an elite athlete." Then something occurred to me and I yanked on his hair. Hard.

"What the hell?"

"That's for humiliating me at shuffleboard, Mr. Professional Hockey Player."

Jax chuckled. "Yeah, that wasn't nice, but it sure was fun."

When the song ended, I untangled myself from him.

He kept his hand on my ass as we returned to our table. Then he set his hand on my thigh after we sat down. The man excelled at multitasking; he poured more champagne as his fingers crept up the inside of my thigh in a sweeping caress.

I snapped my knees together, trapping his hand.

Jax's gaze met mine and he raised one eyebrow.

"I'm loud when I come. I figured you needed to know that before you found out at the same time as the twenty other people in this bar."

Leaning closer, he brushed his mouth below my ear. "And I thought you were being prissy."

"Just because I don't fuck on the first date doesn't mean I'm prissy about sex."

"Even if you were prissy, I'd make it my mission to coax out your inner bad girl." He twisted his hand and pried apart my knees, sliding his fingers up my thigh until he reached my panties. "Have I told you how much I dig that you always wear skirts?"

I shook my head.

"Easy access is sexy." He sank his teeth into my earlobe. "You're sexy. Christ. I don't know how much longer I can keep my hands off you."

My throat was bone dry. I wasn't sure if it was the champagne or him that had gone to my head. When his stroking fingers slipped beneath the elastic of my panties, I tilted my pelvis forward, giving him better access. Then I turned my head and met his hot and hungry gaze. "I'm willing to chance getting kicked out of here for lewd behavior if you are."

"For real?"

"For real. But before I let you hike up my skirt and bang me against the nearest wall, I need to know your last name."

"It's Lund."

"Jaxson Lund. Nice." I nipped his chin. "I'm Lucy Quade."

M ommy, what are you doing?"
  The memory vanished.

I whirled around to see Mimi leaning out of the rear car window. Jax rested against the passenger side door, watching me. I hadn't heard him get out of the car, but I wasn't surprised he'd needed to make sure I was all right. In truth, I was more melancholy than freaked out now that I'd revisited a defining moment in my life. It'd been a life changer for Jax too, and it hurt my heart a little that he'd gone to such lengths to try and reconnect with that happy time in his life.

I smiled at him and then our daughter. "I was just checking out this cool old building that your dad owns."

"Are you done? Because I'm hungry. My tummy is growling."

How could she possibly need more food?

"How about if we hit the Burger Time drive-thru on the way home?" he said to Mimi.

"Yay!"

After telling Mimi to buckle up, Jax opened my car door for me. "You okay with this?"

"This" wasn't referring to fast food. "Now that the shock has worn off? Yes, I am." I poked him in the chest. "But don't throw away that sign, buddy."

"I wouldn't dream of it."

Twelve

JAX

My week from hell started first thing Monday morning. We still hadn't received the proper permits from the city, so renovations at the barcade and Borderlands remained at a standstill.

The final inspection for my apartment got pushed back due to an electrical issue.

That electrical issue would affect half of the apartment building if left unattended, so as building owner, I had to listen to solutions and sign off on upgrades that cost me two hundred grand.

I suffered through a Lund Industries board of directors meeting that dragged on for three hours, so I was twenty-five minutes late picking Mimi up from school and she let me have it.

My counselor had an emergency and postponed our appointment on a week I really could have used a neutral party to talk to.

Nolan reminded me I still hadn't hired a decorator/designer for my new apartment, which meant the only room that would have furniture was Mimi's bedroom, since I'd rented a furnished place at Snow Village.

I hadn't had time to work out since Sunday night.

And Lucy had gone radio silent—no calls, no texts . . . nothing.

Although it was only Wednesday afternoon, it'd been the longest three days I could remember.

I walked into the front offices of Lakeside Ice Arena to drop off Mimi's registration paperwork. No sign of Crabby Gabi, but as soon as Margene saw me she hustled over and bumped my shoulder.

"Hey hey. The big shot is in the building."

I made a show of looking over my shoulder, and Margene laughed.

"Glad to see you've got a sense of humor." She sobered immediately when someone came through the door behind me. Under her breath she said, "Trust me, you're gonna need it."

"Thanks for the warning. I'm supposed to drop off this paperwork."

"I'll take it." She frowned. "Mimi isn't with you? Doesn't she have skills class?"

"I'm meeting her here. Her mother is bringing her."

"Gotcha. Come on. Let's get this over with." She sidestepped me and headed down a hallway.

I followed her into a conference room, where a little gnome of a man was laying into Gabi. And he didn't bother to keep his voice down.

"I don't know how many goddamned times I have to tell you this. *I* am the coach. *You* are just the assistant. Your opinion is just that; it means nothing to me. You know you're lucky to even have a job—"

Margene cleared her throat. "Excuse me, Dennis, but we have a parent here."

His look said "So?" and I immediately disliked him even more.

"His daughter is starting skills class today," Margene continued. "It's always been our practice for the parents to meet their child's coaches."

Surprisingly he offered his hand first. "I'm Dennis Dyklar. You can call me Coach Dyklar."

Wow. Okay. I shook his hand. "Good to meet you. I'm Jax." I felt both Margene and Gabi staring at me for not sharing my full name.

And when "Call me Coach Dyklar" scrutinized me, I thought he'd recognized me. But instead he said, "Been a while since I've met a parent new to hockey. So I have to ask if you're one of those helicopter parents that's always hovering in the background, on guard to rush to your kid's rescue?"

"Not that I'm aware of."

"Good. As long as you stick to my rules we won't have a problem."

Buddy, I've already got a problem with you. "What rules would those be, Coach Dyklar?"

"First off, your kid needs to be fully dressed and ready to hit the ice five minutes before the first whistle. Second, I'm the coach, not you. If I feel you're a distraction, I'll limit the amount of time you're allowed rink side, maybe even deny you visiting privileges entirely."

No way in hell would I walk off and leave my daughter with this guy.

"Third, she needs to be able to handle criticism. Coaches yell at players. A fact of hockey life. Some girls can't handle it. Some girls cry."

"Some boys cry too, Coach Dyklar," Gabi pointed out.

He shot Gabi a dirty look.

She merely blinked at him.

A little tension there.

"Any questions?" Coach Dickhead asked me.

"Just one. Are you her skills coach or her team coach?"

He sighed, as if I'd asked a dumb question. "Both."

"I assumed there'd be a dedicated instructor for skills."

"When I took over the ten-and-under levels, I combined the two positions," he said proudly. "Who better to test their skills than their coach?"

It wasn't about "testing" skills—it was supposed to be about teaching skills. If players didn't learn the basic skills and practice them, how would they win games? And a coach as a skills teacher at this level meant the kids who had a better handle on basic skills would garner more of the coach's attention and more ice time.

"Sorry, Jack—"

"It's Jax," I corrected him.

He waved his hand at me in the ultimate "whatever" dismissal. "I've got to go over some important coaching stuff with Gabi before class starts. Margene can answer any other questions."

All of a sudden I had a lot of questions for Margene.

As soon as we were out of the conference room, Margene faced me and put her finger over her lips, then led me down the opposite hallway into a tiny office.

She skirted the desk to sit behind it. "Close the door."

I did and remained standing, leaning my shoulders against it.

Margene made the "out with it" motion.

"He's the reason why there are openings in the eight-year-old class."

"He's also the reason why we've lost half a dozen really good coaches in the past year alone. He's an egotistical asshole with nothing to back it up."

"Little man syndrome?" I asked.

"And little dick syndrome," she said with a snicker. "Not that I know that firsthand."

"Has he been here from the start?"

She shook her head. "Lakeside has been in operation for four years. He showed up two years ago, claiming he'd coached hockey at a private school on the East Coast. But we've never been able to verify it—refusing to hire him hadn't been an option, since his great-aunt owns this place."

"His is a paid, full-time position?"

"A part-time paid position." She snorted. "That's the reason he combined the skills and coaching positions; now he gets paid to do both." She held up her hand when I opened my mouth to object. "I'm aware of the need for separation, but I manage the rink and set the schedule. I'm not part of the coaching staff, so I have no vote in staffing positions or their teaching decisions."

"That sucks."

"Tell me about it. I've had no recourse except to watch him ruin what had once been a promising hockey program." She slumped back in her chair. "Now that you know our dirty little secret about Dennis the Menace, I imagine you'll seek out other options for Mimi."

I gave her a considering look before I spoke. "I could. I have the means. But what about the other families who are using the facility for recreational hockey? They have to suck it up or quit. And since Lakeside's concept of rec hockey and club hockey in one facility appealed to us, I'll suck it up too." I smirked at her. "But that doesn't mean I'll just accept the way he runs things." I'd bide my time, get a feel for the place and the patrons before deciding how much I wanted to stir the pot.

Margene grinned at me. "I knew you were trouble, Stonewall. Give 'em hell and welcome to Lakeside."

When I returned to the rink, Mimi was already there and dressed. "Hey, girl. You ready for this?"

"Uh-huh."

"Remember what we practiced?"

"When I'm on the ice, my stick is in my hand."

"Very good. What else?"

"Keep my head up and my blade on the ice."

"You get an A-plus for today."

Her grin was there and gone as she shifted her stance. "What's up?"

"Mommy said she saw you going into the office."

"I had to drop off your registration paperwork."

"Did you meet my coach?"

"I met him briefly."

She blurted out, "Is he nice?"

What a loaded question. "Why did you ask that?"

"Because two of the other players said he's mean and he yells all the time." Her eyes were so anxious it slayed me. "Daddy, what if he yells at me?"

I forced an even tone. "You need to listen to him and what he's yelling at you about. If you weren't paying attention and put another player in danger . . . that's a more serious reason to be yelled at than you missing a shot on goal, okay?"

"Okay."

"I've gotten yelled at by coaches my whole life. It's not fun. So no matter what happens, you can talk to me about it afterward, because I know how it feels. You never have to hold anything back with me, okay?"

She nodded.

"Mimi, you're sure you want to do this? Because if you want to walk off the ice right now, you can, no explanation needed."

"No. I wanna play."

I smiled at her. "Then go have fun. I'll be right here when you're done."

The whistle blew, signaling the start of class.

I scanned the stands and saw Lucy near the top. I dipped my chin at her but didn't scale the steps to sit beside her. I had no precedent for what she expected during Mimi's ice time, so I opted to stay in the front row so I could hear the coach and watch my daughter.

Ten minutes into the class, I wanted to punch Coach Dyklar in the throat.

The man had no idea what he was doing.

Where were the straight skating drills?

And blowing that goddamned whistle every couple of minutes . . . I wished he'd choke on it. Maybe he would if I could get away with a quick elbow shot.

The bench beside me squeaked, and a soft, warm hand covered my fist resting on my right thigh.

"I can see how tense you are even from the top of the stands," Lucy said. "Relax."

"I can't. This is so fucked up. He shouldn't be teaching this class, because he's teaching them nothing. It's an utter waste of time for her."

Lucy leaned into me. "I'm a newb, remember? Explain what you mean."

I launched into a running dialogue of everything that was wrong with this scenario.

She didn't interrupt or ask a bunch of questions. She just let me ramble and kept running her fingers up and down my knuckles, trying to soothe me.

When I finished ranting, she pulled a water bottle out of her bag and handed it to me.

"Thanks." That's when I noticed she sat so close the left side of her body was pressed against the right side of mine from calves to shoulders. "You cold?"

"A little. Somebody was thoughtful enough to bring a blanket last time."

"Sorry. I don't have my equipment bag with me."

"Don't apologize. This hot body of yours is warming me right up."

"Good."

After a moment, she lifted her head from my biceps and forced my attention away from the rink to her. "You are upset by this coach if you didn't make a sexy, lewd comment in response to mine."

I gave her a tiny head-butt. "Don't distract me when I'm in meddling hockey parent mode." Then I put my arm around her and tugged her closer.

After watching for a while, Lucy said, "What are you going to do?"

"Nothing, probably."

She snorted. "Like I buy that. You're a problem solver."

"You wouldn't say that if you knew about all the things hanging over my head that haven't gotten resolved this week," I grumbled.

"Welcome to the club, Lund."

Before I could ask for more details on her bad week, the class moved to center ice. "Now why the hell would he do that?" I watched as Coach Dumbass put two kids in the face-off circle. "That kid in the red? Jesus. He can barely stand up on skates. The last thing he needs is to hear about face-off strategies."

"And again, I ask you, Stonewall, what you plan on doing about these problems you're seeing."

"I'll work with Mimi on basic skills."

"And her teammates? What about them?"

"I'd give them pointers if they're around when I'm teaching Mimi."

"So more hours at the rink?"

"Probably."

"I'll start packing my own pillow and blanket."

I looked at her. "You don't have to be here for every practice, Luce. I can pick her up and bring her home."

"Which in the near future will be you riding the elevator and knocking on our door."

Not soon enough.

She placed her hand on my chest. "I'm sorry."

"For?"

"How I left things on Sunday. Saying no to checking out your new digs and then for not touching base with you at all this week."

I brushed a few stray strands of hair away from her face. "Still freaked out about me owning the bar?"

"A little. I'll feel better if you admit it's weird you bought it."

"Nope. Never."

She laughed. "Jerk."

"Since Mimi has a cell phone, you don't have to touch base with me as much. I can talk directly to her."

Her eyes searched mine. "She called you this week?"

"Every night." I smirked. "She needs someone to talk hockey with, newb."

"See?" She whapped me on the chest. "If I don't come to practices and learn about the game, I'll be left out."

I knew how that felt and I never wanted that for her.

Then she slid her hand up my neck and cupped my jaw. "Let me ease some of your tension and take your mind off your troubles for a little while."

I cocked an eyebrow at her.

She still was so freaking cute when she blushed.

"Not that, Mr. Dirty Mind. I'm asking you to come over for dinner tonight."

"I'd love that, Luce." I turned my head and kissed her wrist. "Thanks for asking."

"I need to make a store run first." She paused. "You're okay with sticking around here until class ends and bringing Mimi home?"

"Yep. It'll probably be another hour and a half before we're there."

"That works for me." She scraped her nails through the stubble on my cheek. "I like this scruffy look on you, so don't feel like you have to head home to shower and change before dinner." Then she backed off and stood. "Behave. I mean it."

"What?"

"Don't 'what' me, Mr. Body Slam. You're in an arena, a dude you can't stand is on the ice; it's your perfect excuse to smash him into the boards."

I grinned.

"You aren't getting Mimi thrown out on her first day. So you are benched, Stonewall. Or stuck in the sin bin, or whatever it's called when you are out of play."

"Damn, Lucy Q, I'm almost proud that you remembered some hockey talk."

"Hard to forget how thoroughly you drilled a few of those terms into me. Over and over."

My eyes gleamed when my mind flashed back to that night. In retrospect, it'd been one of the best nights of my life, because that's when I'd known—

"Wipe that hot and bothered expression off your face."

"Then you shouldn't have brought it up."

She rolled her eyes. "See you."

I refocused on the action on the ice. Gabi waited in the ref's crease, but I hadn't seen Coach Dickless call her over even once. There was no point in having an assistant coach if you didn't utilize them.

Finally class ended.

Mimi skated over to me.

"Hey, how was it?"

She pulled off her glove and then her helmet in that quick manner that all hockey players did and that gave me a burst of pride. Then she leveled the "Are you kidding me?" look that was one hundred percent her mother. "You saw how it was, Daddy."

When the pointlessness of the class was obvious to an eight-year-old . . . "You still have to tell me one positive thing about the class."

"I didn't get yelled at."

I fought a laugh.

Mimi craned her neck to scan the stands. "Where's Mommy?"

"She went to the store. I'm taking you home and staying for supper."

Then she grinned that sweet, hopeful, girlish smile that owned me. "Yay! Then I can make you cookies."

"Do you need me to help you out of your gear?"

"I'm not a baby."

Okay then.

She reached the mats and disappeared.

I figured I was in for a wait, so I watched the next group take the ice. Girls, probably in the 14U bracket. I'd read up on the girls' hockey program, and the only difference I saw between it and boys' hockey was the "no checking" rule at all age levels. Gabi skated two laps with them before issuing instructions. The students collectively groaned, and she wore that evil "I'm torturing you for your own good" look that I'd seen on dozens of coaches over the years. I wasn't surprised when she stopped in front of me.

"Is this your group?"

"I'm the assistant. The head coach is out on maternity leave until the season officially starts, so I'm basically running this group." She kept her focus on the ice when she asked, "Why didn't you tell Coach Dyklar who you are?"

"I did. I'm Mimi's dad."

"Come on, Lund. Humbleness doesn't suit you given the career you've had."

"Me bragging about accomplishments in my former pro career isn't going to make him a better coach. He's a know-nothing with a Napoleon complex that he lords over the youngest kids and their parents. I hate that he is the first contact a lot of these players will have with the world of hockey. There are so many good men and women who love teaching and coaching. They should be a kid's first coach. That's where they'll learn love of the game, respect for the rules and teamwork."

That outburst earned me a genuine smile from Crabby Gabi. "I couldn't agree more. And that accurate assassination of his supposed character makes me rethink my initial opinion of you."

"Which was what?"

"That you're an entitled a-hole who throws around your name and money to get things done your way."

"By all means, Gabi, don't hold back on how you really feel," I said dryly.

She blushed, but she didn't apologize.

"Look, I'm entitled. I know that. But rehab forced me to deal with my issues, so I can state with pride that I am no longer a drunken a-hole throwing anything around."

Her gaze narrowed. "Rehab isn't mentioned anywhere in your bio. Is it recent?"

"It's been three years. So fair warning not to invite me out for a drink."

"I doubt your wife would be happy if I did that."

I didn't correct her mistaken impression that Lucy and I were married. "You're probably right."

"Anyway, I didn't come over here to go all fangirl on you. In fact, I wanted to apologize for my a-hole behavior."

"Apology accepted. I won't secretly call you Crabby Gabi behind your back, and you won't make assumptions about me based on my name, deal?"

"Deal."

Then I offered my hand. "I'm Jaxson Lund. You can call me Jax."

She slapped my hand and snorted. "Gabriella Welk. I go by Gabi."

"Welk? As in . . . Lawrence Welk?"

"Yeah. He and my great-grandpa were cousins. I never met him."

"You're from North Dakota?"

"Yessir. University of North Dakota grad."

I groaned. "No way is a former Fighting Sioux player teaching my kid."

"Says the dude whose college mascot is a bucktoothed rat," Gabi retorted.

I couldn't help but laugh. Nor was I surprised that she knew I'd attended University of Minnesota. "Go torture your team, North Dakota. A couple of them are gossiping instead of skating."

She whirled around and zipped across the ice.

As much as I wanted to watch Gabi's coaching style, I had to meet Mimi out front.

Ten minutes later she appeared, dragging her equipment bag behind her.

The girl didn't protest that she "wasn't a baby" when I carried her equipment bag.

Mimi wasn't talkative at all in the car. I'd expected a million questions, but she just stared out the window.

I didn't push. She'd talk on her own time frame.

She did pay attention when I drove into the parking

garage and not the visitor's lot. "Uh, you'll get in trouble if you park in somebody's spot."

"It'll be okay. Trust me." With all that had gone on in Mimi's life, had she forgotten I'd be moving into this building?

When we reached the apartment, Mimi burst through the door, calling out for her mom. For a moment I remained frozen in the doorframe, wondering what it'd be like to have this life. A family meal every night. Helping Mimi with homework or cleaning up the kitchen because it was my turn. My gaze homed in on the wreckage that Mimi had left—her coat, shoes, backpack strewn across the floor. At my place I insisted Mimi pick up after herself. Here, she existed in the familiar chaos she created because it was home. Would she ever consider being with me . . . home?

That's how Lucy caught me, staring at the messy foyer with jealousy and melancholy.

"Jax? Is everything all right?"

I gave myself a mental shake and realized I hadn't even closed the door. "Yeah. Sorry. I was a little lost in thought."

"About?" she asked, reaching around behind me to shut the door.

"About when to show Mimi where I'll—and she'll—be living."

Lucy didn't point out that Mimi would only be living there part time. "Dinner still needs to simmer another thirty minutes. Should we all head up there to take a look?"

"Sounds great."

Mimi sauntered into the foyer eating a carton of yogurt. "What sounds great?"

"We're going up to see our new apartment," I said to her. Her gaze moved between us. "Mommy is coming too?"

"Of course I am. Finish your snack and we'll go."

While we waited for Mimi to return, I dug out my keys and started spinning them around my finger.

Lucy's hand curled around mine and stopped the jingling. "What's with the nerves today, sport?"

I could've tossed out a half-assed half-truth, but I didn't. "I want her to like it. I want her to feel like it's her home too, and not just Daddy's place where she stays sometimes."

First her face showed surprise, followed by another reaction I hadn't seen before—a sheen to her eyes that had me backtracking. "Shit. Sorry. I didn't—"

"Stop." She moved in and set her hand on my chest. "You're doing everything right, Jax. She'll get there, okay? She likes being with you. This move is a good thing because it proves you are settling in."

"Okay, I'm ready!" Mimi announced.

Lucy and I broke apart. "Let's go."

My heart swelled when Mimi reached for my hand as we headed down the hallway. Then she stopped. "We're going the wrong way. The elevators are at that end."

"That's the first part of the surprise." I held open the plastic curtain that shielded the construction debris, and Mimi and Lucy stepped through.

Lucy gasped. "Is that . . . ?"

"A private elevator? Why yes it is."

Mimi bounced on her toes. "It's just like the Barbie Dream-House!"

I chuckled. "I don't know about that, but since your apartment is the last one on this end of the building, I had it installed so you'll be able to leave your mom's apartment and take this elevator directly to my floor anytime you want."

"That is so cool! Mommy, isn't that so cool?"

"It's pretty unbelievable."

My gaze snared Lucy's. "Safety first with her. Always. No one else has access to this elevator. It's coded so Mimi's key will only take her to the top floor. And back down to this floor."

"You had an elevator installed to go between just three floors?"

"It goes down to the first level of the parking garage. The original building schematics left enough space to have two sets of elevators on each floor, so it wasn't as big a deal to put an elevator in since the shaft existed and we didn't have to create access to every floor."

"Can we go up now?" Mimi demanded.

"Yep. Poke the button."

She did and the door opened.

We stepped inside and I hit door close.

Tight fit. The car could hold maybe two more small people. "Okay, Meems. Poke the button for the fourteenth floor."

Lucy murmured, "You're not calling it the penthouse?"

I tugged on her hair and murmured back, "Sassy."

"Daddy, we're not moving."

I held an infrared device in front of her. "Put this on the keypad and then hit the button for the fourteenth floor."

A green light flashed and we started to move. "My key and your mom's key allow access to the top floor, your floor and the garage."

"I get a key?" Lucy said with surprise.

"Of course. You can come up anytime you want."

She frowned at me. "But what if you're—"

"I've got nothing to hide, Lucy. My partying days are behind me. I don't want anyone but my family in the home I share with our daughter."

That's when Lucy truly understood the message I'd been trying to relay to her. Her eyes widened. "Jax."

"You will never have to worry about walking in on some of the situations you were subjected to in the past. I promise."

The doors opened and Mimi sprinted out.

Lucy and I stared at each other.

"I know my promises probably don't mean shit, so here's

the honest-to-god truth: I haven't been with a woman since I sobered up."

Her jaw dropped. "That's been over three years."

I said nothing.

"Why?"

"Because meaningless hookups nearly destroyed me. They definitely destroyed everything that mattered to me."

Those beautiful brown eyes searched mine intently.

I wanted to ask her what she was looking for, but Mimi released a happy squeal and I walked toward her.

Thirteen

LUCY

Jax hadn't been with a woman in three years.

Holy shit.

As I tried to wrap my head around that and his confession about one-night stands, the elevator door started to close on me, prompting me to move.

Plastic sheeting hung everywhere. As I headed toward the sound of their voices, mysterious crunching noises sounded beneath my feet. I glanced down and saw the flooring hadn't been put in yet. Weird. From what I could see this place was still several weeks from move-in ready.

I ducked between two sheets of plastic and found myself in an enormous room. A bank of windows spread along one entire side, providing an unobstructed view of the city. A double-sided glass fireplace served as a breaking point between this room—I assumed the living room—and the kitchen.

Walking into that kitchen was like stepping into a kitchen showcase magazine. A marble-topped island anchored the center of the space in a modified U shape with enough seating around the eat-in bar for at least a dozen people. On the backside of the island was a huge farm-style sink and food prep area. Stainless steel appliances gleamed amidst the coffee-colored cabinetry. The marble countertops were stunning with the craziest pattern of brown, black and flecks of vivid blue that I'd ever seen. That pop of color tied in the front panel of the island—the same blue as in the marble—painted such a high gloss I suspected I could see my reflection in it.

"Holy moly, Jax. I don't even know what to say. This place is breathtaking."

He looked up at me and grinned. "Thanks. I designed the kitchen, and I cannot wait to cook in here."

"I can't wait either! There's two ovens, Mommy, so I can make a whole bunch of cookies at one time."

I noticed Jax's pleased grin that Mimi was looking forward to cooking with him. "That is pretty cool."

Mimi tugged on Jax's hand. "Come on. I wanna see the rest."

"You lead the way. I'll let you guess which room is yours."

We passed a formal dining room off the kitchen. Just beyond that was a theater room with seating for at least thirty. Farther down the hallway was the first bedroom—with an en suite bathroom. The next bedroom had been painted a soft pink, and Mimi squealed.

"This is my room! I just know it."

"Yep. Check out the bathroom."

I followed her into a dream bath, with a shower and a soaking tub. Next to the vanity was a built-in dressing table, with fancy makeup lights and crystal light fixtures. Even the knobs on the drawers were crystal.

"Daddy, I love it!"

Jax beamed when he showed Mimi the walk-in closet, roughly the size of her bedroom in our apartment.

Don't compare. Don't get jealous. He's doing this out of love.

That's when I realized I was all right with this. Maybe because Mimi wouldn't have to go far between the princess-style opulence of this room to her cozy, funky bedroom in our apartment. She literally had the best of both worlds.

"Let's see what's next!" Mimi bounded out.

Jax loomed over me. "You okay with this?"

"Yes."

"You're sure?"

"Jax, you've never really had a place of your own. It's exciting that you get to have everything you've ever wanted in one place."

He looked relieved. "A decade later and you still keep me guessing on how you'll react."

"I will admit total jealousy of the theater room."

"Feel free to use it anytime." He took my hand and towed me out of the room. "I'm installing a commercial popcorn machine."

"Of course you are."

Mimi zipped out of the doorway ahead of us. "Another bedroom and bathroom."

"How many bedrooms total?" I asked him.

"Five, including the master suite. Which is right here."

My heart beat faster for some reason when we paused in front of a set of double doors.

Mimi wormed her way between us and pushed the doors open, and we stepped inside.

My first thought was: How had he known that this was my dream bedroom? The platform where the bed would sit was in the farthest corner of the room, away from the windows and access to the other features of this suite. There were no built-in dressers, so no matter how this space was decorated, it would maintain clean lines. A sitting area opened onto a balcony. The windows wrapped around the corner, providing a different view of Minneapolis.

I followed Jax through another set of double doors that separated the bathroom from the sleeping suite. First thing I noticed was the ginormous walk-in shower. Next to it was a sauna. A soaking tub was wedged in the corner with a great view. The toilet was separate with its own door, twin sinks and an even larger built-in dressing table than in Mimi's bathroom. Which indicated that Jax hoped to have a woman sharing his life and home at some point.

But the real kicker was the his and hers walk-in closets, both with dressing "areas" in front of a gigantic mirror. In the center of the room was a built-in cabinet for accessories and jewelry. I imagined getting ready in here, Lindsey and Mimi both offering their opinions on the outfit I picked for date night with Jax.

I froze. Why had my brain put me in this scene?

Because you suspect Jax had this designed with you in mind but you're too afraid to ask.

"What do you think?" Jax asked, close enough to me that I felt his breath on my cheek.

"I love it. It's kind of its own little retreat in this stunning place that you'd never need to retreat from."

He chuckled.

Mimi jumped in front of us. "So is that it?"

"Milora Michelle," I said sharply. "Rephrase that in a more polite manner."

"Sorry." She peered up at her father. "Is there more for us to see?"

"There's one more area. We have to go back to the living room to get to it."

"You lead the way this time," Mimi said, snagging his hand.

In the foyer, we continued straight instead of hanging a

left. This hallway was all storage, with sliding doors keeping everything hidden but accessible. Jax did pause and slide one door open. "Laundry area."

The space wasn't huge, but I'd never understood devoting a large chunk of living space to a task most people dreaded. This room had the most efficient design of any of the rooms, and my inner organizational geek rejoiced. "No doing laundry in the basement for you," I said teasingly.

We reached a single, oversized French door. As soon as Jax opened it and we stepped outside, cold air assaulted us. Huddling together, looking across the expanse, I was stunned for what felt like the hundredth time today. What was once indoor space had become outdoor space. It was more than a rooftop garden; it was a rooftop backyard.

"Obviously this part will have to wait until spring, but I wanted us to have an outdoor space just like if we lived in a house. I'll have to put in safety precautions because we are fourteen stories up. If there's anything special you'd like to have up here, Meems, we'll have time to work it into the landscaping."

"Are you gonna put like . . . trees up here?" she asked.

"I'd like to. And there will be some grass as well as an area for me to grow herbs."

Herbs. I tried to wrap my head around the idea of Jaxson "Stonewall" Lund snipping mint and marjoram that he'd grown himself. On the penthouse level.

I just couldn't.

"Brrr. I'm going in." Mimi took off down the hallway.

We followed her.

"You think I'm crazy, don't you?" Jax asked.

"Because you'll have a super classy, super cool apartment? Nope. I'm curious, though, on your home gym. Did we miss that on the tour?"

"There's no home gym."

"Seriously?"

"Home gyms are lonely, and I spend enough time alone. I'll keep working out at Snow Village, or with Nolan, or at Brady's place."

I nudged him with my shoulder. "I thought maybe the building owner was adding a gym for the tenants."

"Between the bars and this apartment, I've got enough building renovations to deal with. Every project has had added delays this week."

"I did think your interior would be closer to done. You don't have any flooring in here."

He groaned. "Don't remind me. I'm supposed to pick wall colors. I'm about to say screw it and go with white."

"Don't do that. It'll end up looking sterile. You need to bring warmer tones in. What's your flooring in this part of the layout?"

"Hardwood. Tile in the kitchen."

Then he gazed at me with such puppy dog eyes I laughed. "What?"

"Help me? Please? I have no idea what I'm doing, which is why I haven't done anything."

"Do you have samples of the flooring and paint swatches?"

He walked to the kitchen and returned with a cardboard box. "All right here."

"Excellent. Now I can help you finish your home-work while I make sure Mimi finishes hers."

"Lucy—"

"Is it time to eat yet?" Mimi asked as she skipped into the kitchen. "'Cause I'm starved."

"By all means, let's get you fed before you blow away like a leaf on the wind."

She giggled and hugged me.

Hearing her giggles still filled me with joy. She'd never

been an easy child, and that's what made these moments so important.

I glanced up at Jax. The blatant need to be a part of this haunted his face, burned in his eyes, screamed from his body language as he literally leaned closer. I gave Mimi a kiss on the head and nudged her toward her father.

After I dropped Mimi off at school the next morning, I considered playing hooky from work. The last Thursday of the month had been deemed "Thirsty Thursday" by my coworkers, and we headed out after work for cocktails and conversation.

Normally I loved hanging with my peeps. With so many bar and restaurant options in the Twin Cities, we chose a different venue every month. Tonight's winner was Icehouse, a place I'd dropped in the hat as a suggestion.

I should have been looking forward to getting my drink on since Jax had Mimi for the night. But I couldn't help but worry that a couple of beers might loosen my tongue and I'd ask my girls for advice on the Jax situation, because it was getting harder to ignore that pull between us.

But Jax wasn't just my ex. He was a Lund, and I had to tread carefully on what I shared. I'd never been the type of girl who confessed all, but there were times when I wanted someone to listen and assure me that I wasn't: a) neurotic b) crazy c) an idiot d) all three.

While Lindsey had been great the past couple of years after she'd returned to the Cities, sometimes I sensed impatience that she was the only person in my life that I could be brutally honest with.

My mood must've been apparent, because three of my coworkers asked me if I was all right.

Then just before lunch, Annika—aka the big boss—called me into her office.

I didn't think anything of it, since I had meetings with her whenever we started a new campaign. But our next big PR push wasn't for a few weeks. I'd been waiting for text from the Ad department and had brought up the issue with Lennox, my direct boss, so she could light a fire under their asses and my ass was covered.

After we'd settled in the lounge area of her office, Annika said, "You're distracted today."

How had she picked up on that so fast? "A little. But it'll pass."

She didn't look convinced.

Since she was fishing, I said nothing, just took a sip of my soda.

"No bullshit. What's going on with you and Jax?"

I choked on my Diet Pepsi.

"Aha! I knew it. A spit-take is a dead giveaway. Start talking."

"Is that an official request from the head of PR to a junior-level graphic artist?" I said with an edge to my tone.

That gave her pause. "No, Lucy, it's a request from one family member to another."

"Please don't take this the wrong way, Annika, but I'm not part of your family. Obviously Mimi is, but up until Jax moved back here six months ago, my contact with the other branches of the Lund family outside of work has been limited."

"You're saying I'm your boss, not your friend?"

I looked her in the eye and said, "Yes."

Her crafty smile . . . I'd seen that same type on Jax's face many times in the past month, and I braced myself.

"Fair enough. But just for a moment, let's pretend that our connection is more than merely employer and employee. Let's pretend that I didn't spend an hour on the phone with my cousin Jaxson, listening to him outline a possible freelance PR project. And I'll pretend that he didn't mention your name, oh, at least fifty times during that conversation."

"I'm not surprised he finally called you. I told Jax that you were the go-to person on his PR needs for the relaunches of both bars. I specifically told him that I wasn't qualified—"

"Hold up. I'm serious, Lucy, this is not about LI or freelance work. I asked what was going on because Jax mentioned the two of you being at Mimi's hockey practice, then about your family dinner last night as well as the excellent eye you had for color and how you'd helped him pick wall colors for his new apartment—an apartment that I just found out is in your building, a building he now owns. Add to that, I saw how you two were at brunch on Sunday and the football game the week before that, so convince me this is merely Mimi's parents learning to get along for her sake."

Rather than playing it off as if she had misinterpreted everything, I blurted out, "I don't know what the hell is going on between me and Jax, okay?"

"Finally the truth."

"For as much good as it will do you," I muttered.

Annika leaned forward. "I recognize that look. The one that says you need to talk but you have no one to talk to."

I must've appeared taken aback by her dead-on assessment, because she laughed.

"I've been there. Actually I was in that situation for six months with Axl, when we were together but had to keep it under wraps." Unconsciously her fingers sought the necklace with the diamond-encrusted letter *A* that hung above her cleavage. "Although my issue wasn't questioning how I felt about him. I knew I loved him. I think you're in that questioning-your-feelings stage, aren't you?"

"Yes. It doesn't get any clearer even when I can break

everything down, piece by piece: my fears, my hopes, my happiness."

"Happiness?"

"Happiness that the Jax I knew before and fell for has reemerged. Only he's better, which is both awesome and it sucks because it immediately kicks in my doubts that he could've changed that much, become that much better of a man. So one moment I'm good with how I feel and the next I'm like . . . inconsistent much?"

Annika didn't say anything.

"Jax's subtle ways of letting me know he wants more have gotten less subtle. He hasn't given me more than a peck on the mouth, but the ways he's reminded me of the intimacy we used to have, and could have again, have been more effective and powerful than if he would've stripped me bare and fucked me senseless." The instant that left my mouth I wished I could take it back . . . because hello? I was blabbing about my sex life to my boss.

Former sex life, my libido piped up snarkily.

"Sorry, Annika, that was—"

"Honest and a relief to admit, I imagine."

I nodded.

"Don't apologize. Right now, regardless of your mistaken assumption, I *am* your friend, not your boss. And nothing you tell me will ever leave this room."

I did trust her, which was odd given the fact Jax was her cousin and the Lunds circled their own.

"You had a family dinner last night," she prompted.

"Yes. Meals aren't something we usually share as a family. I made a pork and noodle dish. Comfort food, you know? Because Jax was super tense during Mimi's first hockey practice and he'd had a bunch of setbacks with his projects. We finally toured his apartment, which is pretty spectacular, by the way. When we came down to eat, I cracked open a beer without thinking. I mean, I didn't offer him one, but I had to ask if it bothered him that I was drinking."

"What did he say?"

"That it would only bug him if I planned on kissing him later."

Annika laughed.

"Annika, it's not funny! I got so stupidly flustered, like a teenage girl faced with making out with her crush for the first time."

"How did Jax react to you being flustered?"

"Cocky. But before that . . ." I twisted my bracelet around my wrist, unsure if I should bring up Jax's confession of abstinence.

"Lucy?"

I looked up at her.

"I won't push you to talk if you're uncomfortable. But nothing you tell me could make me any more uncomfortable than that first day you interviewed here and I learned some hard truths about Jax and his dishonesty in his dealings with you and Mimi. I hated that he'd manipulated his entire family. I couldn't let it go; it pissed me off to no appreciable end. So I grilled Nolan, and he admitted he'd confronted Jax about his behavior during that time and they'd had a falling-out that lasted a year." She threw her hands up. "A freaking year that two Lund brothers weren't speaking to each other and none of the rest of us noticed. That fried my circuits, big-time."

That shocked the crap out of me. I hadn't known that Nolan had actually called his hockey hero brother out on his booze-and-broads problems. "When did you have this talk with Nolan?"

"Right after I'd hired you. Then Nolan dropped the bomb that Jax had recently gone through rehab."

My jaw dropped. "You knew?"

"That was the first time I'd heard that Jax had a drinking

problem." She sent me a sad smile. "I wanted to tell you, because I thought you of all people needed to be aware of it, but it wasn't my issue to disclose. However, I strongly suggested Nolan push Jax to talk to you about it ASAP, since it might impact your custody agreement, not to mention it might change the way you and Jax interacted."

I cocked an eyebrow at her. "Is this your way of proving to me that you're trustworthy?"

She shrugged. "Just relaying the facts."

"Part of the reason I got so flustered by Jax's kiss comment last night was because earlier he'd told me that he hasn't been with a woman since he went through treatment."

Annika's eyes widened. "You're kidding."

"No. That's what he told me."

"Do you believe him?"

His expression of embarrassment popped into my head. "Yes, I actually do. That's why I'm in this state. The attraction between us is still there. If we slept together . . . would it be because I'm a safe choice for him to reclaim his sexuality? And would I jump on board with the smexing because I need to prove to myself that I'm enough that he won't stray this time?"

She remained quiet and contemplative for several long moments. Then she sighed. "I hope talking about this has helped you, Lucy, because I have no advice to give you. None. Jesus. I'm sorry. And you haven't even mentioned how it might affect Mimi if you guys got back together and then broke up again."

"Exactly. So that's why I'm a little distracted today." I managed a smile. "But it'll pass. I promise. And believe it or not, before you called me in here, I was trying like hell not to think about it."

"Sorry. I'm a fixer."

"And a meddler," I retorted.

"I blame my mother for that trait." Annika gave me

another considering look. "Aunt Edie didn't live up to her reputation as a human bulldozer when it came to Mimi?"

I shook my head. "She's been wonderful since the day Mimi was born. In fact, she saw Mimi before Jax did. Edie knew what was up with her son, but she's his mother. She had no choice but to support him. The only time I kept Mimi away from her grandparents and her uncle was after Jax threatened to sue for custody. I refused to allow Mimi contact with any member of the Lund family until that was resolved in my favor." I'd been so scared they'd just take her and I'd never see her again because the Lund family did have that kind of money and power.

Annika sighed. "Like I've told you before, no one in our family knew what was going on during that time. Now I suspect it was because Edie and Archer were mortified by Jax's behavior and they hoped he'd straighten up before anyone realized what a drunken, belligerent asshole their son had become."

"You're probably right."

"Anyway, you're distracted—with good reason—so I'm enforcing a mental health day on you."

"Annika—"

"Huh-uh. This is the part where I'm your boss and this is an order. March yourself down to HR and Soon-Yi will give you a certificate for a massage. Then get a mani-pedi and go home and take an uninterrupted nap. Jax mentioned he had Mimi overnight because of your girls' night." She winked. "And you're welcome for me saving you from Thirsty Thursday by sending you home. I know when I'm dealing with major decisions, I'd rather be alone with my thoughts than in a crowd."

"Thank you, Annika. For everything today. I feel a little more settled after your impromptu therapy session."

"Anytime." She leaned over and squeezed my hand. "I mean that. Whenever and wherever you need to talk, I'm there for you."

"Same goes."

"Remember you said that when my man is gone and I wanna get my drink on to forget he's on the road."

The day I'd dreaded turned out to be blissful.

After a massage, a facial, a mani-pedi, a deep-conditioning treatment for my hair and a decadent late lunch complete with dessert, I returned home. While I missed Mimi, the silence in the apartment was a welcome change. I napped, fully naked, something I couldn't do with Mimi around, and when I woke up, I cracked a small bottle of prosecco I'd been saving.

Lounging on my couch in my robe, sipping bubbly, listening to random tunes on Pandora . . . I couldn't remember the last time I'd been so relaxed.

My cell phone buzzed on the coffee table. I leaned over to see a text message from Jax.

> JL: Hey Lucy Q. I know you're out whooping it up tonight, but could you bring Mimi's equipment bag to hockey practice tomorrow afternoon? We forgot it ☹

> ME: NP. But I didn't go out, I'm home.

> JL: Are you OK?

> ME: I just needed a mental health day.

> JL: Because of work? Or Mimi? Or . . . me?

I snorted, seeing he'd listed himself as the last possible source of my emotional rollercoaster.

ME: Definitely you ☺ I have lots of things to think
about.

JL: What can I do? Do you need me 2 bring you food?

It wasn't like I could ask him to swing by the liquor store
for more prosecco.

ME: I'm fine. Listening to tunes, having a cocktail.
Hey, you know what song just came on? Lose My
Breath by Destiny's Child. Remember when we
danced to it?

JL: Like I could EVER 4-get that nite.

I squinted at my phone, looking for the innocent blinky
eyes emoji. Aw, screw it. I sent the text without the emoji.

ME: You can't forget because I asked if you were a stripper?

His response was slower. The ". . ." flashed at me for
several long moments.

I topped off my glass and set my phone aside, picking up
the trashy entertainment magazine that was my guilty pleasure. Then my phone buzzed. Twice.

Don't look. Just keep flipping pages.

But I was curious, so I checked the message.

JL: Because that's when I knew you were the only one
for me ♥

JL: Then and now.

"Oh please." I snorted and then texted him a GIF of some TV actress snorting. Because I found it funny, I sent him a different one. And then another one.

And that's when my phone rang.

Shit.

I answered it with, "Aren't you supposed to be watching our daughter and not spending all your time screwing around on your phone?"

"I am watching her. She's in the kitchen finishing the dishes."

"Wait. Mimi is doing the dishes?"

"Yes." He paused. "Don't you have her load the dishwasher after supper?"

It was less hassle just to do it myself. But I wasn't going to admit that to him. "Why did you call?"

"Seriously, Luce? After you sent me the GIF with the woman laughing like a donkey?"

I snickered. "I love that one."

"I figured you did since you sent it to me five times."

"I did not! I sent it once. Maybe twice."

"Scroll back through the message thread if you don't believe me." Another pause. "Are you okay?"

"Perfectly fine."

"You sound . . . off."

"Yeah? Well you sound annoying."

He laughed.

Jerk. With the sexy jerk laugh.

"Mimi and I were about to go out for ice cream. Want us to bring you some?"

Yes. The bubbly had kicked in my sugar craving, but I answered, "Nope. I'm good."

"You sure? I remember how much you loved MooLattés from DQ, Lucy Q."

I closed my eyes. When he'd been around early in my

pregnancy, he'd been so sweet and eager to feed my cravings. Whether for food or sex. Sometimes both as he'd licked whipped cream off my—

"That's it. There's something going on with you that you're not telling me, so we're coming over." Then he hung up.

"You don't just get to barge in anytime you feel like it, sport," I said out loud, so at least I felt like I'd gotten the last word in.

Mature, Luce, real mature.

My phone buzzed with a text. I had to scroll through five GIFs to see what he'd said.

JL: Mocha or vanilla?

ME: You don't have to

His demand of MOCHA OR VANILLA? popped up again before I finished typing my first response.

ME: CHOCOLATE JERKFACE

I pictured him laughing because my contrariness amused him.

JL: Is chocolate jerkface a new flavor? If they don't have it is just plain chocolate OK?

I had no problem finding the middle finger emoji.

JL: ☺ C U in 30

was still in my robe when they showed up twenty minutes later.

At least I'd managed to toss the empty prosecco bottle in

the garbage so it didn't look like I'd been lounging around having a liquid supper even though I totally was.

Mimi bounded over and hugged me. "Daddy said it wouldn't be fair to have ice cream without you."

"Did he now?" I said, smoothing her hair down.

"Uh-huh. And I sorta forgot my hockey bag."

I gave her a smacking kiss on the forehead. "Lucky thing Daddy didn't have anything better to do than to go for an ice cream run and bring you over here to fetch it." I still hadn't looked at Jax, but I felt his burning gaze on me.

"Are you mad, Mommy?"

"Not at all. I'm always happy to see you, sweetheart."

She grinned. "You're still coming to my hockey practice tomorrow? Even though you don't have to bring my bag?"

Then it clicked. My eyes narrowed. "Milora Michelle. Did you forget your bag on purpose so I'd have to show up at the ice rink?"

"Uh . . . maybe. But I really, really want you there, and I don't want Daddy sitting alone."

I saw no machinations on her earnest face. She just didn't want to leave me out—or maybe she didn't want me to opt out. "You sweet, sweet girl," I murmured. "Of course I'll be there."

"Yay! Can I eat my ice cream in my room?"

"Sure," Jax answered. "Take your time. Your mom and I have to talk anyway."

Mimi's gaze moved from her dad to me and back to her dad. "You're not gonna fight again?"

"Nope. We're past that, aren't we, little mama?"

"Absolutely, big daddy," I cooed back.

As soon as she was out of earshot, Jax crossed the room and loomed over me.

I blinked up at him.

But his focus wasn't on my face; he'd glued his gaze to the

gap in my robe. A gap that left no question about what I had on under the fluffy terry cloth.

Not a damn thing.

"Where's my ice cream?"

That caused him to shift back.

"Right over there. I'll go get it."

As soon as his back was to me, I scrambled off the couch and rounded the corner into the kitchen, where I oh-so-nonchalantly leaned against the counter, waiting for him.

Jax handed me the plastic cup with a muttered, "Here," but he didn't give me the space I expected.

"Thanks."

"What's going on with you?"

I plucked the cherry off the top and ate it. Then I dug my spoon in for the first taste of ice cream. "Nothing is going on."

"Then why did you need a mental health day?"

"Why did you choose today to disclose every moment we've spent together to Annika? Yes, she's your cousin, but she's also my boss. So I had to field questions about what's going on between us."

"What did you tell her?"

I scooped more chocolatey goodness onto my spoon and slipped it into my mouth. After I swallowed I said, "Damn, this tastes so much better than I remember."

"Lucy. Stop hedging."

"Jaxson. Stop badgering. I'm trying to enjoy the ice cream that you insisted on bringing me." Hah. He couldn't argue with that.

But the man reached over, plucked the cup out of my hand and held it out of my reach.

"Hey!"

"When you answer my question to my satisfaction, I'll give you a bite."

"And if I don't answer to your satisfaction?"

"Then I get a bite." Smirking, he brought the ice cream–filled spoon to his mouth and ate it. "That was a penalty shot. Now . . . mental health day?" he prompted.

"The truth? You confuse the hell out of me. Annika noticed my distraction and demanded details. But since I don't know what's going on between us, how can I explain it to someone else?"

He held the spoon in front of my mouth.

After I sucked it clean, he didn't shoot off another question. Hmm. Seemed Mr. Nosy was having difficulty concentrating.

Then he snapped out of it. "You aren't happy that things are undefined between us?"

"They're defined; you're Mimi's dad and I'm her mom."

"Try again." Jax overfilled the spoon with ice cream and a good swipe of whipped cream before he popped it in his mouth.

I made a frustrated noise. "I hate when you push me. Hate it."

"I hate when you throw up a wall."

Had we made any progress in changing our communication style or were we back to square one?

"You told me something you hate about me. Now tell me something you love—and I mean love, not like." He held the spoon to my lips again. "Have a taste while you're narrowing down the list—I know it's hella long."

I laughed. "That, right there, is something I've always loved about you. You have a quick sense of humor." I eased forward to take the ice cream. "Your turn. Tell me something you love about me."

He said, "Your legs," without hesitation.

"It can't be a physical attribute."

"Naming your tits isn't an acceptable answer either?"

"Ya think?"

Jax helped himself to a bite of ice cream. Then he set the cup aside and caged me against the counter.

My heart rate shot up a hundred beats, and I craned my neck to look up at him.

"Everything." He kept those beautifully troubled eyes on mine as his hand curled around the side of my face. "I've always loved everything about you, Lucy. As far as what's going on between us besides parenting as partners? Maybe this will clear things up for you." His mouth crashed down on mine.

Then I was kissing Jax like I hadn't kissed him in a decade.

Nine years, my subconscious reminded me.

Whatever.

But as passion exploded between us, it felt like we'd never been apart.

Kissing Jaxson Lund wasn't something I could ever forget. He poured every ounce of his lust into me, fueling mine, reminding me of how it'd been between us.

Spontaneous.

Hot.

Desperate.

Fast and hard and hungry and dirty.

So very dirty and slightly obscene the way this man kissed me.

Every.

Single.

Time.

And time stopped for me. My head spun with each swirl of his tongue. My lips throbbed where he sucked on them. Nipped at them. Licked them in a long, sensuous stroke of his wicked tongue.

Jax felt my blood pounding as he slightly pushed his thumb into my carotid artery, as if he needed to gauge that my response to this—to him—was as powerful and all-consuming as before.

It was.

It *so* was.

When I shifted closer to him, that's when his rumble of satisfaction vibrated through me.

He slid his hand down my throat, pressing his open palm on my chest before he slipped his fingers beneath my robe.

Jax never eased up on the kiss as he sought my skin with both hands. And where I expected his passionate greed, he gifted me with soft caresses bordering on devotion.

I spun further and further into the black hole of desire as Jax annihilated my walls with each sucking kiss, every insistent sweep of his tongue against mine.

I clawed at his shirt, needing something to anchor me as that need dug into my very existence. Having this physical connection was a frightening thing. Once I'd had it, I craved it. Which made it so much harder when it was ripped away.

No wonder I'd opted to build a wall around this part of me.

No surprise that Jax was the only man with the determination to knock it down.

Jax's lips left mine so he could drag an openmouthed kiss from the base of my jaw to the hollow of my throat, and then slowly, slowly, slowly back up.

As he breathed heavily in my ear, chills skittered across my skin.

When he finally spoke, it wasn't what I expected.

"Luce, I'm about five seconds from coming in my jeans, so I have to stop."

I smiled and stroked his hair. "Okay."

He nuzzled my throat and pulled me completely against his body.

That's when I realized he was actually shaking. "Jax?"

"Fuck. Just give me a minute." His hold on me tightened,

and he'd buried his face so deeply in my neck I had no idea how he could breathe.

I hoped he got himself under control before Mimi burst in, as she was prone to do. I didn't know how we'd explain it.

He released me and took a step back. He righted my robe—wearing his usual cocky smirk—and smoothed my hair back, before tilting my head to meet his gaze. "That's what's going on between us."

When I started to speak, he shook his head.

"Please listen first. I want a chance with you. Maybe this is a surprise, maybe it's not. But don't discount how serious I am. Yes, it's complicated as fuck-all, but there's one way we can simplify everything."

"How?"

"Tell me that this isn't one sided and everything we've talked about has allowed you to believe that I've changed."

"I know you have. That's why I didn't shove you away when you shoved your tongue down my throat."

He smiled and pecked me on the lips. "You loved it."

"Your take-charge side has always been impossible for me to resist, sport."

His eyes searched mine. "You want this, right?"

My heart hesitated, but my mouth didn't. "Yes. But I want to take it slow. Like baby steps slow."

"I can do that."

"And if it's not working out, and we call it off, we act like adults."

"You already act as if this is going to fail. Like it's just us killing time with each other until someone better comes along."

Jax had it all wrong, but the hurt in his eyes caused me to switch gears. "Fine. But both Channing Tatum and Josh Duhamel are single now, and if I run into them—"

His mouth was on mine again, owning mine again, every

muscled inch of him plastered against me, his hands in my hair as he proved he knew exactly how to turn me on.

When Jax finally broke the kiss, he murmured, "Think about that if you ever 'run into' one of them."

"Who?"

"Exactly."

"Ah, yeah. Sure. No problem."

Scrambled brain, please come back online.

When he started kissing my neck, I pushed him back. "You're the one who said we had to stop. So keep those lips to yourself, buddy."

He laughed softly. "Good point."

"But I am serious about us letting this unfold organically."

"Organically," he repeated.

"We won't make a point to tell Mimi we're together; we'll just spend more time as a family. That'll ease her into it. We need to keep the schedule of her splitting time between us."

"Agreed."

"Organic also means no big announcements at a Lund gathering that you and I are moving forward."

"Who am I allowed to tell?" he said tightly.

"Anyone who specifically asks." I poked him in the ribs. "Don't pout. I'm not denying that we're in a relationship; I'm just not broadcasting it."

An odd look crossed his face.

"What?"

"You won't get all prissy if I want to put my arm around you? Or if I hold your hand in public?" His gaze dropped to my lips. "Or if I kiss the hell out of you?"

"I'm never prissy." Okay. That *had* sounded prissy.

"I meant prickly. Shrugging me off. Scooting away."

"Not unless you stick your hand down my pants."

"Hey, I did that one time." He grinned. "I much preferred slipping my hand up your skirt."

"Every chance you could get. Not that I discouraged your amorous attentions, but we will have to act with more decorum with Mimi around."

Speaking of . . . Mimi strolled into the kitchen.

"Got my stuff and I'm ready to go." She wormed her way between us to give me a hug. "See you tomorrow, Mommy."

I kissed the top of her head. "Sweet dreams, sweetheart. I love you."

"Love you too."

After she was out of sight, Jax kissed me with the sweetness I needed.

"Eat your ice cream before it melts."

Then he was gone.

Fourteen

JAX

I'd had enough of playing the "hurry up and wait" game in every aspect of my life.

It'd been three weeks since Walker had obtained the first round of permits for the bar remodel. I'd seen four construction workers on-site during that time and none of them had been swinging a sledgehammer.

Whenever I'd tried to get answers, all I heard were crickets.

My apartment finally had paint on the walls. At this point I didn't give a damn if I had to sit on beanbag chairs in the living room. I just wanted to be in my own space. I intended to hold that construction company to their "move in next week" promise.

Lucy and I were taking such tiny baby steps in this relationship that we'd come to a complete halt. We hadn't spent family time with Mimi—or not as much as I thought we

would. Lucy and I hadn't been alone for more than five minutes since that discussion in the kitchen.

I understood she'd gotten swamped at work, which meant
I'd had Mimi at my place four days out of the workweek instead of only on the weekend, but there weren't texts between
us or even phone calls. Definitely wasn't any type of physical
contact—even a damn hug would've been welcomed. And
since I'd agreed to her pace, I couldn't do fuck-all about it.

Then the other kick in the ass was the situation at Lakeside and Mimi's hockey practices. No changes—except for
now Mimi had a game once a week, a game none of them
were prepared to play in with their lack of basic skills.

After spending the morning with Dallas and Simone regarding the bars' reinvention, I was both excited to move
forward with their plans and pissed off that we couldn't move
forward.

So Betsy, the office manager at Flint and Lund, was shocked
to see me in person shortly before noon on Friday, especially
when I sped past her and stormed straight into my cousin's office, only to find Walker facedown on his desk, apparently taking a little snooze.

"Is this why my project is at a standstill? Because you're
literally asleep on the fucking job?"

Walker lifted his head, his eyes wild with the look of someone who'd been abruptly woken up and had no idea where he
was.

"Jax? What the hell are you doing here?"

"Interrupting nap time," I said with a sneer.

Betsy slipped in behind me. "Sorry, Walker, he blew past
me before—"

"It's fine, Bets." Walker cracked a yawn and stretched.
"Have Jase meet us in the conference room in five."

"Will do." She shut the door behind her.

Walker gestured to the chair across from his desk. "Have a seat."

"I'll stand. I don't plan on being here long."

His blond eyebrow winged up. "Because?"

"Because I owe you the courtesy of doing this in person."

His eyes narrowed.

"Today I'm asking the city building permit division to reissue the permits Flint and Lund have obtained for my property to my real estate corporation, Stonewall Enterprises, so I can move forward with construction with another company."

He pushed to his feet and slapped his hands on the desk. "Now wait just a goddamned minute. I—"

"I'm done waiting. While I appreciate your intention to take this project on with such short notice, it's become apparent in the past six weeks that Flint and Lund has priorities other than this project."

"You're firing us?"

"Yes." I set my hand on the door handle. "I checked to make sure that accounts payable had sent payments for all invoices. The last one was dated three weeks ago. Since new work hasn't been done since then, there shouldn't be outstanding invoices. But if there are, send them to my attention. See you."

"Jax. Wait. Can we at least talk about it?"

"We could've talked about it anytime in the past three weeks, but anytime I called you? All I got was the runaround."

"If I thought you were—"

"Serious about this project *you* would've taken it seriously?" I said tightly.

The embarrassed look on his face said it all.

Fuck. This is what I'd been worried about. I'd even mentioned my concerns to Nolan, but he told me I was paranoid and impatient. But the truth was right there.

I could've let it go.

I should've let it go.

But . . . I didn't let it go.

"Let me guess. Because I walked away from a position at LI, you thought remodeling the bar was a cover that I used as an excuse to do nothing but fuck around in my retirement? Or maybe because I've owned the bar for a few years and hadn't done anything with it, you figured there was no rush on getting this project underway?" I paused, forcing myself to keep my gaze locked on his. "Or this is the most fun option . . . you decided I wouldn't stick with it, like I hadn't stuck with Lucy or being Mimi's father. Since you're also aware I put Dallas in charge of reinventing the spaces, there's a double whammy of irresponsibility—the oldest, alcoholic Lund and the youngest, flightiest Lund, who've both declined to work in the family business, will get bored, or we'll find out there's too much work involved, and we'll just flit on to the next thing that catches our fancy."

Walker said nothing.

"That's what I thought. In hindsight, I'm glad that I didn't ask your company to work on my apartment remodel. God knows what excuses you would've given me for that." I opened the door. "What sucks for me is I suspected this lack of interest was personal, based on the kind of guy I used to be. I can't honestly blame you for your hesitation in agreeing to get your company involved, Walker. But it sure would've been easier for all of us if you would've just lied and said Flint and Lund was too busy to take on any new projects."

"Jax—"

"Don't worry. That's what I'll tell anyone in the family who asks why you're no longer associated with the remodel. At least that'll allow me to keep some dignity in this situation."

I walked out.

Sweet baby Jesus I needed a fucking drink after that.

I craved the numbness like I hadn't craved it in a while. And it seemed I passed by every goddamned liquor store in the Twin Cities on my way to the city administration building.

As I sat in my car, I did ten rounds of breathing exercises, but they didn't help calm me, or block out that little voice that kept urging me that one drink wouldn't hurt.

That one voice was so loud that I needed twenty, or thirty, or fifty voices to drown it out.

I looked up the closest place for an AA meeting and headed there as fast as my wheels would take me.

The AA meeting reset my brain and my attitude so I could move on with my day.

With the reissued permits in hand, I met with the new construction company. A sizable check guaranteed they'd start the project first thing Monday morning. Money talks . . . so does the Lund name, and I had no problem using both to get this project back on track.

Neither Simone nor Dallas was fazed by the rapid change in the situation. They assured me they'd deal with all the issues that went with closing down a business—laying off the employees, moving the existing bar supplies into storage, breaking the news to the regular customers. That allowed me to deal with the next item on my list for today—taking Mimi to a drop-in hockey game at another ice arena.

Nolan appeared while Mimi and I ate an early supper—the man had an uncanny ability to show up during mealtimes.

I knew why he'd shown up. He and Walker had always been tight. So Walker had called him to admit how much he'd screwed up with me. But Nolan's opinion wouldn't change the outcome; I'd already reassigned the project.

My brother helped himself to a plate of shredded pork tamales—the meat wrapped in cabbage leaves instead of corn tortillas, making it healthier—a couple of slices of fried parsnips, an alternative to the usual fried plantains, and a sweet broccoli and green pepper chopped salad.

He and Mimi chatted before he addressed me. "Sounds like you had an interesting day, bro."

"It was a productive day for a change." I sipped my water. "It's unusual to see you on a Friday night. No little fishes on the hookup for this weekend?"

"I'm taking a page from your 'I can change' book and staying away from my usual haunts."

"Like ghost haunts?" Mimi asked. "Because Dallas said she's gonna take me on a ghost tour."

Nolan's sharp look wasn't unexpected.

"Mimi knows about Dallas's plans because I told her; she didn't hear it from Dallas at the bar."

"Good to know." After a few moments, Nolan said, "What are the two of you up to tonight?"

"I'm taking Meems to another ice arena for a drop-in hockey game. For comparison to the way things are being run at Lakeside."

"Is that allowed?"

I shrugged. "My understanding is she can play with a girls' team and on a mixed team until she reaches the ten-year-old bracket. I want her to explore all of her options." I smiled at her. "And this is something you want to try, isn't it, squirt?"

"Yep. Are you coming to watch me play hockey, Uncle Nolan?"

He smiled at her. "I'd love to come, short stuff. Thanks for inviting me."

I scowled at him. I'd been looking forward to brooding by myself.

"Daddy, did you tell Mommy about the drop-in game?"

Shit. "Ah, no, sweetheart. I forgot. You can tell her about it tomorrow."

Mimi shook her head. "She said she didn't wanna miss a single game. You *have* to tell her."

Great. This night was turning into a freaking party. "I'll text her once we know that there's a spot for you to play, okay?"

"Okay."

I glanced at the empty plates and then the clock. "You've got time to load the dishwasher before we go."

Nolan waited until Mimi was in the kitchen before he said, "What the hell, Jax? More hockey? Are you sure this is what Mimi wants, not what you want?"

"First of all, piss off. Secondly, I won't know how other places run their games and what their coaching staff expects from her age group if I don't expose her to other opportunities. And since you've butted into my business again, you're in charge of getting her signed in tonight. That way she won't get special treatment if I'm recognized."

"Whatever. Now I wish I would've stopped at home after work, because these definitely aren't hockey game clothes."

He wore one of his fancy suits with the mismatched patterns that looked ridiculous to me, but I'd always been a conservative dresser. "I'd offer to lend you some clothes . . ." But none of mine would fit him.

"Thoughtful of you to offer, asshole. But then again, you're all about spreading the family love today, aren't you?"

I flipped him off.

H aving Nolan check Mimi in to the drop-in game worked well.

We sat close to the players' bench, and I wondered if I'd ever feel more comfortable in the stands than on the ice.

As soon as Nolan took the seat next to mine, he asked, "You get in touch with Lucy yet?"

"Nope."

"Do you want me to text her?"

"I'd rather you didn't. I want to focus on this and not have to deal with another fucked-up situation in my life, okay?"

"Uh. Sure." He paused and got in my face. "Fuck that. It's not okay. What is going on between you two?"

"Nothing. Which is why I want one lousy hour for total concentration on the one goddamned thing in my life that I'm good at."

No surprise my little bro had nothing to say to that.

To compare apples to apples, Mimi was playing on an eight-and-under team comprised of girls and boys. The rink setup mirrored the setup at Lakeside for Mites games: half ice with inflatable bumpers on either side to keep the players contained. Unlike Lakeside games, neither team had a dedicated goalie; it was everyone's job to defend the net.

"Is it my family pride showing, or has that girl gotten way better at hockey?" Nolan asked me at the end of the second period.

Even when I'd thrust her into a new situation, she kept her focus on listening to her team's coach and implementing everything we'd worked on the past few weeks. "She is better. But you can clearly notice her improvement because these teams are playing hockey, not standing around deciding what to do with their sticks."

Just then Mimi got the puck and she had a moment's hesitation. I found myself doing the one thing I swore I wouldn't; I stood up and yelled, "Breakaway!"

Nolan muttered something about staying incognito, but my eyes were glued on Mimi as she skated to the opposite end.

I bit the inside of my cheek to stop from yelling additional instructions.

Come on, girlie, go for it.

She more or less pushed the puck into the net rather than hitting it in, but a goal was a goal.

Then her stick got caught in the net and she hit the ice.

Face-first.

She lay there and didn't get up.

My instincts overtook my common sense. I launched myself onto the ice, reaching her after the ref did, about the same time Mimi sat up. Crouching beside her, my guts formed a knot when I noticed she was bleeding. I tilted her head back and looked at her through the mask. "What happened?"

"I thot a goal!" she lisped.

Why was she lisping?

My focus dropped to her mouth. Sure enough. One of her teeth on her upper gumline was gone.

I was a fucking dead man.

But for now, I was trying to gauge if she had other injuries as I said, "I saw it, squirt. That breakaway was perfect."

"Wherth Mommy? Did sthe thee my firth goal ever? Did sthe video it?"

Lucy was gonna kill me twice for this.

"Mommy is not here yet."

"Mimi, are you okay to play?" a familiar voice asked above me.

I glanced up and saw the referee was none other than . . . Gabi.

The universe was having a glorious time screwing with me today.

"Are you as surprised to see me, Lund, as I am surprised to see both of you?"

A swish of skates sounded behind me. The other ref asked, "What's the holdup?"

"The player lost a tooth after colliding with the goal. Her dad is helping her off the ice."

"No!" Mimi said. "Don't make me go! I wanna play."

For fuck's sake. Seriously, universe?

"Maybe you should sit on the bench for a few moments," Gabi suggested. "Catch your breath. Get a drink and wipe the blood off your mouth."

Blood. Why wasn't my little girl screaming at the sight of blood?

"Therth not that muth blood," Mimi scoffed.

I heard a chuckle and saw that Nolan was taping us.

He wouldn't find it so funny if I slammed his smarmy ass into the boards.

"Here, Daddy."

Mimi held out her mouth guard. Inside the blood-dotted plastic mold was her baby tooth.

"Wanna thave it for the thooth fairy."

I gently dumped it in my hand and stood up.

Gabi tried to confront me. Although I had several inches and at least seventy-five pounds on her, I felt small enough that it seemed she towered over me.

"Unauthorized persons on the ice usually results in automatic forfeit. But I'll let it slide this one time due to an injury. But if you ever do anything like that again at any game where I'm officiating? I will throw you out of the rink. Understood?"

"Yes, ref."

After I exited the ice, I turned to say something to Mimi, but she'd already skated off to the bench.

It was probably wrong to feel proud that she got right back in the game.

The second thing out of Nolan's mouth after "Is Mimi all right?" was "Dude. You are so dead."

Tell me about it.

Rather than freaking Lucy out and getting her to drive over here when the game was almost over, I took the chickenshit route and texted her.

ME: Hey, are you around? Mimi wants to swing by for something.

LQ: I'm home all night. Is everything all right?

No, you're going to lose your shit when you realize that I broke at least two of the "hockey rules" we laid out . . . within the first month.

Instead of sending a text, I sent her a thumbs-up emoji, so technically that wasn't lying.

Next to me, Nolan clucked.

Asshole.

Mimi's team won with her one goal, and she was on cloud nine.

That's probably why it was taking her so long to emerge from the locker room.

It also gave Gabi the chance to skate over.

Awesome.

"Cheating on Lakeside already, Lund?"

I bristled. "I could ask the same."

"I can't ref at my home rink, and I'm required to ref, so I have no choice but to rotate to other rinks for games. What's your excuse?"

"And who are you?" Nolan inserted.

Gabi ignored him as she waited for my response.

"You know why Mimi needs to explore other options. Besides, it was just a drop-in game."

"Where she scored a goal. Now she won't want to play with her assigned team. It's only a matter of a few practices before she'll be begging you to move her to this rink, or one of the other rinks with a coach who isn't a clueless d-bag."

"I can't solve the problems at Lakeside."

"You haven't even tried. Geez, Lund, I thought you of all people would call that little sucker out. But you just sit in the stands, during games and practices, doing nothing. Nothing."

"Hey," Nolan said sharply, "I don't know who you are or what you think gives you the right to speak to him that way, but simmer down, sister."

Again, Gabi didn't even acknowledge my brother as her eyes were too focused on melting my resolve with her death-ray stare.

A whistle blew behind her and she turned and nodded before facing me again. "You've shown you can put up and shut up. It's past time for you to man up, Stonewall, and you know it." She turned and skated off.

"Who is that?"

I scrubbed my hands over my face. "Gabriella Welk, the assistant coach for Mimi's team at Lakeside."

"So? Who is she?"

"So, she's also *the* Gabi Welk, outstanding player for Fargo North High School and winner of back-to-back state hockey championships, who was offered full-ride scholarships to every major college in the country with a winning women's hockey program—including the University of Minnesota—all of which she declined and signed on with the University of North Dakota in hopes of bringing a women's Frozen Four championship to UND. She was a finalist for the Kazmaier Award. She also played for the U.S. Women's National Team for six years, and was part of the team that won two Four Nations Cups, in addition to winning three World Championships. She was a key player on the U.S. Olympic Women's Ice Hockey Team in the 2010 and 2014 Olympics, winning two silver medals. Then she was chosen as the first female assistant coach to the UND men's hockey team, but she resigned in protest last year when UND eliminated the women's hockey program. She moved to the Cities after her younger sister Dani transferred from UND to the U of M to play hockey, so Gabi could continue to coach her since Dani's playing on the U.S. Olympic Women's Ice Hockey Team in February representing the U.S. in Pyeong-Chang. Lakeside was the only place Gabi could get hired on such short notice that allowed her to keep a flexible schedule."

Nolan gaped at me. "How in the hell do you know all of that off the cuff?"

I sighed. "Margene. She likes me. She likes to gossip. She loves to brag on Gabi because according to her, Gabi is the one thing that Lakeside has going for it."

"Well, watch yourself with her."

"Why?"

He looked at me like I was an idiot. "Because Gabi's got a crush on you, Stonewall."

"Right. She basically told me I was an entitled prick the first time I met her. Only thing she wants to crush is my skull."

"Lucy had the same reaction to you, if I remember correctly."

Lucy. Jesus. I still had to deal with that tonight.

I stood. "I'll fetch Mimi. And you get to go to Lucy's place with me."

"Pass."

"Nope, you have to come."

"Why?"

"I'll need you to accompany my body to the morgue after Lucy kills me for Mimi's hockey injury."

Fifteen

LUCY

Once again Jax would catch me lounging in my robe, drinking.

But it'd been a stressful week and I deserved a drink to unwind.

Think that's how it started with him? One drink to relax turned into twenty and next thing you know . . . you're an alcoholic?

That caused me to reevaluate pouring a second vodka tonic.

How stressful had my week been anyway? Sure, I had plenty on my design plate. I had mock-ups to finish with Jonna, team leader for social media brand, and Annika had asked me to pull ad campaigns from a decade back just to make sure there weren't similarities to the upcoming project.

Now people sought me out for my opinion and I felt I'd earned my spot on the team on my own merits.

The only downside had been less time with Mimi. She

seemed to be adjusting well to spending more time with her father—and not just at the ice rink. I knew Jax expected more out of her when she stayed with him, even assigning her simple chores. But when she was with me, she didn't help out at all. In fact, she'd regressed a bit, acting bratty in the mornings before school. I'd decided to give it another week, and if she hadn't changed, then I'd bring it up with Jax.

Which brought me to thoughts of Jax, who proved that he could follow my request of tiny baby steps when it came to advancing our relationship. Maybe I hadn't believed that he'd follow through with it. I half expected he'd just bulldoze his way into my life like he always had before. My disappointment that he'd followed the rules for a change made no sense.

And I'd lacked courage to take that first step even when I'd been desperate for more physical contact after he'd had his hands on me. I'd relived the times he'd forced me to lie still as he mapped every inch of my body, first with his skillful hands and then with his even more skillful mouth. Even thinking about it now, desire unfurled in my core like a slow-blooming flower.

The door to my apartment opened. Before I moved off the couch, Jax came around the corner.

Alone.

His cheeks were flushed and he acted . . . nervous.

"Jax? Where's Mimi?"

"Now, don't freak out—"

I vaulted off the couch, demanding, "Where is she?"

Mimi stepped out from behind her dad and said, "I loth a thooth!"

Ignoring her grin, I dropped to my knees to take her face in my hands and saw the hole in her gumline next to one of her permanent front teeth. "What happened?"

"I thcored a goal! My very firth one ever in a hockey game!"

"But you didn't have practice or a game scheduled for tonight."

"Daddy took me to a different ithe rink! Whereths' drop-in gameth."

I pulled her upper lip back to inspect her gum for bruising.

"Ouchth!"

My stomach clenched at hearing her in pain. "It hurts?"

"Only when you pull like that. Thop!"

My hands fell away. "Where else did you get hurt?"

"Noplathe, and it didn't bleed hardly at all. Wathn't even blood on the ithe."

"Omigod, that's the takeaway from this? No blood on the ice?"

Stay calm.

I studied Mimi's sweet face. Her lip was swollen from the impact she'd taken. In that moment she looked so much like her father that I wanted to punch him in the mouth so they'd have matching swollen lips. This was his fault.

While Mimi chattered on about her goal and the game, I only half listened as my brain was otherwise engaged in where I could hide Jax's body once I finished with him.

I noticed a pause and found Mimi, Jax and Nolan—how long had he been here?—staring at me expectantly. I mustered up a fake smile for my daughter, and my stomach clenched at seeing that gap in her answering smile. Yes, she would've lost that tooth eventually, but the fact it had been forced out of her mouth made it worse.

Nolan's hands landed on Mimi's shoulders. "You know what, short stuff? Show me how to use the fancy security system your dad had installed in the elevator that goes up to the new apartment. Then you can give me the tour."

Mimi looked at me. "Can I thow him, Mommy?"

"Ask your father. It's his place, not mine."

Jax handed Nolan a set of keys. "Remember what we talked about, Meems. No going outside. Inside only." Then he exchanged a look with Nolan and walked them to the door.

I should've told him that he was free to give the tour because I was too pissed off at him to speak. Instead I walked to my sliding glass door and stared out, taking in the barren treetops illuminated by sodium streetlights.

My heart already pounded something fierce, but when I heard him move in behind me, my pulse tripped double time.

"On a scale of one to ten, how mad are you at me?"

"One hundred and ten thousand."

He didn't laugh, but he understood I wasn't trying to be funny.

Then he said, "I'm sorry."

I waited, expecting him to tack on that she hadn't really gotten hurt, but he didn't.

"You broke one of the first rules we established of keeping me in the loop about all decisions."

"I know. I'm sorry."

"Then you broke another one by not letting me know she'd sustained a hockey injury, and our agreement was I was to be told about all of them, regardless of how small you perceived them to be."

"I know that too, and I'm sorry about that too."

"When did it happen? First period? Second?" Then it hit me. "It happened right before that text you sent me, didn't it?"

"Yeah. At the beginning of the third period. In my defense, the game would've been over by the time you got there."

"In your defense, are you going to claim it was just a baby tooth?"

"Yes."

I whirled around and then Jax had my full attention when he wrapped his hands around my face.

"Luce. I'm sorry. I fucked up. I should've made sure you were there."

"Maybe it should be more important that your child's mother is in attendance, not your child's uncle."

"You're right."

"She got hurt playing hockey, Jax. In the first month."

"But she also scored a goal and she had a great time playing," he pointed out softly. "While I know you don't want to hear this, she is one tough little cookie, Luce. I tried to pull her out of the game and she refused. She insisted on finishing."

That brought tears to my eyes faster than seeing Mimi's holey gumline.

"Ah, shit, don't cry."

But I couldn't stop. I was mad and confused and relieved.

Jax didn't help matters by saying, "She's fine. I was on the ice with her immediately after it happened. And she even managed to slip me the tooth for safekeeping for the tooth fairy visit tonight."

"Is that supposed to make me feel better?"

"It should make you feel better that Mimi isn't upset about it."

His logic dictated that I could just kiss good-bye the hopeful thought that she wouldn't become obsessed with the sport.

"But this isn't about Mimi anymore, is it?"

How did he do that? Know when I transferred one emotion to the next issue, making it one jumbled mess. And I'd always considered myself the intuitive one in our relationship.

"Ask me if I've broken any other rules."

My jaw seemed hinged shut.

"Talk to me, Lucy Q. Come on. Yell at me if you need to."

I shook my head—or should I say I tried to, but he had my face firmly trapped—so I closed my eyes.

"Shutting me out? I thought we were past that. In fact, I could've sworn we agreed to start over three weeks ago with a new relationship. But things have remained the same old, same old between us. I had to remind myself that no, I hadn't been drinking and imagined kissing the hell out of you in the kitchen. I hadn't imagined the feel of your skin beneath my hands. I hadn't imagined the way you arched into me or that little hum you make when you get turned on . . . did I?"

I felt the tension vibrating from him as he awaited my response. "No."

He moved his body closer to mine. "If I didn't imagine it, then why haven't you let me touch you, or kiss you, or hell, really even let me talk to you for the better part of the past month? Have you changed your mind about us?"

"God no."

"Look at me." When I hesitated, he said, "Now."

I opened my eyes and he was right there, those baby blues mere inches from me.

Whatever he saw there had him softening his tone. "Tell me."

"I said I wanted to take it slow, figuring you'd agree but ultimately follow your own agenda because you've never taken anything slow, Jax. I went on a date with you half an hour after we met. We had sex on our fifth date. I met your family two weeks later, and two weeks after that you'd practically moved in with me until you left for training camp in Chicago. Throughout that season we were together, you insisted on buying me plane tickets so we could be together at least every other weekend. You've got no clue on how to take baby steps, because everything with us has been a giant leap."

"But you said slow, right?"

"Yes, but your definition of slow and mine are different once again."

Confusion flitted across his face. "You're saying I've followed your rules exactly and I've still managed to fuck this up?"

"Well, when you put it that way . . . it sounds a bit—"

"Like I can't win no matter whose rules I play by?"

I bristled. "It's not about winning, Jax."

"The hell it's not. But I'ma let you in on a little secret." He mock-whispered, "I'm playing for keeps."

He must've seen my silent surrender of "Me too," because a look of triumph flashed in his eyes.

Watching me, his fingertips slowly followed the curve of my neck down, skimming my collarbones until he could flatten his palms and slip them beneath the lapels of my robe.

His rough-skinned hands ignited little fires across every millimeter of my skin.

I fought a shiver, even as I started to burn.

Angling his head, he placed his mouth on the shell of my ear. "Fair warning: I'm not gonna play fair. I remember exactly how to make you hot and wet."

At that point, my brain overloaded and "Prove it" exited my mouth in a half dare/half demand.

"Gladly." His breath flowed faster. "If I put my mouth here"—he touched his lips to the artery in my neck and lightly sucked, causing me to gasp—"you make that sexy fucking sound."

He sucked harder and I gasped louder.

"That's it. Let me hear you."

I'd always been loud in bed, a quirk that drove Jax wild. Apparently that hadn't changed.

Nor had he forgotten where to touch me to make my knees wobbly. He dragged the ragged pads of his thumbs across my nipples as he breathed in my ear. Hot, rapid bursts of pure male need. Gauging how long I could take it until I broke and begged him for more.

"My Lucy Q," he murmured in that masculine rumble, so low pitched his words were nearly indecipherable. "Don't think. Don't talk. Just feel."

"But Mimi—"

"Left her apartment key on the floor next to her equipment bag," he said, smiling against my throat. "And I double-locked the door."

"Oh."

"Last point I'm gonna make," he whispered as he brushed his mouth up and down my neck and his fingers caressed my breasts. "My rules are in play now. So anytime, anyplace I want to kiss you . . . I will. Starting now." His hands went to the sash on my robe as his mouth sought mine.

Jax bestowed a soft exploring kiss on me. Not sweet, just thorough with a slow rise of heat that filled me from top to bottom. He maneuvered me back toward the couch, settling my butt on the puffy side arm.

He pushed the robe down until it bunched at my lower back, which trapped my hands.

I jumped at the first touch of his tongue flicking my right nipple.

I flat-out moaned when he started to suck.

Then it was on.

Jax pulled out all the stops to remind me he remembered exactly how to please me.

Hitting that perfect spot between pleasure and pain as he worshipped my breasts with his mouth and his fingers. When he feathered the backs of his knuckles down the center of my body, my belly rippled, my blood heated and I automatically widened my knees when he reached his destination.

After him being abstinent for a few years, I wondered if he'd be tentative. If he'd use gentle touches and ask permission.

Nope. The man dove right in, growling his approval in my mouth as he found me wet and ready.

A few well-placed rapid strokes of his thumb on my damp flesh and I started coming around his fingers.

The cocky jerk grinned—he actually freaking grinned wide enough that it broke our frantic kiss.

But I wasn't about to complain when he dropped to his knees and kissed me exactly the way he'd warned me he would—anytime, anyplace. No holds barred, with relentless attention, just constant licking, sucking and nibbling until I detonated against that wicked mouth.

As he waited for me to catch my breath, he started the caressing, kissing, biting thing on the insides of my thighs that he remembered drove me wild.

I couldn't stop squirming until he glanced up at me with the sexy warning in his eyes that told me to stop or he'd stop.

That immediately quelled all movement on my part.

My body buzzed like I was still a live wire waiting for the next set of sparks to short-circuit my brain.

Jax built me up again, pushing me into the gauzy atmosphere of lust, where the anticipation for that rush of pleasure was almost painful.

When I couldn't take any more, he gave me what I wanted. What I needed. What I'd been missing all these years. What I'd never had with any man but him.

I might've released a little scream when the epic orgasm started. But I couldn't hold back. It was just so damned good.

As I became aware of my surroundings, I felt the cocky jerk grinning as he kissed the inside of my knee.

"Jax—"

Loud knocking sounded from the foyer. I could hear Mimi saying, "Whyth the door locked? Hey! Let uth in!"

Still wearing that smug male smile, Jax stood and adjusted the front of his pants. Then he kissed me, sharing the taste of me as he righted my clothing.

After a hard tug on my belt, he backed off from the kiss to ask, "Any questions about my right to kiss you, Lucy Q?"

"Not a single one."

———

Typical Monday at work.

I'd managed not to think about my atypical Friday night . . . for all of two hours, and then I was back to dissecting it.

But my next stop would put a lid on the hot and steamy thoughts of Jaxson's mouth driving me over the edge twice and his sneaky-ass way of getting me to do a favor for him.

After the elevator doors opened on the LCCO floor, I almost said forget it, poked the door close button and returned to my own space.

But the receptionist saw me before I could escape. "Hello, Lucy." She cocked her head, looking behind me after I emerged. "Mimi's not with you?"

"Not today. Would it be possible for me to have a quick word with Edie?"

Her gaze flicked to the phone. "She's on a call, but she should be done soon. Would you care to wait?"

"Yes, thank you."

Too nervous to sit in the waiting area, I walked over to the artwork directly across from the elevator. This was new and super funky cool. Immediately I'd known that Walker's wife, Trinity, had created it. I'd always admired her quirky creativity—she and I were friends before she married a Lund—on the arts and crafts circuits at local fairs, where we'd both been selling our handmade goods. She'd turned her artistic talents into a legit career in the art world, whereas now, I made jewelry and other crafts with Mimi, strictly for fun.

At first glance the large piece appeared to be a photo of the Twin Cities, but upon closer inspection, I saw it had been painted, with 3D images that looked like dialogue bubbles dotting the canvas. I peered at them and realized the buildings in the bubbles were pictures of properties that LCCO—

Lund Cares Community Outreach—owned. The community center where Jax and I had our second date was the first one I focused on.

Information about each place had been typed out and shellacked above the photo. As you stood back and looked at the piece as a whole, you could see the vast outreach that LCCO had. That floored me.

"It's a beautiful piece, isn't it?" Edie said behind me, startling me.

"Yes, and it's a powerful statement piece too. I had no idea that LCCO owned so many properties."

"We had rapid growth for a few years when the real estate market suited our needs. We've reached the stage where we either need to hire more staff or slow the growth. And since our husbands are nearing retirement age, it's been slow and steady." She smiled. "Enough about that. Come on back to my office."

As I followed Edie, I admired her outfit, a long-sleeved dark gray velvet burnout shirt, topped with a flowing scarlet-colored chiffon duster, and wide-legged trousers, cuffed at the bottom, allowing peeks of her scarlet, black and gray heeled loafers. I reminded myself that was why I'd come here: The woman had unparalleled taste.

Her secretary's desk was unoccupied in the outer office in her two-room suite as we passed through to Edie's office. There was no ostentatious show of wealth anywhere in the LCCO headquarters. I imagined it would be hard to solicit donations if it looked as if you didn't need them.

"Everything is all right with Mimi?"

"Yes, except for the tooth that got knocked out Friday night."

"Oh dear." Her resigned look said it might be the first tooth, but it won't be the last. "I'm hoping it was just a baby tooth."

"It was."

"Good. So what brings you here?"

"It's about your son. The man needs a personal assistant," I blurted out. "And somehow I've ended up in that role, which is a situation of my own making."

"Lucy, hon, you're not making sense," she said gently.

Okay. Breathe. "It started when we took the tour of his apartment and he mentioned being so overwhelmed that he hadn't chosen wall colors for the main rooms. I don't understand how he picked floor coverings without knowing the color of the walls. I offered to help him pick paint colors, which ended up being me choosing the colors. I chose a soft brown for the main room and the hallway, and he . . ."

"Please don't tell me he didn't like it."

"No, he loved it. The problem is now he trusts my judgment implicitly and he's asked me to choose furnishings for the rest of the apartment! How am I supposed to know what he likes, Edie?"

She tapped her fingers on the desk. "You did live together for a while."

"He stayed in my apartment with my cheap furniture from IKEA the first summer we met and was a part-time roomie during my pregnancy up until he returned to the hotel he lived in in Chicago during the season."

"That should've been my first clue that he was so . . . unsettled."

I knew that look. She'd taken on guilt for not recognizing her son's issues.

"Anyway, go on."

"The place he's renting in Snow Village came furnished. This apartment is the first place he's owned, that he wants to be a home. How can he not know what kind of style he likes? He wants me to create a more a personal space, which means way more than just furniture."

"Have you asked him why he didn't hire an interior designer and decorator?"

"Yes. He grumbled that they'd fill every nook and cranny with stupid-looking shit and ugly, trendy furniture that no one wants to sit on."

Edie smiled. "Stupid-looking shit sounds exactly like something his father would say."

"Then he told me the real deal breaker for hiring a professional is they believe money is no object and they want no oversight." I exhaled. "How is that any different than what he's asking me to do? I have an unlimited budget, which scares me because I've never had that as an option. His only criteria? The furniture has to be in stock. Nothing custom made or ordered because he expects his apartment to be move-in ready."

"That is a bit of a catch-22, isn't it?"

"Yes." I took another breath. "I'm here to plead for your help. Not only don't I have a freakin' clue what Jax wants in his home, I don't know why he asked me, instead of you."

Another *tap tap tap* of her perfectly manicured fingernails on the desktop as she studied me. "Lucy, hon, you know why he asked you to do this."

Dammit.

"My concern: Is Jax manipulating you with his sudden 'decorate my apartment' scheme? Demanding you choose furnishings you love to make it a home that you'd want to live in with him, when you haven't given him any sign that's a possibility?"

It appeared Jax had taken my "don't broadcast the status change in our relationship" literally, as he hadn't even told his mother. "Edie, Jax and I are starting over. It's still new enough we're taking it a day at a time, keeping two separate places and not upsetting Mimi's life all at once. We'd prefer to ease her into the change in our relationship because there's a lot at stake."

Then Edie did the oddest thing; she squealed happily, hopped up, pulled me out of my chair and into a bear hug that stole my breath. "I'd hoped this would happen for so long."

"Really?"

"Yes. During his dark days, when even I didn't like him very much, I'd lost hope. But now . . ." She squeezed me again. "Now my heart is filled with joy at the thought you'll become the family you were always meant to be."

Good to know she approved. "I'm relieved you're happy, Edie."

"And I'm relieved that my son will be happy again." She stepped back and gently framed my face in her hands. "He told me that you are the love of his life."

Lucky thing she held my jaw or it would've hit the floor. "Jax told you that? When?"

"He actually told me that twice. Right after we met you for the first time and before he went into rehab, when he talked about how spectacularly he'd fucked up with you."

Ooh, Edie dropping the f-bomb. "And Mimi?"

"That's something entirely different for him." Her eyes shimmered with tears. "I'm grateful that you've taken a leap of faith with him and are moving on from the past." She lowered her hands but kept full eye contact with me. "I know firsthand how hard it is to forgive."

Wait. Was she telling me that Archer . . . ?

"This isn't something I ever talk about, because it's in the past, but I feel it's important for you to know, even when no one else does. Maybe especially because of that."

"Jax isn't aware?"

"That his father cheated on me? No. I've never told my sisters-in-law, my parents or my siblings. The only person I told was my best friend, and she passed on about fifteen years ago."

It was difficult watching her collect herself; this wasn't an Edie I recognized.

"Anyway, our situation happened early. Archer and I fell in love fast, became engaged quickly, but we hadn't set a wedding date. He came back from a business trip, acting weird. I jokingly asked if he was acting guilty because he'd cheated on me, not expecting that he'd confess that's what had happened. He told me it hadn't meant anything, he was drunk . . . she was drunk . . . he didn't even remember her name."

She closed her eyes, took a moment and inhaled before she continued. "I broke it off with him. Once a cheater, always a cheater, right? No redemption, no forgiveness, cut and dried, we're done, and I'm gone."

I nodded, forcing my mouth to ignore my brain's *like father, like son* comment.

"This happened in the summer. I left the Cities and headed to our family's cabin near the Canadian border, needing time to sort my life out. I'd been up there three weeks when Archer showed up. He admitted he'd screwed up and after I'd left he finally understood that making excuses for his behavior had made it worse; he should've been making amends.

"He loved me, Lucy. I knew that. I loved him too, which is why it was so hard to believe that walking away from each other was the best option after one mistake. I told him he could have me or he could have every other woman in the world. He chose me; he chose us. It took us a few months to get back on track, for me to choose him and most importantly to choose to forgive him. I never told anyone about it, not out of embarrassment, although it was humiliating, but I knew people would think I stayed with him because of his money. Being married to a billionaire buys a lot of forgiveness, you know?" she said sarcastically.

I wondered if people would say the same thing about me when they found out Jax and I had gotten back together. "And you never worried or wondered?"

"That he'd cheat on me again?" She paused. "No, and not because I watched him like a hawk. When I forgave his behavior I had to trust him again. Having my trust meant everything to him. He's never violated it in the thirty-nine years we've been married. I have the best life I could've ever hoped for, with a man who loves me with all that he has." She offered me a wistful smile. "Everyone's ability to forgive is different. There's no right or wrong way, so I don't pass judgment on what works for other couples. I'm telling you how it worked for us."

She didn't need to tell me her experience to try and sway me into giving Jax another chance—I'd done that on my own. But it did add another positive reinforcement moment that I'd made the right decision for us.

Stepping forward, I hugged her. "Thank you, Edie, for your insight and honesty. I promise this will stay between us."

"I know it will, dear, or I wouldn't have told you." She gave me a very motherly peck on the forehead. "Now, let me grab my laptop and a tape measure, then we'll head to the big empty apartment and figure out what'll make it a homey place you'll all want to live in."

And that was that. End of discussion, move on to the next thing; classic Edie Lund.

She'd soothed me in a way I hadn't known I'd needed. I could learn a lot from this woman, and I was grateful she'd be an even bigger part of my life—more than just Mimi's grandmother.

"Sounds good. And on the drive over, you can tell me how to survive being a hockey mom."

Edie laughed. "Oh, honey, that conversation might take years."

———

Thursday, as I stood outside the front door of the bar formerly known as Borderlands, I decided this was the most bizarre week I'd had in a long time.

After Edie had told Selka Lund that Jax and I were back together and we were working together to furnish Jax's apartment, Selka had told Annika. Annika then chewed me out for not telling her about the change in my relationship with Jax first, and then she'd given me Tuesday and Wednesday off to play interior decorator.

As much as I appreciated—and needed—that time to finish the "favor" for Jax, I couldn't refuse when Annika sent me to deliver her top secret PR plans directly to Jax. Her excuse for not delivering it herself—heading home for a nooner with Axl—sounded suspicious. Not the nooner part. Whenever Axl made a surprise appearance at the office—especially during the hockey season—we all found some other place to be. I questioned why it had to be me, in person, during the workday, instead of me handing the packet to Jax during Mimi's hockey practice tonight.

As I debated on whether to enter through the hole in front of the building where the door used to be, or heading around back, two construction workers carried a load of demolition debris out the opening and tossed it into the Dumpster by the curb.

Other than pacing in front of the building that day Jax confessed he owned it, I hadn't been in Borderlands since the night I'd cried in my nonalcoholic beer after my pregnancy test came back positive . . .

I'd been avoiding Jax for two days. I responded to his texts, but whenever he called me—like six times a day—I wouldn't pick up. My excuse? I was sick. There was truth to that excuse.

I'd been nauseous and tired, fighting colds and flu symptoms since the first part of the year. When I realized spring had snuck past me, I had to admit the lingering sickness wasn't the flu and I'd gone to the doctor.

I'd expected a bullshit diagnosis of a virus that would run its course—thank you for the fifty-dollar co-pay—but the results were shockingly unexpected.

Pregnancy.

I'll admit I lost my shit with the PA, demanding answers on how I could get pregnant when I was on birth control. I never missed a dose.

But I had been on an antibiotic as I fought a sinus infection that I blamed on being in various airports during the height of winter sickness season. And during that time, Jax had a five-day winter break and we'd spent most of it in bed in his Chicago hotel room.

So combine a sex marathon with weakened contraception and ta-da . . . we'd made a baby.

I had no idea how I'd break the news to him. Would he think I'd done it on purpose?

No way had I wanted a baby. Jesus. I was only twenty-four. I was all about my career as much as he was about his. I'd just gotten a promotion at work. I knew nothing about babies or being a mother.

And yet, the pregnancy had happened. I had months to prepare for the baby's arrival the first part of December. Jax wouldn't be happy. Having his girlfriend living in a different state already added stress to our relationship. Having his child living in another state . . .

Hence the reason I'd been avoiding him and why I'd chosen to drown my sorrows in nonalcoholic beer, in the one place in Minneapolis that made me feel close to him: our bar.

Our bar because it was the scene of our first sexual encounter.

Our bar because it was where Jax had confessed his love for the first time.

Our bar because we felt free to be us—no one recognized Jax. We spent time dancing, talking and fooling around, making memories just like any other young couple in love.

Feeling morose, I didn't glance up when a shadow fell across the table. I said, "I'm fine, Vic," assuming it was the bartender.

"From what I can see, Lucy Q, you're a helluva long ways from fine."

The shadow belonged to Jax.

Holy shit. Jax was here. In Minneapolis.

"Jax? Aren't you supposed to be in Chicago getting ready for the playoffs?"

"Yes, but I have a girlfriend who won't talk to me and it's driving me fucking crazy."

"How did you find me?"

"I will always find you."

Dammit. I was not going to cry.

"I needed to see you in person, baby, to look in those beautiful brown eyes and find out what's going on."

Baby. God. Maybe after I told him about the baby, our bar would be where it all ended.

Jax scooted into the booth across from me. He set aside the bottle of beer without looking at it, picked up my hands and kissed the center of each of my palms. "I'm here. Talk to me."

"I don't know how to say this."

His body stiffened. "Are you breaking up with me? Because I promise once the playoffs are over I'll be focused on you—on us—one hundred percent. The 'hawks haven't been in the playoffs for so freakin' many years that we're all so pumped—the players, the fans, the whole damn city! I can't imagine what it'll be like if we make it to the finals, say nothing if we win the Stanley Cup." He released my hand to pantomime mind blown.

That's when I knew I couldn't tell him about the pregnancy. Not yet. Not when he'd reached a career goal—hell a life goal—of his team playing in the Stanley Cup Playoffs. He couldn't do anything about the pregnancy and he couldn't be with me, so it'd keep until he could be excited about another major event in his life.

"Luce?"

I smiled at him. "Silly man, I'm not breaking up with you." I reached over and scraped my fingers through his playoffs beard. "Although I might if you don't shave this scruff the second the season ends. I hate when I can't see this handsome face."

"Done." He turned his head and kissed my wrist.

I loved the small pieces of sweetness and affection he showed me, although anyone who watched him on the ice would argue that Stonewall Lund was incapable of being sweet.

"Now will you please tell me what you don't know how to tell me?"

And I came up with the perfect white lie. "I won't be able to travel to any of your playoff games. Management is expecting more out of me with this promotion."

His eyes searched mine. "That's it?"

"Yep. I know you're disappointed, and I want to be supportive—"

He leaned across the table and kissed me to stop my babbling. "To be honest, it's a relief. The coaches are really cracking down on outside influences, including family, and trying to keep us focused. Not to mention that playoff tickets are hard to come by and I gotta give mine to my family first. Plus, babe, you don't even like hockey. Admit it."

I teased his lips with little sugar bites. "True, but I happen to love a certain hockey player."

Jax took over the sweet kisses, replacing them with hungry, openmouthed soul kisses that ignited my lust instantly.

Even after almost a year together, his passion knocked me sideways. That he could express his love for me, his need for me with just the way he kissed me. The infrequency of our physical connection made us reckless.

Which Jax demonstrated in the next breath when he demanded, "Back room. Now. I haven't fucked you for two goddamned weeks and I'm dyin'." He sucked on my lower lip. "Dyin'. I think my balls might've fallen off from disuse. You'll have to examine them very closely."

I laughed. "Better go slip Vic fifty bucks to look the other way."

"Baby, I need you so bad I handed him a Benjamin as soon as I walked through the door."

C an I help you with something?"

I blinked and the memory disappeared, making me aware that I'd been standing in the same place while it'd played out. I turned toward the woman and smiled. "I'm here to drop off something for Jax."

The woman scrutinized me, which wasn't particularly fun because she was stunning. Tall, slender, flowing chestnut locks straight out of a shampoo commercial, her placid face flawless—without makeup. Assessing gray eyes that suddenly lit with recognition.

"Holy shitballs. You're Lucifer."

"Excuse me?"

"Sorry. You're Lucy. Jax's . . ."

I raised an eyebrow. This next part oughta be good. "I'm Jax's what?"

"You're Jax's Lucy." She offered her hand. "I'm Simone. Jax's business partner in the bar."

Of course you are.

"Jax isn't here, but I could take that for you." She pointed to the thick manila envelope clutched in my hand.

"Sorry." I managed to give Jax's incredibly beautiful business partner a smile. "Strict instructions from Annika that this is for Jax's eyes only. I thought she'd spoken to him and he knew I was coming."

She shrugged. "No idea about that. He had some kind of meeting that's gone on longer than he planned."

Vague much with the *some kind of meeting*? I said, "An AA meeting?"

Simone shook her head. "He usually goes to the Monday meeting."

Now I felt stupid; I hadn't known that. Jax never talked about that stuff with me. But apparently he did with Simone.

Go away, jealousy.

"You're welcome to wait inside, but I'll warn you, it's a serious mess."

"I can see that. But surely Jax's office is exempt from the mess? I'll wait there."

"Well, Jax doesn't have his own office. We share the space."

Of course you do.

"Come in, and watch your step."

The inside had been gutted to the rafters in the ceiling. The only thing left was the enormous hand-carved bar. I said, "You're keeping that?"

"Yes. It'll be the cornerstone element of the speakeasy."

I had a pang of nostalgia when I realized the wall that separated the bar from the back room had literally bit the dust too.

Then I heard, "Lucy?"

I watched Dallas amble toward me, wearing a dusty pair of overalls and a yellow hard hat and carrying a clipboard. She looked so damn cute—not that I'd call her that to her face. "Dallas. Looks like you're in your element."

She gave me the widest smile I'd seen from her in ages. She'd stopped smiling altogether the last few months she'd worked at LI. "I am! Since we got underway with the new construction company, things have gone as smooth as a kale and acai smoothie straight from the blender."

That comparison actually made sense. Then I realized she'd said, "new construction company," which meant Jax wasn't using his cousin Walker's company, a development he'd forgotten to share with me. I shot Simone a look out of the corner of my eye. Seemed to be quite a bit Jax hadn't shared.

"Anyway, what are you doing here?"

I held up the envelope. "Annika sent me to hand deliver these to Jax."

"Gimme gimme."

"Keep those grabby hands to yourself, sister. This info is for Jaxson Lund only. It says so right here."

Dallas squinted at the envelope. "I don't see anything."

"Because it's written in invisible ink that only the recipient can read."

Simone snorted.

"That is hilarious." She cocked her head, not caring that her hard hat slipped to the side, and perused me head to toe. "But you I can read as easily as a newspaper. Why are you so tense? And why am I seeing a dark spot on your aura, like an unresolved memory that recently resurfaced?"

I withheld a shudder. The woman was spookily intuitive. I wonder what she'd see between Jax and me now.

Sexual frustration in his aura probably.

"Be patient, Lucy," Dallas said softly. "You're missing one important piece before everything falls into place, but you won't find it in the past."

Gooseflesh erupted.

Then Dallas was hugging me . . . and tugging on the envelope for Jax. "Nice try."

She smirked. "Can't blame me. Before you go, if you want a tour of the upstairs, come find me."

After she left, Simone said, "No matter how many times I see her do that, it still freaks me the fuck out."

"No kidding."

We ended up at what looked like a freestanding closet. Surely this couldn't be . . .

"Welcome to our office."

Inside wasn't as rough as the outside, but it was jam-packed with paperwork and odds and ends. I moved a box of coffee pods from one of two chairs. I expected she'd leave me here, but she plopped into the chair opposite mine, apparently ready to chat.

Great.

"Look, Lucy, I'm sorry I called you Lucifer."

"No harm done. It's been a while since anyone has called me that, which tells me you've been involved as Jax's partner longer than I realized."

"Four years. We met at the height of his hockey career and the lowest point in his personal life. It was the common thread between us." She set her elbows on the desk. "There's no need to skirt the truth. Jax and I slept together a few times early on until we recognized we were better off as friends. I've got no interest in him besides a business partnership. That said, we are very close."

"Why are you telling me this, Simone?"

"I want to be clear that I'm not the competition."

I returned her forthright stare. "I appreciate you saying

that. But my competition for Jax's love never has been another woman; it's been hockey."

That response shocked her. Then a smile bloomed across her face. "Damn. He wasn't kidding about your brutal honesty. He needs that, now that he's back in a place mentally where he can handle it." She paused. "He wasn't kidding about your eyes either. He swore they were the most arresting shade of brown and when he met you it was like you could see into his soul."

"Jax said that?"

"Granted it was in his drinking days. Then he'd play 'Brown Eyed Girl' over and over on the jukebox until I threatened to have it removed."

"Will it bother you if I say that Jax hasn't said anything about you except you're his business partner?"

Simone shook her head. "He compartmentalizes his life. In some ways it's good; in some ways it's not. He keeps the bar stuff from you. He keeps the personal stuff from me."

Just then Jax burst into the room saying, "Simone, have you seen—"

"Lucy?" she supplied.

His gaze zoomed in my direction and stayed there. Two strides later, he stood over me. He smiled and murmured, "Hey, beautiful," and then he kissed me. More than a chaste peck on the mouth, less than a tongue teaser. "What are you doing here?"

"Annika didn't tell you I was coming by?"

"Nope. It's a happy surprise, though."

I handed him the envelope. "PR stuff."

"Have you looked at any of it?"

"Not my business, sport."

He kissed me again. "Have you had lunch?"

"Yes," I fibbed. I'd eaten a protein bar and a banana on the drive over here. "Why?"

"Because it's rare that we can have a meal together. Just the two of us."

I smirked. "Are you angling for a nooner?"

"Jesus. No."

"Pity," I said softly. I curled my hand around the side of his face. "It was surreal walking through here. I was sad to see no back room."

"I watched them tear down the wall. Damn thing was flimsy."

"It did shake pretty hard. But I always attributed that to you, Jax, not poor construction."

"You always made the earth move for me too, baby."

We stared at each other with stupid smiles on our faces until Simone cleared her throat.

"Uh, I'm still here, guys."

Jax blushed. Then he pushed himself upright and offered me a hand. "Do you have time for a tour?"

Just then the whole upper floor shook, and someone yelled, "Look out!" before another loud crash sounded.

"Another time, okay? I'm already behind from missing two days this week."

"Gotcha. Need me to get Meems?"

"Could you? And keep her tonight? And take her to school in the morning? Oh, and let her know that I won't make it to her practice?"

"That's asking a lot, Luce."

I poked him in the ribs. "Don't even. I spent one whole day fretting about the favor you asked and two whole days getting it done."

"I appreciate it. I rewarded you for the favor beforehand, if you'll recall." He tacked on that wicked sexy smile and my entire body went hot.

"Only thing I can do is promise to return the favor," I cooed back.

Heat flashed in those blue eyes.

"Omigod. You two are so obnoxious with this new relationship thing," Simone said.

Dammit. I'd forgotten she was here. Jax had the power to make me forget everything but him.

We both looked over at her, and I was shocked to see her smiling.

Jax said, "What?" tersely.

"A happy Jax? Never thought I'd see the day. I love it, even though you are both too cute for me to take in large doses or I might vomit."

I returned her smile and stood on tiptoe to give my man one last kiss. "See you later."

$\mathcal{S}ixteen$

JAX

Watching Mimi's team get shut out again caused my blood to boil.

They'd played four games and lost four—even when it technically didn't matter because there'd be no tournament at the end of the season. What bugged me about this situation was not only weren't the kids having any fun, they weren't learning anything except frustration.

Coach Dickface let them wander around on the ice with no plan, no encouragement and no coaching. The poor kid who'd gotten stuck playing goalie had only been relieved by another team member after he'd lain on the ice in the middle of the second period and wouldn't get up.

The boy reached the bench, sobbing from exhaustion and humiliation because he'd let nine goals past. Nine breakaway goals on a half-ice court because his teammates had been milling around the opponent's net, too late to help defend their own net.

The coach sneered at him. Whatever he said to the boy brought Gabi to her feet, and she got in the coach's face, but he waved her off as if she were a pesky fly. I didn't agree with this philosophy of a dedicated goalie anyway. Each kid should rotate into the position at the very least, or like in the Red, White and Blue Hockey league for the Mites age group, all six players on a team skated and they all defended their own net.

I doubted the kid would be back next week. This team had already lost four members due to "personal issues" according to Margene, so there wasn't a full roster of kids to rotate in and out. Which meant more ice time, but that wasn't necessarily a good thing.

"Jax." Lucy rubbed her hand up and down my spine. "Glaring and swearing under your breath isn't helping anyone." She rested her cheek on my biceps. "Can you take it down a notch?"

"I'll try." Other parents behind us were equally disgruntled. For home games I arrived early to get a front row seat, which allowed me to hear what happened on the bench. Lucy sat to my right and Nolan sat on my left. My parents had attended once, and we'd managed to keep the entire Lund family from descending to support Mimi. She didn't need that kind of pressure.

After the game, Dad had taken me aside and asked why I'd chosen community play over enrolling Mimi in a club hockey program. My answer—Mimi was trying the game to ensure she liked the sport before we committed her to club hockey—had surprised him, because growing up, he'd insisted on the best of everything for me, and I've no doubt that played into my success as a hockey player.

While Dad attended as many games as he could when I was in youth hockey, he had enormous responsibilities at Lund Industries, especially after my grandfather retired. So he hadn't been the one hauling my ass out of bed at four A.M. and driving me to my first hockey practice of the day. He hadn't been the one picking me up after school and taking me back to the rink. That'd all been Mom. She'd done it with a smile on her face most days—and a huge cup of coffee in her hand.

Early on Mom realized that hockey wasn't a hobby sport for me; it was everything. In retrospect, that's probably why she refused to let Nolan play. At the time she claimed she wouldn't raise her sons to be rivals and hand them sticks to beat each other with. But looking back on the sheer number of hours it entailed getting me to practices and games and hockey camps . . . I suspected she'd had her fill of the hockey mom life with me. Yet even through my adulthood, she'd attended my college and pro hockey games. I'd never asked her if my retirement was a relief. And here I was, less than a year after retirement, back in the arena with her only grandchild following in my footsteps.

"You okay?" Lucy asked, adding another couple of strokes down my back.

I loved having her affection, from the soul-stealing kisses to something as simple as a touch. "Not really."

She whispered, "I'll bail you out if you get thrown in jail for taking a swing at him."

"Are you advocating violence, Lucy Q?"

"Just this one time, so make it good."

Laughing, I turned and kissed the crown of her head. "He's the type that'll sue, so no threats. Besides, that's not a side of me that our daughter needs to witness."

The instant that phrase left my mouth I knew it'd come back to bite me in the ass.

And it did, sooner than I'd expected, when Coach Dumbass opted to pull the goalie with five minutes remaining in the third period.

After the visiting team scored two more goals in less than a minute, another parent started raising a stink.

"Come on. Give 'em a little dignity, Coach D."

"Have a heart."

Someone else said, "He doesn't have a brain, so as far as I'm concerned his heart is in question too."

Lucy snickered beside me.

Gabi spoke to Coach D loud enough that I heard it. "Come on. Ask the ref to end the game. Pulling the goalie makes you look like a fool."

Wrong thing to say.

"You're out of line and that means you're out of here," he said, pointing to the locker room entrance. "Leave the ice."

She laughed. "Make me, little man."

He yelled for a time-out, then he turned his venom on her, ignoring his team skating toward him for instructions.

"You think you can boss me around and get away with it? You figure you're such a big shot that you're immune from repercussions? Wrong. I will have you fired, just like that." He snapped his fingers in her face. "Now get off my bench."

And that did it.

I stood up. "If Coach Welk leaves the ice, so will my kid."

"Mine too," someone said behind me.

Then the bleachers shook as every parent stood in solidarity.

His face had turned the color of an eggplant. "You're all banned, hear me? From games and practices in this rink. I'll see to it."

"Try and keep me from my kid even one second of ice time, Dennis, and you'll see exactly how I earned my nickname."

His eyes widened. I knew he knew who I was, but he'd never acknowledged it to me.

Until that moment when he opened his big mouth. "You've got no power here, Lund, so get over yourself."

"I don't want power. I want my daughter to learn the skills to play hockey, and that's not happening with you as her coach."

"Stonewall is right," a woman chimed in.

"If it was one of us complaining about your lack of coaching experience and skills, it'd be one thing. But *all* of us?" another guy inserted. "We're done letting you call the shots."

"Yeah, where's the rink manager?" someone else said.

Margene had been sitting at the officials' table. But as soon as Gabi signaled to her, she skated over.

"What's going on here?" she demanded.

That's when the ref got involved. "We've got a serious delay of game, so wrap this up and deal with it later."

"No," Gabi said. "We're forfeiting."

Coach D sputtered like a teakettle about to boil over. "You d-d-don't. She c-c-can't—"

"As the assistant coach, she can make that decision," Margene retorted. To the ref she said, "Call it."

The ref skated to center ice and blew the whistle.

That's when I realized whatever was going on between the coach and the parents, the kids didn't need to witness it. I turned and faced the group of about twenty-five behind me. "Who can supervise the kids in the locker rooms while we deal with this?"

Two hands went up, and then they were herding kids away.

Margene looked at Coach D, furiously texting on his cell. She said, "Put it away, Dennis, and quit tattling to your aunt."

"That's not who I'm texting," he snapped back. "I think the *Tribune* sports section would love an exclusive on how Stonewall Lund is a bully and a troublemaker at a private ice rink where his daughter is enrolled."

That smarmy little fucker.

Lucy's hand on my arm kept me from launching myself at him. Or maybe her death grip was so she wouldn't go after him after he brought Mimi into this.

While Coach Dipshit grinned like he'd just won the lottery, Gabi reached over, plucked his phone from his hand and smashed it beneath her skate.

Between the laughter and the clapping, I don't know how I heard Lucy's relieved intake of breath.

Then Margene blew her whistle to quiet everyone down.

Oddly enough, Nolan spoke first. "I'll advise you, Coach Whoever you are, that the forms Mr. Lund signed are to protect his minor child, and any disclosure to the press that puts her—or any other child on this team—in the spotlight because of you purposely disclosing privileged information will have immediate legal repercussions."

"Who are you? His lawyer?" Coach Douchebag sneered. "Of course Mr. Lund can't go anywhere without an entourage."

"I'm a lawyer," one of the parents said, "and I couldn't have phrased it any better. You are skating on thin ice, Coach Dyklar, if you'll pardon the pun. Don't make this worse on yourself by playing an 'alert the media' card you don't have. I highly doubt the owner of this establishment, even if she is your relative, will want to tangle with lawsuits resulting from your reckless behavior endangering children."

A harried-looking older man I'd seen around the rink moved quickly to reach our fun little lynching party.

"Coach Olin is head of personnel at Lakeside," Margene said by way of introduction.

"I was here doing paperwork when the ref tracked me down. What's this ruckus I've heard about how a coach called forfeiture?"

Coach Dickweed immediately jumped in with accusations, which Gabi countered, but with them talking over each other the main point had gotten lost.

Margene blew her whistle again. "I'm a neutral party." She shot Coach D a hard look when he snorted. "I'll give the play-by-play."

After she finished speaking, the head of personnel said, "You'll both get a chance to tell your side of the story. That won't happen tonight; it may not even happen this week with this bug that's been going around. The only action I can take is to suspend you both from coaching until this is settled."

Gabi managed to look crestfallen and murderous.

Coach Dickhead kept a smug smile. He didn't care about getting suspended, but Gabi assisted with two other age groups. This was a huge blow to her and her players.

"If you're suspending both coaches, who's gonna coach our kids?"

Murmurs sounded in response.

"Again, that is a matter for personnel to handle. But we're short staffed, so it might be a few weeks until a replacement coach can be arranged."

"What if a parent from this group could coach in the interim?" Lucy asked, shocking the crap out of me.

"I imagine you have someone in mind?"

"Stonewall would make an excellent coach," Gabi blurted out. "I've been watching him working with his daughter on her skill set, and I don't need to list his accomplishments to prove he's qualified."

Lucy squeezed my arm when I started opening and closing my fists.

There were a chorus of *yeah*s from the other parents.

Coach Olin's expectant eyes zoomed to me. "You on board with this, Lund?"

Blood rushed to my head, and I had to swallow twice before I could eke the words out. "I'll already be here, so yeah, I'll do it. Both the skills class and game coaching."

"Happy now?" Coach D said to Gabi. "You got what you wanted—your precious hockey pro working here."

Gabi's face bloomed pink.

Next to me, Nolan muttered, "Shit."

Coach Olin said, "Enough, Dennis. My office. Both of you. Now."

Margene said, "You'll have to fill out all the applications to coach in USA Hockey before you leave tonight, so we can get them faxed in ASAP and don't miss the registration cut-off deadline."

"Some of the paperwork should already be on file with them, since I helped out at training camps and skills events the last year I played in the NHL."

"Excellent, Jax. After you get done here, meet me in my office."

Through the excitement buzzing around us, Lucy stood on her tiptoes and whispered, "You got rid of him and you didn't even have to throw a punch."

I caught her lips with mine and kissed her, not giving a damn who watched.

The pleased little hum vibrating from her let me know she didn't care either.

"Daddy?"

No reason to break away guiltily. We said we'd deal with this as it happened, and Mimi just happened to return when I was kissing her mother.

"Hey, squirt. Are you all right?"

How would she react? Happily? With confusion?

Her gaze moved from me, to her mom, to Nolan, to the coaches on the bench removing their skates and back to me. "Did Coach Welk get in trouble?"

Or option C, choosing to ignore it entirely.

"She and Coach D have to sort through some issues with their bosses, so in the meantime, I'll be coaching your team."

"You will? Like coaching everyone?"

"That's what team means."

She scowled.

A niggling sense that she wasn't happy about this development surfaced. "What's wrong?"

"But you'll still coach me alone sometimes, right?"

"Wouldn't dream of missing our ice time together, Meems."

She smiled widely, showcasing the gap in her gumline. "Yay! Can we go out for ice cream now?"

"I bought ice cream at the store today," Lucy said. "We can make sundaes at home."

"But I wanna go out for ice cream with Daddy."

"Then it's a lucky thing that I already asked him to come over."

But belligerent Mimi had settled in. Lucy noticed it and she tried to hustle Mimi out. "Come on. You'll ride with me. Daddy will be right behind us after he's done with his paperwork."

"No. I'll wait for Daddy. You can go home and get stuff ready."

Lucy's patience thinned. "Watch your tone or the only thing that I'll be getting ready is you for bed without any ice cream."

"That's mean."

After everything that had happened in the last hour, I wasn't about to ignore Mimi's attitude. I leaned across the railing. "Go with your mother now, Milora Michelle. And no back talking."

Her eyes filled with tears. "I don't want any stupid ice cream. And I don't want you to come over if you're both gonna be mean to me."

Nolan muttered under his breath.

I looked at Lucy and she mirrored my WTF? expression.

But she rallied first. "Have it your way, Mimi. We'll skip the ice cream tonight. Say good-bye to your dad."

"Bye," she said sullenly, not coming closer for a hug.

Lucy said, "I'll call you," and followed Mimi as she stomped off.

"Man, it's like an alien inhabited her body," Nolan said. "Haven't you told her you're back together yet?"

"Nope. If she reacts that way when she sees us kiss I don't know how she'll take it when I'm at her place in the morning after I've spent the night. Or if Lucy is at my place."

"Isn't that the dream of most kids whose parents have broken up? That they get back together and life will be unicorns and sunshiny rainbows once again?"

"It's different for us, because there's never been an 'us' as a family." I didn't have time to brood about Lucy having to deal with Mimi's bratty attitude alone, because the parents who'd been milling around finally descended.

"Your questions will be answered as soon as I have answers," I said. "Assuming I'm approved to coach, let's keep the same schedule for now for skills and practices. Margene will update you with changes."

Nolan accompanied me to Margene's office, which I hadn't expected.

Margene didn't chatter with me or my brother, which allowed me to get the paperwork done faster. But I was curious about one thing.

"What can you tell me about the woman who owns this place?"

"*Eccentric* is frequently used to describe her. She bought the land—or if you believe the rumor, she won it in a poker tournament—intending to build a paintball gun recreation area. Something happened with the zoning that didn't allow it. Someone advised her to build an ice rink. So she did. She initially wanted the space to be strictly for figure skating—guess she had a crush on Dick Button back in the day, that's how old she is—but hockey has grown so rapidly she banked on that instead. She did insist on having an hour blocked out on Saturdays and Sundays for ice rental for kids' birthday parties." Margene shook her head. "She's great to work for, but there are a few things, like hiring Dennis, that make no sense."

"Is she ever here?"

"She drops in. She likes to catch us unaware. But she hasn't been in for ages, and all my correspondence with her is either through her property manager on the phone, or via email. Why do you ask?"

I shrugged. "Just wondering if I oughta be on the lookout for a granny type coming after me with a cane or a walker for insulting her nephew."

Margene and Nolan both laughed.

Then I said, "It'd probably be best if I went on the offensive and asked to meet up with her first."

"She'd like you all right. Big, handsome athlete who's a master on the ice."

Nolan coughed, "Suck-up."

She merely grinned at him. "Telling it like it is. I'll see what I can do about hooking you up with her."

I cringed. "Jesus. Don't say it like that."

"Dirty mind," she chided. "Now get outta here so Gabi can sneak in and blister my ear."

In the parking lot, Nolan said, "Thanks for the interesting evening, bro."

Then it occurred to me that it was Saturday night, his sacred "hang and bang" club night. "What's going on with you? Why aren't you out trolling like the tomcat you are?"

"I told you. It's gotten old. Or maybe I've gotten old." He brushed a speck of lint from his navy wool coat. "Or maybe I just like hanging out with you. We've never gotten to do that on a regular basis before."

What a sweet little shit. I shocked the crap out of him when I said, "Aww. I'm touched, and prepare yourself, bro; I'm coming at ya for a hug."

During the backslapping, tight-squeezing, laughing hug, that sneaky sucker managed a quick shot to my kidney. I'd forgotten we used to do that, and I laughed, even when it stung. "Nolan, you dirty-fighting fucker. Good thing I love you, bro, or I'd be rubbing that *GQ* face on the concrete."

"You'd have to catch me first, and the only time you're faster than me is when you're on skates." He adjusted his wool scarf. "And back atcha, showing the love tonight. Speaking of . . . are you going home? Or over to Lucy's?"

"What do you think?"

texted Lucy that I was on my way over.

She answered the door before my second soft knock. "Hey. You didn't have to come over. Mimi is already asleep."

"Did she . . . ?"

"Get mouthy? No. She didn't bring up that she saw us kissing either."

I kicked off my shoes and hung up my coat. "You're sure she saw us?"

"Jax, baby. Everyone saw us."

My arms circled her and I tugged her against my body. "Did that bother you?"

"Only in that we haven't given Mimi a heads-up that we're . . . God, if I can't come up with the right words for us, how are we supposed to explain it to her? *Boyfriend and girlfriend* sounds juvenile. We're not lovers."

Lucy paused, waiting for me to tack on *yet*, and I wanted to, but the thought of telling her the reason I'd been holding back with her made my heart race, and I had the urge to flee.

"Jax?"

I looked into her eyes, seeing confusion. "We tell her that we're replacing yelling with kissing." Then I kissed her. And she melted into me like she always did. When I broke the kiss and lifted my head, pain shot down the side of my neck, and I winced.

"What's wrong?"

"Wrong angle for my neck. No worries, though. That kiss was worth it. Your kisses are worth everything."

Lucy stepped back and propped her hands on her hips.

Never a good sign.

"Even if we can't define what we are to our daughter, we both know this is an intimate relationship. Intimate means more than sex—it also means we tell each other things."

My heart picked up speed.

"Is there something important you forgot to tell me, Jax?"

There's no way that she knows. Don't act paranoid. "Such as?"

"Such as you replaced Flint and Lund as your general contractors on the remodel."

I exhaled, silently thanking the universe for a reprieve, even when I knew it was temporary.

"I had to hear it from Simone."

"To be honest, I don't know how to be a normal couple, Luce. I haven't been part of a couple since we were together, which for me has meant I had no one to talk to about the daily life stuff. There's been no 'How was your day, dear?' with anyone else. I talked hockey with my teammates, I talked about addiction issues with my counselors, I talked health concerns with my doctors, I talked bar business with Simone, I talked property management issues with Chris, I talked career issues with Peter, I talked to you about Mimi and I talked to my family. That's it."

"So neatly compartmentalized," she murmured.

"It works for me."

Lucy moved in and smoothed her hands over my pecs. "Well, it doesn't work for me. If I'm part of your life, I want to know about all of that because that's what makes up your life. Okay?"

"Okay."

"And you can start by telling me who the hell this Chris 'property management' person is, because that's the first time you've ever mentioned that name."

I gave her a quick peck on her frowning mouth. "This building isn't the only property I own."

"Shocking."

Such a smartass. "Stonewall Enterprises is the company I started for property investments. Chris is a former college teammate who manages everything and advises me on potential purchases. My cousin Brady is such a numbers geek that he runs my financials for fun. As of right now, Stonewall Enterprises owns the entire block that the bar is on, an office building in Wayzata and one in Burnsville. Last year I acquired an abandoned strip mall and several parcels of land adjacent to it. I've looked at a dozen options to turn it into something besides a big money suck, but nothing has been decided."

She stared at me.

"What?"

"This is what you deal with all day?"

"Yeah. Why?"

"How did you ever think you could do all that and run LI?"

"Hey, I came to the conclusion that I couldn't sooner rather than later, remember? That counts for something."

Then she got right in my face. "No wonder your neck hurts. So here's what's going to happen. You will strip down to just your socks and underwear. Stretch out on my bed and let me massage your neck and back."

Half-naked with Lucy touching me . . . I'd jacked off to that thought more times than was healthy. How could her bossiness piss me off and turn me on?

Because this is your Lucy, the one you fell in love with because she's always had that special ability.

A firm tug on my hair brought my attention back to her.

"Let me take care of you, Jax. While I'm massaging away the aches and pains of the day, you can fill me in on what happened with Walker, and we can both use the time to remember the intimacies of being a couple."

I was too choked up to say anything; she'd known what I needed before I did.

I kissed her forehead, took her hand and led her into her bedroom.

Talk about surreal, stretching out on Lucy's bed—happily she still slept in a king—like a starfish, with Lucy sitting on my ass and her hands working magic on my stiff muscles.

The crisp cotton sheets didn't have her scent, meaning she'd probably just changed her sheets. In anticipation of me coming over tonight?

A sharp slap landed on my shoulder blade. "Don't tense up."

"Sorry." I'd kept the tension from my body as I told her about Walker. I'd voiced my concerns that I hadn't heard from Brady or Jensen, so I assumed they were pissed off at me too. Annika wasn't mad; she hadn't understood the delays either.

We talked about my potential new gig as a hockey coach.

We talked about her taking on more management responsibilities when Lennox went on maternity leave.

We talked about the furniture delivery schedule for my apartment.

We talked about taking a baking class with Mimi.

We talked like a normal couple reliving the week's events, which was a milestone for us.

While we talked and Lucy had her hands all over my

back, shoulders and arms, I'd kept my dick from going fully hard by imagining an ice bath.

But as soon as we stopped talking, the sensuality in her touch overwhelmed all of my senses.

When she leaned forward her hair trailed against the underside of my arms, making the skin there tingle. She pressed her fingers into my flesh so deeply that I felt the bite of her nails, which spun me into the past and all the times she'd dug her fingers into my ass, my shoulders, my spine, the nape of my neck as I moved inside her.

I thought I could keep it together by imagining walking naked through a snowstorm, but that's when she went in for the kill. She scooted down so she could lay her upper body on top of mine.

Her naked upper body.

Her breasts pressed into the lower curve of my back. Her fingers circled my wrists. Her breath fanned over the damp spots she'd created as she kissed and licked the slope of my shoulders.

And her scent. Christ. That lemony sweetness eddied around me when we were skin to skin, and I wanted to rub every inch of her all over every inch of me.

At least a dozen times.

"This body of yours, sport." She sighed dreamily. "It's beyond fucktacular. Muscles, muscles everywhere I touch." She licked the back of my neck, and I shuddered beneath her when she sank her teeth into that spot. "Everywhere I taste."

Another delicate lick near my hairline sent goose bumps down my arms, and my erection jumped as if she'd tongued me there.

"I want you," she whispered in my ear. "I want you so much I can't think straight."

Yes. Finally.

Her left hand moved up and down my left arm in a constant

caress as she dragged her mouth across the slope of my shoulder, alternating kisses with the tender scrape of her teeth. She nuzzled my neck and breathed me in, and when she exhaled, that sexy hum of pleasure vibrated throughout my entire body, like a tuning fork that had hit the right note.

Then she started to rock her groin into my ass, and my body remembered what to do, how she needed me to move. As soon as my hips left the bed, Lucy snaked her hand between my body and the mattress, grabbing hold of my hard-on through my boxers.

Reality crashed down as if I'd been doused in an ice bath and then shoved outside into a subzero Minnesota winter night.

Panicked, I rolled away from her, dumping her back on the mattress. At first glance she still wore that naughty smile, believing that she was about to get lucky.

It sucked watching that smile fade into disbelief as I jumped back into my jeans.

"Jax. What is wrong?"

"I can't . . . We can't do this right now."

"Yes, we can."

I snagged my shirt and yanked it over my head. "No. I'm sorry. I have to go."

"Go? *Now?*"

Her bewildered expression ripped at me, but somehow I got my belt fastened. "Yes."

"At least give me a reason why you're literally running out of my bedroom."

Think fast. Then the perfect excuse popped into my head and I hated myself for it. "Mimi is in the next room, Lucy."

"Jax, she's sound asleep."

"I . . . it just freaks me out, okay?"

"You are freaking me out. Can't we—"

"No. I've gotta go. I'll call you tomorrow and we'll figure out Mimi's schedule."

I booked it out of her bedroom, grabbed my coat and shoes—without putting them on—and hoofed it to the elevator on the opposite side of the building.

Before I got into my car, I noticed my shirt was covered in feathers.

What the hell?

You knew if you kept chickening out this would happen.

Bullshit.

That's when I noticed my down jacket had a hole. Every time I moved tufts of white floated out. Good to know I wasn't morphing into the chicken on the outside to match the chicken that clucked inside me like crazy.

I took it as a bad sign anyway.

I tossed the coat in the garbage and shivered all the way home.

Seventeen

LUCY

"Y es. Right there. Perfect."

The deliveryman picked up his clipboard. "Sign here and here."

I scrawled my name and handed it back. "Thank you so much."

"Not a problem. There's more on the loading dock, so I'll see you tomorrow."

"Not me. The owner will be here to take delivery." I smiled. "Go easy on him. He doesn't know where anything is supposed to go."

"In his own house? Damn. I guess that's rich folks for ya."

I walked him to the elevator, and after he reached the ground floor in the garage, I switched off delivery mode. Now only Jax's, Mimi's and my keys would run the elevator. Pretty nifty safety feature.

Mimi sat in one of the new barstools, coloring. She'd been

unnaturally quiet since Saturday night. I hadn't pressed her to talk, knowing she'd inherited my trait of talking on my time frame, no one else's.

Jax had been scarce since that night too, after he'd panicked at the thought of having sex with me and ran.

Paranoid much? That's probably not true.

I could say that to myself over and over, but it didn't convince me or take the sting away. What was worse, Mr. Let's Talk It Out refused to talk to me the one time I actually wanted to have an intimate conversation with him.

Now I knew how shitty it felt to have someone bail on you without explanation.

I'd handled his rejection—because face it, that's what it was—in a mature manner; I got myself off with my trusty vibrator, imagining the lust on his face as he watched.

Then I followed that action with another action—I shut my phone off and went to bed.

But he hadn't called, or texted. Not at all on Sunday, Monday or Tuesday, leaving me more confused than ever.

Jax should've been all over me, especially after being a freakin' monk for three years.

Following that logical train of thought, he wouldn't have suffered from performance anxiety. The cocky man knew precisely how to satisfy me, as he'd proven the previous weekend.

Maybe he was afraid of being quick on the trigger the first couple of times?

Maybe he'd been telling the truth about being worried that Mimi might overhear us.

I was loud in bed. It's never bothered me, and Jax loved that I was so vocal.

But things were different with a kid in the next room. The few times I'd actually had a guy stay over, Mimi hadn't been around.

God I'd grown tired of being in my own head with these stupid, paranoid thoughts.

Jax needed to explain what happened. Until he did, we couldn't move forward, and dwelling on it, dissecting it, wouldn't change a damn thing.

I refocused on Mimi. "Hey, girl. You ready to go downstairs?"

She shrugged. But her feet started to swing beneath the barstool—a tell that something was bothering her.

"Something on your mind, sweetheart?"

She looked up at me and nodded.

I saw such sadness on her face that my heart stumbled a little. "What is it?"

"I haven't seen Calder in forever."

Now that hockey sucked up a big chunk of her free time, even the nights she stayed at Jax's, she arrived too late to play with Calder.

"Can he come over here and play?"

"This weekend? We'll figure out a way to make it happen. I promise."

"No, Mommy. Today."

Today had been an in-service day for the teachers, giving the kids a day off in the middle of the week. I checked my watch. Almost two. Even if Calder could come over, we had to leave for hockey practice in three hours, which wouldn't give them much time.

"Please?"

"I'd love for him to come over, Meems, but you have hockey practice—"

"It's not practice, it's skills class, and I don't wanna go."

I froze. That was the first time she'd wanted to skip anything hockey related. "You're sure?"

"Uh-huh. So can we call him?"

"We can try. But it's late in the day to be asking, so you'll be okay if he can't make it?"

"I guess. But even if he can't come, I still don't wanna go to skills class."

Oh boy. "I'll call his mom." I scrolled until I found her name and hit call.

She answered, "Rowan Lund."

"Rowan. It's Lucy."

"Hey, Lucy, how's it going?"

Weird wasn't a socially acceptable answer, so I said, "Good. Say, I know it's late notice, but Mimi wondered if Calder could come over and play for a while today. She misses him."

"Omigod, seriously? That would be a sanity saver. He had to come to the gym with me today since there's no school, and he's been a little terror."

"I know the feeling. You're at the U of M right now? We'll be there in like . . . twenty? Will that work?"

"Yes. He'll be thrilled. Thanks so much."

As soon as I hung up, Mimi was practically bouncing up and down. "So? Can he?"

"Yes. We're picking him up, so grab your coloring stuff and we'll drop it off in our apartment and get our coats."

Mimi hugged me. "Thank you, Mommy. This is gonna be the best day ever."

C alder was a sweet kid. I got a huge kick out of seeing him and Mimi playing together.

Mimi was a grade ahead of him in school and thought that entitled her to boss him around. But also, as an only child, Calder was used to getting his way. Listening to them bicker and compromise kept me entertained throughout the afternoon.

They were munching on chocolate caramel cookies they'd made—Calder insisted on sprinkling coarse sea salt on the chunks of caramel before we popped the cookie sheets in the oven. Surprisingly that gave them a different, better flavor. He proudly informed us he'd learned that secret on *Chopped*.

Then I'd hauled out my crafting supplies so they could make friendship bracelets before we dropped Calder off.

When my phone rang and the caller ID flashed JAX, I had a moment of panic because I'd forgotten to call and let him know Mimi wouldn't be at practice.

I answered with, "Hey, Jax. What's up?" as if I didn't know.

"Where's Mimi? Class starts in ten minutes."

Rude much? "She's not coming to class today."

"What? Why not?" A paused followed. "Is she sick?"

"She's fine. Calder spent the afternoon and they're having a great time."

"Too great of a time for her to make it to hockey practice?" he snapped. "Or is it that you don't want to bring her because you're upset with me?"

Oh hell no.

I walked into the kitchen out of the kids' earshot. "Don't make assumptions when you haven't been around either of us the last four days. If you had, then you'd know something was bothering Mimi. I don't know what it is, but she told me she wasn't going to skills class—regardless if Calder had come over or not. She's had a fun afternoon, being a kid playing with her best friend, and she's happier than I've seen her all week. The world won't end if she misses one practice, Jax. And you have a problem if you can't see that."

I swore I heard his teeth clack together in frustration.

"Call her later. I'll make sure she has her cell phone on." I hung up. If he wanted to argue and accuse, he could show up and do it in person.

S ince Jensen was out of town, Rowan suggested we take
the kids to Chuck E. Cheese's so neither of us had to cook.
The kids were in heaven. Rowan and I had a lot in common
and we enjoyed hanging out in what we jokingly called a
"Lund-free" zone. We hugged good-bye and promised to keep
in touch more frequently, and we meant it.

I juggled the box of leftover pizza and my keys when we
stepped off the elevator, so I didn't notice him before Mimi
did.

"Daddy?"

I saw him sitting on the floor across from our apartment.

"Hey, Meems. I heard you got to play with Calder today."

"It was so much fun!" Her nose wrinkled. "Why are you
sitting on the floor?"

Good question. He had a six-thousand-square-foot apartment three floors up, with killer seating; I oughta know, I
picked it all out.

"I was waiting for you. I missed you, squirt. A lot." He
reached out and tugged her onto his lap.

Mimi curled into him, nestling her head between his neck
and shoulder. "I missed you too, Daddy."

And . . . my ovaries exploded. My heart melted. I wanted
to dogpile them with relief and happiness. But I didn't move
and interrupt their moment.

Jax kissed the top of Mimi's head. "Can I tell you something?"

"Uh-huh."

"You hurt my feelings tonight."

She lifted her head and looked at him with confusion. "I
did?"

"Yep. See, tonight was my first night as the fill-in coach for the skills class. And I was kinda nervous about teaching all those kids. But then I thought, it'll be okay because Meems will be there. And then you weren't. It made me sad and hurt."

"Did you cry?"

I bit my cheek to keep from laughing. Crying was Mimi's pain barometer.

"Well, I wanted to, but I didn't think it would be very cool for the players to see me boo-hoo-hooing at our first practice together."

Mimi giggled.

I watched her studying him; the look on her face indicated she was about to make a confession.

Jax noticed it too. "Remember our promise to each other to always be honest when it came to hockey stuff?"

When had he had that conversation with her?

"Uh-huh."

"What's the real reason you didn't want to come tonight?"

"Because I don't want you to be my team coach."

If that answer shocked him, he hid it well. "Okay. Can you explain why?"

"Because coaches yell, and I don't want you to yell at me. I want you to come to my games and watch me. If you're everyone's coach, then you'll be watching them too and then maybe I'll never get to be a better player."

It'd never crossed my mind that that's what had upset Mimi Saturday night, not seeing her dad kissing me—if she'd even caught that.

"Did it hurt your feelings that I said that?" she asked in a small voice.

"Not at all."

"Am I bein' bratty not wanting to share my daddy?"

"God no." Jax kissed her forehead. "I'm glad you told me this. Because it does change a few things, but sweetheart, some of those things can't be changed. When I agreed to be the fill-in coach, it was as good as a promise. If I go back on my promise, that means not only do you not get to play in any hockey games, none of the other kids on your team get to play either. Do you think that's fair?"

Mimi twisted the ends of Jax's hoodie string around her finger as she thought it over. Then she said, "No, that wouldn't be fair."

"Do you think you could share me for a few more games? Until it's decided if Coach Welk will be assigned to your team or until they find another coach?"

"I guess that'd be okay." She paused and looked at him. "I hope they pick Coach Welk. Did you know she played in the Olympics?"

"Yes, I did."

"*Two* different times?"

"Pretty amazing, isn't it?"

"Uh-huh. And her sister is gonna play in the Olympics soon."

How did Mimi know that? None of it was a surprise to Jax either. How much time had he spent with Coach Welk?

"Is there anything else you wanted to talk about?" Jax asked her. "Anything at all, maybe even something not about hockey or coaches?"

"Nope." She hugged him and scrambled off his lap. "Wanna come in and have some of the cookies that me 'n Calder made?"

"I'd love that."

When he pushed himself up from the floor, I noticed he winced. He'd used his body as a battering ram for most of his life, so I suspected he was paying the price for that now. But I didn't recall ever hearing him complain.

I continued to stare at him as he moved closer to me.

In that moment, I fully grasped the multitude of changes Jaxson Lund had gone through; I saw the different aspects that had come together to turn him into this amazingly complex man. A man strong enough to walk away from a sport he loved, from booze, from a family business that didn't fit him . . . from me Saturday night, when I knew he'd wanted to stay, but the timing had been wrong.

That's when I knew I loved him, this Jax, the man he was now. A man who was becoming the father Mimi needed. A man creating a career outside a hockey rink. A man looking for a home of his own. A man who'd asked for my forgiveness and had earned it. A man I wanted to spend the rest of my life loving, and laughing with, and yelling at, and listening to, and holding in my arms every night.

"Lucy?"

He'd said my name with wonder and surprise from whatever he'd seen on my face.

Mimi sighed and grabbed the keys from my hand to open the door. She went into the apartment, leaving Jax and me alone.

"Luce, baby, are you okay?"

I smiled at him, the smile that had him smiling back at me. "Actually I've never been better. Come in and have some cookies."

"They'll have to tide me over until I get home since I didn't eat supper."

I handed him the pizza box. "Have at it."

"Thanks." Then he looked at me suspiciously before he cracked the cardboard lid open and peered inside. "Of course there's green olives on it."

"Beggars can't be choosers, dude. And you better get used to green olives on your pizza, because Mimi and I both love them. You are officially outnumbered."

The dining room table was still covered in crafting supplies, so Jax ate the leftover pizza, six cookies and a glass of milk standing at the counter.

Mimi chattered on about the things she and Calder had done, including a ride in the elevator up to the new apartment. "Daddy, when are we gonna move in?"

By "we," was Mimi including me?

"The moving company is packing up your room on Friday and bringing my stuff as well as what I had in storage."

"Can I stay over in my new room Friday night?"

"Yep. After the hockey game." He wiped his mouth with a napkin and wandered over to where Mimi sat, working on another bracelet. "Whatcha doin', squirt?"

"Making a friendship bracelet for Coach Welk for when she is our new coach."

Jax smiled. "That's sweet. I'm sure she'll love it."

"Do you wanna make one?"

"For Coach Welk? No."

"No, silly, make one for someone else. One of your other friends. Like Uncle Nolan."

My eyes met Jax's over Mimi's head, and we both grinned, imagining fashionista Nolan with a brightly woven, slightly misshapen plastic beaded bracelet beneath his Armani shirt and Van Cleef and Arpels cuff links.

"You'll show me how to do this?" Jax scooted a chair closer to her and plopped down. "Because I've never been artsy or crafty."

"That's not true," I pointed out. "When I was pregnant with Mimi you untangled those three balls of yarn that were all twisted together."

He looked at me with surprise. "I'd forgotten about that. Then you knitted those tiny yellow and green booties from it. I remember being floored by the thought that the lump in your belly would eventually be out and wearing those booties." A guilty expression crossed his face.

"She never wore them because they were lopsided. Crocheting wasn't my best crafting skill."

"What was?"

"Soldering jewelry. I rocked at bending metal too." Then just to see how he'd react, I tacked on, "But I especially loved handling hard rods."

Jax's head whipped my direction.

He didn't buy my innocent expression . . . but he didn't respond with a veiled lewd comment either.

My naughty smirk stayed in place as I walked away, leaving them to spend time alone together.

I'd unloaded my research—aka other companies' ad campaigns and marketing blitzes—for the new spa products campaign geared toward late teen/early twentysomething women, and dove in.

Since I'd freelanced from home during Mimi's toddler years, I could block out everything and concentrate on the project at hand.

Mimi's tap on the shoulder startled me. "Hey. You done already?"

Jax chuckled. "It's been an hour and a half since we've heard anything from you."

"Sorry. I was in the zone."

"Go back to it. After Meems is ready for bed, I'll listen to her read and tuck her in."

Mimi hugged me. "Night, Mommy. Thanks for the best day."

"You're welcome, sweetie. Love you."

And I returned to the zone without problem, not breaking free from it until Jax flopped next to me on the couch.

"Man. She was wound up today."

"She used to be like that every day. It was exhausting."

"I can't imagine."

I gathered the materials I'd spread out everywhere and stacked them on the coffee table. Then I faced Jax, who wore a sheepish look. "What?"

"Remember when we first started dating and you made me tell you a few things that I was bad at?"

I nodded.

"After tonight we can add crafting to that list." He held out a tangled object that I assumed was a bracelet. "Go ahead and laugh."

"Well, it's not . . . totally hideous. It's completely unwearable, but you earned a solid C for effort."

He laughed. "Mimi insisted I make it specifically for you and give it to you, now that you and I are friends."

My gaze zoomed to his. "Is that all she said? That we're friends? Nothing about—"

"Seeing us macking on each other rink side?" He shook his head. "Maybe at her age that's all she's capable of seeing, since she thinks most boys are smelly and stupid."

"You have a point. She's never seen me in a romantic relationship, so she would call this a friendship."

Jax reached out and twined a hank of my hair around his finger. "What would you call it, Luce?"

"Confusing."

He said nothing for several long moments; he just continued that motion of wrapping and unwrapping my hair. Finally he said, "About Saturday night . . ."

I shocked him by shifting to sit on his lap with my knees tucked beside his thighs and pressing my fingers over his lips. "I've had just as much time to think about it as you have. Yesterday I came to the realization that I owe you an apology."

He tried to protest, but I shook my head and pressed harder against his mouth.

"I talk, you listen. I told you I wanted everything between us to unfold organically. And my offer of a massage didn't have ulterior motives . . . at first. But as soon as you let me touch you, I remembered how much I loved touching you, and rather than being content with that one small step, I pushed it.

I pushed you into a place you didn't want to be, and I'm sorry. So sorry, Jax. I made you uncomfortable, it made you leave and that made me mad. When I simmered down, I realized *I* was in the wrong, not you for removing yourself from a situation you weren't ready to be in. So I am sorry, okay?"

His fingers circled my wrist, pulling my hand from his mouth. But those vivid blue eyes that I loved roamed over my face, as if he was searching for something.

"What?"

"Thank you."

"For?"

"For understanding. For being better at this stuff than I am. For proving you've changed as well." He returned to twisting that section of my hair. "We agreed to not bring up the past, but I have to say that the old Lucy wouldn't have been able to let that go. You would've given me the silent treatment until I cracked and had to pick a fight so we could talk about it."

"True." I groaned. "And I always considered myself the more mature one in our relationship."

"Yeah, well, I reverted today when I accused you of keeping Mimi out of practice because of what'd happened between us Saturday night. Sorry for that, by the way."

"Apology accepted."

Jax tugged me closer by the hair, until my mouth was mere inches from his, until those soulful eyes were right where I could see every emotion I felt mirrored in his. "Can we kiss and make up now?"

"God yes. Please."

The kiss destroyed me from the first touch of his lips to mine.

Achingly sweet.

Unhurried.

Tender.

Passionate.

Fresh and hungry and possessive and perfect.

So freaking perfect that I almost burst into tears—but then I would've had to relinquish his lips, and that wasn't happening anytime soon.

Jax finally had to pull my hair to get my attention.

I buried my face in his neck and closed my eyes, letting my silence say everything I couldn't.

Eventually I moved to sit beside him.

"Tell me about your week so far."

He clasped my hand in his. "I've worked out with Nolan every morning. Dealt with remodel issues, which there always seem to be a fuck-ton of. Had a meeting with Chris about some swampland he wants me to buy."

"Seriously?"

"No. It's partially designated a wetlands area that might as well be a swamp for all the good it'd do me to own something I can't develop. I spent last night reading up on skill drills and making a practice graph so the kids didn't have another wasted hour on the ice."

"How did it go tonight?"

"Great. The kids were attentive and excited, and I hadn't seen that response in any of them with Coach D. I wish Mimi would've been there."

I squeezed his hand. "Next week. And I have to hand it to you, you did an amazing job talking it out with her tonight. I'm relieved that you got her to admit why she was upset. And if I thought she'd react that way to you becoming an official team coach, I wouldn't have suggested a parent take over the position."

"If it wasn't you, it would've been someone else. I had an open discussion with the parents tonight, before I knew how much it bothered Mimi, that my coaching was a temporary fix. Gabi is next in line for the position and to run that program. I'd never step in front of her." He sighed. "And to be honest, I don't want the commitment. The only reason I'm there is for Mimi. If she decides hockey isn't for her, I don't want to be stuck coaching other kids for an entire season."

"I'm happy to hear that too."

"Along those lines, tomorrow afternoon we're meeting with Agnes Lindholm, Lakeside's owner, about getting Gabi reinstated as coach."

"Who's we?"

"Me and Gabi."

That didn't sound right. "Why Gabi? Why not Margene?"

"Because Agnes loves that former Olympian Gabi is a Lakeside coach. Quite a feather in her cap, according to Margene. We're hoping when she hears what an unbelievable asshole Dennis has been to Gabi . . . Jesus, you should hear some of the shit he's said to her. I couldn't believe it when she told me."

How much time had he been spending with Coach Welk that he'd become her confidant?

"Plus, get this," he continued. "Dennis refused to give Gabi time off to go to the Olympics! The Olympics that her sister is playing in. What a tool. Gabi was worried she'd have to quit Lakeside, and I can't imagine that Agnes would let that happen. Anyway, I have no idea how long it'll take because Agnes defines eccentric, and yeah, I realize that's coming from a Lund, so I won't be able to get Meems from school tomorrow."

"That's all right. I can get her. But if you're planning on her staying in your new digs Friday night, can she be with you all day Saturday and spend Saturday night too?"

"Sure. What's going on with you?"

"It's getting close to Lennox's due date, and we're spending Saturday dividing up her responsibilities. Annika is not happy about it, because Axl is home over a weekend without a game scheduled. But we're so busy during the week that we haven't had time to do this and Lennox is freaking out."

"Are you telling me that Lennox is forcing you all to work Saturday? Even her boss?"

I laughed. "Yep. That's Lennox. She wants to make sure no one fucks up anything while she's on maternity leave, especially the boss."

"Maybe I should bring Lennox along when we talk to Agnes."

"Or maybe you should just bring Agnes flowers. That'll soften her up."

His brow furrowed and he said, "Flowers?" as if he'd never heard of them.

"All women love to get flowers."

Jax nudged my chin until I met his gaze. "I've never given you flowers, Luce. Not once."

What was I supposed to say to that?

"I could've given you so much and I gave you nothing."

"Jax. I never wanted things from you. I only wanted your time."

He closed his eyes. "I couldn't even give you that."

I kissed him. "No dwelling on or brooding about what can't be changed."

Then he gave me a huge-ass grin.

"What?"

He picked up the friendship bracelet. "This counts as jewelry, right?"

"Only in the loosest definition of the term."

"But I can give you this." He tried to hold my wrist in place so he could tie it on and I resisted. "Will you wear this friendship bracelet that I handcrafted for you?"

"Uh. No."

"Then I'll just have to give you something that you will

wear, won't I?" He kissed my surprised mouth. "Challenge accepted. Now gimme another kiss to hold me until I see you again."

"You're not staying over?"

He shook his head and returned to kissing me.

I didn't push him for a reason. He had so many irons in the fire that he probably needed a night to himself.

Eighteen

JAX

I was about to lose my shit with Mimi.

And didn't that just make me the worst father in the world?

Fuck, but the kid was being a brat today.

At least I hadn't called her a brat to her face. That counted as parental restraint, right?

I'd been muddling through this attitude of hers for six hours. Six. Hours.

I'd let her sleep in this morning after we'd had a late Friday night watching movies in the new theater room. Sleeping in on Saturdays usually tamed Mimi's morning beast, but it had awaked in full roar mode, which made me wonder if Mimi had reverted to that behavior and Lucy had been letting it slide and not telling me about it.

Mimi refused to come out of her room for breakfast.

I didn't insist; I figured I'd have to pick my battles with her today.

When she emerged an hour later, still in her pajamas,

asking me to make her pancakes, I told her she'd missed breakfast and would have to wait until lunch to eat.

She started crying.

Like a total sucker I said she could have cereal. But she didn't want cereal. Now she wanted yogurt. When I told her I hadn't bought yogurt, she looked at me like I'd forgotten her birthday. Then she informed me that "Mommy always buys me yogurt" and that she was going down to her apartment to get some.

I said no and she threw a screaming Mimi fit.

I let her.

Realizing I wouldn't relent, she announced she was taking a bubble bath in her new tub. She sneered at my offer to help her, reminding me that she wasn't a baby. But I ended up in her bathroom anyway, throwing towels on the floor to sop up the water and bubbles after she'd overfilled the tub.

After that fiasco, I hoped to see my sweet, contrite girl offering an apology for screwing up, but that Mimi was nowhere to be found.

But I caught Demon Mimi jumping on the bed.

Then I found her standing on the counter looking for ingredients to bake cookies.

The kid about gave me a heart attack because it was a big drop to the floor if she would've lost her balance.

That stunt earned her fifteen minutes in time-out, which turned into another fifteen minutes because she would not keep her butt in the chair. That forced me to sit across from her so it felt like I was punishing myself.

I cooked macaroni and cheese for lunch—at her request—which she refused to eat more than three bites of because it "looked funny."

After lunch I settled her in the theater room, so I could have an hour to myself to go over the paperwork from the meeting with Agnes.

Mimi lasted ten minutes before she was "bored" and asking if she could get her "good" toys from the apartment.

I said no, knowing she'd ask me ten minutes after that to go back down there and get something else.

So she ran off and hid.

I was starting to question whether a six-thousand-square-foot apartment was a good idea, because there were a fuck-ton of places for a resourceful kid to hide.

When I finally found her, I chewed her out.

She'd burst into tears again and sobbed that she wanted her mommy.

At that point, I wanted my mommy too.

I'd had three very stressful days in a row, and I just wanted to chill in my new place. Instead of the lazy, fun Saturday I'd envisioned for us—cooking together, watching a movie, setting up her bedroom—I'd been smacked with the ugly truth that I actually disliked my child today.

Oh, I loved her, and tomorrow things would be back to normal, but for today . . . I'd had it. I didn't know how Lucy did it, besides the fact she had no other options and had to figure out a way to deal with hell-girl, but I was throwing in the towel and calling for backup.

The phone rang four times before she picked up.

The first thing out of my mouth? "Help."

My mom arrived half an hour later with my dad, which was a surprise.

Mimi launched herself at Grandma.

After calming Mimi with soft, soothing words, Mom handed her off to Grandpa.

My dad grabbed Mimi's coat and backpack, sent me an encouraging smile and disappeared into the elevator with my daughter, who hadn't even bothered to say good-bye to me.

Yep. I had this parenting gig down cold.

Not.

As I stood there feeling stupid, mean and sorry for myself, staring at the elevator door like a lost puppy, my mom wrapped her arms around me in a huge hug.

I closed my eyes and enfolded her more tightly in my arms, catching her familiar scent—Chanel No. 5 perfume, hair spray and coffee. Even in heels the top of her head barely reached above my sternum, but for just a moment, I was a kid again, when Mom's hugs made everything better.

We remained that way for a while, even when I tried to pull away because I knew Dad was waiting for her. But she squeezed me harder and held on.

When I sighed and released some of the tension in my body, she finally let me go.

She stepped back only far enough to place both her hands on my cheeks, allowing her to gaze into my eyes. "Every parent has a bad day with their child. It's normal. You've done nothing wrong, son. You just need a little break from each other. That's it."

"You're sure?"

"We raised two bullheaded, bright, boisterous boys, who oftentimes stomped on my last nerve before setting it on fire, so yeah, honey. I'm sure."

I groaned. "I'm sorry."

"You were a kid. Kids are the most self-involved creatures on the planet."

"I'm sorry that I grew up to be a self-involved man." I released a slow breath as she studied me. "You've just rolled with everything I've done, or not done. Been beside me every step of the way, even through the rockiest parts, and I know I don't say it often enough, but thank you. I want to be the kind of parent to Mimi that you've always been to me. The kind of parent you still are to me." I smiled. "You are the very, very best mom in the whole entire universe, and I love you more than Christmas."

Her eyes filled with tears and she lightly tapped my cheeks. "That's for making me cry. And I still have that card with the effusive praise you made me when you were ten." She smirked. "I had to take it out every couple of months and reread it during your teen years just to remind myself that my sweet child did exist somewhere inside the sulky, stinky teenage boy."

I laughed.

"Don't worry about Mimi. She'll be fine with Grandpa and me. It's you I worry about." Her eyes searched mine. "How long has it been?"

Since I've had a drink?

Since I've had sex?

Mom clucked her tongue because apparently she'd read my mind. "Not those things, son. How long since you've played?"

And she knew. She always did.

"Months. It's not like I have anyone I can play with."

"Go to the rink and suit up anyway."

"Mom—"

"You're missing that part of who you are, Jax. Of who you've always been. Reconnect with it even if it's just skating by yourself as you pretend the Red Wings are on your tail and shooting pucks like you're on a breakaway in game seven of the semifinals."

Once again, she'd nailed exactly what I needed. "I hate that you're always right."

She laughed. "I know."

When she reached the elevator, she turned. "Text me the five W's as soon as you've figured it out so I don't worry."

Some things never changed; Mom demanding the five W's—our family code for who, what, when, where, why— before she and Dad let me or Nolan leave the house.

"I will. And, Mom? Thanks."

As soon as she was gone, I picked up my phone and checked the Lakeside app to see if there was free ice.

Then I realized after Thursday's meeting I could demand ice time whenever the hell I felt like it. Luckily I wouldn't have to do that today. Two hours from now the rink would be empty, and I couldn't wait to be on it.

I told Margene to lock the door after she left for the night.

I skated onto the ice, warming up stiff muscles. Breathing in that familiar scent of cold. Hearing the scrape of my skates and the overhead blowers.

In all the Saturday nights I'd spent in ice arenas, it'd never been like this: just me.

Playing hockey with yourself isn't as fun as playing with a team or even one-on-one. But playing hockey with myself was better than not playing hockey at all. I ran speed drills, forward and backward. I shot the puck across the blue line and chased it down. I nailed a couple of slap shots and wristers. I used the posts to bank it in. With each shot on goal I felt the tension leaving me, along with massive perspiration.

I took a breather and drained a bottle of water. When I faced the ice, another skater had joined me.

What the fuck?

Gabi removed her helmet and smirked at me. "You like playing with yourself, Stonewall?"

I shrugged. "It's the only time I have decent competition."

"Ooh. Burn. Prove it. Let's play a little one-on-one and see who comes out on top."

"You don't wanna play with me, Welk."

She skated away from me backward, toward center ice. "Sure I do. That's why I'm out here and suited up." She popped her helmet back on. "Unless you're afraid of being shown up by a woman."

"In your dreams, North Dakota," I retorted. "I'm not playing you. I'd squash you like a bug."

Stick in hand, she gestured to the empty arena. "No one here but us. Wait. What's that I hear?" She pretended to cock her head. "Is that . . . clucking?"

Oh hell no.

I reached her before she made a single cluck. "Fair warning that I won't go easy on you because you're a girl."

"Fair warning that I won't go easy on you because you're an overconfident male."

I held the puck out, she slapped it out of my hand and she immediately controlled it.

But I caught her and forced her away from the net with a shoulder shove, flipping the puck outside of my blade, pushing it forward as I raced to the other goal.

Gabi caught me on the left side, stealing the puck and skating around the backside of the net, coming out on the right along the boards.

I bodychecked her. Not full strength, but enough to knock the puck lose.

That hit didn't even faze her.

The little shit reached the puck before I did and whizzed around the backside again, coming forward in a zigzag pattern. I blocked her first shot, snagged the puck and cut her off as I zipped down center ice, and took the slap shot.

I raised my arms in victory.

She waited in the face-off circle and smacked her blade on the ice.

"One, zip, North Dakota," I crowed.

"Quit yapping, Gopher, and drop the puck."

I dropped it, she got it and she showcased her stickhandling skills as she played keep-away, a one-on-one training drill I recognized, trying to mesmerize me into watching the puck.

Nice try, girlie. It won't work.

When I brought my stick out, I might've hooked her skate and sent her sprawling.

And when she caught me on the backside of the net, she might've high-sticked me.

The demon in her eyes said, *No refs, no rules, no regrets.*

She was a helluva player, but I tricked her with a deke and scored goal number two.

We skated side by side to the players' bench where we'd left our water bottles. Once we could hold a conversation, she said, "Wanna go best three out of five?"

I laughed. "Glutton for punishment today?"

She smacked me on the arm. "Now I'm warmed up, old man."

That's when I heard a commotion and turned around to see a group of guys moving into the spectator seats. I squinted at them, but I sure as hell wasn't hallucinating.

My brother and my cousins Walker, Brady and Ash plopped down like they were here to watch a game.

When Gabi said, "Who are they?" I knew she had nothing to do with them being here.

Then that tall Swede, known as the Hammer, also known as my cousin Annika's husband, skated onto the ice. And the cocky bastard wore his goddamned Wild uniform.

The jerk sprayed us with ice as he came to a stop.

He granted me a smirking once-over—I was in all-black practice clothes, wearing none of my team's logo—and said, "No team pride? Sad day, dude."

"What are you doing here?"

He skated away, leaving me no choice but to follow him. Gabi trailed behind.

I looked at Nolan and each of my cousins. "You're a little late for an intervention. It's been over three years since I've had a drop."

"Yeah, if we would've known then what we know went down now, we would've intervened a lot fucking sooner," Walker said.

Nolan elbowed him. Hard. "Shut it."

"Why are you here?"

Axl spoke up. "Because his wife"—he pointed at Brady—"is making the PR department work at LI on a Saturday. There's no game tonight, today's practice was for pussies, and my wife isn't home. I've got a lot of pent-up energy to get rid of. I heard you were here, skating around lost and alone, so I thought I'd kill time and show you up." He grinned. "Win-win for me, loser."

"You're on." I looked at Nolan. "Mom called you?"

Brady said, "No. Aunt Edie called Lucy to tell her that she and Uncle Archer had Mimi overnight. She mentioned you were here, Annika and Lennox overheard and they passed it on to us."

"We're here for the bloodbath," Ash said, rubbing his hands together. "So get to it."

I looked at Axl. "You won't get in trouble for this?"

"Not if no one knows."

All eyes zoomed to the one unknown: Gabi.

"My lips are sealed, but dude, there is no way I'm missing Hammer versus Stonewall."

"What are you doing here anyway?" Nolan demanded. "I thought Jax was playing alone?"

Gabi looked at me. "Is Mr. Fancy Pants ever not a rude asshole?"

Everyone laughed. Nolan was the least assholish guy of all of us.

I shrugged. Then I looked at Axl. "Full out?"

He grinned. "Ain't no other way to play, old-timer. Let's do this."

Gabi volunteered to drop the puck, and she reminded us of the one-on-one rules—which varied from club to club, but it was basically don't be an asshole and take the long shot every time.

We skated to the center ice face-off circle, and I happened to look over at my family.

"What the hell, Walker? Are you wearing a . . . Hammer-quist jersey?"

"Yep." Walker pointed at Brady, who also wore one. "Gotta support our sister's man."

"Annika made you wear them, didn't she?"

Brady said, "Yeah. She's scary as shit when she's in hockey-wife mode. Oh, and Jensen said to tell you if he was here he'd be wearing a Detroit jersey to show he's neutral."

"He's an idiot if he's a Detroit fan," Gabi sneered.

I held my glove out for a fist bump.

Then I saw Nolan and Ash were both wearing my old jersey. They each gave me a cheesy thumbs-up.

"We gonna stand around or is the ass-kicking gonna start?" Axl demanded.

"Start it."

In my pro years, once I was on the ice or on the bench, everything outside of the game ceased to exist. I was singularly focused. That competitive spirit hadn't left me, but it had mellowed. I could've knocked Axl on his ass several times and I didn't. Dick move to prove I still could, and I wouldn't take the chance on injuring him no matter how full out we were playing.

But ultimately his defensive skills kept me from scoring—lucky fucker got in two shots—and playing him, a guy in his prime damn near a decade younger than me, just reminded me why I'd retired.

Yet, being on the ice with a player of his caliber also made me realize how much I missed playing. I couldn't be the only former NHL player who longed for a game.

There were senior leagues and men's leagues I could join. Ego aside, it wouldn't be fair to play with those guys, even though I knew some semipro guys did. Just like with coaching, I didn't want the time commitment of joining a league. I wanted to round up old warhorses like me, who wanted to play for fun.

That was something I'd look into now that I had a vested interest.

Axl clapped me on the back as we skated back over to where the Lunds sat.

"You didn't show off too much, Axl, but you beat this old man and I'm beat. Skating with kids . . . no comparison."

"Speaking of . . . when can we come to one of Mimi's hockey games?" Walker asked. "Is it true you're coaching?"

I looked at Gabi. She gave a slight shake of her head. For some reason it didn't feel right to discuss Mimi's emotions about me coaching her team or disclose what had gone down at the meeting since it affected the Lakeside staff and we hadn't talked to them yet. "I'm the temporary coach. It's still up in the air as to who will take over and when."

"We haven't been introduced," Ash said to Gabi. "I'm Ash Lund. Jax's cousin. And you are?"

"Not buying your charm, cuz, if she's not buying mine," Nolan said crossly.

Gabi removed her hand from her glove and offered it to Ash. "Pleasure to meet you, Ash. I'm Gabi Welk." Then she offered her hand to Walker and Brady. "You Lunds really are all for one and one for all like Jensen warned me."

"You met our little brother Jensen?" Walker said.

"When we were over at Jax's place in Snow Village. I'm not a huge football fan because . . . hockey, but it was cool to meet The Rocket."

A phone buzzed and Brady pulled his cell out. "Workday is over. Lennox is on her way home. Later, guys."

Before I could ask Brady how Lennox was feeling, Axl

piped up, "That means Annika is out of there too. Thanks for the game. See ya."

"Anytime."

Gabi skated to the women's locker room, and it was just me, Ash, Nolan and Walker.

I pointed at Walker's phone. "No urgent messages from Trinity?"

"Nah. Liam has been crabby and teething all week. Trin probably crashed. She's tired." He smiled. "Since she's pregnant again."

"Christ, Walker, Liam is barely a year old."

"I know. We want to have our kids close together. Wasn't planned, but whatcha gonna do?"

I muttered, "Climb off her?"

"Never," Walker said with a laugh. "Besides, she loves being a mom."

That made me think of Lucy. She was a great mom, but she'd never been one of those "I can't wait to have kids" kind of women. Our accidental pregnancy had freaked her out, and she hadn't told me about it until hockey season ended.

I hadn't blamed her, but at the same time, I had resented her. Especially when she'd refused to move to Chicago. How was I supposed to be supportive to her and the baby when we didn't live in the same state? Since my team had reached the semifinals of the Stanley Cup Playoffs that year, our off-season had been shorter than usual. The coaching staff, management, my teammates—we'd been under even more pressure to make the next season a winning season, which we had because we'd won the cup the next year. I couldn't spend much time in Minneapolis and that had marked the beginning of the end for us.

When Walker said, "Listen, Jax," my attention returned to him. "I'm sorry I put you in the position that you had to fire my company." He scratched his beard. "There's no excuse for how unprofessional I acted. None."

"Everyone fucks up, Walker. Yeah, it sucks that your screwup was on my dime and my time, but I've moved on. I'm not gonna hold a grudge, especially not against family."

"Man, I appreciate that. And I'll throw it out there: If you keep buying these weird places and need restoration, call us."

I flashed him a feral grin. "Don't push it."

"Even if I give you an 'I was a judgmental asshole' discount?"

"Now we're talkin'. I won't rule it out."

"I appreciate the second chance." He stood. "See ya." He slapped hands with Nolan, Ash and then me.

Before I headed to the dressing room, Ash said, "Dallas really loves working on your projects. Thanks for looking out for her."

"She's earned her spot running the team. She also knows anytime it becomes too much, she can bail. No harm, no foul. I just want her to be happy in her work environment, because I know how much it sucks when you're not."

Ash gave me a considering look. "Think she'll ever return to LI?"

"No idea. I don't think she knows the answer to that, Ash, but do me a favor and don't bring it up. Let her be my shining star for a while."

"I will, because she needs that."

"Thanks for coming tonight, guys, and for the support. Wasn't expecting an audience."

Nolan said, "I wasn't expecting to see you playing alone with Gabi, Jax. Think that was smart?"

"She's a pro, and the closest I've come to finding a player on my level who doesn't hold back. It was fun to blow off some steam with her, and I think she needed it too."

He opted not to share whatever had put a wrinkle in his forehead.

I glanced at Ash. "You two hitting the town tonight?"

"After we change clothes," Nolan said. "Thank god Flurry has a dress code."

"Have fun."

"What are your plans? I mean, you could come out to the clubs with us," Ash offered.

"Thanks, but those days are long behind me."

In the locker room I ditched my gear and took a fast shower. By the time I dressed in my street clothes and headed out, I saw I'd missed two texts from Lucy.

LQ: Everything OK? Edie said Mimi is having an overnight with them.

LQ: I'm home if you want to talk.

The time had come to have the talk with her that I'd been avoiding.

ME: OMW

Before I walked out the main entrance, I heard arguing. I stepped into the hallway and saw Gabi and Nolan locked in battle. "Hey. What's going on?"

"Nothing," Gabi snapped. "Your brother was lost so I was telling him exactly where to go."

Nolan snarled something I couldn't make out.

"Do I need to stay and referee you two? Or can I go home to my"—I almost said *wife*, but Nolan would question that, so I amended it to—"family?"

"Go ahead, bro. I'm sure Lucy is anxious for time alone with you since Mimi is with her grandparents."

What the hell? Did I even want to know what that meant?
Nope.
Gabi said, "Go. I'll lock up."
"See you Monday."

Nineteen

LUCY

'd had a serious case of déjà vu when Edie called me and said Mimi was spending the night with her and Archer. That had been the norm during Jax's visitation periods with Mimi, although I hadn't been aware of his drinking issues at the time; I'd merely chalked it up to Jax opting to do something other than spending time with our daughter.

When I'd quizzed Edie on why Jax and Mimi weren't playing house in their new apartment, she told me he'd gone to the ice rink and suggested I contact him after I finished working.

There hadn't been enough space in my brain to worry about Jax's Saturday plans, when my head was about to explode with scheduling and spreadsheets and team assignments and computer upgrades. I'd always known Lennox defined efficient, but I hadn't realized she'd done the work of like three people. I selfishly hoped she would come back after her maternity leave, because I did not want to do her job.

Our weekend work attire had been casual, but I needed movement and comfort, so I slipped on my trusty robe immediately after I got home. Once again Jax would catch me lounging around half-naked while I finished a PB and J for supper.

Three knocks sounded.

He could've come in, I'd left the door unlocked, but he waited for me to let him in. I considered teasing him that he wouldn't find me doing anything remotely interesting behind closed doors, but I still wasn't sure how he'd react to sexual banter.

I opened the door and almost swallowed my tongue.

With that gorgeous face, Jax always looked good. Tonight, though, with his hair damp and scruff darkening his cheeks and a look in his eyes that bordered on wild, he was devastating.

Then he aimed that wild look at me, his gaze dipping to my cleavage and back up to my mouth. "Lucy. I . . ."

He seemed so forlorn that I stepped into his arms without hesitation.

Jax buried his face in my neck and lifted me off the floor, his hands gripping my ass as he carried me into the living room.

Okay then.

He gently lowered me to my feet, his mouth searching for mine and finding it.

The kiss was sweet and resigned and slightly desperate. In our past when Jax kissed me like this, I'd find myself pressed against the nearest flat surface—vertical, horizontal, it didn't matter—with his hands tearing at my clothes.

Thank god I was barely clothed. We could get straight to the next phase where his hands and mouth and need fired my blood so fast he could drive into me without hesitation because my body was ready for his.

But something clicked in him and he eased off.

His big hands were actually shaking when he framed them around my face.

"What?"

"I love you."

Why were his eyes so tormented when he told me that?

"I love you so fucking much. It's been a goddamned dream to get a second chance with you. To be with you and work on being us again."

"But?"

He shook his head. "No buts. There is something I need to tell you. Something that might change everything back to the way it used to be." He dropped his hands from my face and stepped back. "It's an ugly thing, Luce. Really ugly."

"I've dealt with ugly before."

"Not like this, you haven't." His hair nearly stood on end from where he'd been running his hands through it. "I don't . . . You haven't asked how I went from being a social drinker to being an alcoholic."

"I wondered. But is that really something I can ask? Because what if you didn't know? What if you couldn't remember how it was not to give in to that urge to drink until you felt better or felt nothing? You didn't drink more than I did whenever we were together, but I wasn't around you all the time. You hid it from your family, your teammates; it would've been easy to hide it from me." But I didn't give him the real reason I hadn't asked: I was afraid he'd tell me it happened after he'd checked out of our relationship.

"That's fair. The truth is a mix of those things. I needed booze to help me have fun. Then I needed it to help me sleep. Then I needed it for everything else. Alcohol started making my decisions. And I made some bad ones obviously."

"Jax, just tell me."

"Over the years the secrecy surrounding my drinking

problem was eating away at me. The last year before I got help, I couldn't even look at myself in the mirror because all I saw was a liar and a coward and a drunken loser. A lonely loser who used random sexual encounters to feel something for a few minutes other than despair. But the booze took that away from me too; I'd black out with no memory of where I was, how I'd gotten there or who I had been with."

I don't want to hear this. I don't want to know this about you. I don't know that I can handle it.

I gave that whiny, scared, judgmental voice a hard mental slap. If he'd found the guts to tell me this, I'd find the courage to listen.

"But the kicker? What finally sent me to rehab? I had some health issues and I found out . . ."

The paused killed me. Killed me.

"I'd contracted a sexually transmitted disease."

Do not react. Not yet.

Jax jammed his hand through his hair. "I didn't know when it'd happened or who passed it to me or if I'd unknowingly passed it to someone else. Random encounters also meant I had no way of finding out." He closed his eyes. "I couldn't help but think it's what I deserved. I knew everyone in my life I'd ever hurt emotionally or pissed off would be fucking gleeful that I'd got my comeuppance. My stupidity and arrogance and self-involvement and entitlement had brought me to the lowest point in my life. I checked into rehab two days later.

"I dealt with the booze addiction and my new reality as being a lifelong carrier of an STD all at one time, because they were so wound up together I couldn't separate the cause from the effect. It's been a helluva lot easier telling people that I'm an alcoholic than I have HSV-2 and I'll be on medication for the rest of my life."

"Who knows?"

"That I have an incurable STD? My team doctor, my personal physician, my counselor." Jax lifted his gaze to mine. "And now you."

That shocked me.

"Mimi can't get it from me. But you can. There's the ugly truth. In fact, if we have sex, there's an eight percent chance that you'll be infected. Even if we use condoms. Even when I take Valtrex every day to control outbreaks. Even when I haven't had any outbreak for eighteen months. Not one sexy thing about that, is there? When I first found out I had this, I felt lucky that I hadn't ended up with HPV, Hep C, or syphilis. Then after doing research, I discovered that herpes two, like AIDS, can't be cured. I just have to learn to live with it. And tell any potential partner that I have it, so knowing that, I decided I wouldn't subject anyone to the slightest chance of exposure and chose abstinence."

My thoughts spun so fast I couldn't grasp a single one.

"I knew I wouldn't get involved in another intimate relationship that was temporary." Jax looked away, took a deep breath and returned his gaze to me. "I want you, Luce. I want you like fucking crazy. I love you. I want to spend my life with you and be the loyal, loving man you deserve. I'm not telling you this because I want you to throw caution to the wind and get naked with me right now. I'm telling you this because I want you to think about what it would mean for you, and for your health, if we become lovers. If you can't get past it . . . I understand that too. Maybe too well."

I frowned at him. "What's that mean that you understand too well?"

"I'd hoped after I started getting my life back together if I made the changes I needed to become a mentally healthy man, that maybe there would be a chance for us to try again. We loved each other fiercely once. We were good together until I screwed it up. I wanted to fix it. But there is no fix for the physical risk you'd take every time we'd be intimate. That night when you gave me a massage? I panicked. I wanted your touch, craved your attention, so much that for the briefest moment I forgot I couldn't just say yes and lose myself in that sexual relationship that was as natural as breathing to us. We had to talk about it first."

"And the night you went down on me?"

"There's no risk for you on the receiving end. That's no excuse for not telling you. But it just seemed so right, and as always with us, it happened so goddamned fast."

All of this was going fast. "So what now?"

"So now . . . you know." He exhaled. "I love you, Lucy Q. I've always loved you. No matter the outcome of this between us, I'm here for Mimi for the long haul."

"I don't doubt that, Jax." I paused and seized the chance to talk about something else. "What happened with her today?"

"She woke up like a character out of *Evil Dead.*" He locked his gaze to mine. "She's a safer topic for both of us, but I don't want to talk about her."

"I don't know if I can continue to talk about this. What good will it do?"

What will it change? hung in the air between us, followed by silence.

Jax watched me closely. When I didn't say anything else because I didn't know what to say, he said, "I understand. I'll just go."

"But . . ."

"There's no reason for me to stay."

"Jax."

"It's okay. We'll touch base tomorrow." He started backing away.

I swear by the time he reached my apartment door he was running.

And I didn't try and stop him.

———

After Jax left, I cracked open a beer and my laptop.

I needed to know the health issues, realities, complications about HSV-2 for myself.

Holy crap was there a lot of information. Everything I could possibly want to know about the STD. I must've hopped from article to article for over an hour, because the next time I reached for my beer it had gotten warm.

I closed my eyes and let the emotions I'd kept in check wash over me.

The one I expected to be the most prevalent, the "I told you so" smug feeling of satisfaction that he'd gotten what he deserved . . . was absent.

Neither did I feel manipulated by him telling me he loved me so he could finally get laid. Because if this secret was about pride, I'd be the last person he'd want to know. He'd cheated on me. It'd been a key factor in destroying our relationship. He had to fear that I'd laugh. Or I'd have no sympathy whatsoever. Or that I'd walk away because he wasn't worth the risk.

Mostly I felt sad that he'd accepted he'd have to spend his life without intimacy.

Being around him the past few months hadn't stirred up bad memories of our time together, but the good times, of which there'd been plenty. The bad times happened at the end. The worst times happened when we hadn't been together for years, when he took out his frustration with his life on me in the one way he could hurt me—financially. There was a two-year period where it seemed like he dragged me to court every other month to argue over child support and custody rights.

It'd been a shitty time in my life, but I'd survived it without turning to booze. Or random sexual encounters. I had something more precious to worry about than my pride: my daughter.

When I looked at Jax now, there was no trace of that self-hating, self-destructive man. All I saw was a man who knew what he wanted and was patient enough to wait for it, even when there was no guarantee that he'd get it.

I knew I'd fallen in love with him again, but I hadn't wanted to put myself out there first.

He'd taken the risk.

Now it was my turn.

Twenty

JAX

Tonight I regretted not putting in a home gym.

I could use a workout with a speed bag. And a punching bag. Beating the shit out of something held immense appeal.

In the scheme of things, Lucy could've reacted worse. A lot worse.

And I'd bailed before I saw something replace the shock on her face.

Like fear. Or regret. Or smugness.

I scrubbed my hands over my face and replayed everything that had happened earlier. Had I made a mistake not telling her sooner?

Yeah, I could imagine how that conversation might've gone.

Hey, Luce, while we're getting to know each other again, after I've been out of your life for eight years, and you might consider trusting me . . . before I can prove to you that I've changed . . . you oughta know I have an incurable STD, so whatdya say we give an intimate relationship a shot?

If I would've confessed all at the very start, we wouldn't have gotten to this point where I knew she felt something for me and our past hadn't destroyed all chances of a future together.

I hadn't fully prepared myself, however, for the stress I'd be under for however long it took for her to decide whether I—we—were worth the risk.

Maybe I'd watch a movie to take my mind off it, because there wasn't a chance in hell I'd be able to sleep tonight.

But I didn't move. I remained in the living room, brooding in the near dark as I stared out the windows, hating that my poor life choices had brought me here even as I understood without me making those bad choices, I wouldn't have wised up, become a better man, cleaned up my act. I wouldn't be here for my daughter or have this new relationship with Lucy. I'd be drunk, reliving my glory years, blaming everything and everyone but myself for my crappy, lonely life.

I'd decided to cook something when I heard the elevator ding.

Or maybe it was wishful thinking.

Then I saw a reflection in the window and movement behind me. My heart rate quadrupled before I slowly turned around and saw Lucy standing there. I honestly was so dumbfounded I couldn't form a single word.

Her hands were jammed in the pockets of her robe. It took a while before she found her voice.

"I can't imagine how hard that must've been for you, Jax. Telling me you love me and want a life with me and then having to tack on an 'oh, by the way, I have HSV-2' statement that might end everything between us."

"Has it?"

She didn't move. She didn't speak.

The next minute was the most excruciating of my life.

When she shook her head, I finally understood the need to fall to your knees in gratitude.

Lucy said, "Once again you put yourself out there first, leading by example. So before we dissect how our being together will change our day-to-day lives with Mimi, I want tonight for us."

"Us talking about the precautions we'll need to take?"

"If you want." Then she untied her robe and it hit the floor. "But I'd rather you just take me to bed."

What spurred me out of my shocked state of seeing the sexy woman I loved standing before me naked was seeing the sexy woman I loved standing before me naked holding a strip of condoms.

I must've growled when I charged for her, because she took a step back.

Then my mouth crashed down on hers, and my hands were all over her—fisted in her hair, caressing her face, trailing down her neck, covering her breasts, squeezing her hips, palming her ass. Dizzying to realize this beautiful woman had chosen me.

"Bed. Now," I gritted out.

"No," she said, chasing my mouth to steal more kisses. "That's too far away. Right here. In front of the fireplace."

Somehow, even with her clinging to me, I backed us up ten steps and snagged the remote that turned on the fireplace. Orange, yellow and red flames burst to life. No slow build, just instant heat.

That summed us up perfectly.

"Jax," she panted against my neck, "take off your clothes."

"Luce. Have some patience."

"We've passed that point, sport." She wiggled away from me. "Let me help."

Lucy slipped her hands underneath the front of my shirt,

her palms stopping on my pecs. "Your heart is going a million miles an hour."

"It tends to do that when you're touching me," I said gruffly.

"Do that sexy, he-man, one-handed shirt removal maneuver and I'll touch you some more."

Didn't have to tell me twice. *Whoosh*, my shirt landed on the floor.

"God. You still have the most fucktacular body."

Even when I wanted to watch her touching me, I closed my eyes and focused on the soft brush of her thumbs across my nipples. The delicate manner in which she dusted the tips of her fingers across my collarbones. Then she smoothed her hands lovingly down my arms, from the cup of my shoulders to the bones in my wrists.

As her sweet mouth followed the path her fingers had taken, I locked my legs to keep them from shaking. My breath came hard and fast. Each pull of air was saturated with her lemon and flowers scent, and I was drowning in need for her, for this to actually happen so I knew it wasn't just another damn dream.

I stayed still when her hands squeezed my hips for a few seconds, and then my pulse—and my cock—jumped when she hooked her fingers inside the waistband of my sweatpants and slid them down until they fell to my ankles.

I was naked.

She was naked.

I felt like a virgin and suspected I'd last as long as one too once I got inside her. Three years was a long time to be abstinent; nine years was a lot longer to wait to recapture this intimacy with the only woman I'd loved. Christ. I didn't want to disappoint her, but I didn't—

"Jax." Lucy's hands curled around my face and her lips were a breath from mine. "Stop worrying. Stop holding back."

She took my mouth in the fierce kiss I needed, her tongue owning mine. When I groaned with frustration because I needed more than just kissing, she ripped her lips free. "Baby, you already know how to love me. So show me. Remind me."

My fears faded. Her confidence in me bolstered my confidence. I growled, "Condom."

She slapped a square package on my chest so fast I wondered where she'd been keeping it.

After I rolled the rubber on—ignoring her protest that she wanted to do it—I fell to my knees on the rug in front of her. I dragged my mouth between her hip bones until her entire body trembled. My tongue followed the rise of her mound down between her legs. The sweet, sticky wetness I discovered did me in completely.

I brought her down to the floor and levered myself over her.

My arms shook as I indulged in a few more kisses on her beautiful face, the corners of her eyes, her jawline and the tip of her chin. A sheen of sweat coated my body, and I hadn't done anything strenuous.

Yet.

"Slow and sweet next time," she said as her grabby hands latched on to my ass and her legs circled my waist.

"You said that the first time, at Borderlands."

"I remember. And you nearly fucked me through the wall, Stonewall. Let's see if you can fuck me through the floor."

"God I love you."

I drove into her without finesse. I couldn't have gone slow and sweet if my life depended on it. The hot, wet, tight clasp of her sex nearly undid me right then.

Between Lucy yelling, "Yes, yes, yes," and her nails gouging my ass as I pumped and thrust, I reached the detonation point far too fast. But Jesus, nothing in my life had ever felt this good.

When she started biting my neck, I didn't have a fucking prayer of holding back. "Lucy, baby, I can't—"

"Go over. I want to watch you."

A kaleidoscope of colors exploded behind my lids as I started to come. My body kept the rhythm as my brain flitted away, letting me feel every hard throb, every suctioning pull of her muscles contracting around my shaft. Even as the orgasm ebbed, she clutched me tight, her soft words of love seared into my soul.

I collapsed on top of her with one last full-body shudder, burying my face in her neck.

Lucy let me stay that way for a little while as I tried to realign my worlds, but I wasn't a small guy, and when she'd had enough, she lightly tapped my ass, indicating I needed to move.

Lifting my head, I gazed into her eyes, letting her see every bit of emotion I couldn't put into words.

The emotions in her eyes mirrored mine.

Thank god.

Before I left the haven of her body, I took a little detour to her chest, kissing and licking and teasing until she squirmed and arched beneath me.

"Jax, I—"

"I know whatcha need, baby." I eased out of her and said, "Hang on." Then I plucked her up and carried her into our bedroom, where I made good on my promise that the second time would be slower and sweeter.

Yawning, after we thoroughly exhausted each other, I stretched out and pressed the side of my face into the pillow. I was too damn comfortable to even reach down and pull the covers over my naked body.

I'd half drifted off when the mattress dipped.

Lucy curled up next to me, resting her cheek on my shoulder blade and throwing her leg over the back of mine, pulling the covers over both of us, just like she used to do.

Her contented sigh echoed mine.

I just wanted to bask in the aftermath of two mind-scrambling orgasms, and by bask I meant . . . fall into a coma and sleep.

I'd reached that almost dreaming state when her soft voice tickled my ear.

"I'm so glad you told me everything, Jax, and there are no more secrets between us."

"Mmm." My brain sort of went back online, and I mumbled, "That's not true. I have another secret."

"You do?"

"Mm-hmm."

"What is it?"

"I bought the ice rink."

Twenty-one

LUCY

"You what?"

Jax had to be kidding.

I heard him snore. What the hell? He couldn't just drop this into pillow talk and then nod off.

Maybe he was half dreaming when he said that.

I sat up, yanked the bedding away—momentarily distracted by his amazing ass—and poked him in the ribs. Twice.

"Luce, I'm tired."

"So am I. But I will keep poking you. Tell me you're joking."

He turned his head and looked at me sleepily. "No joke. Can we talk about this in the morning?"

"Nope. Now."

A weary sigh escaped him and he rolled to his back.

"How did you end up buying Lakeside?"

Jax groaned and said, "Because that Agnes is a pushy old broad who's been wheeling and dealing her whole life and she suckered me in," with what sounded like affection. "We had an appointment with her at her mansion in St. Paul."

We . . . meaning him and Gabi.

"We get there and Agnes has this elaborate high tea planned, served in her fancy-ass dining room, on china that belonged to Napoleon or something."

I snickered.

"What?"

"I'm trying to imagine two ham-handed hockey players lifting their pinkies as they sipped from centuries-old tea-cups and noshed on miniature French pastries."

Jax flashed me his sweet grin. "You have no idea. Anyway, by the last dessert course I'm antsy because Agnes has grilled us on everything from our upbringings to our hockey careers to our favorite movies. While I'm not drinking, Agnes keeps pouring champagne for Gabi, which loosens her tongue, and that wasn't helping us move things along. Finally some butler dude reminds Agnes she has another appointment so she gets down to 'brass tacks'—her word choice, not mine. Immedi-ately she turns into this shrewd businesswoman who appar-ently knew my grandfather, the other Jackson Lund. He screwed her and her husband out of two big business deals sixty years ago, buying up smaller companies they'd intended to invest in. I'm thinking to myself . . . I'm screwed. Then she informs me that 'Jackson, the unpleasant toad' had actually done them a favor, forcing them to reevaluate their business goals, and they ended up multimillionaires."

"Wow. That's weird. Then again, the Lunds have been movers and shakers in the Cities for what . . . a hundred and fifty years?"

"It gets even more bizarre. Agnes believed it was karma that I—Jackson's namesake—came to her for a favor. To 'settle the score' she offered to sell me Lakeside, allowing me to take whatever action I want with the building and the staff. Her price was fair, Luce. Strictly from a financial perspective, I would've been an idiot to turn it down. Then that crafty old fox said she'd only sell me the ice rink if I also bought a run-down bowling alley in Rosewood that she's been trying to get rid of for over a year.

I blinked at him. "You own the ice rink *and* a bowling alley?"

"The papers I signed would attest to that," he said dryly.

"Who knows about this?"

He scratched his chin. "Me. Gabi. Agnes. Her butler/personal assistant guy. And now you."

I poked him in the ribs. "I've made it to the short list?"

Jax's eyes softened and he reached up to touch my face. "You're at the top of all my lists from here on out, Lucy."

I moved closer and kissed him. Twice. "What happens now?"

"Staff meeting on Tuesday. Dennis is gone. The other instructors will be informed they're on notice. Lakeside will be making changes for the next year. Not sure exactly what, except Gabi is reinstated and she'll take over coaching Mimi's team. I'll still handle the skills class and I've got a few other ideas, but Tuesday's the big day." He brushed my hair away over my shoulder. "Will you come to the rink on Tuesday? Work your PR charm with the parents and kids while I'm dealing with the coaches?"

"Jax. I don't know anything about running an ice rink."

He chuckled. "Funny. Neither do I."

"I'm serious. This is your business."

"No, baby, this is *our* business. Now that we're officially a couple, I want us front and center at Lakeside, not just me. All that means is we can tout it as a family-owned business."

"I won't have to do anything like manage ad budgets and

submit wage increases to payroll? Because I'm already taking on a ton of new responsibilities when Lennox goes on maternity leave."

"I just want your public support, even if in private you tell me I'm crazy for letting an eighty-five-year-old woman bully me." He caressed my arm. Those rough-skinned fingers sent tingles rippling across my flesh. "And I'll actually have a real office at Lakeside. No more sharing a closet space with Simone at the bar or borrowing the conference room at Chris's office."

"Makes sense you'd have your base of operations there since you've spent most of your life in an ice arena."

"Hiring competent managers also means I won't be stuck behind a desk. I want oversight in these businesses I've invested in . . . not being forced to make day-to-day managerial decisions. I have more important things to do."

"Like?"

"You." Jax flipped me onto my back and stretched out over me. "That will take up a lot of my time." He pressed his lips to the corner of my jaw, then he started a meandering path of kisses down my neck. "A lot, my Lucy Q, so you won't need to question what's my number one priority."

Early on Sunday morning, after Jax and I had made love for the fourth time—the man was insatiable—we'd had a detailed discussion about our expectations going forward, both as a couple and as a family.

Neither of us saw any reason to keep the truth of the change in our relationship from our daughter, because it wasn't temporary. Jax wanted me to move in immediately, and I agreed was no need for a transitional period. Intimately existing space, both of us being present in Mimi's life both eager to make that our new normal.

family brunch and the invite to

watch the Vikings game at Walker and Trinity's place. Jax picked Mimi up from his parents' house and took her out for ice cream so they could talk about their issues from Saturday. I could've gone with him to serve as a buffer in case things got tense. But they needed to find their own way to sort out conflict, especially now that things were about to change in Mimi's world once again.

Mimi was shocked to find me moving things from my bedroom into Jax's bedroom. She was even more shocked when we admitted we'd fallen in love again and the new apartment was where we'd all live together as a family.

Was Mimi happy about that? Not at all.

Several of the hurtful things she'd hurled at us were aspects of becoming a three-person family unit that Jax and I hadn't considered, including Mimi having to share her Daddy time with me, after she'd just gotten Daddy time, if we would be kissing all the time which was gross, if Daddy would make her do chores, if I'd let her watch cartoons before and after school, if she'd have a babysitter when we had Mommy and Daddy date nights like Calder's mom and dad did, how would she choose who helped her with homework or who she read books with every night, and it wasn't fair that she'd only have one bedroom when she used to have two.

But the real kicker was when Mimi said she never wanted us to have another baby, because we'd probably love the baby more than her and forget about her.

In the midst of her selfish concerns was real fear that she'd become less important in both of our lives. That's when we realized we needed help to make this new family dynamic work. Family counseling sessions brought to mind broken families—not families that had been renewed like ours, but neither Jax nor I were willing to sacrifice Mimi's happiness for our own. But neither were we willing to let an eight-year-old call the shots.

Thankfully Jax's counselor understood the stress the situation would put him under and set up an appointment for us with one of his colleagues.

Mimi had been quiet since Sunday night. She watched her dad and me together with equal parts suspicion and fascination, because we hadn't bothered to hide our happiness. There were no half measures with Jaxson Lund in public or private. In front of our daughter or behind our bedroom door.

Lucky me.

Tuesday I showed up at the ice rink after work to support Jax when he spoke to the staff. I'd almost made it to Jax's new office at the end of the hallway, when I heard someone call out, "Lucy?" behind me. I wheeled around and faced Gabi.

"What's up, Coach Welk?"

"Can I talk to you about something?"

"Sure."

She jammed her hands in her back pockets. Then she blurted out, "I want you to know I'm not looking to screw around with Jax. I'd never do that. I'm not like that." She paused to breathe. "I know it must seem like we've spent a lot of time together, but it's all been business related . . . well, except for when he took me to Snow Village so maybe I could jump the line on the waiting list for an apartment. Besides that, even when we played hockey Saturday night, Jax has been one hundred percent professional with me. In fact, he's the one who insisted that everyone stop calling me Gabi and start referring to me as Coach Welk. I have no interest in him romantically, okay? If he and I end up spending work time together, it'll only be about work. You have my word."

I tried to keep my face blank. Where was this coming from? I couldn't imagine that Jax had suggested she state her intentions to me. Had someone else brought it up with her? Because it seemed too specific to be a random convo. "I appreciate your honesty, Gabi, but can I ask why you're telling me this?"

Confusion distorted her expression, followed by disgust. "Because Jax's brother was a real dickhead about it Saturday night. He said I'd better figure out where I stand, because the last place he'd ever let stand was between you and Jax. Then he spewed a bunch of other stuff, but I was so mad I didn't hear it all. But his warning about me getting too cozy with Stonewall was loud and clear."

That dumbass. I'm sure he had good intentions, but he'd gone about it the wrong way. Nolan had no business trying to circumvent a problem that wasn't there. Not only that, it made Jax look like he needed help keeping his pants zipped. I guessed that Gabi hadn't said anything to Jax, because she and I wouldn't be having this discussion if she had.

I smiled at her, which freaked her out, because she took a step back, and I couldn't help but laugh. "Sorry. This is just a bizarre conversation, so bear with me, okay?"

She nodded.

"First of all, it takes guts to be proactive instead of reactive, and I appreciate that. Just from the little I know of your history at Lakeside, I understand why you'd want to deal with any issues right away. I'm happy and relieved that Jax has a person like you on his team and on his side through the upcoming changes. Maybe I should be jealous because you and Jax have hockey in common. But there's no question in my mind that you and Jax are friends. And I'm grateful that he has a colleague who understands that part of his life.

"That said . . . Jax and I have waded through some rough waters to get to this point, so he won't do anything to screw this up. Neither will I. We are a solid unit." I smiled at her again. "I appreciate your candor. Between us? Feel free to tell Nolan to mind his own business next time he decides to tell you what to do."

Gabi grinned. "Oh, I will, believe me. I wasn't sure how my boss would react to me giving his brother a piece of my mind."

"Better that than giving him a piece of your stick."

She blinked at me. "What?"

"Umm . . . isn't that a hockey saying? Something to do with part of your hockey stick getting in on the action?"

"You mean the phrase 'he got a piece of that'? That's from baseball."

I sighed. "I suck at hockey lingo."

"You ever want a crash course on it, hit me up."

"Thanks. I may need to do that if Mimi sticks with it." I bumped her with my shoulder. "Sticks with it? Get it?"

Gabi rolled her eyes.

"Come on, that has to be a hockey pun."

"It was, it just wasn't a good pun. Later, Mrs. L."

She walked off before I could correct her that Jax and I weren't married.

I walked through Jax's open office door and saw him leaning over his desk. "You're looking all official and owner-like."

"Shut. The. Door."

Terse words. That's when I noticed Jax wore his brooding face. "What's the matter?"

"Shut the damn door, Lucy."

Fine, Mr. Crabby.

Turning, I pushed it closed, rather than slamming it, and found myself pressed chest first against the door, watching Jax's hand as he twisted the lock.

He'd twined his other hand in my hair and pulled slightly in a lover's signal to expose my neck to him, which I did without hesitation.

His mouth brushed my ear. "That hallway has great acoustics," he murmured, "which means I can hear everything." He nuzzled my neck and repeated, "Everything."

Why was he telling me this . . . Oh. Crap. He'd heard me talking to Gabi.

"You don't have any idea, do you, what it meant for me to overhear that I have your full trust, when you didn't have a clue I was listening? To hear you tell Gabi that she'd never be a threat to our relationship because you are that fucking confident in us and in me? Christ. I've never been so relieved. So humbled." He kept rubbing his lips back and forth across that same section of skin until gooseflesh broke out. "And so turned on. Fuck, woman. I need to show you that I'll never take that trust for granted." He planted soft kisses from below my ear across the underside of my jaw. "I need to feel you, soft and wet and warm all around me."

"Now?"

"Right now." He dragged more kisses down my throat. "Please."

From the heat of his mouth, of his words, of his body pressed against mine, I'd started to drift to that sensual daze that Jax could invoke with little effort. And the *please* . . . I loved that as much as I loved *right now*.

My soft moan was all the encouragement he needed.

Jax rucked my skirt up to my hips, hooked his fingers beneath the waistband of my tights, then shimmied them and my panties down my legs to the tops of my boots. "I love that you wear skirts."

I knew he loved hobbling me, only allowing my legs to spread so far, forcing a tighter connection and less movement on my part, since I tended to be squirmy.

"Unbutton your blouse," he said against the curve of my shoulder, "then put both hands on the wall."

And I loved his commanding urgency, his rapid breath flowing against my skin.

Behind me, I felt his hands yanking down his sweats and

boxer briefs. Then his mouth was gone from my skin for a moment when he ditched his long-sleeved T-shirt.

My fine motor skills vanished entirely when I heard the crinkle of the condom wrapper, followed by the heavy weight of his erection nudging me.

Apparently my clothing removal wasn't fast enough. Jax tugged my blouse free, peeled it down my arms and chucked it on the floor. My bra quickly landed next to it.

Then his muscled chest was as hot and heavy as a sun-warmed rock against my back. I hissed in a breath when his right hand dove between my legs and his left hand impatiently swept my hair aside so he could sink his teeth into the nape of my neck as he impaled me.

"Oh god."

"Gotta be quiet so no one can hear how much fun we're having," he whispered, moving my hand to a better position on the wall to brace myself.

That fizzy, flipping, buzzy sensation overtook me when he started to thrust.

Yes, definitely fun, but so much more than that. "Jax."

"You can touch me all you want later," he growled into my ear.

We'd become attuned to each other so fast it'd scare me if I dwelled on it. Instead I blanked my mind to everything except how Jax made me feel—alive, desired, beautiful.

His.

The relentless rhythm he set never faltered as he kissed the slope of my shoulder. The man was a multitasking master, keeping his hand spread between my hip bones over my mound so he could stroke me and hold me in place as his other hand toyed with my breasts.

"Tell me you're close," he panted against my temple. "Christ, I need to work on my stamina, because I'm about to blow."

"Then do it. Do it as you're kissing me."

"Lu-cee." He said my name as a drawn-out groan, the last syllable vibrating against my mouth before our lips met in a hungry kiss.

He slammed into me twice more and then his body shuddered against mine.

I loved the energy I felt in that moment moving from him to me, proof of how powerful this love was between us.

Jax didn't break any part of our connection, his hips still pumping slowly, his fingers still stroking me, that perfect mouth of his still owning me with every sweet suck of my tongue and every damp slide of his lips across mine.

After he ended the kiss, he nuzzled the side of my throat as he pulled air into his laboring lungs. "I love you. So fucking much."

I pushed upright from the wall and reached back to clamp a hand on his ass cheek, and twisted my other arm over my head, wrapping it behind his neck. "Mmm. I love you so fucking much too."

"We should quit our jobs and spend every hour that Mimi is in school in bed. Can you imagine how killer my stamina would be?"

I nipped his jaw—hard—and he hissed. "You have like ten businesses you're running. Speaking of . . . Maybe this isn't the time to bring it up—"

"Unless you're bringing up being ready for round two . . . I don't even want to think about work when I'm still buried inside you and my dick is still half-hard." His hands gravitated to my hips and he gently pulled out. Then he kissed my temple and retreated.

I righted my own clothing and turned around to see he'd gotten dressed and was wiping off his hands with antibacterial wipes.

Then he said, "If I make this my main office, I'll have to install a private bathroom."

No communal bathrooms for the rich. I understood it went deeper than that, but I opted not to comment. When he offered me the wipes, I took one of those without comment too.

Three knocks sounded on the door and Jax grinned at me. "Maybe my lack of stamina isn't such a bad thing. Not enough time for us to get interrupted." He planted a kiss on my mouth. "But I still owe you one later tonight."

Jax opened the door and Margene paused in the doorway. "What's up, Margene?"

"Gabi asked me to come and get you. She needs you"— she looked at me—"both of you in the arena."

My stomach clenched. "Mimi?"

"Yeah, but she's not the injured party." Margene's eyes held wariness. "The boy she bodychecked is."

Twenty-two

JAX

Margene didn't say another word as we left the office and entered the rink.

Gabi had separated the kids—Mimi on one end of the players' bench and the kid she'd supposedly bodychecked on the opposite end.

I withheld a groan. Of course the kid in question had to be Thomas, the biggest boy on the team. My gaze scanned the spectators' area, but I didn't see his parents.

Before I stepped onto the ice, I looked at Lucy. "Stay here."

"Like hell, Lund. This isn't a coaching problem or an owner's problem but a parenting problem."

Gabi stopped me right off the bat. "Two things, Stonewall. First, you're a parent in this situation and understand that I cannot give Mimi special treatment. Second, I don't know why your brother was here for just a practice, but he caught the incident on his camera if you want to look at it."

Nolan ambled down, leveling animosity at Gabi before he

looked at me, then Lucy. "It's cued up to the right spot. Hit play."

Lucy leaned in and we watched on the small screen as Mimi skated, hell bent for leather, right at Thomas, slamming him into the boards with a perfect body check. He went down; she skated around him and added insult to injury by spraying ice in his face.

Jesus.

I watched it again. Then I said to Nolan, "Could you forward that to me, please?"

"Of course. But you should know why—"

"You aren't a parent, pretty boy, so your comments are irrelevant," Gabi snapped. "Thank you for your assistance and take your seat. Or leave."

"You're welcome, Gabriella."

"Coach Welk," she snapped.

"Where are Thomas's parents?" I asked Gabi.

"He said his dad is out of town this week and his mother dropped him off because she had to get his sister to dance class. She should be here shortly." Gabi pointed to the seats off to the left of the bench. "We'll deal with this when practice is over. The other players shouldn't lose ice and coaching time when none of them are at fault."

I muttered my agreement.

The next forty-five minutes were as hellishly long as I suspected they'd be.

At least the other kids were having a great practice. They'd shown dramatic improvement.

A harried-looking woman I remembered from the showdown with Dennis seemed confused as to why her son sat on the bench. When she tried talking to him, he ignored her.

Mimi hadn't looked at us even one time either.

Not that Lucy would've known if she had, as she was furiously texting with someone. Casually I said, "Remember our first meeting and I was annoying cell phone guy? You're about there, babe."

"Wrong. I'm not talking at a thousand decibels. I'm having a silent discussion with your brother."

"That's so much better. Now I have to think about you and Nolan text fighting about him warning Gabi off Saturday night. It's not like I don't have enough to worry about, with Mimi getting suspended the first week I own this facility. Or the deeper issues of her sudden aggressive behavior on the ice stemming from her unhappiness at home. And Margene asking if Lakeside is still hosting a huge holiday party for all the members. Which reminds me that Thanksgiving is next week, then it's Mimi's birthday and Christmas will be here before we know it. So do we spill the beans to our daughter about the fat man in the red suit? Because are kids still supposed to believe in him at her age? Then it's New Year's and Gabi is gone to the Olympics in South Korea for three weeks, which puts me right back in the coaching position that Mimi doesn't want me in. Will that give her an excuse to revert to this behavior we're dealing with today that she knows is wrong because she needs my attention?"

Two cold hands landed on my cheeks, and I found my face being turned toward Lucy's.

"Breathe with me," she said quietly, but firmly.

"Lucy—"

"Do the thing with your hands. Open, close. Open, close. Come on, Jax."

"How'd you know about that?"

"I watch you, man of mine, just as closely as you watch me." She brushed two soft kisses across my lips. "Now, unless you wanna make out with me, right here, right now, to take your mind off all this stuff you finally shared with me, take a deep breath in."

I did and curled my hands into fists.

"Good. Let it out."

I released the tension and my fists on the exhale.

We did that two more times until she dropped her hands and I could do it on my own.

Pushing me toward that structure helped me sort through my chaotic thoughts and compartmentalize what I could. The rest of it . . . I let go.

Lucy reached for my hand. "Better?"

"Yes. Thank you."

"I should be thanking you. I'd started adapting that technique when I was stressed at home, instead of reaching for booze, which is a good habit now that we're living together."

I squeezed her hand. "I don't expect you to give up alcohol."

"I'm not. I'm fine being an occasional social drinker. But our home will be booze-free."

I brought our joined hands to my mouth and kissed her knuckles. "I love you."

The whistle blew, forcing our attention away from each other.

Gabi dismissed the rest of the team and signaled for us to come in directly behind the bench.

"What's going on?" Thomas's mother asked.

"We had an incident earlier. Mimi"—she gestured for her to stand up—"bodychecked Thomas. It's a long-standing rule in hockey that there is no checking in the eight and under age group during a game, say nothing of in practice, and there's never any checking at any age level in the girls' or women's divisions." She looked at Mimi. "Which I've repeatedly reminded everyone."

"Oh, thank the lord," Thomas's mother said. "I thought maybe Thomas had crashed into her."

Wait. What? She wasn't angry?

"It was more than a simple crash, Sheila," Gabi said

carefully. "Mimi went after Thomas on purpose and knocked into him hard enough he'll have bruises on his bum."

Thomas's mom harrumphed. "I'll bet her coming after him wasn't entirely unprovoked, was it, son?"

Thomas hung his head and muttered.

She poked him on the shoulder. "Speak up so everyone can hear you."

"No, ma'am."

"What did you say to her?"

"That girls shouldn't play hockey with boys because they aren't tough enough and they can't even bodycheck. And the only reason Mimi was on the team was because of her dad being famous."

Beside me, Lucy sucked in an indignant breath.

Sheila forced Thomas to turn around. "We've talked about this. That is bullying and baiting and completely unacceptable." She poked him in the chest. "You are a big kid and it doesn't matter if you bully with your body or your mouth. And I won't stand for it, Thomas."

Gabi seemed at a loss for what to do, then she rallied. "Lakeside has a zero tolerance policy for disregarding standard hockey rules as well as a zero tolerance policy for bullying." Her gaze moved from Thomas to Mimi and back again. "Since you both broke the rules, you're both suspended for one game and one practice session. Sitting on the bench tonight doesn't count. I'm disappointed in both of you. Very disappointed. Head into the changing rooms and apologize to your teammates. You're supposed to be a team; you work together, not against each other. Now scram and get changed."

Then Gabi looked from us to Thomas's mother. "The matter is settled. No need to further hash it out. Obviously as parents you can do whatever you want as far as additional discipline. But when I was a kid, official discipline from the coach was worse than anything else—except my parents not allowing me to play hockey at all as punishment. So keep that in mind. I've already been the bad guy today." Her gaze flicked to someone behind us. "It's a role I'm familiar with. Now excuse me, I've got another class to teach." She skated away.

I hadn't expected that. Neither had Lucy. She leaned over and said, "Can Gabi run the entire hockey program?"

"Yeah, but she doesn't want to. She wants to coach."

"Jax. Who's going to be running it?"

"Me. For now." I stood. "There's a few things I need to wrap up before I come home. I won't be long." I leaned down and smooched her mouth, just because I could.

After owning the rink for just a few days, I knew the place could eat up my life in a way that the bar never did. And if I created a nice office space for myself, I'd end up being there all the time, which defeated the purpose of starting over with Lucy and took time away from Mimi.

But I couldn't just tell Margene to handle everything either. That'd been the issue with Lakeside—an absent owner and no one on the staff knowing who was in charge. I'd have to interview potential managers once we determined the long-term and short-term goals for the facility.

Life had been so much easier when all I had to worry about was playing hockey.

The next week the family counselor we'd chosen had requested to meet with Mimi alone for the first appointment. Lucy and I met with her afterward and were shocked at all the things the counselor had found wrong with our child. It took every ounce of restraint I had not to lash out at the supposed professional for her comments about Mimi being egotistical, manipulative and unmotivated as well as suffering from ADHD and only child syndrome—I hadn't even known that was a thing.

By the end of the hour, my hand had hurt from where Lucy had squeezed it so hard. Her tears soaked my shirt after we finally escaped from the counselor's berating. It just reminded me how lucky I'd been in finding a counselor who helped me through my recovery, because not all counselors were created equal.

It was the first crisis Lucy and I faced together as parents. We weren't sure how much truth there was to the counselor's claims and if we'd downplayed Mimi's behavioral issues because we loved her and chalked it up to Mimi being . . . quirky little Mimi. Figuring out the next step—whether we should contact a different counselor or muddle through on our own—ate at both of us, especially when Mimi wasn't acting out and seemed to accept the new reality that she lived with her mom and dad together as a family.

Thanksgiving week started out with a bang, Lennox giving birth and my cousin Brady being over the moon about their baby boy, Jaden Ward—whom I'd already nicknamed JW. Lennox's absence from the PR department meant Lucy had to stay late to catch up, leaving me and Mimi to make Thanksgiving preparations.

I'd lived my entire life clueless about family holiday expectations. My folks and brother showed up wherever we were playing Thanksgiving week because there wasn't a break in the hockey schedule. Since the rest of my family would be scattered—Ward and Selka, Rowan and Calder, Walker and Trinity and their son were traveling to Detroit to watch Jensen play; Annika would be on the East Coast for Axl's back-to-back games; my uncle Monte and aunt Priscilla, Ash and Dallas would be with Priscilla's family down South—that left my immediate family. Now my immediate family included Lucy's sister, Lindsey, their mother, Jill, and her companion, Benny. So bighearted Lucy had invited everyone to our place for the big meal. A meal that she passed off to me when she had to deal with both Lennox and Annika being gone from LI at the same time.

My mom volunteered to help, but dammit, I had my pride. I'd been taking cooking classes for a few years. How hard could it be? Plus, I had Mimi as my trusty helper.

But we ended up staying late at Lakeside on Wednesday night, and by the time we returned from the grocery stores—which had taken two hours because who knew all the stores would be that busy?—it was after eight P.M. and we hadn't cracked open a single can for pumpkin pie.

The kitchen disaster started when Mimi dropped an entire bag of flour on the floor from counter level.

We burned the pies, filling the kitchen with black smoke that set off the smoke detectors.

A can of whipped cream spontaneously blew up in the refrigerator.

I realized I didn't have a pan large enough to roast the gigantic turkey, and the turkey was still mostly frozen.

We forgot to buy potatoes. How had that happened?

Lucy came home to find me and Mimi sitting on the kitchen floor, eating raw chocolate chip cookie dough for supper because that was the one thing we hadn't fucked up.

Did she lecture me?

Nope.

Did she sigh and take over food prep?

Nope.

She grabbed a spoon and joined us.

In that moment, my life was absolutely perfect.

In the hour following our cookie dough binge, Lucy called five shelters, found the one that needed volunteers, ordered an astronomical amount of food from a dozen different carryout places and hired a delivery service to pick it up and drop it off in the morning.

Our family dinner plans changed. The guests who thought they were dining with us ended up helping us serve food at the shelter. Then afterward, we had everyone back to our place for pizza, ice cream, homemade cookies and games. We'd ended up with extra guests—Gabi, whose parents were in Tampa with her sister Dani as she prepared for the Olympics; Simone, who had no family; Martin and Verily, my former neighbors from Snow Village; Flynn, one of the coaches at Lakeside, and his wife, Suzie; and a surprise visit from my Lund cousins from Duluth, Zosia and Zach, who were flying out of Minneapolis the next morning for a fishing vacation in Florida.

Everyone said it'd been the best Thanksgiving they could remember and they couldn't wait to do it again next year.

A family tradition had to start somewhere, and for once I'd been a part of starting something.

Sunday afternoon we got to meet the newest Lund when we dropped a meal off for Lennox and Brady. Seeing JW . . . I got a little melancholy. I hadn't been around during Mimi's baby years and hated that I'd missed so much.

And Mimi, who'd declared "I never want you to have another baby" earlier in the month, completely changed her mind upon seeing her new baby cousin. She announced she'd break the pinkie promise she'd made with Calder that they'd run away if either Lucy or Rowan got pregnant.

Kids. Never a dull moment with them.

The other good thing that came out of the visit to Lennox and Brady's was meeting Lennox's best friend Kiley, who was a counselor and a social worker. Lucy spilled her guts to Kiley about the other counselor's diagnosis of Mimi, which spoke volumes of how much it'd bothered her, because she never brought strangers into our business. Kiley said she'd be happy to observe Mimi in a couple of different social situations and give us her honest opinion.

Soon after, we helped Kiley out with a holiday party for the kids in her program. She attended one of Mimi's hockey games and a practice, plus she and her husband and their toddler daughter had dinner with us. Lucy and I were relieved when Kiley assured us that Mimi was exactly as she appeared: a kid adjusting to changes in her life and using that to her advantage—just like any other normal kid. To show our gratitude for Kiley's help, I gifted her vouchers for both Lakeside and the bowling alley for her program so she had options for the kids' activities.

Nails skated down my arm, pulling me from my thoughts.

"Whatcha thinking about so hard, Daddy-o?"

I glanced at Lucy, lying in bed next to me. "If the next four weeks will be as busy as the past month."

"The holidays are their own kind of crazy. Add in December being birthday month for Mimi, and I'm facing end-of-the-year wrap-up at LI . . . for us, December is extra crispy crazy."

"Extra crispy crazy?" I smiled at her. "You've got fried chicken on the brain."

"Can you blame me? My brain is fried," she admitted with a yawn. "I mean, Mimi's birthday party requests weren't excessive; the build-your-own-cupcake station is getting to be standard birthday party fare. But where on earth did she get the idea for fried chicken and waffles? And a mashed potato bar?"

"I caught her and Calder watching old episodes of that show on MTV where the kids have over-the-top birthday parties, so that's probably where she saw it. High five for talking her out of having a chocolate fountain, mamacita."

Lucy hit her palm to mine. "She's already hinting for a

sleepover party for next year, but I told her not until she's ten, so we've got a year to prepare for it."

Slipping my arm under her lower back, I rolled her on top of me.

"You are such a beast that you can maneuver me around with one arm."

"You love it." I pushed her hair over her shoulder, letting my fingers glide through the silky softness. "I hope we'll have another child by Mimi's tenth birthday."

As she stared at me, I noticed her deep brown eyes weren't bright with possibility.

"What?" I asked her warily.

"I love you."

Here we go. "And?"

"And babies are a lot of work. Before you get that 'Shit, is she gonna lecture me again about not being around when Mimi was a baby?' look on your face, my concerns have nothing to do with what happened back then. It's about now. Because your non-hockey-playing life is so overloaded with Stonewall Enterprises responsibilities that you don't have time for a baby."

Okay. So that stung.

"I've done the baby thing by myself once. That was enough." She scooted forward and braced her hands on the mattress, one on either side of my head. "Although it feels like we've been together for a long time, it's only been a few weeks. We all need time to get into a solid groove as a family before we start adding new members. That means no babies for a while. And no puppies or kitties or fish or ferrets or hamsters or guinea pigs or potbellied pigs or whatever critter of the week Mimi has been not-so-subtly hinting would be a great Christmas gift for her."

"Luce. Do you *want* to have another baby or two with me?"

"Yes." She feathered her lips across mine in barely-there kisses. "But the old-fashioned girl inside me wants us to be married before another baby happens."

That caught me by surprise. Lucy had never hinted that she wanted that. "I asked you to marry me, and you turned me down."

"You haven't asked me recently," she cooed.

"Lucille Quade, will you do me the honor of becoming my wife?"

"Where's the ring?"

I squinted at her. "What?"

"You can't propose without a ring." She nipped my chin. "I'm only doing the marriage thing once, so your proposal better be epic and not something you blurt out in bed because you felt pressured."

Where had all of this come from?

From the girlie, romantic side of her that Lucy rarely acknowledges, which allows you to ignore all that hearts and flowers shit that you're bad at anyway.

I narrowed my eyes at her. "Don't get your hopes up that my proposal will be some epic thing like Jensen did for Rowan." My cousin had popped the question at a U of M football game, where Rowan was the collegiate cheer team coach and he'd hired the marching band to spell out MARRY ME ROWAN during halftime. "Or like Walker did with Trinity." That proposal had happened in front of our entire family at a barbecue. "Or like that fucking showoff the Hammer did for Annika." Axl had gone all out during the Wild's last home game of the season, proposing to her on the ice in front of the crowd at the Xcel Energy Center. "Brady is the only one who's shown any sense." He'd bought the rings, booked the ticket and whisked Lennox off to be married on an island, just the two of them.

"Uh, no thanks. All of those are far too public. It's a life-changing moment for two people, and it should be private."

There was my practical Luce.

"Anyway, back to the original issues. To have a baby, you do realize we'd have to stop using condoms."

I snorted, but my heart beat faster.

"Speaking of condoms . . . I'm tired of them."

It's for your own good, woman.

"I know you're protecting me, Jax." As she spoke she teased my mouth with hers and kept our gazes locked. "You're meticulous about hygiene. Maybe that's why you haven't had an outbreak in a year and a half. I don't have to tell you that the virus isn't transferable through your sperm and there's still a two percent chance you'll infect me even when you're not showing symptoms even if we use condoms."

"Jesus, Lucy, what—"

"I love making love with you. Love it. I crave it. You can make me beg you for it. But since we've renewed our intimate relationship, you haven't let me go down on you. Not once. That's not protecting me, baby. That's denying me."

She sank her teeth into my lower lip and tugged. "I want you in my mouth, no condom. I want to feel your hands on my head, pulling my hair, as I take you over the edge and drink you down."

My dick jumped to attention.

"Please," she whispered against my jaw. "Let me have my wicked way with you."

Before I answered, Lucy pushed up onto all fours and started kissing her way down my body. Slowly, giving me a chance to change my mind.

But she was right. I wanted this.

Propping myself on my elbows, I watched her enjoying my body. Her little hums of approval as she licked my nipples.

Her deep inhale as she nuzzled the hair between my pecs. Then an actual growl as her tongue traced the groove of flesh between my waist and hips known as an Adonis belt. She went a little crazy there, and that in turn made me crazy, especially when the ends of her hair randomly arced across my flesh—little tickles of sensation and my body tightened in anticipation.

When Lucy reached the end of—or the start of, depending on your perspective—my happy trail, she looked at me as she swirled the flat of her tongue around the head of my dick.

That visual was permanently etched in my brain as was the next one: her sucking my shaft in deep until the tip hit the back of her throat.

Watching her watching me, I understood why she'd pushed me on this—intimacy shouldn't have boundaries. She'd broken the last one with every lick, suck and sexy, flirty look from beneath her long eyelashes.

And I'd forgotten how amazing this felt.

One thing I hadn't forgotten? She liked it when I took charge. I curled my hand around the bottom of her jaw as I began to move my hips. "I'm not gonna last."

Her smirk said she knew that.

After she'd blown my top, she crawled up my body, lazily dropping kisses across my skin, turning me into a mass of gooseflesh from head to toe.

"There. Now that wasn't so bad, was it?"

I cracked one eye open. "I don't know. Maybe you'd better do it again so I can be doubly sure."

Twenty-three

LUCY

I hadn't gotten good and pissed off at Jax for weeks.

Weeks.

But as it was now the twenty-third of December and I'd yet to see the Santa gift for Mimi that he swore he'd purchase, I'd reached the pissed-off stage.

He'd been burning the candle at both ends since he'd taken over Lakeside, as he'd also been dealing with the bar remodels, some issue at the office building he owned that he was being very vague about, as well as the bowling alley. He'd missed half of our cookie baking night with Calder, Rowan and Jensen. He'd arrived just in the nick of time to Mimi's school holiday program. And I suspected the man hadn't shopped for a single Christmas gift.

Which was why I showed up at Lakeside when I knew he wasn't there so I could snoop through his office and see if he had gifts stockpiled that he hadn't brought home.

Margene chased me down the hallway after I booked it past her office.

"Hey. Lucy. Jax isn't here."

I know. "That's okay. I'm just looking for something he might've left here."

She stepped in front of the door, the bells on her elf hat jangling. "You can't go in there."

"Why not?"

"Because it's two damn days from Christmas. What if he's got your present on his desk?"

I couldn't help but ask, "Does he? Have you seen it?"

She shook her head.

"Of course you haven't, because I doubt the man has bought even one gift. But it's not my gift I'm worried about, Margene. He wanted to be 'one hundred and ten percent' involved in the Santa thing, so I let him take care of it. It's roughly thirty-six hours before that gift needs to be under the tree for Mimi. And if he's dropped the puck on this . . ."

Her shoulders slumped. "I ain't gonna lie. I'm here all day, every day, and I've not seen Jax carrying in any packages, nor has FedEx or UPS delivered any boxes with his name on it for the past week."

"Just fucking awesome." I leaned against the opposite wall. "Better start looking for another job because I'm gonna kill him."

Margene snickered. "Maybe he had that stuff sent to his folks' place? Or even Nolan's? Knowing that little snoopy miss would find it here and—"

"Because hiding it someplace other than in our six-thousand-square-foot apartment with locking cabinets and tall shelving that Mimi couldn't possible access even if she had a ladder . . . makes so much more sense?"

She reached out and patted my shoulder. "Men suck at

holidays, sweetie. The decorating and the shopping and the cooking and the wrapping and the freaking out about being in charge of everything—that falls on women's shoulders every year. Even when we swear next year we'll go the minimalist route—fewer gifts, simpler meals, less social obligations. My husband was as surprised as the kids when they opened their gifts on Christmas morning, because he didn't have a damn clue what 'we'd' bought them."

"Jax has spent one Christmas with Mimi. One. And it wasn't even an entire day." I breathed in. Breathed out. "I'm not looking for perfection. But I feel like this is the last year the jolly man in the red suit will still hold that magic for her. I want Jax to get to experience it with her. If her Santa request isn't met . . . she'll be disappointed. And I'll be upset because her disappointment is one hundred and ten percent avoidable if I would've taken care of it like I always do."

"Maybe that's where Jax is right now," she said a little loudly. "You need to have some faith in him."

"I guess."

Margene reached over and hugged me. "Go finish the million other things that need to be done in the next day and a half. I'm sure when Jax gets home later tonight, and you ask him, he'll assure you he did what he'd promised."

I hugged her back. "Thanks, Margene."

"Do you want me to tell him you stopped by?"

"Nope." I put my gloves back on and rewrapped my scarf around my neck.

By the time I'd reached my car in the parking lot, I'd already gone to the next item on my long list.

JAX

Three raps sounded on my door. "You can come out now. She's gone."

As soon as I opened the door, Margene laid into me. "Please tell me Lucy has it all wrong and you've got Mimi's Santa gifts squirreled away in here."

"Dammit." I ran my hand through my hair. "I knew I was forgetting something."

"Jaxson Lund! You are in such deep doo-doo."

"I know, I know. But I've had a million things on my mind . . ."

"Not a valid excuse, especially not this time of year when we women have to do every damn thing ourselves."

Do not defend yourself. In this moment it doesn't matter that you have Lucy's gifts in your car.

"You do know what Mimi wants from Santa, right?" Margene demanded.

I had a vague idea. "Of course."

"Is it something you can trot your butt out to the store and buy right now so I'm not ordering funeral flowers for you next week before I start searching for a new job?"

"Hilarious, Margene. I can buy what Mimi wants, but it'll take me a few hours to get it."

She pointed at my cell phone. "Well, what are you waiting for? Get. It. Done." She slammed the door behind her.

It wasn't very often I exercised my right to use the Lund Industries corporate jet, but this qualified as an emergency. The first call was to my dad to make sure the plane was on standby and ready to go.

The second phone call was to my mother.

"You forgot to get Mimi's Santa gift, didn't you?" was how she answered the phone.

Awesome.

"Yeah. I need your help. Like right now. And I'm hoping that you don't have one of your ten million social engagements tonight, but I'm so screwed, Mom. Please, please, please save my ass and help me save Christmas."

She laughed. "Oh, this is so good. If I do this, you will owe me big-time, understand?"

"Anything."

"Anything?" she repeated with curiosity, which meant the return favor would likely haunt me, but beggars and all that.

"Yes, anything."

"All right, boy, hit me with the five W's."

"I'll fill you in on the flight to Chicago."

Twenty-four

LUCY

I yawned and clutched my coffee mug. My third cup and it was only six thirty in the morning.

But it was Christmas morning and Mimi had no problem getting up at the ass-crack of dawn.

"Want me to make another pot?" Jax murmured sleepily beside me.

"No. I'm good."

"Mmm. Me too. This robe is so comfy I just wanna nap."

After the Santa-extravaganza, Mimi had forced us to open our gifts from her first, which were super fluffy bright red matching robes, personalized with MOM and DAD and MIMI and 2017. It was such a sweet gift and Jax had been surprised by it too, so I'd have to thank Edie for taking Mimi Christmas shopping.

"Mommy! Look at this one!" Mimi held up a tiny pair of bright purple ski pants.

"Those are awesomely cute."

"And the jacket doesn't even *match*, just like a real snowboarder's outfit."

Jax chuckled.

I leaned closer and whispered, "Did you buy the entire American Girl store?"

"Damn near. You should see the camping gear. It is way cool."

Jax had scored high points with "Santa's" gift: an American Girl doll who looked like Mimi. There were boxes of clothes and accessories, everything from the hockey uniform the doll came outfitted in, complete with helmet, stick and tiny Chicago Blackhawks sweater with LUND and her dad's number across the back, to a lion tamer's outfit and a chef's uniform.

"She's gonna want to play dolls with you, Daddy-o."

He kissed my cheek. "I can't wait."

For the next hour we watched an animated Mimi inspecting every item in detail, so it was a perfect, lazy Christmas morning where we could just . . . be.

Upon reaching the last box, a strange look crossed her face.

"Something wrong, sweetie?"

"I don't see the outfit I really, really wanted."

That surprised me, given the fact she sat among the rubble of a dozen outfits and accessories, and it wasn't enough? When had she become so greedy?

"Which outfit was that, squirt?" Jax asked carefully.

"The big sister outfit with the baby carrier. So when you and Mommy have a baby, me 'n my doll match."

And I just melted. Mimi hadn't said anything about us having a baby since we'd met Brady and Lennox's boy, JW. In typical Mimi fashion, she'd needed time to process it before she'd accepted the idea.

"See? Even Mimi's on board with the baby project," he whispered.

Then why haven't you asked me to marry you?

Maybe in this day and age it seemed silly to want that piece of paper and a ring, but I did, even when I had the promise of forever from Jax every time he told me he loved me.

After we ate breakfast, a delicious overnight French toast that Jax and Mimi had prepared the night before, Mimi wanted to open the other gifts.

Jax and I had agreed to buy only one thing for each other, so I had a serious case of present anxiety at seeing his lone present from me beneath the tree.

We waited until Mimi had opened all of hers before she handed us the last two boxes.

"Mommy should go last," Mimi said slyly and tossed the wrapped box to her father.

Jax shook the present. "Hmm. Whatever could it be?"

"Open it!" Mimi said, bouncing on the couch with excitement.

He tore the paper like the Hulk, sending Mimi into a fit of giggles.

That sound. The huge grin on Jax's face. This was how our family was supposed to be, cuddled up together in our robes and laughing. This was the best Christmas present ever. Did I really need a ring to make it better? No. I sent a silent thank-you to the universe that we'd finally ended up here.

"Uh, Luce?"

I glanced over at Jax's very handsome, very confused face as he dangled a key between us.

"My gift to you requires us to take a little field trip. No, you don't have to get dressed." I stood and took Jax's left hand. "Help him up, Meems."

Linking hands, the three of us took the elevator down to the eleventh floor in silence, which was a feat for our daughter. We stopped in front of our old apartment and I said, "Go on in."

"I'm scared."

"Don't be silly, Daddy."

"Yeah, Daddy-o, don't be silly."

Jax gave me a smacking kiss before he opened the door. The apartment had been emptied.

But I'd brought two items into the empty space.

Jax looked at the Borderlands sign sitting on the plain metal desk, and then back at me. "What's this?"

"Your new office. Or it will be once it's designed to your specs. I've already talked to Walker. He's eager to make up for mishandling the bar remodel, and he's agreed to finish this in a timely fashion." I moved in and wrapped my arms around his waist. "You need an office of your own, Jax. But it doesn't need to be in the bar, or at the ice rink, or at the bowling alley, or even next to your manager's. This apartment is empty, and the elevator is coded to this floor. If you feel like you need to work in the evening, you don't have to go far. There's space for a small conference room if you want one, and you'll have a dedicated area to display your sports accolades. You can even have video camera surveillance routed here once the computer system is running, so you can keep an eye on your businesses and employees without having to be right there. Plus, you'll have a private bathroom, just like all the bigwig Lund executives at LI do." I pointed to the sign. "All you have to do is look at that and you'll know you're in your happy place. And if you need further assurance, hop on the elevator and you're home with us."

"Lucy. I . . ."

I'd never seen him at such a loss for words.

Mimi started skipping around with her doll, chattering away to it, giving us privacy.

"Did I overstep my bounds?"

"Never. I'm just so floored that I don't know what to say. This is the perfect solution. I don't know why I didn't think of it."

"Because you've already got enough going on. And Walker is giving me the discount he promised you, which is the only way I can afford to do this for you."

"Thank you." He rested his forehead to mine. "You really knocked my Christmas gift outta the park. Now my gift to you seems lame in comparison."

"I'm sure—" was all I got out before Jax's mouth landed on mine.

He kissed me with the mix of sweetness and passion that lit me up like a Christmas tree.

This was one of his I'm-in-charge kisses, forcing me to be patient.

This was one of his seduce-you-now, conquer-you-later kisses.

This kiss filled me with his love until I was overflowing with it.

I poured it right back into him.

"Are you still kissing?" Mimi said with a put-upon sigh. "Come *on*. Mommy still needs to open her present."

"Okay, kiddo, let's go."

My gift from Jax was a gorgeous necklace, five different-colored sapphires in five different shapes—an orange rectangle, a green circle, a pink diamond, a purple square and a blue oval—spaced on a platinum chain.

"I helped pick it out," Mimi said proudly.

"You did great, because it's perfect. I love it. Thank you."

"You're sure?" he asked anxiously.

"The presents are just icing. Us being together, that's the real gift, Jax."

"You always say the perfect thing."

ours later, after we'd made the rounds to family and friends, Jax and I were sprawled in our bed, naked and panting after he'd "gifted" me with two orgasms to cap off my perfect Christmas.

He kissed my shoulder and said, "Baby, you asleep?"

"Yes. Santa is only supposed to come once a year and you've already doubled that in one night, so hands off, big guy."

"I've always been an overachiever." His gentle fingers pushed my hair out of my face, and he leaned down to peer into my eyes.

My eyes narrowed at him. "What?"

"I promised Mimi I wouldn't tell you this until Christmas was over because she didn't want you to be mad at her. It's twelve thirty, so technically, Christmas is over . . ."

"Tell me."

"When she moved her hockey bag out of your car into mine, she spilled her orange Creamsicle shake all over the floor and the back seat of your car," he said in a rush.

"When did this happen?"

"Yesterday morning after she and I finished running errands."

My mouth dropped open. "There's been ice cream sinking into the interior of my car for a day and a half and you're just telling me now? Do you *know* how much a sour milk product reeks?" I paused. "Is that why you insisted on taking your car today when we went to spread Christmas cheer?"

"Yeah." He gave me a sheepish smile. "Sorry. We did get most of the mess cleaned up right after it happened. Anyway, I kept my promise to her and now you know."

"I know what I'll be doing first thing tomorrow morning," I grumbled.

"I can take it and get it detailed for you, if that'll put a smile on this beautiful face."

"Nope." I poked him in the chest. "You promised Mimi you'd play with her new toys tomorrow, buddy."

"All day?"

"All day and all night, probably. The girl's got stamina."

"Mmm. So do I." He planted kisses down my spine. "You can stay just like that, all sexy and sleepy, and I'll do all the work."

For five seconds, the next morning, after seeing the enormous stain in the back seat—orange food dye was nearly impossible to remove—I considered selling my car rather than having it detailed. But my frugal side won out and I drove to the super deluxe car wash closest to our apartment.

With an hour to kill, I grabbed a magazine and a Diet Mountain Dew. The lobby was completely empty—not a surprise since it was only nine a.m. the day after Christmas. Thankful for the quiet time, I settled in.

My alone time lasted about ten minutes. The door banged open, and I heard a man yakking on his cell phone at a thousand decibels, but I couldn't see him.

The sound of his voice made the hair on the back of my neck stand up.

"Yeah? Well you suggested it when I told you money was no object, and I think she's really unhappy with it." Pause. "Why? Because she gave me a thoughtful, personal, perfect gift and all she got from me was a crappy Cartier necklace."

I rolled my eyes. Crappy Cartier? I don't think so.

"What the gift said was that I don't listen to her. I didn't get her what she really wanted. She tried to hide her disappointment, but damn, I don't think she realizes that those beautiful brown eyes of hers reveal every emotion."

I kept my head down, playing along as he recreated the scene.

Annoying man on his cell phone?

Check.

Annoying man pacing around me?

Check.

From the reflection in the glass that allowed customers to see their cars going through the automated portion of the car wash, I watched every inch of his six-foot-four frame pacing, those long, muscled arms gesturing wildly.

He couldn't see me smiling at him, as his head was down and his baseball cap put his face in shadow. Not that he'd looked my way even one time to see if his loud, one-sided conversation might be bothering me.

Because it was bothering me that he thought I hadn't liked his beautiful gift to me.

He stopped moving. "Fine. You think it's stupid as shit I'm doing this, but I want her to know her worth to me." Pause. "Look. I'm done with this convo. I'll call you later, bro. Bye."

My heart threatened to beat out of my chest when he stopped in front of me, but I nonchalantly flipped through a couple of magazine pages.

Then he plopped down on the bench directly across from me. I felt his gaze moving up my legs from my heeled suede boots to where the hem of my wool skirt ended above my knees.

"Ever have one of those days?" he asked me.

"One of those days where you're enjoying a rare moment of quiet and some rude guy destroys it with an obnoxiously loud phone conversation? Why yes, ironically enough, I *am* having one of those days right now."

Silence.

Then he laughed. A deep rumble of amusement that had me glancing up at him.

Our eyes met.

That punch of lust hit me like it always did.

"Jax. What are you doing here?"

He leaned in, resting his forearms on his knees. "Making conversation with the most beautiful woman I've ever seen. Do you know what today is?"

"No clue, dude."

"In Canada, it's 'Boxing Day,' which I never understood. Why would the day after Christmas be devoted to a sport where guys beat the crap out of each other? I always thought it'd be more appropriate if they called it 'Hockey Day' because . . . well . . . Canada and hockey, aay."

I snickered.

"Anyway, my Canadian teammates cleared up the 'Boxing Day' confusion for me. Boxing Day is when you box up leftovers from your Christmas feast and share them with the less fortunate." His eyes searched mine. "Did you know that's what it meant?"

"Nope. I took it literally too."

"Good. Because I have something in a box for you . . . but it's not leftovers."

I forgot how to breathe when Jax shifted and dropped to one knee in front of me.

Then a brown velvet box appeared in his palm. He studied my face with wonder and devotion. "Lucy Quade, I love you. I've always loved you. Getting a second chance with you is more than I deserve, and I'll devote my days to making your life as full and happy as you've made mine. Every day with you is better than the day before. I want a lifetime of that, with you by my side as my wife. So will you marry me?" He lifted the lid on the box.

I leaned in to get a closer look, but my eyes were already swimming with tears.

Jax plucked the ring out and gently took my left hand. He kissed my ring finger before he slid the ring on.

The stone in the ring was so big I swear it threw prisms across Jax's face as I lifted the ring up to look at it closer.

"Holy crap, Jax, it's huge."

"I've been waiting a long time to hear you say that, my Lucy Q." He laughed when I whapped him on the biceps.

I turned the ring, this way and that, absolutely mesmerized by the extreme sparkles coming from a singular stone. "I've never seen a diamond cut into this shape."

"I dealt with a bunch of jewelers before the guy found this one. I wanted simple, and classy, a huge heart with the highest level of clarity so it perfectly matched how I see . . . you."

"You're gonna make me cry."

"Baby, you're gonna make me cry if you don't say yes."

"Yes, I'll marry you, you crazy annoying man." I gave him a skeptical look. "This was a damn good setup for a proposal. How long have you planned this?"

Jax grinned. "Remember when you said you wanted things to unfold 'organically' between us? I knew neither of us wanted a public proposal, so I'd intended on proposing to you on Christmas Eve after Mimi had gone to bed and it was just the two of us. But after that spill, I realized I could use that to my advantage. You're a creature of habit; I knew you'd come here, so I called and rented the place for an hour."

"You just rented it? You didn't buy it?"

"Smartass. I don't buy everything."

I set my hand—left hand, of course, so I could admire my new sparkling heart-shaped engagement ring that had to be at least ten carats—on his chest. "I love that you thought of this and I love you, Jaxson Lund." Then I kissed him with more passion than I usually did in public.

Jax groaned against my lips. "Let's go home and cele-brate. Naked."

Guilt swamped me: I realized I hadn't thought about Mimi at all. "Where's—"

"Mimi is with my folks."

"Did she know you were going to propose?"

"No one did. This belongs to us." He grimaced. "Gotta move these creaky old hockey player knees." He stood and sat next to me. "Can this be a super short engagement?"

"How short?"

"Are you busy this afternoon?"

My first reaction after laughing was to argue with him that we couldn't possibly get married today . . . but I realized I never wanted the pomp and circumstance, I just wanted him. And that's precisely what he'd offered. "I went on a date with you thirty minutes after we met. In keeping with tradition, getting married half an hour after you proposed is so—"

"Us," he finished.

This man.

Then Jax kissed me in that cajoling way I couldn't resist. I'd already made up my mind, but I let him "convince" me a little longer.

"So what do you say?"

"I say yes."

Epilogue

JAX

A finger poked me in the side, startling me. I jolted awake and cast a bleary eye on my daughter.

"Daddy. Come *on*. Mommy said it's time."

I noticed Lucy's side of the bed was empty. Whoa. I hadn't heard her get up. It hadn't been that long ago we'd gone to bed.

"Where is she?"

"Waiting for us." Mimi bounced up and down. "Hurry up! This is so exciting!"

At least this wasn't happening in the middle of the damn night. "I'm coming. Give me a minute."

She harrumphed and skipped out of the room.

Yawning, I dressed in the sweats and T-shirt I'd only taken off an hour before. Maybe it was selfish to hope this didn't last long, but damn, I was so freaking tired, I couldn't wait to crawl back in bed and sleep.

I wandered down the hallway and paused in the doorway to the theater room.

The buttery scent of popcorn wafted out. Lucy had also lined up chips and dip, cans of energy drinks, cookies and red licorice. I grinned. She'd picked up on hockey players' superstitions pretty damn fast; we'd had the same exact snacks every time the U.S. Olympic Women's Ice Hockey team played. I loved that she'd become so invested in the sport and the players on her own—no prompting from me—but Mimi's obsession had a lot to do with it.

My heart damn near burst in my chest when my wife turned and looked at me, giving me that beautiful smile that belonged solely to me.

Her smile faded and she scowled. "Jaxson Lund. You get back there and put on your U.S. Olympic Women's Ice Hockey team jersey now, before the final game starts!"

Maybe she was taking the superstition thing too far? The entire Lund family—including the babies—had worn the same lucky Vikings jerseys after the "Minnesota Miracle" game that had clinched the NFC divisional title against the Saints, only to have the Vikings lose the NFC championship game to the Eagles the following week. We all still moped about the lost opportunity to play the Super Bowl in our home stadium.

"Daddy, go! Gabi got these for us special and we have to wear them for every game!"

Two against one. "I'm going."

We settled in to watch the USA versus Canada in the gold medal game. Lucy had a bunch of questions, which I mostly answered, but Mimi chimed in before I could on about half of them. The kid was a sponge, and a natural athlete who worked hard at improving her skills. Even if she decided not to pursue more competitive hockey, we liked watching college and NHL games together.

Mimi and Lucy screamed themselves hoarse during the

game. The shoot-out finish where the USA beat the Canadians 3 to 2 was one of the best hockey games I'd ever seen.

But as I watched my wife and daughter hugging each other, chanting, "USA, USA," I knew my life was pretty damn sweet. Hockey would always be part of it, but not the most important part.

As they'd wound down the celebration, Gabi sent us a text—a picture of her with the team and their shiny gold medals—and Mimi lost her mind. The kid bounced off the walls for the next hour before we finally tucked her in bed.

Lucy sent Mimi a soft look before she quietly closed the door to her bedroom. "Do you think tonight will be a defining moment in her life?"

I pulled her into my arms and kissed the top of her head. "Maybe. But she also mentioned that she and Calder might pair up and start training to become ice dancers after that Olympic competition ended. And I know you heard her comment about practicing bowling so she could join the national junior league bowling team."

Lucy sighed. "Too many ambitions, and she's good at anything she sets her mind to. She gets that from you."

"I think in the long run, the defining moment in her life will be when we became a family and she realized she'll have our love and support together no matter what she chooses to do."

"Perfectly said, Mr. Lund."

"Come on, Mrs. Lund, let's see if we can't make another little miracle tonight."

JENSEN

Getting a head-butt to the groin was the perfect capper to my crap day.

I stepped off the elevator on the second floor of my apartment building, pulling my roller bag behind me. When I turned the corner—*wham!*—a hard head connected with my crotch.

Grunting, I crumpled against the wall for a moment, thighs clamped together to try to block out the pain.

Motherfuck did that hurt.

When I didn't hear a "Gee, mister, I'm sorry," I glanced up to see my crotch smasher sailing down the hallway, long brown curls bobbing as if she didn't have a care in the world.

That pissed me off.

"Hey, little girl," I yelled.

The figure spun around and glared at me. "I'm *not* a girl."

"With that long hair I assumed—"

"You have long hair," he pointed out.

"I'm not wearing a dress," I shot back at him.

"It's not a dress. It's a *hakama*."

"Looks like a damn dress," I muttered. I closed my eyes and silently willed the throbbing pain in my groin to go away.

Stupid visualization exercises never worked.

Sighing, I pushed off the wall and opened my eyes. I said, "Look, kid, we . . ."

But he was gone.

Where the hell had he disappeared to so fast?

He'd probably slipped into an apartment. But I knew everyone who lived in my building, and no one had kids.

Maybe in the two weeks you've been gone someone new moved in.

That'd be an issue since Bob the building manager was supposed to restrict families with kids to the other building.

Did this kid's parents know he was running the halls unattended? Did they care?

If I ever ran into them, they'd get a piece of my mind about their son's behavior.

Why don't you shake your fist in the air too, you grumpy old man?

I'd cop to being grumpy, but I wasn't old. No matter what my body felt like some days.

I shambled down the hallway to my apartment. After unlocking the door, I dragged my suitcase inside.

The piney scent lingering throughout the space indicated the cleaning service had been here recently. When I snagged a sparkling water out of the refrigerator, I noticed my personal chef had delivered this week's meals. Now that I wasn't on vacation, I had to get back to healthy eating. Training started in roughly eleven weeks, and I already had enough to overcome without showing up looking like a lard ass.

My damn balls throbbed, so I grabbed an ice pack out of the freezer and hobbled into the living room. As soon as my butt connected with my square-shaped sofa, I breathed a huge sigh of relief. God I loved this couch. Sort of pathetic that I'd rather have it beneath me than a woman.

I heard my phone buzzing in the outside pocket of my suitcase, but I ignored it. I wasn't in the mood to talk to anyone. I needed time to chill. Yeah, I'd just returned from vacation, but only the last week had been flop-on-the-beach-with-a-beer time. I'd spent the previous week at the clinic in Florida with the doc who'd done my surgeries. He and his sadistic outpatient review team had performed every stress, mobility, agility and functionality test ever invented on my body to gauge the success of my surgeries last year.

They marveled at the progress I'd made since my last visit. They told me I'd surpassed their initial expectations for recovery. They listed all the medical milestones I'd passed. But they hadn't told me the one thing—the *only* thing—I wanted to know: Would I ever play football at the same level as I had before the injury?

An injury that had kept me off the football field all of last season.

Actually, it'd been a combination of injuries. A late hit had knocked me out. So in addition to getting a concussion, at some point during the play I'd dislocated my kneecap—not that I'd been aware of that injury at the time. When I'd finally come to in the *hospital*—that had been freaky as hell—I hadn't been able to feel *anything* from the waist down due to paralysis.

Paralysis.

Even now I can't wrap my head around that word.

When I think back, it seemed as if it'd happened to someone else. My neck in a cervical collar. My arm in a sling. As I lay in that hospital bed, I felt nothing. I'd wanted to scream but I couldn't get enough air into my lungs to even speak.

Then the drugs kicked in and I drifted back into the black void.

Upon awaking several hours later alone in my hospital room, I tried to wiggle my toes, roll my ankles, shift my thighs, force any kind of movement, but I just ended up sweaty and frustrated.

And scared. Holy shit I'd experienced fear in that hospital bed like I'd never known.

Sleep became my refuge. For twenty-four hours the doctors watched me for signs of improvement or decline. When I groggily complained about the throbbing pain in my right knee, the doctors did another full, thorough and painful examination. They determined the hematoma on my spine had caused the temporary paralysis. When the swelling decreased, so did the paralysis.

I'd never welcomed pain like I had that night. I refused pain meds. I wanted to feel every twinge and every burning, stabbing pain—it was better than never feeling anything again.

Two days after the paralysis scare, my family loaded me into the Lund Industries private Learjet. The medical professionals associated with the Minnesota Vikings organization recommended a surgeon in Florida, so I was off to Pensacola for diagnosis and surgery.

My shoulder injury required surgery, and the recovery time was four months. It was one of the most trying times in my life, despite the fact that the surgery had gone well and the prognosis for recovery was excellent. While I appreciated the unconditional support my family provided, they'd been extremely smothering.

During the second week of physical therapy, when I became frustrated with my lack of progress increasing my walking speed, I asked for another set of tests because I knew something else was wrong. The tests revealed I'd ruptured my Achilles tendon. The knee injury had masked that issue, and my knee turned out to be the least of my worries.

An Achilles rupture can be a kiss of death to a football player. I could name a dozen careers abruptly ended by that particular injury. After the surgery to repair the rupture—which I couldn't schedule until my knee was one hundred percent—the recovery time was a year. So sitting in the doctor's office in Florida, I knew I'd miss the entire *next* season.

Although I'd signed a three-year contract, this type of injury was a game changer. The team could pay me the remainder of my guaranteed salary and cut me from the team, turning me into a free agent. But if the Vikings released me due to their medical concerns, what other NFL team would want to take a chance on me?

None.

Thankfully I'd had the best year of my career prior to the injury, so I'd been placed on the injured reserve list. The big bosses assigned me a sports medicine therapist/trainer. Dante was a cool guy. He knew when to push me and when to back off. He and I spent a lot of hours together, yet I never forgot where his loyalties were. He'd accompanied me to Florida for my one-year postsurgical checkup—so he could accurately report the doctor's diagnosis back to the coaching staff. I guess they didn't trust that I'd be totally honest.

After the week in Florida, Dante tagged along with me to Mexico. While he sampled tequila and women at the exclusive resort, I spent hours walking on the beach and staring at the ocean, trying to figure out what to do with my life when playing football professionally was no longer an option. Because I could be facing that decision in as little as three months.

Right now I was exactly where I claimed I'd wanted to be the past two weeks: sitting on my comfy couch in my apartment. So why was I so restless? Why was I lonely?

I tipped my head back on the cushion and stared at the ceiling.

You're lonely? Call your brothers. Or your sister. Or your parents. Or your cousins. They'd be here, or ask you to meet them someplace in a heartbeat.

But my feet didn't move. My will was as lazy as my body today. When I held out my hand toward my suitcase, my phone didn't magically fly into it like Harry Potter's broom did when he called out, "*Accio!*" That'd be a cool power. It'd be even cooler to have a magic wand that fixed everything.

I shifted the ice pack on my groin. I must've been sitting there longer than I'd been aware of because the gel had become gooey and warm.

Don't be a brooding asshole. Do something productive.

Maybe my neighbor Martin would be up for a video game marathon. If nothing else, the dude made me laugh, especially when he talked about the things he'd seen and heard around the apartment complex. I'd bet he knew who the nut-smashing kid belonged to.

Since Martin lived across from me, I didn't bother to put on a shirt before I stepped in the hallway. If he bitched about me being shirtless, I'd point out that my brother-in-law Axl—former tenant of my apartment—had strolled around buck-ass naked most of the time. At least I had my bottom half covered.